THE TEMPLE OF
OPTIMISM

THE TEMPLE OF
OPTIMISM

James Fleming

talk
miramax
books
HYPERION
NEW YORK

Library of Congress Cataloguing-in-Publication Data

Fleming, James
    The temple of optimism / by James Fleming.—1st ed.
    p. cm.
    ISBN 0-7868-6676-4
    1. Country life—Fiction. 2. Derbyshire (England)—Fiction. I.
Title.

PR6056.L42 T46 2000
823'.92—dc21   00-040963

FIRST EDITION

1   3   5   7   9   10   8   6   4   2

THE TEMPLE OF
OPTIMISM

One

GREY BOLSTERS of cloud rolled across the sky, their bellies tinged with pink. Like elephants, he thought, or Daphne Cuthbert's jowls. He leaned a little further out of bed. Everywhere it was the same, from one horizon to the other. He scratched his ribs. So today was to be no different at Winterbourne from any other in this strange month of June 1771. Wise men would wear a hat in the certainty of rain, fools would not, and both would be right. The cattle would stare silently into the river Eve and the leaves hang flabby and moist. The smallest noise would travel for miles. Everything would be middling and dull. It was not at all the weather that Nathaniel Horne was used to among the hills of Derbyshire.

He crossed his hands over his plump, furry stomach and lay back twiddling his thumbs. The conversation of birds going about their vital, early-morning business, the distant noises from the stables, the rumbles from the kitchen area, all were congenial to him. He liked to be where things happened. Movement of any sort was attractive to his impatient, capricious mind. He was a person in whom the sight of a fresh hole in the ground excited the same rustle of anticipation as the words *Terra Incognita!* evoke in an inveterate explorer. 'Ah,' he would say, peering down – or up, or along; at any rate fixing his brown and marvelling eye to what he pronounced as the arperture and fiddling inside it with his stick – 'can it be that the mole still sleepeth, and that the lion roareth not?', or 'Doth Mrs Brock snore while Adam delves?', or any one of a number of homely biblicisms that he had composed out of an instinctive sympathy for the animal kingdom. A hole in which one of his men was working attracted him as surely as a catapult a

3

schoolboy, for it combined the best of both worlds: an underground mystery and the chance for a pow-wow. Hard on the heels of why? would follow an amiable inquisition about the man's health, his wife's sores, the ease of digging, the composition of the soil and then, more likely than not, some loosely tangential anecdote that had happened, as they conversed, to bound fully accoutred into his fructuous brain.

Anything concerning drainage was a source of endless fascination to him. To watch the deep square drain in the stableyard being unblocked left him with a sense of total fulfilment. As Amos Paxton, his steward, poured in a bucket of water at the top, he'd scamper on his chubby legs to its mouth in the orchard to see it cleanse. 'Exemplary,' he'd chortle, dashing his hat against his knee. Or 'That'll let the air in, eh lads!' jabbing with the tip of his cane at the flotilla of horse turds that bobbled like rotten apples beneath his fleshy nose. In this respect, as in many others, Nat Horne had retained into middle age a pleasing sort of childishness.

His favourite expressions were mudgy me, by Jove and by Jupiter. Some of his friends even called him Jupiter Horne to his face. But he was never disconcerted or thought they presumed too far. He just grinned and pronounced himself extraordinarily flattered.

He clasped his hands behind his head and smiled the reposeful smile of a man content with his lot and having before him the prospect of an agreeable day doing nothing urgent.

In point of fact he had never done anything urgent throughout his fifty years, unless one excepts the vicarious urgency that is involved in riding a horse flat out in the name of vulpicide. It was merely the impression that he gave. His entire manner proclaimed the end of time if the blacksmith had not finished shoeing the oxen by such-and-such an hour, or the fleeces been bagged by noon. But he never meant it. It was the way he was, sea water without brine.

To matters of domestic economy he was indifferent. In the mornings he would breakfast by himself, for preference off a snipe and a poached egg, his small jaws agitating rapidly as he considered his day. After a conference with Paxton, he'd perch himself jovially atop Pilot, the towering grey gelding that he'd bought principally for its name, and set out to inspect his projects, aflood with bustle and enthusiasm, proposing this and belaying the other: exhorting, interfering and contradicting himself but always with such good humour and absence of condescension that not one person on Winterbourne estate ever thought the less of him. 'It's the master's way, it can't be helped,' his men would say as they shifted a hundred drainage pegs eighteen inches to the left. No one could take against an employer with a face that glowed like a conker and such a cheery way of carrying on.

At midday he would return for a slice of cold pie. Perhaps he would then have a nap, curled up on the sofa. And perhaps he would not. It all depended on the events of the morning. For instance, the trill of a skylark wavering above the moors might inspire him to enumerate all the birds that sang as they flew. Then nothing would satisfy him until he had established whether the plink of a blackbird as it flitted from bush to bush was from pleasure (which made it eligible) – or from alarm (which disqualified it). Or it might occur to him as he inspected the stables to make a pet out of a bat. (Thus, in fact, did he once spend an entire summer and so greatly amused his neighbours until, at a dinner the Cuthberts were giving for the bishop, he produced it from his pocket and invited the company to observe its appetite for liver.) Or he might be overtaken by a desire to devise a mechanism for quantifying the flow of water from a well. Or for weeks be heard trying to measure in a certain hollow the distance required for the perfect reflection of one syllable of echo. (In 1768 he described the results in a paper he read at the Assembly Room in town. But since he got carried away by the excitement of it all as he ran up and down the stage shouting 'Pantaloon', which was his test word, no one was able to hear his conclusion – 105 feet a syllable – and he had to go round later repeating this nugget.)

These were what he termed his Private Enquiries, as distinct from his morning labours which he classed as Agriculturalism.

At four p.m. Digworth smote the gong, first in the hall with three stately taps of a pro-forma nature and then, should his master not appear, on a valorous thumping circuit of the terrace, crying out between each series of blows, 'Cutlets today, Mr Horne, beetroot soup, kidneys, suet pudding . . .' This was the summons for the main meal of the day for Nat and his wife, Lady Blanche.

Afterwards he surrendered himself to the duties of a husband. Once a week in the winter he would take the trap into Buxton and partner his friend Major Seddon, late of the Fencible Regiment, in a rubber or two of whist. It was a game that he played noisily and with sly skill. Sometimes in the summer he'd go with his terrier and his fishing rod for a walk beside the little river Eve. But these, it was clearly understood between them, were concessions by Blanche.

Fox-hunting in its season had been a favourite pastime until he had fallen out with the owner of the hounds, his neighbour at Overmoor.

Blanche was of a less brisk disposition and especially so before her morning cup of chocolate. No one was more aware of this than Nat after twenty-three years of marriage. And since he loved her (he looked down fondly to where she lay beside him, her knees drawn up towards her chest and her head half-hidden by the covers), he adhered loyally to the terms of their truce: that so long as he did not move or speak before Digworth brought up his hot water, he was free of all obligations towards her (except on Sundays, holy days and when they had callers) up to the moment the four o'clock gong struck.

So on this morning as on others he lay by her side and waited, quivering, for the crackle of Digworth's catarrh in his dressing-room. It occurred to him that he might have Digworth shave him in the afternoon. Was it today the Scarletts were coming, or was it on Thursday? And was there actually a difference between one day and the next? Time should be treated like dough, he thought, and chopped up to suit one's needs and not according to some fusty convention.

He wiggled his toes and watched a spider with an oval, putty-coloured body tiptoe up the bed-curtains. By Jove but he'd been lucky to snare a wealthy wife! He traced with a fingernail the twist of gold thread that spiralled through the blue-grey bed-curtains. By Jove yes, that'd been a stroke of unmitigated good fortune finding himself acceptable to a peer's daughter. Not that he'd been out tuft-hunting, mind you. Absolutely not. It had been from the first a marriage of love as far as he was concerned. Well, perhaps unmitigated was an exaggeration. Blanche's marriage portion had made a difference. One had to be candid about it. It had allowed him to do all sorts of things at Winterbourne that he could never have managed from his own resources. But it had added to their union a *couleur* that he sometimes regretted. It was a matter of pride, really.

A lock of dark hair had escaped from her nightcap and settled laxly across her thin cheek. When they were married they'd laughed at the contrast between her cap, which invariably greeted the morning as neat as new, and his, which when it could be found at all, had the appearance of having been savaged by a mastiff during the night. But that had been years ago. Before Edward was born. Before laughter became less plentiful.

He picked his nose and started to fidget. He crooked a finger round the hem of the bed-curtains and again examined the sky. The fish bellies were losing their lustre and the clouds congealing into one huge canopy the colour of lava. Invisible in the depths of the horse chestnut tree that grew on the edge of the lawn, two wood pigeons gurgled to each other as they brazened and strutted amidst the foliage. He heard the skeek of a kestrel a long way off. He heard Digworth shuffling around in his dressing-room. His eyes lit up. There was a tap on the door. It was enough – and with a haroosh of the covers he plunged through the bed-curtains like an opera singer who hears five hundred voices baying for an encore. Within seconds he was shouting down the stairwell for his chocolate, his breakfast, Amos Paxton, his hat, horse, dog, the gardeners: in short, for everyone and everything that his imagination had listed as imperative for his enjoyment of the day. And when no one responded, he set off for the nether regions of his large and crumbling mansion with his nightshirt billowing round his little legs and his slipper heels cracking on the stair treads.

Blanche, who had been awake for a good hour but had not wished to advertise the fact, uncoiled herself and flung an arm across her eyes. At a distance that was altogether insufficient, she listened to doors slamming, the joyful yelps of Trump, the rumble of Paxton's voice and the clatter of something dropped on stone flags. To Nat talking nonsense to Trump as he climbed back up the stairs. To Nat washing, Nat singing, the window being lifted, to Nat addressing the weather as if he were Harry Hotspur on the eve of battle. Had it ever been otherwise?

She laid a finger across her lower lip and pressed it against the gum. Yes, that night three years ago when it had been so cold that he'd had to get up twice to bank the fire. Had stolen every one of the blankets. Had lain doggo even when Digworth brought up his water and eventually, as quiet as a mouse, had disappeared to return carrying the thermometer in his gloved hands.

'Look at it, my dear,' he had said in a voice of awe, 'fourteen degrees of frost in the kitchen larder, in the *kitchen larder* would you believe.' Then he'd put the thermometer in the bed, jumped in after it and for the next hour (in fact until 32°F was achieved) informed her with sepulchral glee of the upward progress of the mercury.

It had been, she decided, the only day of their married life that had commenced without a fanfare. Was it impossible for him to do anything quietly? Did he have to attack every hour as if it were his last? Frankly she was sick of it. There were times when she couldn't have cared twopence if he and Edward and these great barracks they lived in all flew off to the moon. She had been faithful to him, faithful, dutiful and sharing. She had fulfilled the most painful and humiliating obligation of a wife by giving birth to the tiresome Edward, and she felt she was owed something in return.

She had never disguised from him her contempt for their neighbours. She had never for a moment pretended she felt other than she did about the discomforts of Winterbourne from the day he had brought her there as his bride and their carriage got stuck on the moor. Once, on a bitter February evening when the draughts coming under the door had made even the carpets shiver, she had taken off her mittens and shown him her chilblains. She had looked him squarely in the eye and said she could not tolerate another winter in the place. They must buy a town house in London: nothing excessive, just so long as it had some decent rooms where she could entertain her friends. But she had known immediately it was hopeless. His face had puckered like that of a child whose kite has lodged in a tree. 'You mean, go to town just as the fun is starting here? No hunting or duck shooting? I couldn't do that. Go to London for the winter? I'd sooner die.' So she had desisted. If it meant choosing between London and Nat, at the end of the day she'd rather have Nat.

It was not, she thought as she shook out her long black tresses, that he was a scoundrel. He did not beat her, ignore her or patronise her. When he needed her money (which was whenever he called her his little treasure), he was civil and, so far as she could tell, truthful. He did not gamble for anything more than a few pennies when he went off to play whist. He was not a rake. He was still handsome and, in his own fashion, charming. No, on not one point of his externals had she any right to complain. The real problem was that a little of him went a long way. He was everywhere at once. To reflect was unthinkable, to idle anathema. No sanctuary existed that was completely free of his Jack-in-the-box personality. Total strangers became his best friends at the drop of a hat and with their retinues would invade Winterbourne for weeks on end, filling the house with their nonsense and denying her a moment's peace. He was, she knew, the most exhausting man on the planet.

'Help yourselves,' he'd boom, his brown eyes sparkling as the newest troupe spilled into the hall with their dogs and children and without an instant's hesitation began, like gold miners, to drive home their pegs in this adventitious El Dorado. 'Only two things you need to know at Winterbourne: grog's in the cupboard that way, the necessary place in the cupboard *that* way. All that's mine is yours. Stay the winter if you can, the duck'll give capital sport by and by. Her ladyship'll be delighted, won't you, my ruby?' And then with absolutely no concept of propriety, not even a flicker of *comme il faut*, he'd give her waist a blustery squeeze in exactly the same way as he did to Cook on her birthday. It was embarrassing beyond words. She deserved better.

'Your coat, Mr Horne, don't go forgetting your coat now. It'll likely rain before the day's out.'

'Blast it! Oh very well, Digworth, if you insist. Come on then, Packy, time we were off.'

Footsteps crunched through the gravel towards her window. So, they were on their way, Nat and his faithful Paxton, to make their customary tour of all his little projects. That's what he was, a dabbler: a noisy, bumbling dabbler. She heard him say something about having the windows reputtied. The footsteps stopped. She knew they were inspecting the sills. Nat whistled philosophically through his teeth. Then the gravel stirred as they set off again. No wonder he had insisted on having gravelled paths instead of slabbing them down as others did. Nothing silent could ever happen in gravel. Perhaps she should suggest they replace the drawing-room carpets with beds of gravel so he could march up and down having conversations with it and never disturb her.

'Tom Glossipp came to see me last night,' Amos was saying. 'Asked if we'd be counting the lambs soon.'

'Why ever did he want to know that?'

'Pardon me saying so, Mr Horne, but he did the lambing again for us this spring, if you remember.'

Nat struck his forehead with the flat of his palm. She heard it plainly.

'Bless me, so he did! Memory's like a sieve these days. Of course he did! Good lad, Tom. Nice and gentle with his hands. Can't think what we'd do without him. Tell me, Packy, did we agree to pay him by the lamb or, ahem, for *le tout* lambing, if you follow me.' (They halted directly below her window.)

'By the lamb, sir. A farthing for every lamb living at June 1st and as the day's passed and he's seemingly got a need for the money –'

'Trump! Trump!' Nat's roar seemed to emanate from under her very bed. 'What the devil d'ye think you're doing rolling in that shite, you scabby little muck-worm, you. Come into heel this instant, d'ye hear me?' His voice faded to a purr. She heard him click his fingers and imagined the creature fawning at his boots with a besotted look in its eyes. And then he'd bring it into the house with him and let it jump on the sofa so that the servants would have to clean everything. God, but he knew how to try a woman.

'Very well then, Packy, we'll ride out to Britannia in the afternoon and count our way home. Tra-la-la, tra-la-lee, la, la-la lee. Now I was thinking last night . . .'

They rounded the corner of the house and made off into the pleasure grounds. Soon only the sound of his distant rallies with the gardeners remained to displease her. She picked up her rosewood hand mirror and, as she waited for Margaret to bring in her chocolate, arranged her hair in girlish licks across her forehead.

'Will there be anything further, my lady?' Margaret asked later, putting down the nail scissors. Blanche considered. She must speak to Mrs Croft about provisions. Her sewing basket needed a good clear-out. She really should go to the schoolroom and see how Edward was faring with his new tutor, the beetle-browed Mr

Dryce, MA. There were flowers to be cut if they were dry enough. Then she might read until Nat returned for his midday repast. If he did. A few pages of *Pamela* would divert her. But there was another thing –

Though generally speaking immune to intellectual effort, Nat had recently discovered the pleasures, if she could use that word, of *Tristram Shandy*. 'I say, little ruby,' he'd chirrup of an evening, uncrossing his legs, removing his spectacles and as usual interrupting her without any consideration for anyone but himself, 'this fellow's extraordinarily droll for a parson. Wish we had more like him. Just listen to this, will you? What's happened is that Uncle Toby's had a misadventure. Mind you, we can't be sure but that's how it looks –' and then he'd read out the most frightful whimsy, bouncing round in his chair, pinching his nostrils and shrieking with laughter like a drunkard as the tears rolled down his cheeks. There was one passage in the book that had particularly caught his fancy. Somewhere in one of Shandy's interminable digressions, it was remarked by – she forgot whom – that of all the pleasures of bachelordom, the freedom to sleep diagonally across one's own bed was among the greatest. 'The majesty of genius,' he said wistfully, 'only an original could have put his finger on it so unerringly,' and when she retorted indignantly, but wasn't that what he did anyway, he responded, 'Oh surely not. I lie as straight as a cucumber.' But it was true! He slept like an octopus! Arms and legs all over the place, grunting, groaning, twisting, nudging and kicking at her until she was consigned to an outpost no wider than a sandbank. And so it went on. If she was really unlucky, he'd lean forward and tap her on the knee and say, 'Oh I *must* read that to you again, isn't he the funniest parson you ever did hear of?'

Once she had thought to humour him by reading a chapter for herself. But she had soon desisted, thinking to herself, why do I need to be any further acquainted with Mr Shandy when I have him living in the house with me already?

This thought put her off the idea of reading. She decided instead she would check the linen press after seeing Edward, and so instructed Margaret to meet her there with the housemaids at eleven. Then she scrutinised her fingernails down her long nose and slid angularly into the chemise Margaret was holding for her.

Two

GLAZED AND gelid by winter, brightly purling in the summer
months between walls of yellow irises and frothy, clean-
scented cow-parsley, the little river Eve formed the spine to the
body of Winterbourne. Its head lay in the numerous springs that
rose in the oval of hills behind the village. Sweetly clear, the
fingerlets rushed down the woody slopes and were united in a
short gorge, from which the stream debouched over a shelf of rock
into a deep round pool of translucent green. At the tail of the pool
was a cattle ford. About twenty yards below this stood the
wooden cantilevered bridge that carried the road from outside
over the Eve and up a steepish incline into the hamlet of
Winterbourne, where it stopped. Its energy spent, the river then
sauntered through a green vale shaped like the fanned tail of a
courting bird.

At the broad end of the tail it ran through a number of rushy
pastures that were called the Out Ground. These abutted the
moorland. At this point, where the Eve met a ledge of hard rock, it
turned abruptly to the right. Here the water backed up during
winter floods to form a considerable lagoon which, because of the
unceasing movement of the river, froze but rarely. As soon as their
usual haunts iced over, ducks and waders of all sorts came in their
hundreds to feed at the Rushes, as the marsh was known.

From June onwards all the old women and children from the
nearby villages descended on the place to harvest the rushes for
their winter lights. It was a sight to see them cross-legged in their
family groups, fingers and tongues going nineteen to the dozen as
they nimbly peeled the rushes in such a way as to leave only one
narrow rib from top to bottom to support the pith. Often enough

Nat had tried his hand at it, but he was too clumsy and so ended up by making himself comfortable in the midst of their pleasant chatter, which was perhaps what he'd had in mind all along.

Beyond the Rushes lay the moor with its mixture of heather and sweet summer grasses, and the lichen-covered ruins of Britannia.

None could say with assurance why they bore this name or the purpose they had once served. According to local lore (which is to say, according to Amos Paxton), it had been in ancient times a shelter and trysting point for the cattle herds, since it was here that the road out of Winterbourne joined the old droving way into Buxton. But whatever the reason, it was a convenient landmark for the tinkers and packmen and all who still used the moorland road. Many was the picnic Nat had had there as a child. Everyone knew where Britannia was.

At the root of the tail and therefore looking down the vale towards Britannia, was Winterbourne. It consisted of seven cottages, one built of stone and the rest of thatch over wattle. In these lived Walter Hamilton the blacksmith, Moley Dibdin the jolly trapper of eponyms, Tom Glossipp, a pensioner, and Nathaniel Horne's other employees. At harvest time and haymaking (which on his poor soil did not make a large noise), a gang of workers and their families came out from Buxton to help in the fields. Amos Paxton occupied the stone cottage. It was neat and square like its garden, and situated next to the corn mill. The millstones were turned by water carried in an open ditch from the Eve. It was one of Amos's principal duties to oversee this vital operation. Around lay in a jumble the rest of Nat's grey-slated, dilapidated farm buildings: granary, cattle sheds, the smithy, stabling for the plough teams and miscellaneous hovels for dogs, chickens, geese, implements and all the what-have-you of an agricultural undertaking. The remainder of the cottages fronted in a row on to the lane leading out of the village to the rectory and the church.

The advowson to the living was held by Nat. Only once had he been called upon to exercise it, many years ago when the existing incumbent, the Reverend Percival Hughes, had been inducted.

On a rocky outcrop above the village, and so dominating it wholly, was Winterbourne House and its terraced gardens. It was reached by a steep rough road running through a grove of yew trees which had been planted by Nat's father. It was this man who had also erected, at a short distance from the house and with the last of his fortune, a handsome range of stables for the family's carriages and riding horses. His portrait, darkened by smoke, hung above the fireplace in the hall. It depicted a taller and sterner version of Nat standing in a brown velvet suit and pointing with authority at the new stables. Besides one gleaming, spurless boot sat dutifully the great-great-grandmother of Trump. Her name, Hilda, had been artfully woven into the roots of the tussock upon which her haunches rested, but by now this could be verified only by the use of a ladder and candle.

Behind Winterbourne the land lay quite differently. For at a bowshot or so from the village it soared dramatically upwards into a rugged horseshoe of hills across which spread a beech wood of imperial beauty, the purest emerald in May and all hues of gold and fox-pelt bronze in the mists of autumn. On the further side of this range, the ground fell gently away through bracken and rough cattle grazing until it reached the Buxton to Derby turnpike. From Britannia to the highway the land belonged exclusively to Nat Horne. It was an area of a fraction less than three thousand acres and so offered him ample scope for pootling.

It was after two o'clock when they arrived at Britannia. Amos Paxton was a thick, square-shouldered man of forty-five. His forearms were like logs and each blunt-nailed finger as solid as a spigot. He had an honest, open face, a rather wedge-shaped nose and eyes the blue of cornflowers. Rarely was he seen without a mouse-grey felt hat squashed on top of his prominent ears. He and his wife Mary had one living child, a son called Davie.

All his life Amos had spent at Winterbourne. He knew as well as he knew his own name which fields gave an early bite in April, the hollows where the ground lay wet and clogged the bush harrows, and the most intimate foibles of the milking cows. He could judge without leaving his bed whether the Eve had flooded the Britannia road. The position of every rotten floorboard in the corn loft was imprinted on his mind like a map. The run of the drains, the number of cartloads to empty the dung yard, the volume of flour required each week in the kitchens, the width of every gateway to an inch – of all these details, which are so vital to the easy operation of an estate like Winterbourne, Amos Paxton was the absolute master. Practical, phlegmatic and conscientious, he was the perfect foil to Nat Horne. No worldly ambitions corrupted his sleep. So long as he could serve the family that had employed him and his father and his grandfather, and could each winter find enough straight stems in the hazel coppice to work up into the intricately carved walking sticks for which he was justly famous, his soul was at peace. Winterbourne was his life. As it was for Nat, so it was for him. And for this reason they had grown more than usually fond of each other over the years.

A hundred yards short of Britannia, Horne reined in. Around him the track and the soft peaty ground to either side were pitted and scored with ruts.

'See how deep the doctor went in,' he said, pointing downwards, 'and it's only a little piss-pot affair he has for a trap. Can you imagine the trouble we'd have been in if it had been some barouche full of her ladyship's friends from London? What a trouncing we'd have taken! Mudgy me, it was bad enough as it was, what with her full of grippe and shivering fit to die.'

'Aye, four oxen it took to pull the mannie out. It was lucky Tom Glossipp was riding past or the doctor'd have had a long walk of it.'

'That horse of his, that nice little chestnut, was it ever right in itself afterwards?'

'Can't say, Mr Horne. Never heard one way or t'other.' They continued to Britannia and halted beside the ruins.

'Y'know, Packy, one of these days we'll have to do something about this road of ours. We can't go on like this. A day or two of rain, that's all it takes to turn it into porridge. Waters and tempers rise in tandem. The doctor can't get in, her ladyship can't get out – you'd think the Jacobites were banging on the door when she gets one of those moods on her. Dear me, it was lucky she wasn't living here the day they did arrive. Do you remember that? Scared Cook witless they did, all those glinty little Scotch eyes suddenly staring at her through the window.'

Amos looked at him sideways and fiddled with his reins. 'Us could put in a new road,' he said tentatively.

'Us could. Right enough, us could. But where the devil would we put it?'

'Come along a bit higher up, p'raps?'

'How now, Packy, take the book and score one lamb for Tom. Lying behind its mother under that boulder with the splash of yellow lichen. See where I mean?'

The day was well advanced by the time they had worked through the Out Ground and returned to the home pastures.

Nat felt hungry. And the work had kept him away from his private enquiries, which at that time were divided between the means of sustenance of an unnaturally large newt with a warty black spine and a yellow belly that he had discovered at the bottom of a well and the question as to whether buzzards always circled clockwise.

'Parson's coming in behind us,' remarked Amos. 'It'll be another kind of lamb he's thinking on, I reckon.'

Nat looked round. Sure enough, up the road from Britannia the Reverend Hughes was riding at a shambling trot, hunched over his saddle bow, his fat, black-gaitered legs dinging on his pony's ribs with every step it took. Nat splashed through the river to meet him.

'By Jove, Reverend, been at it again?' he said with a smile, indicating the laden saddlebags that hung on each side of the horse. 'We'll soon have to extend the parsonage if you continue to stock your library at this rate.'

'Only a few morsels that caught my eye in town,' replied the other in the thin tones of an older man. 'That chapman who comes up from Derby each month – whatsisname, you know who I mean – is as familiar with my weaknesses as you are yourself.' He bent forward and patted his bags. 'Still, the price was short and the type's dense. Elliott on the Pentateuch looks interesting – I've had one of his before. I like his style. He's not afraid to get to the pith of the matter. But as for the rest I hardly know what I've come away with. You know how it is for us disciples of Caxton. Something clicks, a cloud of madness comes over one, and before you know where you are, your purse is empty and Hood – that's the fellow's name, knew I had it somewhere – is grinning at you as if he'd saved your soul. Which I suppose he has in a manner of speaking. Now if you'll excuse me, Mr Horne, I'd like to get my children unpacked and spend a little time coddling them before it gets too dark. Light like this is hard on an old man's eyes. Dear me, such a gloomy piece of weather we've had this month. Jonah himself could not have been more benighted than we have been.'

He tipped his hat to Horne, made a regal, circular motion with his hand in the direction of Paxton and kicked on his pony. A breeze had arisen which caused the swallowtails of his clerical bands to flutter up round his throat.

'Our minister is a happy soul,' Nat said as he rejoined Amos. 'Do you remember the pother I was in over whether to appoint him or that other fellow who could reel off the names of every pontiff and patriarch since the birth of Abraham?'

'Going back some you are now, sir. Aye, the Reverend's happy enough, though the missus did say he'd had a terrible go with the stone not long ago. Had no end of trouble passing it. As big as a bantam's egg, or so she heard. Did you know it was his sister who has the learning now of young Master Cuthbert . . .?'

They rode companiably along beside the Eve. A field away, Winterbourne House rose defiantly atop its eyrie as though on guard against invading forces. A coot scuttered noisily across the water into a clump of reeds. In a backwater under the opposite bank a couple of tiny bursting bubbles showed where a chub was feeding.

'Otter's back again,' Amos said. 'Expect she'll be rearing a litter somewhere hereabouts. Two, no three, years it's been since she was last here. Do you see her marks on the strip of mud by the flags?'

But Nat's eyes were elsewhere. For the clouds, which throughout the day had smothered Winterbourne in a blanket of grey, had suddenly thinned and broken over the hills before them. Like a window opening in a fortress wall, a round embrasure had appeared in the gloom and from it, buttressed on either side by towering fleecy mounds, streamed a funnel of daffodil-coloured sunlight. It descended at an angle across the mountain bowl, brushing the crowns of the beech trees with a palette of gold, green and all shades of black. From the very heavens it poured, catching, it seemed, in its long liquid gleam every mote and speck that could fly. And at its toe, trapped in the epicentre of its trumpet-shaped cone, lay Winterbourne House, shimmering like a jewel. Its windows flashed and blazed. Every detail of its huge carcass seemed magnified a hundredfold, from the finials on its chimney pots and the gilded curlicues on the weathervane, down through the family escutcheons graven on the lead gutter heads to the worn steel rims of the boot scrapers. Edward's toy sword, which he had thrust into a molehill on the lawn, shone with the intensity of Excalibur and cast behind it a shadow as slim as a pencil. In the space of a minute, the house had sloughed its skin of decrepitude. Refulgent, splendid and arrogant, it reared above them like a fiery-scaled dragon.

Nat sat on his horse transfixed. He put out a hand and gripped Amos's shoulder. 'Look at it, Packy. Just look at it will you, man? Did you ever see anything so glorious in your life? It's like a miracle. It reminds me of a picture I once saw showing Elijah being scooped up into heaven. Whoof, down came God's hand and up the ray he walked, his cloak flapping behind him. I tell you, it fairly gives my heart a wrench to see the old place so bright and young after all it's been through. Think of it, Packy, think of all the happiness and all the misery that have happened under its nose. Do you suppose it knows about them? Do you think it has a mind of its own, like you and me? Houses aren't just stones and mortar. They have spirits. You can feel them all around you the moment you open the front door. So why shouldn't they have minds as well? My God, it's, it's . . .'

His voice tailed off as he followed the shaft back to its molten eyeball hanging over the hills. Suddenly he started to squirm in his saddle, plucking at one ear lobe. 'That's what we'll do, we'll come through the hills with it, we'll put a road up through the wood, over the hill and down to the turnpike, a right spanker that her ladyship can be proud of till the day she dies. That's the answer! That's what we'll do! O fantastic mudgy – to hell with Britannia, damnation and the devil to its bogs and slithers. A pox on the lot of them, that's what I say!'

Every window in the mansion was now on fire, splintered by a thousand leaping pricks of flame. They saw Blanche come round the corner on to the terrace. She lifted her face to the sun and closed her eyes. Between her fingers was a single white rose. The buttons on her dress twinkled like stars, the pendant at her throat glinted as she moved her head to sniff the bloom. She called down to them dreamily.

'I must go to her –'. Nat threw Amos his reins, slipped his

stirrups and ran clumsily across the field, waving his stubby arms above his head. Amos watched him climb the fence and scramble up to the terrace, where his wife stood waiting, her elbow cupped in the palm of one hand and her black eyes tipping the rose petals. Then he led Pilot away to the stables, feathering his hat round his skull and wondering how anyone could make such a fuss about a sunbeam.

That evening Nat did not read *Tristram Shandy*. He had Digworth light a fire in the library, open two of his best burgundy and fetch out the wax candles. He spoke encouragingly to Mrs Croft in the kitchen. He went upstairs and after a good deal of thought, selected his maroon coat and breeches. Edward's door was open, so he entered and, because the image was still fresh in his mind, began to tell him a story about a pixie sliding down a moonbeam.

'Do you know how old I am, father?' asked the boy scornfully. Nat looked at him with amazement. It had never occurred to him that children could be other than three or four. That there could be an intervening stage between suckling at his mother's breast and demanding a sub, a stage when a boy might wish to learn and a father could share some portion of his wisdom without impairing his dignity, struck him as wholly novel and delightful. It was yet another marvel in this blessed day of his. His face crinkled with pleasure as he pulled up a chair. 'When can I come duck shooting with you?' Edward asked. Man to man, they discussed the business thoroughly. They turned to other essential subjects.

Edward enquired about the newt, which he yearned to keep in his room. Of its own accord, the conversation shifted to how wells worked and where so much water came from.

'Gallons and gallons of the stuff every day – imagine it, journeying from deep within the earth to this one point –'

'How much is a gallon, father?'

Nat fetched out Edward's pot. 'About that much, I'd say.' Their eyes met and laughed.

'How many gallons a day does that make?'

'By my calculations 13 gallons a minute, 780 gallons an hour and 18,720 gallons a day. Which is to say about 300 hogsheads. Of course it depends how wet the year has been.'

'That bat you kept, do you think it would have eaten the newt or the other way round . . . ?'

Nat kissed his son goodnight and ran down the stairs whistling, more completely happy in his heart than he had been for a long time. He even contemplated sliding down the banisters.

Blanche heard him from the drawing-room but for once she did not object. What he had said to her on the terrace and, more importantly, the manner in which he had said it, had brought back to her in a rush all her memories of the Nat she had once known and worshipped. Not the garrulous and inconsequent buffoon who was starting to go deaf, the middle-aged Shandy who preferred his steward's company to her own, but the youth who had stolen up and captured her with a swarm of butterfly kisses as he offered her his heart for eternity. They had spoken to each other with their eyes also, caught echoes they'd both thought buried and, as that miraculous beam of light faded into the glim, entered arm in arm by the garden door.

The single rose stood in a vase between them as they ate and drank. Digworth was banished from the room. Afterwards they walked through to the library and unrolled the estate map on the table. Their heads touching, his arm twined through hers, they let their forefingers prowl side by side over the contours that the new road should follow. He called her his little treasure. She did not mind. He was again her man. It was, she realised, all she had ever cared about. 'Do you remember . . . ?' she asked, leaning her head against his shoulder. He put his arm softly round her waist and they went upstairs rather earlier than usual.

Three

FOR THREE years the beech woods rang to the blows of the woodcutters' axes and the groans and oaths of the human debris that Nat, for no greater outlay than a few evenings' duck flighting and some pretty words in the magistrate's ear, had contrived to draft from the assizes.

Downwards trundled timber cradles laden with grey, shaven boles and upwards crawled a procession of carts charged to the brim with gravel and bottoming for the great enterprise. Trees crashed, picks rattled on stone, men laughed, swore, ached and sometimes vomited. Horses flirted in spring and neighed to each other through the autumn fogs. Arch stones were keyed into place with wooden fenders, and gabions swayed into their beds by a windlass of Paxton's engineering. Breechings snapped since this was the labour of humans, and one man, a red-haired giant convicted of vagrancy, broke his leg and screamed awfully. Overseen affably by Nat from Pilot's comfortable back, and sternly by Amos as with his plans and measuring rods under his arm he strode through the labourers and the draught horses, the dust, the mud and the noise, her ladyship's road inched upwards through the woods. Every Friday afternoon Blanche had Vinson, the coachman, drive her up in the dog cart to make an inspection of the works. When progress was less than she had hoped for, she frowned, and tapping Vinson on the shoulder, descended smartly to the fire waiting in her sitting-room. But usually she was delighted and, reclining at a safe distance from the sweaty gangs, took out her pencil to draw up lists of friends for house parties.

For Edward, of course, it was paradise. Mr Dryce, and with him rules of quantity, deponent verbs, the awkward aorist and the prophecies of Daniel were relegated to mornings only, leaving the rest of the day free for acts of blissful anarchy behind his father's back.

At the crest of the hill, the road paused to take in the view and then, with swoops and rushes, unwound itself like a serpent until, on one fine day in August 1774, it slid triumphantly into the turnpike directly opposite the convivial property of Arthur Smith, innkeeper at the Green Man. The last load of gravel was emptied, spread and raked. The stonemasons tapped home the last block of ashlar on the last parapet of the last bridge. Shovels were stacked. Brows were wiped. The deed was done.

Nat's pride knew no bounds. His face shone like a bonfire as he bustled round shaking hands and clapping backs. He leapt on to the parapet, wobbled, recovered, laughed at himself as loudly as anybody, and declared it 'the bonniest day in my life'. He called for three cheers for the men, three cheers for Edward for not having got himself killed by a lump of stone, a shovel or Mr Paxton, and three cheers for the finest wife in the kingdom. As the last Hip Hip Hoorah! faded into the air, he plucked from his head his father's bell-bottomed wig, which he had disinterred from the cupboard beneath the stairs expressly for the occasion, and tossed it aloft. It fell like a nest of wriggling spiders into the dust and was borne away between Trump's sturdy jaws to be buried in a rabbit hole pending later experimentation.

'Damned good dog,' he shouted, grinning from ear to ear, 'damned brave animal to touch a Winterbourne wig, what! Now come on lads, three cheers for the little lionheart, Hip, Hip . . .' Edward tugged at his sleeve and he hopped back on to the parapet.

'Blow me if I won't forget my own name next. I christian this road – here, come up beside me, my ruby, and we'll do it in style.' Blanche lifted her skirts and stepped primly on to the parapet beside him. Edward jumped up on his other side, not a bit self-consciously. Nat put an arm round each of them. 'Steady as she goes, my darlings – I christian this road – LADYSWAY!'

Amos puffed out his chest and grew ten feet tall. His son Davie, who had hidden in the culvert under the bridge, began to cry. Tom Glossipp snapped open his fiddle case. Vinson did something no man there had ever seen during the last three years: he removed his coachman's benjamin. ('Oooh' cheered the labourers lying on a bank in the sunshine.) Arthur Smith bowled a firkin of ale across the highway. Madge Smith clapped as he struck the bung. The Reverend Hughes sniffed at it and pronounced a benediction on the works of man and God alike: wished he was ten years younger and said as much. And overhead small white clouds like putti drifted through the azure sky and gazed serenely down upon this pleasant, pastoral scene.

But the longer Nat thought about it as he lay in bed that night, the more he convinced himself that his accomplishment deserved more. Not everyone could have built a road so rapidly, cheaply and artistically. Not everyone could have done it at all. So was he to be fobbed off with a barrel of beer and a bit of scratching and scraping in the middle of a highway? By Jupiter, no! He wanted something more resplendent, something with some fizz to it. That's what they'd do, throw the house open, have a party, rattle the floorboards until the sun came up and show the county the stuff Ladysway was made of. In short, do the thing properly. Having thus hit upon a new escapade, he spreadeagled himself across the bed and instantly fell asleep.

Tom Glossipp and young Handy, his musical cohort, were alerted. Sheep were slaughtered. Oysters, winkles, beer and claret were portered to Winterbourne in glorious quantities. Floors were scrubbed until they shone with the healthy glow of a quarterdeck. The silver was polished and the firedogs burnished. All the corpses of all the moths and butterflies that had trustingly gathered for warmth in the echoing state rooms and had there expired and been translated into so many wizened lozenges, like date stones, were consigned by Digworth to a mass burial in the sunshine.

The appointed day dawned and with it a rustle of excitement that was palpable for miles around as folk laid out their partying clothes. Trump was marched off to spend the night by the Paxtons' hearth. Edward was put in charge of the flagpole and had Digworth accord him an extended roll on the gong as he crawled out of his bedroom window and loosed the toggle of the gules of St George.

'It's too absurd, really too absurd,' said Daphne Cuthbert to her husband as the pair of matching bays strained against their breast straps on one of Nat's steeper gradients and the coachwork groaned like a ship on a sullen sea. 'Can you imagine what it'll be like in winter? A touch of ice and the horses'll be on their knees. That's all it'll take, a touch and no more. Just like Nat, never had an ounce of common sense in his dear head.' She waggled her jowls in affectionate criticism and fluffed out the skirts of her green-and-white striped ball gown with mottled fingers.

'A road like this certainly does a horse no favours,' conceded Mr Cuthbert. A small man with a narrow mouth and disputatious eyes, he was one of those to whom a party was no more exciting a prospect than death. 'Always pulling too hard on the way up and running too loose on the way down. There'll be breakages on Nathaniel's new road before winter's out, you take my word for it.' He unholed the window strap a notch and fell to calculating the equine depreciation rate per annum that his host could expect. The evening air flowed sluggishly into the carriage. They came to another tight corner ('A regal sweep', Nat had proclaimed it). The wheels scrooped through the gravel as the coachman nursed the vehicle round. An immense boulder, veteran of some prehistoric era, loomed up at Mr Cuthbert's shoulder, so close that he could have reached out and touched it. He leaned forward and rapped at the glass with the knob of his cane.

'Damn your eyes, Shattock, do you want the thing to climb in and sit beside us? I'm warning you, one scratch on the paintwork and it'll be down the road on foot that you go.'

Daphne Cuthbert drew out her fan. Rivulets of sweat were coursing through the rouge on her grainy cheeks. She let down the window on her side and stuck her head out.

'Oh Mr Cuthbert, you must come and look at what's happening below. Isn't that the Scarletts' coach stopped at the turn down there? Why, if they baulk at that, whatever will they do when they get here? No, they're on the move again, hooray! the day's saved. And there's the Flowers behind them, I'd know that coach of theirs anywhere, always looks as if they use it for carting dung. Oh and do look, my dear, I beg you, there's a perfect whirligiggle going on down there now – the Dipples have pulled up – I do hope they've brought Dickie with them, such a personable young man – and the Askews' coachman has got down from his box . . . He's walking up to them looking ever so pompous – now they're shouting at each other and waving their whips around. How do I know what

24

they're saying? Really, Mr Cuthbert, you do have the most ridiculous expectations sometimes – and . . . Well I never! It can't be! What on earth can have come over Nat!'

She retracted her head and sat on the edge of her seat dripping with excitement. 'You'll never guess, never in a month of Sundays, who's coming up behind the Askews.' She put her hand on her husband's thigh and shook it as if it were a loose banister rail. 'It's Sir Anthony! Himself from Overmoor, no less, bowling up the hill in his racing fly with the hood down and that young wife of his, Daisy Garland as was, sitting beside him as pretty as a picture wearing the hugest hat you ever did see. Well! To think that after all the bad blood that's passed between Winterbourne and Overmoor these past years, here's Sir Anthony and Lady Apreece coming to a ball in Nat's house. Glory me, whatever shall we see next? I declare tonight'll be a night to beat all others.'

And so indeed it was. From near and far flowed a stream of gentry in carriages, farmers on horseback with their wives a-pillion, shepherds, rat-catchers, horse-copers, professional men in their traps, men on ponies, men on donkeys, men on foot with their families, everyone who at one time or another had crossed Nat's ebullient path. All knew each other (or about each other, which was often better), all, rich and poor, high and humble, grew happier by the minute as Digworth and his minions passed among them with tray and flagon. From every window an arc of candlelight silvered the newly scythed lawns and box-edged terraces, and in every state room soared a babble of conversation as Nat's guests exchanged fortissimo their views on all that breathed, ate, fornicated and died in their rural universe. And over them presided the mellow figure of their host, gliding from room to room like a duck patrolling its brood.

How d'ye do's to right and left, Joves and Jupiters and mudgy me's, bowing, embracing, nodding, chaffing, sympathising.

'Dashed sorry to hear about your pig, Mrs Foulkes. May I recommend the services of Mr Dawkins, the finest pig doctor in the kingdom? Here, Will, a patient.for you . . .'

'Your leeks are positively exuberant this year, Robert. Come, let us find a quiet window seat so you can give me a few hints . . .'

'Ah, Sir Anthony, how *extremely* good of you to come.' (At which those standing nearby posted their ears on sentry-go.) 'Now what have you done with your beautiful wife? Have you hidden her from our rough eyes? Very considerate of you, my dear fellow, she is a flame that us poor moths are nervous to approach.'

'By Jove, Mrs Tudge, how ravishing you look tonight –' and he bent to kiss his laundress's wrinkled hand, upon which she blushed like a tomato and so added immeasurably to his enjoyment. Simple, lovable Nathaniel Horne! He had a fond word for everyone and they for him. The force of his personality held them in thrall.

At nine o'clock Digworth flung open the double doors of the ballroom. From its cavernous interior, furnished solely by clumps of wooden candlestands in the corners and a line of benches against each wall, could be heard the hesitant notes of Tom Glossipp and David Handy tuning their fiddles. Feet began to tap. Men craned their necks to seek their wives, bachelors flaunted their wares and maidens studied the floorboards. As for dance cards, whoever would dream of such paraphernalia on a night like this?

At the same time, unnoticed and to tell the truth, unlamented, Blanche slipped quietly upstairs to her boudoir. What she termed the lower ingredients of the company tired her. She had no wish to be jostled in their rude dances, have her toes trampled on and awake in the morning with arms bruised to the colour of woad. It was Nat's party and she gladly acknowledged the fact. He could handle it very easily – better, in all probability – by himself. She had circulated, conversed and been seen: her duties were finished. As for Edward, let Mr Dryce MA take care of him: that's what he was paid for.

'I do believe I have the makings of a headache,' she said, placing her fan on a console table and stroking her forehead with four white fingers.

Nat looked at her, reading her mind perfectly. 'Shall we disturb you?'

'So long as you enjoy yourself, my dearest husband, nothing will disturb me.'

She went upstairs, poked up her fire, slipped off her shoes and rested her feet on a stool furnished with blue ticking. The noise from the ballroom reached her distantly. She took out her pencil and paper and tapping her teeth drifted off into heady contemplation of guest lists, dinner placements and the *goûts spéciaux* of the nobility.

'Will you allow me the honour?' Nat said gravely to his son, as Tom Glossipp struck the opening chords of 'Speed the Plough'.

Thereafter, to the last wild revel amid guttering candles and the threat of dawn, there was not a moment that those present forgot until their dying day. Jigs, gallops, reels, glides, minuets and all manner of country dances poured in quick succession from the repertoire of Glossipp and Handy. With heads aslant and knees flexing, they fiddled away as if their lives depended on it. Moley Dibdin begged the pleasure of the magistrate's wife. Mr Wiseman, the lawyer from Derby, bowed and was accepted by Nat's dairymaid, who had put on her red jig shoes for the occasion. Amos Paxton (who was now seen by all to be as bald as a silver dish), led out old Mrs Dipple for the third petronella – and none thought it unfit. It was an evening when horses high and hobby were left in their stables, when the goodness that people hope to find in their fellow journeymen was seen actually to exist and when a common purpose united everyone in pleasure. Except for the necessary pauses when the fiddlers were reprieved and Digworth dispensed various liquids and Mrs Croft's raisin cake, the benches remained empty. The dingiest maid and the shyest youth alike were whisked from their seats. If anyone was at a loss for the correct step, friendly hands were ever ready to steer a body to its proper station.

'Marry, but this is a rare frolic and no mistake,' sang Thaddeus O'Donnell, a travelling cattle dealer with laughing eyes, a terrific purple nose and a scar down one cheek where he had been caught by a horn, as he swung Daphne Cuthbert on his forearm. 'Niver have I seen such skipping in this godless land, niver, iver, in all me days. And isn't his honour the greatest skipper of them all?'

It was true. Everywhere, it seemed, danced Nathaniel Horne. His small feet twinkled, twirled and pointed in their shiny, silver-buckled pumps. His fubby legs bent and leapt with the energy of a man of twenty. His cheeks glowed, his forehead shimmered, a furnace of passion burned from the depths of his flashing eyes. The night was his. Nor did he forget his son Edward. Could he not remember the awful solitude of youth on these occasions? Could he not imagine the feelings of a gangling twelve-year-old as from the edge of the curtains he observed these wild cavortings, aching to be part of them but knowing not how? So when, before very long, Digworth whispered in his ear that Mr Dryce had immured himself in the library with Mr Cuthbert, the book of Job and two bottles of port, he made a note to keep an eye on the boy himself.

'Mr Dryce? Has he, by Jove,' he said, sitting himself down between Mrs Cuthbert and Thadie O'Donnell (whose face was running like a weir). 'Has he indeed? – then he's a dog. A beetle-browed dog who should know better.'

'Indeed he should, a truly deplorable state of affairs,' agreed O'Donnell, taking several pieces of Mrs Croft's cake and storing them round his person. 'You know, this is the most truly beautiful cake ever to grace this sinful world. When you see her, will you give the compliments of Thadie O'Donnell to the lady who had the baking of it, your honour? Bejasus but the crumbs can be hard on a man's throat.' He looked across Nat to where Daphne Cuthbert was doing a brisk trade with her toothsome pink fan. 'Would it be an impertinence, madam, to suggest that a brimmer of his honour's punch would chase the dew from your ladyship's brow more speedily than that device you have in your pretty hand? Or will your husband dash me to the ground for my insolence? Wait now till I see if I can finger him among this terrible lot of folk.' The three of them leaned back against the wall as O'Donnell surveyed the room.

'Let me see now, let me see . . . I picture the gentleman as having the countenance of a wolfhound, all slavering and snarling at the sight of O'Donnell having speech with his lady, thighs like oak trees, a neck like a beer barrel – do I go too far, madam? This tongue of mine is foriver getting the better of my wits – and a brisket as broad as a church door. To be sure, it's like his honour's bull that I see the fellow.'

Nat turned to him laughing. 'No, no, Thadie, you couldn't be more mistaken. Mr Cuthbert is constructed on altogether more meagre lines. Is that not so, Daphne? Is not meagre the word to describe your good man's brisket?'

Mrs Cuthbert's damp jowls flobbled with mirth. She lowered her fan and said judiciously, 'Meagre conveys too full an impression. I think I would prefer leafy.'

'And in any event, you have nothing to fear from him, my friend, since he is, as we speak, dissecting the prophet Job in the library. It is he who is closeted with the dog. Or so Digworth has just informed me.'

'Faith, but it's a good sharp saw he'll be needing then. That Job's no better than a scrawny wee tinker by my way of thinking. How can it be, I ask myself, that a man owning all those fat cattle, with all that meat parading daily under his nose, can be no more than a rattle of old bones? Poor doer, eh, your honour? Speaking of which, would your honour be after wanting a piece of his cake? It's my opinion that the weight of it in my pockets will upset the lines of my tailoring when I take to the floor again. No? But you'll not think the worse of the man if O'Donnell does? Such a truly beautiful piece of baking . . . ' and so saying he took out a whang of raisin cake, which he ate off his palm, like a horse. He wiped his hands on his homespun breeches and placed them on his knees.

'Is the leafy fellow alone in there with the prophet?' he demanded.

'No, he has Mr Dryce for company, as I said.'

'And so you did, so you did. The dog who should be caring for the boy Edward. Do you want that I fetch him out? T'isn't proper that a fellow of his age has no one to show him how to skip. Just say the word, your honour, and I'll drag the devil out by his ears.'

'But Mr O'Donnell, were you not on the point of entertaining me?' intervened Daphne Cuthbert tartly.

'And so I was, madam! Curse me for the ill-mannered churl that I be!' He sprang up, a patter of crumbs falling about him. 'Thirty seconds and no more, I give you my word as an honourable man. Am I not an honourable man, your honour? And will you also be telling this to the leafy fellow should he tire of the prophet and have a wish to dissect me instead? For I've a mortal fear of a man until I sees him. Now, was it thirty seconds that I said?' He ambled off towards the door, a ramshackly figure with a streaky grey mane spilling over the back of his collar.

Nat watched Tom Glossipp point his toe, flick the hair out of his eyes and tease a wistful chord from his instrument. Of course Thadie had been right. Of course Edward should be learning how to skip. No son of *his* should go graceless into the world. He spied him leaning beside the open window, looking bored and supercilious. Fashionable dancing he could come to later. He would scarcely be able to avoid it when he went south. But for now he should kick his heels up and let himself go. It would serve him well when he returned from London if he had discovered for himself the pleasure that ordinary people gained from music. And it should not be with just anyone. It must be with the fairest woman in the room so that as he set and swung her he would feel pride, confidence, boastfulness and perhaps, who could say, a twitch of young lust.

'By Jove yes!' he said and jumped to his feet. He looked at Daphne Cuthbert passaging her fan. 'My dear, you must excuse me if you will for one tiny moment – '

'Daisy Garland's your girl, Nat Horne,' she said, 'off you go. It'll do Edward a power of good. Make him feel like a hundred guineas. See if it don't. Ah, Mr O'Donnell, at last, I've a thirst on me like – '

'A shovelful of sand, was that what was on the tip of your tongue, dear lady? I fear I was delayed. Thiry seconds is a very liquid measurement where I was born. Was that liquid I said? To be sure, it must have been since the brain is famous for being father of the deed.'

'I'm not sure you have the phrase entirely correct.'

'It's curious you should say that, madam, for as I spoke, I said to myself, O'Donnell, you have planted the words as you do your beans, which is to say, in a manner that is not as line astern as they should be. And another thing –'

'Which we may call secundo – '

'Quite so, a lovely word that never strays far from my side. Secundo, therefore – ah, but this is a matter of such delicacy that I shall be embarrassed to make it known except behind the shield of your machine – spread it thus: exactly, madam, you have taken my notion as gracefully as Venus stepping from the ocean – and it is this – faith but I blush even to give it the time of day – do you promise you will not belabour me or make an adverse report on me to his honour if I say I am wondering how, on a point of anatomy – but this is bold, madam, this is boldness to fill a ship, I beg you spread your fan till it creaks – how – and this is my point, both secundo and the last I shall have to say on the subject – how can the brain be a father if it has no whim-wham?'

'Mr O'Donnell! Mr O'Donnell! I am shocked at you. I am completely overturned. This is upper-case boldness indeed. You must do a penance. You shall dance with me immediately.'

Daisy Apreece's eyebrows rose. Her hazel-brown eyes sparkled as she looked from Nat to Edward. What a sweet idea! The poor boy, abandoned on this of all nights! But of course she would, nothing would please her more! She had a melodious voice, rather deeper in tone than might have been expected in one so small. She was wearing a low-bosomed russet-coloured dress, cut on the full, with a black velvet sash. At her neck swung a smoky blue pearl enclosed within an oval of filigree'd gold. She looked to Sir Anthony for approval. With the gesture of a man who has been wed for sufficiently long to feel secure in the possession of his legal property, he waved her away and resumed his conversation. And thereafter it was pretty much as Daphne Cuthbert had predicted.

Dawn had yet to break when the Cuthberts left. The sky was indigo, the air still, humid and pregnant with thunder. Mr Cuthbert was spooned into his carriage by Digworth and fell asleep, gurgling in the corner like a pug dog. Mrs Cuthbert said thank you but she was perfectly capable of looking after herself. Thadie O'Donnell put his head in at the window and kissed his way from the tip of her fingers to the soft gusset of flesh above her elbow. Shattock climbed unsteadily on to his box. Nat gave them all a valedictory salute and stood back. His shoulders drooped. If there was one thing that saddened him more than the death of dogs and horses, it was the departure of guests. Thadie O'Donnell linked his arm through Nat's. 'Now why don't we find that dog of a tutor and give him a bit of a thrashing?'

'Thadie, I believe you are tosticated.'

'It is possible. And yourself, your honour?'

'I should like to be. To have had all my friends under my roof, to have fed and wined them, to have danced with my son – what greater happiness can there be? And now they are departing. Soon it will be over. Yes, Thadie, let us go in and tosticate ourselves like men.'

Four

'WHEE!' SHE squealed as they gathered speed on the hill down to the turnpike. 'Whee!' she cried and 'Whee!' again as Shattock hurled the coach through the first of Nat's regal sweeps. Volleys of sparks squirted into the night as the iron-rimmed wheels screwed against the road metal. Trees, shrubs, boulders, the startled faces of departing party-goers, swooped into the yellow pools of the coach lights and in a flash were erased. A thorn bush thrust its spiky fingers through her open window. The panting of the horses mingled with the rush of the hot night wind and the jangle of harness. The swingle bar rattled in its coupling. Torrents of gravel spewed against the floor beneath her. Rumbling and lurching, they sped through the blue-black night, Shattock's arms spread wide as, like a charioteer, he flung his team down Ladysway.

She slid back the panel and poked him in the back. 'You are going too fast. You must hold back, do you hear me?' She knew it was ridiculous. The man was clearly as drunk as a cobbler. But she thought it should be said. For the record. She could tell her husband she had said it if they broke an axle.

'You are going monstrously too fast,' she shouted again as a man on a pony took to the hillside. They swerved to avoid a hare. The coach kissed the bank, the wheels struck a fang of bedrock and they took to the air. With a crash they descended, pitching Mr Cuthbert into her lap. He opened and closed his mouth, choked on his saliva and, pressing his head against her thigh, began snoring again half an octave lower. God, but she longed for a pee. Never mind, first things first. Lightning flashed above them. In its dazzle she saw a bridge racing up the hill towards them. So narrow! And their speed so frightful! 'Aim for the centre, you imbecile, or you'll kill us.' Shattock turned on his box. She glimpsed a splash of teeth. 'Cockadoodledoo –'. She gripped the strap and closed her eyes. Cockadoodledoo! She'd give him cockadoodledoo all right, she'd give it him where it counted . . .

For two seconds the hooves drummed on the bridge. Then the pitch changed as they hit solid road again and went rocking down a straight towards the east and the palest glimmer of dawn. The gradient eased, the horses slackened their pace. She saw in front the ghostly ribbon of the turnpike and a flicker of light from the Green Man. The coach glided to a halt: the tempest abated. Shattock bowed his head between his knees. His whip slid to the ground. Mr Cuthbert snorted and opened his eyes. They all got down and standing besides the steaming horses, regarded each other uncertainly, in the way that people do when the lights go on after some great dramatic entertainment. Mrs Cuthbert returned from the bushes. Her husband squinted at the stars spinning through the sky. Then they remounted and turned south towards home.

'Nat's the lucky one,' she said between yawns, 'he's only got to go upstairs and tumble into bed.'

But Nat was not the lucky one. Only five months later the county was shocked to the marrow by the news of his ghastly death. None could believe it. So spontaneous a man, so humourful and kind, so sincere, so sympathetic to the human condition – and now no more. Nathaniel Horne of Winterbourne dead, drowned in the Rushes: it was not possible. There was neither man nor woman who did not experience a profound feeling of loss when the word got around. Could a just deity really exist? Wherein lay the mercy of a God who on a whim, at the toss of his head, could finish a man like Nat while all around he let the vilest scum scamper freely? At least, they said, trying as people will to salvage some meaning from the unintelligible, Edward had not been there to witness it.

That winter of 1774 was crueller than any could remember. The autumn rains had been incessant. The land springs, glutted after a run of wet seasons, flooded the corn vales and drowned the seedlings beneath a carpet of silt. Wiseacres shook their heads and spoke of famine when the time came to reap the grain. Then, in the middle of January, a piercing north-easter settled in and with it a frost that gripped the land in an iron claw. The sky was pinched and grey. In the blackened pastures the frost-rimed rushes stood pale and erect, like clumps of candles. Among them the sheep scraped disconsolately at the moss until they could take no more and lay down to die in the night in ditches and behind walls. Birds were unable to feed and dropped lifeless from their roosts. Tramps were found stiff in farmers' outhouses. Streams dwindled and ceased. Meat was so frozen that it could not be spitted. The weather was unsparing.

Nor was the day of Nat's funeral any different, excepting that for the first time there was a growl of snow in the wind. As they walked or rode to Winterbourne, the mourners smelled it and shivered. Some came up the Britannia road, crossing themselves as they passed the Rushes but refusing to look directly at it, forbidding their imaginations to grind out the details of Jupiter Horne's death throes. Others arrived up Ladysway. Singly or in silent shuffling groups, over two hundred people gathered that morning to bury Nat. Many were openly weeping. They crowded the church and when it could hold no more stood outside the porch in Breughelian misery, stamping their leather boots to keep warm. Their breath rose in misty columns.

The service was short. There were no words of pomp, for none could be found who would trust themselves to speak. Upon everyone lay the pall of mortality. With closed faces, they looked stolidly to the front. Numbly, automatically, they knelt, rose and intoned the responses. The bitter words of prayer raked at their hearts but were unable to penetrate, so powerfully was Nat still among them. No artifice of mankind was capable of reaching within those sealed and private chambers wherein tussled sorrow, compassion, fear and incomprehension.

Thin flakes of snow began to drift down from the hills as Nat was borne to his resting place. And now, as they watched his coffin swaying through the graveyard, the mourners thought, Had he really been so small? The Nat they knew, so bursting and sputtery, crammed within such pitiful bounds? Or had the water somehow shrunken his body and spirit during the night before it was recovered? And so, whether they liked it or not, their imaginations were driven into hateful and explicit visions of his agony. Yea, by drowning, whispered the earth-loving countryman within each of them: slowly, in the dark, in the slime, in terror – and at last they saw it all. They looked at Amos and thought, Surely there was something he could have done? But when they caught a glimpse of his face, and when they noticed how tightly he pressed his cheek against the coffin as he helped carry it from the church, they thought as one, Thank God it was he and not I.

The cordsmen took their places. The parson and Lady Blanche faced each other across the pit. She and Edward bowed their heads. Percival Hughes's quick words vanished into the starving sky.

Edward released his mother's hand. He watched his father's friends file past, saw them stare at the coffin as they flung down their offerings of soil. Some glanced at him as they turned away, and nodded. What did they mean? What was he required to feel? Nothing was clear to him. Mr Morris, his new tutor, had spoken to him about death and how it could have a different meaning for everybody. How it was a beginning as well as an end. He had done so in a dignified and kindly manner and Edward had been grateful. But it was not enough. He understood, because Mr Morris and his mother had told him so, that he would not see his father again. But he could not decipher the connection between his being and his unbeing. How was it that someone so personal to him, so silly, so wonderful, so jam-packed with spirit and enthusiasm, such a friend, could suddenly become nothing? Without any warning, asking permission, or saying goodbye. How could he have done such a thing to his son? Had he meant so little to his father? But death, he supposed, had entered the lives of all these people. They had known it at other times and in other places. They had buried their dead as he was now doing and still they breathed, moved, grieved and lived. In a few minutes they would be sitting down to the wake. They would eat and drink, repeat his father's jokes, say mudgy me! and by Jove! in just his tone of voice, tell their favourite stories about him – and then leave. In a month or two something else would have happened and Nat's memory would be no more than another pebble spinning in the daily stream of their thoughts. But for him it was different. He had more at stake – he *must* have more – because he was his father's son. And yet, as his feet squelched in the greasy puddle he had made on the lip of the grave, he was aware that he had nothing because he understood nothing. It was like snatching at the wind. He could not be as these people were, but he had no idea what he should be instead. There was obviously a key to it, but where should he look? How would he recognise it? Would anyone help him? Cold, lonely and resentful, he joined his mother at the head of the mourners and walked back down the lane to the house of his childhood.

Five

'YOU ARE not alone, Mr Spratchett. He is an enigma to us all. Yes, no, maybe – who can say how he will respond? I am sorry, but at present I can do nothing to suggest how the matter is to be carried forward.'

Nicholas Hawkesworth laid aside his spectacles. A red spot, the size of a farthing, showed where they had rested on either side of his nose. He rubbed his eyes with his knuckles and placed his palms flat on his desk. His fingers were like twigs, their joints very prominent.

'As I said, Edward is an enigma. He has been my friend and client since we were at Cambridge, but even now I feel I know him little better than when we met. April weather is more constant. Ah well, it is how it happens. Our profession would be a poor one if all men were alike. A dish of tea? The consignment is newly landed, I am told. Lewis will be glad to serve us. No? I understand. The avoirdupois of business, eh Mr Spratchett! But where should we be without it? Oh, one thing more before you leave: by when do you need a decision?'

'Her ladyship is not a well woman, not well at all. Her physician is adamant that she must leave the country before the winter sets in. The damp, you know, it is like acid on her lungs. May we say by September 1st? Will that be time enough for our enigmatic friend to decide upon these points?'

Spratchett gripped the arms of his chair and straddled to his feet. His stomach settled into its new alignment. He took his wig from the nail and spread it upon his round, bald head. He eased the crotch of his breeches with one finger. 'By the end of the month, then? We are agreed? Remember me, if you please, to your good lady . . .' Nicholas smiled and handed him his cane.

The other lawyer having departed, he sat down and addressed a short note to Edward Horne. The detail could wait. For the present it was important only to entangle his curiosity. Then he unlocked the false bookcase on the opposite side of the room from that by which Spratchett had left, and passed through a door faced in scarlet baize into the welcoming domesticity of his home.

'Tighter, Fanshawe.' Again his servant leaned forward to adjust the knot of his cravat.

'Don't strangle me, man.'

'If you were to lift your chin, sir . . .'

Edward felt Fanshawe's hands fretting at his throat. He looked down the back of his neck. His dark curls were speckled with dandruff. Ants' eggs.

'And now my cinnamon coat, if you please.' He swivelled his lithe body before the wall mirror. He advanced a leg. Very fine, these new breeches. Snug, trim, racy: very fine indeed.

'My canary waistcoat, do you think, Charlie? Or would it be somewhat too peacocky against the cinnamon? Do you suppose Miss Nelson would prefer a quieter contrast? Now read me Hawkesworth's letter again, his exact words, mind you, without any of your usual twiddlum-twaddlum about lawyers' pomposity. There was something in his phrasing that caught my ear. Not his normal pish. These buckles are positively revolting, Fanshawe. What the deuce do you do all day?'

Charlie Anstruther lifted a pallid hand to review his fingernails, but otherwise did not stir from the mantelshelf along which he had draped himself. 'Scrope's our man for reading,' he drawled, taking a file to the tip of one nail. 'Too oathy hot for a fellow to read and stand at the same time. Hey there, you fat sneaksby, wake up and remind Edward what his poxy lawyer wrote in that letter that came this morning.'

Because of the way that the curtains fell round the window seat, all that was visible of their friend was a pair of buckled shoes. There was a badger-like groan. A hand emerged from behind the lime green brocade and trawled beneath the seat. The paper rustled and disappeared. There was a long sigh.

'What a chap does for his friends . . . Very well, a fellow called Hawkesworth, who professes to have your every interest burning in his heart, has been honoured by a visit from a fellow called Scratchett. Says they're cooking something up, please send more money. Doesn't actually say that of course, but any fool can tell it's what they mean. Then it goes on – I tell you, Horney, no joking but this has the ring of an expensive letter – here we are, this is what you're after, pom-pom pom-pom, blow the bugle, sound the fife, the truth approacheth, limping a little as usual: "A proposition has been made –"'

The curtain flew back and Harry Scrope's untidy, amiable face appeared.

'A proposition! Hear that, will you! Even money it's the Nelson lot behind it. Old sugar-bags the Jamaican wants to marry his daughter off before his slaves get too uppish and he finds himself a pauper. I'll have a wager on it. Here, Charlie, give me a wager –'

Anstruther yawned. 'Y'know, Edward, if you take my advice, you'll steer well clear of all propositions. When a man makes you a proposition, it's a guinea plays a codpiece he's after the shirt on your back. If I was you, Adonis, I'd make a run for it. Go to Norfolk. Shoot a few partridges.'

Edward held out an arm and wriggled into his cinnamon coat. It had black braid facings and cuffs. He shook out the sleeves. 'A cravat pin? Is it asking too much that you remember my cravat pin, Fanshawe? But I know he mentioned something about it being a bit of a gamble. You missed that out. Read it again, Harry.'

'You ain't half a puzzle. Here's us swanks, Charlie and me, with a lifetime's acquaintance with all manoeuvres adjacent to the boudoir, laying short odds from what we've seen of you and Miss Jamaica on the gallops that you've landed a plantation heiress – and what do you do? Do you fetch your whip out and drive for the post like a good 'un? Oh no! You fret and fart over one piffling word your man's slipped in to cry the thing up. Pay no attention, it's only a friend speaking, but I have to declare that your judgement can be pretty rum at times. Oh I say ha ha that was a cracker. Rum – plantation – comical, eh? Oh very well, no needs to look at me like that.'

A blue-tasselled valance hung from the window seat on which

Scrope was sprawled. He began to roll one of its velvet buttons between his thumb and forefinger.

'All right, I concede. These are his exact words, straight as they fell from his inky tool. "I am aware that the allowance you receive from your mother is not so munificent as to permit daily, or should I say nightly, attendance at an institution known to us both where games of chance –". What pomposity! What utter bombast! Let this man henceforth be named Signore Pomposo di Orotundo.'

'It shall be posted in the *Gazette* on Thursday.'

'Must I continue? This is all too painful for a plain-speaking Yorkshireman. Oh very well, if you insist.' He held the letter above his nose and put a hand behind his head. '"But I believe you will find Mr Scratchett's proposition an engaging substitute. There is a gamble involved, you should know this in advance. If you are able to come and dine with Letitia and myself tomorrow, etc. and so on, I remain glubble glubble Pomposo Principe di Orotundo."' He tossed it away. 'There you are, his exact words.'

'I thought he was only a *signore.*'

'Well, he's a prince now. Very able chap. Gone up in the world.'

'In any case, we must note the word "engaging". We must dub it significant.'

'I tell you, Edward, your fortune is as good as made. The Jamaican has had enough. The weevils of old age have got to his brain. He wants to be shown more front doors and fewer basement steps. How nice, he is thinking, to dandle a grandchild on my creaking knee, how diverting to hear the patter of tiny feet in place of my physician's clumping boots. Make no mistake, what he craves above all else is to purify his sallow lineage through an alliance with creamy, vigorous, English sap. And you, my dear chap, by reason of your liaison with his sumptuous daughter, are sitting squarely in his sights.

'Can the import of the proposition be any other? Would you not agree, Charlie, that the mercury is in the ascendant for Horney here?'

'Nothing more certain. So long as our hero does not flinch.'

'Well?' demanded Edward truculently. He felt tired and bilious. His engagement had not been a success. She had been indisposed (she said). The favours that he had anticipated had not been available. He had behaved badly and he knew it: had sulked on being rebuffed and left with tasteless alacrity. And then, as he was going, he'd argued with the footman. With a footman! In fact he'd nearly struck him for refusing to lend him an umbrella. And how it had been raining, with never a chairman to be found. In the end he'd had to walk through the thunderstorm to Arthur's so that when, in the early hours, Anstruther and Scrope had tipped him into a hackney chair, he'd been both wet and drunk. To add insult to injury, he'd been awakened by Fanshawe not with the compassionate twinkle that a servant should reserve for a peccant employer but with a spiteful leer, to say nothing of a great deal of wholly unnecessary noise. And he disliked receiving unexpected letters from lawyers.

'Well?' he repeated, throwing himself into his host's chair, his peevish expression saying more clearly than any words could, Better not be wasting my time. Hawkesworth regarded him dryly. What had his father said when he completed his apprenticeship? 'M'boy, to succeed in this profession of ours, you must be able to read a client's liver as plainly as his will.' He went to the oak corner cupboard and unlocked the cellar keys.

'I do believe a glass of wine before we eat will make our evening more congenial, don't you, Edward?' He tossed the keys in the air, rattled them mischievously beneath Edward's nose and left the room.

It was the brandy that had done it. He should have known better. Anstruther always swore that Arthur's had the vilest liquor in town, that they strained it from the dregs of the barrel. Dear God, but he wouldn't make that mistake again.

He put his feet up on a stool and looked mumpishly round Hawkesworth's comfortably disorganised drawing-room. The walls were ivory coloured and carried a dense hang of small Dutch pastoral scenes, several of them skew-whiff. It irritated him that one so neat in his office habits, and with a wife as proper as Letitia, should be so contrary in the manner of his private furnishings. He pressed his fingers against his temples. Swaying trees murmured to him through the open windows. Pulses of young, clean air whisked in and out and rummaged through the curtains. The growl of London was muted. Everything had been refreshed and invigorated by last night's storm, the crabby humours of the capital purged. As he sat listening to the rustle of leaves and watched the last of the sunshine dart up and down the flaking trunks of the poplars, he began to draw from them some of their blitheness. Nature was so calm as she pattered round with her mop and bucket, staunching and renewing. Would that he could exchange Fanshawe for her! What a servant she'd make, discreet and even-tempered, always ready with a smile when one awoke. Would never ask for pay. And without a speck of dandruff anywhere.

He closed his eyes. It was good to be alone. The quiet, the little breezes, the tap tap tapping of the curtain cords against the shutters, the transient shadows that flickered beneath his eyelids – it was marvellously restful. It was what he needed.

Presently, and with a feeling of shame for his earlier churlishness (of which at the time he had been only half-conscious: the words had been extruded from his mouth of their own accord, plop plop, like eggs from a mechanical hen), he got up to inspect the picture above the mantelshelf. It was a Dutch representation of the battle of the Medway. Snow-capped wavelets, puffs of cannon smoke, the blazing dockyards, despairing Englishmen, de Ruyter on his quarterdeck with epaulettes the size of garden rakes – the artist had not spared himself. Edward stood before it with his thumbs in his waistband and his coat bunched behind his back. One could almost say the man had been there himself, it was so detailed and realistic. And yet . . . he'd wager it hadn't been like that really. He took a step closer, scratching his ribs. Flapdoodle, the lot of it! And he was just thinking contumaciously: this barrel-chested, jaw-jutting, clanking old sea dog doesn't actually give a rap for the battle, his ship or the drowning sailor (bottom left); a guinea says his uppermost concern is how quickly he can get home to a bucket of good Dutch gin and inside his wobbling frou, or if not inside his, inside someone else's – when the door behind him opened. He gave a jump and turned. He saw Hawkesworth with one bottle in his hand and a second under his arm. At his heels came Letitia, a trim, auburn-haired woman with the eyes of a bantam hen, and a manservant carrying a stool from which to light the candles.

'I was just thinking –', he started.

'I know, Edward,' Letitia said, going over to fasten the windows, 'you were just thinking, How tiring to have to oblige a couple of frumps like the Hawkesworths when I could have been at Arthur's with my friends. See how well I know you! But come, sit down here beside me and tell me about yourself.'

Nicholas placed a glass in his hand. He sipped at it. In no time he was back in the saddle.

Letitia Hawkesworth liked Edward. She found him handsome. The aura of tragedy that touched him was attractive to her: the death of his father, his mother's illness, all those acres in Derbyshire that neither of them visited (why ever not?), his perpetual air of being lost in some wilderness. He needed protecting, she thought. She dimly imagined a webby unlit *thing* rushing towards him, poised to engulf him the instant he stepped out of his private shelter and into a world of which she was certain he understood nothing, a world of cannibals, sharks and harpies. She fluffed herself out at the head of the dinner table and spread her napkin. How would he respond to his mother's proposal? She enjoyed these intricate unwrappings of family history with all their revelations of thwarted ambition and rusty deceptions. It was like dealing with a crate of broken crockery. Would this handle agree to be reunited with this cup, or had age and discolouration made them incompatible? Were all the pieces present? Covertly she watched him drink his soup.

His head with its curly black hair was bent forward, his lips parted. Small, irregular teeth: white pliant fingers tilting his soup dish away from him. His napkin, which he had tucked into a buttonhole in his coat, cascaded down his shirt front like a snowdrift. His eyes, the steady grey of dry slate, were fixed on Nicholas. (They were discussing the affairs of the New River Company, a perennially fascinating subject to her husband.) He spoke rarely, a question now and then about their dividend history or the ownership of the King's Cog, little more, and when he did it was with a light, almost colourless voice. He might be inclined to haughtiness, as Nicholas said, but it was hard to see him losing his temper. She could not picture him ranting or throwing his arms around. There was humour in his face, round the edges of his eyes and mouth, and when he did come out and declare his opinion forthrightly on some point or other of the company's operations, it was with a wry and economical wisdom. Nicholas paused. Or perhaps he had finished. She found it hard to tell the difference these days. His voice slithered to a standstill, and the Company's stopcocks, flumes and other recondite matters of commerce trickled peacefully away in the direction of the unoccupied seat at the far end of the softly spangling table. Edward finished his soup and wiped his mouth. Then for some reason he laughed, a small explosive bark so unconnected to the silence that had momentarily enveloped them as to suggest he had all along been thinking about something totally different. His eyes danced, his face creased with pleasure and turning to her he smiled so beautifully that she felt quite shaken up.

A maid entered to change the plates. Letitia wished now that she had ordered a fish course. Nicholas was always telling her that there was no better moment to introduce a nervous subject than when people were eating fish. It was such a finickety business. All those tiny bones. Every sort of manoeuvre – intellectual, emotional and diplomatic – was rendered practicable by the impossibility of simultaneously speaking and eating fish. No hasty decision was ever reached over a side of young pike. No man could complain afterwards he'd been pushed into a foolish mortgage or obliged to concede a preposterous dowry if he'd taken the precaution of filling his mouth with steamed pike before he replied.

The meal progressed. Wine and conversation flowed pleasantly. But Letitia began to grow impatient. She was inquisitive to know how Edward would deal with his mother's offer. She had fed and entertained the players. She had earned her seat in front of the orchestra pit. What if she grew sleepy and had to retire before the performance started? That would never do. She wanted to hear the trumpets tootle, to see the drum skins dimple and fiddle bows leap. She wanted to see the curtains part and the actors foregather. She wanted her money's worth.

'What news of your mother then?' she enquired, adding encouragingly, 'Nicholas says Mr Spratchett gave him so indifferent an account that he was really quite worried. Do tell me he was mistaken.'

The stridency of his name pushed Augustus Spratchett instantly into the limelight. A quicker trajectory was imparted to the proceedings. Even if either party had wished to, it was impossible any longer to ignore the reason for the meeting. The outline of the proposition, and thereby the form and temperature of the gamble involved, surfaced like a sounding whale in the swell of their conversation. Letitia pushed her plate aside and sat back in her chair with a motherly wiggle of her bottom as Nicholas, frugally at first, but then with increasing confidence as he realised he had Edward's complete attention, launched himself into the affairs of Lady Blanche.

The candles were trimmed. The port was fetched. Letitia was informed that her continued presence was indispensable. And by the time they had drunk their first glass, her ladyship's propositions lay stark upon the mahogany table. She would settle Edward's existing debts; give him a small sum in cash; and make over to him the entire property of Winterbourne without entail. (Which aspect the lawyer very properly emphasised.) *Per contra*, she would be relieved of the burden both of his annual allowance and of the rent on his spacious lodgings, immediately and for the rest of her life.

'In a nutshell, Edward, her health is poor, she worries that she may last longer than her money, and she is eager to live abroad among her English friends in Florence, where she understands that everything is much cheaper. Knowing that she may never return, and mindful of the duties of a mother to her only child, she is anxious to settle her affairs. Cleanly, fairly and expeditiously.

'For your part, you can either continue in London as you are or you can cut loose and go to Winterbourne. You cannot do both. That is the gamble I spoke of.'

'But no entail, eh? So I could sell the place if I wished and return within the week, is that not so?'

'Yes. Perhaps not within a week. I have never thought of you as the type to do anything within a week. But in theory the answer is yes. Derbyshire is not short of wealthy men – Arkwrights, Strutts and so on – oh, I could list any number of prosperous families from those parts, good breeders all of them and each one keen to see their sons settled. You should have little difficulty finding a buyer for a property such as Winterbourne.'

'I see.' Edward stroked the stem of his port glass.

But he did not. It was thirteen years since he had left Winterbourne. He had neither returned nor wanted to. The memory of that departure had stained his mind ever since. He had shovelled it to the back of his consciousness together with all the other images of his childhood. And now he was being asked to take them out again and reach an accommodation with them. Could he do that? There were other considerations too. It was all very well to say he would sell it and return to London a wealthy man, but supposing it took a year instead of a week – what would he do all day? What did he know about agriculture? What friends would he have there? What about Caroline Nelson?

'The pleasures of London are very solid, you know,' he said at length, glancing from Nicholas to his wife and back.

'Tell me, Edward, what do you suppose is going through your mother's head at the moment?' asked Letitia.

He looked at her in a puzzled way. The last occasion he and his mother had met had been about six months before, for coffee at the Cocoa Tree. It was not something they did often. He never asked himself why: some stones were best left unturned. She was late. He was reading the new issue of the *Gentleman's Magazine*. Suddenly he felt her presence at his shoulder. He dropped his paper and half rose. This cobweb with violet pouches beneath her faded, sunken eyes, this tiny figure who was gripping her parasol as if it alone stood between her and death, could this be his mother? God, but she'd gone downhill fast. Shocked, embarrassed and yet at the same time fascinated by the fragility of this stranger who was not a stranger, he was for a moment transfixed. They sat and drank and talked of this and that, foraging among the few interests they had in common. He had spoken too heartily. 'It's a shame we do not have more cousins to discuss,' he said loudly as the flow slackened. She lunged across the table. Her nails dug into his wrists. Her eyes shone with the fervour of devotional lamps. Her face was inches from his. Every chisel mark of anguish was as clear as linenfold. 'Edward, my son, my dearest son –'. It was almost a whisper. She opened her mouth again – he could see it as if it had been yesterday, a great knot of words stumbling over each other in their anxiety to be born – and then a carrot-headed youth holding a plate of chops and turnips shoulder-high knocked into the back of her chair. Her parasol fell into the sawdust. She glanced at it. She looked up at the waiter with an expression of hurt and bewilderment, and when her eyes again met his, they were dead. The lamps had been extinguished. He was looking into two lifeless backwaters. The moment, the only such moment he had ever known with her, had gone, slain in the womb by this single act of gaucherie. For a second they sat without moving. 'My poor Nathaniel, he is waiting for me. I must go –'. She patted the back of his hand, a couple of feathery taps, that was all, rose and left. Not one word more did she say. He watched her out of the window as she walked down the street, a lonely widow fumbling with her parasol in the summer drizzle. What had she wanted to say? How the devil could he tell?

No, he said to Letitia after a long pause, he really could not imagine what was going through his mother's mind.

But she had seen those grey eyes turn in on themselves and heard the defiance in his voice. He knows, she thought. He knows well enough. But he cannot be a fugitive for ever. A candle sputtered and expired in a gutter of smoke. Its odour pervaded the room. She gathered her skirts and pushed back her chair.

'You have no choice, Edward. Accept the word of another mother. Go to Winterbourne and go soon. As Nicholas says, you can always sell it.'

IT WAS early on a flawless autumn afternoon that the post-chaise he had engaged in Derby deposited Edward Horne outside the Green Man. He descended stiffly. The vehicle bounced away down the turnpike at the head of a lengthening plume of dust. The journey had been long. He felt liverish and unslept. His clothes were the same as he had worn to the Hawkesworths and clung to him like old fish wrappings. He picked the straw off his coat and looked around, frowning. It was lonely. The incessant jerking and rumbling of the Manchester coach, the stopping and starting at all hours, the fug, the frowsiness, the smell and the inanity of the conversation of his fellow passengers, all these he had thought bad enough at the time, but now, as he stood in the horrible silence, he would have given his right arm to have them back again. It was frightening it was so quiet. The country air struck him as bogus. It had no body to it. No, this was not what he'd had in mind when he'd recklessly told the Hawkesworths that so long as they sent his things on by carrier, he'd leave for Winterbourne on the very next coach. Damme if I won't! he'd exclaimed, thumping his glass on the table. And now here he was, already pining to be back in his familiar haunts.

His glance flickered over the half-timbered walls and ivied chimney of the Green Man. He supposed he was being observed from some part of it. A great spyer on folk had been Arthur Smith, he remembered. Cumbersome in his movements, obsequious in his manner, and with quick magpie eyes that never fixed a man in the face but prowled up and down his coat buttons, measuring and probing. Perhaps he'd died. Thirteen years was a long time.

A pony was tied up beneath a dusty clump of sycamores,

shaking its head and swishing its scrunty tail against the flies. Chickens were scratching between its hooves. He watched them cock their heads and eye him with the glittering prurience of their species. Behind ran a brook with a footbridge leading to a pasture in which lay a black cow under an oak tree. An old dwindled man emerged from the hovels behind the inn and limped across the bridge. Muttering to himself, he poked at the cow's rump with a hazel switch. The gruff slither of words carried clearly to Edward. The animal swayed to its feet, blinking in the sunlight. It licked at its flank and regarded the cause of its disturbance with apathy. The man lowered himself into a bowl of entwined tree roots and cross-legged began to whittle at his stick with a knife. With its empty milk bag slapping against its legs, the cow ambled across the pasture to the stream. It lifted its dripping muzzle and looked pensively at Edward. The man too looked across at him, made as if to rise but instead gave a vague flourish of his switch.

How sordid and provincial it all was. Edward snorted and, slinging his coat over his shoulder, set off up Ladysway.

'Just like his mother.' Madge Smith, a plumpish woman with an orderly face and a plain kerchief round her head, moved a bowl of whey and another of raspberries to one side and placed her elbows on the sill. 'Same sort of glued-up expression. Didn't much care for what he saw, that's for certain. Wonder why he didn't come to the door. You'd have thought that after all these years he'd have been curious to learn if we were still here.' She rubbed a hole in the window grime. 'Must be having his baggage sent on behind him. Funny him arriving out of the blue like that. No word of warning, no horse, not even a little parcel of things to tide him over. Do you suppose Amos knows he's coming?'

Arthur Smith stropped his jowls with the back of his hand. He had a plunging, hound-like face in which his small eyes seemed set too high for comfort. His shirt was grey with age and he wore a stained moleskin waistcoat with brass buttons, the top one unfastened.

'It's a queer business, like you say . . .' He hoicked around in his mouth with a dirty forefinger. 'D'ye remember that night Sir Anthony rode over soon after her ladyship went off to town? Didn't he say how we were to be sure and tell him when any of the family returned? D'ye remember?' He flicked a gobbet of mutton gristle on to the floor. 'Can't recall a year when the flies were so bad. D'ye remember Sir Anthony saying that, Madge?'

'Think I'd forget a night like that? Door flew open and in he stamped all done up in his storm cloak, leaving puddles from one end of my floor to the other like plates of soup. Think I'd forget that in a hurry? And then ha ha ha in that lordy voice of his and did we have something for the inner man on account of the 'trocious weather.'

'And more fool I for giving him a nip of the contraband,' said Arthur unhappily.

'Next thing we knew he'd sat himself in my chair with whole rivers coming out of his boots –'

'It were my chair he sat in, Mrs Smith.'

'Right you are, your chair it was. Anyroads, it don't matter as they both had to be burnt on account of the worm they'd taken.'

'And then he said, "A bird can't fly on one wing alone", and held out his glass.'

'Couldn't refuse him, could us, he being who he is?'

'No more'n we could dress in silk and satin. How many wings did that bird have before it could fly?'

'Doesn't bear thinking about. But he left in the end. A buster of a night it was too. Wasn't that when the bridge was swept away?'

They stood by the window watching Edward's lean figure disappearing up Ladysway.

'Strangest thing of all was having that groom of his, Thirkle it must have been at the time, ride down from Overmoor the next morning asking if we knew where Sir Anthony was. Never did fathom where he'd spent the night, did us?'

'Queer folk the gentry, Madge. Different from the likes of you and me. No way of knowing what really goes on inside their heads. Sweet as liquorice one day and the next day bang! it's off with your topknot. Never know where you are with them. Mind you, old Mr Horne wasn't like that. Steady as a sundial, he was. Sir Anthony shouldn't have spoken about him like he did. Still, he's dead and gone so I suppose it didn't do anybody any harm. D'ye reckon he still means it, what he said about keeping an eye out for the family?'

'Well you're not going to discover by standing there, you great lummox. So off you go to Overmoor and tell himself who's walking up Ladysway. Could be something in it for us, you never can say. Off with you. Off! Off!'

Flapping her arms in front of her, she shooed him from the kitchen.

A red admirable jinked across the road in front of Edward, its wing bands glinting in the sunlight. He took out a lawn handkerchief and mopped his brow. A blister was starting to form on his right heel. He sat down and packed his shoe with elder leaves. From all directions, the shining face of beauty beamed down on him: the sky, the trees, the hills, the noble prospects shimmering from afar in the heat of a golden September. About his feet, bents nodded their seed-laden heads as a breath of wind stole through their hairy stems. But he saw them not for what they were, not for the gifts from the tray of a kindly god, but only for their value in the eyes of an Arkwright, a Strutt or a Boulton. He felt put upon. He should have stuck to his guns and remained in London. He should never have listened to Letitia. Where was the fun to be had in a place like this? Where was a man to have a good rub-a-dub with his friends?

He rose. A bee rushed past him, braked, and returned to inspect at its leisure this unfamiliar obelisk. A huge dandelion sprouted from the bank beside him. He slashed tetchily at it with his cane and watched its myriad seeds float away in a cloud. Now if each of them was an Arkwright's guinea – no, he could never live off that; if each of them were a hundred guineas and the whole was invested in the Funds at three per centum per annum . . .

A movement below caught his eye. A man had come out of the Green Man and mounted the pony. So Arthur Smith was living. Even at that distance his style of riding was unmistakable, all loose and floppy, like a man who was on a horse for the first time, like a Venetian. He watched him shamble off up the turnpike. A second horseman appeared at a walk from a piece of woodland that straddled the road. The two met and stopped. Edward saw their heads move as they spoke. Arthur pointed up the hill. The other shielded his eyes and also looked upwards. They folded their arms across their saddle bows. The horses sniffed at each other. Arthur raised his hat. They parted.

The newcomer reached the inn, waved – that must be to Mrs Smith – and passed on heading south, straight as a broomstick in his saddle. Ha! the parson. And a new one into the bargain. So Hughes had gone to meet his maker. Well at least there'd been some changes since he'd left. At least something happened here. He picked up his coat and continued.

It was the church he saw first as he descended between the beech trees, squatting on a mound beneath its dumpy steeple. Then the parsonage, polished and trim; then the cottages beside the lane, the barns and the cowsheds, and, finally, on its rocky plateau, the great spread of Winterbourne House. He halted in a gap between the trees. Though he had been thinking of little else (through wishing to see for himself how it would strike the eye of a buyer), the sight still caught him by surprise. Fractured memories that he had believed extinct swam into his mind and nibbled at its edges. He swatted at them as, more slowly now, he limped into the sunlight. Beyond and below the house, green fields stretched out on both sides of the Eve towards the Out Ground and the Rushes. On the horizon the moorland wavered bluishly in the haze. 'And may the incense all be mine' – the line came to him from he knew not what long-departed schoolroom. A cockerel shook its wings from the top of the dung heap. A few seconds later its diminutive call reached him. 'Peacocks,' he whispered to himself, 'I see peacocks here.' And with these two random thoughts that sprang from nowhere, like gateposts in a fog, he reopened his account with Winterbourne.

He chose to go through the farmyard rather than directly to the house. He needed a meal, a drink, to announce himself. What he might do next, he had no idea. At some stage he would have to speak to Amos. Somehow or other, this week or the one after, he would find a chance to float through his mind the possibility of his stay being regretfully curtailed.

Dogs thrust their snouts beneath chewed doors and snarled toothily at him as he walked past. Hazelwood hurdles were stacked against the walls, half-hidden by nettles and dockens. Scattered over the bare brown soil were lozenges of sheep droppings. Flies crawled fatly upon their segmented slopes. He picked his steps with care. A succession of odours offered themselves: simmering bones from the flesh house, the tang of rotting manure, the richness of fresh sawdust, the reek of stale milk from the byre, the sharpness of animal urine. On a sort of clothes line hung the curing skin of a cow, its empty leggings trailing in the dust. Half a dozen doves with lustrous blue necks were clustered in a semicircle round a heap of oat husks. More memories. He could not help himself but smile.

A scurry of piglets came racing round the angle of the granary, all pink and bobbing, absorbed in a game of their own devising. They saw him and with a chorus of snortles, raced back the way they'd come. He turned the corner. In front of him, frozen in the action of filling their pails at a circular, stone-capped well, were a man and a woman. They were both rather younger than him, the former strong and sunburned with a scrap of blue cotton knotted round his neck. The man looked carefully at Edward and said something to the girl. She placed her leather pail on the parapet and with a flash of white calves and a ripple of long brown hair, made off at a run.

The men shook hands uncertainly. 'Father's been expecting thee,' said Davie Paxton.

Superficially, time had not been unkind to Amos Paxton since the death of Nathaniel Horne. He walked more slowly and stooped a little. Rheumatism troubled him when the weather was damp. His eyes were clouded as if by a sea mist and he was apt to forget his hat when he went to cut sticks in the coppice. But within himself he had aged terribly. It was true that the responsibility for Winterbourne was not entirely his. Once a year after harvest a mannie would ride up from Derby, make a cursory inspection of the buildings, take a pinch of hay and hold it to his nostrils, trickle a few oats between his fingers, hem and haw over a glass of small beer and, having pronounced upon Amos and his works a paternoster on behalf of her ladyship, depart as quickly as he decently could. But that was only once a twelvemonth and awhiles he had to carry the burden of Winterbourne alone. It was a lot to ask of a man past his prime, that he care for so much as if it was his own. Will either of them return? Where will it all end for us? he'd demand of Mary, his wife. But she could give no answer.

During the early days, when the rattle of an arriving carriage was a daily hope, they often talked among themselves in the evenings about Nat, raking through their memories to pass the time. But in the end even this became self-defeating. For to have stood by and watched another man drown was not a wound that could be dressed and thought no more of, like grazing a shin or spraining an ankle. The more they spoke of Nat, the more grossly his death renewed itself in Amos's memory, until now it clung there unquenchably, gorging itself upon his emotions as if it were an immense leech. The blame had not been his. No one could have saved Nat. A thousand times his family had told Amos this, but still he was oppressed and his sleep troubled.

What then was a man to do?

'You and Davie must come to Overmoor. I need a foreman I can trust,' Sir Anthony Apreece said one morning, horsing unexpectedly into the yard with a couple of brace of hounds. 'And Mary and Davie's Annie, of course. There is a fine house waiting for you. You and I can farm in the modern style. You would be a proud man at Overmoor,' he added, jingling coins in his pocket.

'But I'm a proud man here. And you've rooted out your hazel coppice. So where'd I go for my sticks?'

'You can ride over here any day you choose. That cannot be an objection.'

'From Winterbourne I hail and here I'll stay till I die, like my folks afore me, thanking 'ee, Sir Anthony.'

Besides, he said to Mary that night, there'd always been something about the man that struck him as, how should he say – ticklish. Uncertain. To do with his temper. He couldn't quite put his finger on it and would rather not have the opportunity to do so.

So he stayed, growing each year more gnarled and rheumy and each spring singing a little less into the tufty ears of his plough horses as they plodged through the biting April showers. But conscientious he remained, as ever. 'A day of reckoning will come,' he said to Tom Glossipp as they crouched beneath a hedge with their dinner of bread and dripping and salted bacon, 'mark my words if it don't, Tom. Just when we're least expecting it, like when we despair of ever seeing the sun again after months of rain, there'll be a to-do of carriages and folk bustling down Ladysway and Mr Edward saying, What's all this about then and why hasn't that been seen to? The day'll come all right and when it does, I'm not the man to be found wanting.'

But that spring there had been a disaster he was powerless either to avert or restore.

It had happened one mid-afternoon on a day of ceaseless rain. He and Davie and the woodmen had been sheltering in the byre, watching Tom Glossipp deliver a calf. It had not been an easy birth. Every year they had trouble with this cow, a red brindled beast with a wild eye and curvy, sharp-pointed horns that could pin a man to the wall or break his skin with one toss of its head. It had taken the five of them to get her into a pen and hold her, while Tom guddled amongst her vessels with his gentle hands as she strained and roared and savaged them with her rolling, white-rimmed eyes. In the end they had to put a rope round the calf's hooves and it slid wetly out with no bother. Now they were standing around to see if it would suck of its own accord. Tom was wiping his forearms with a handful of hay and expressing his ardent wish that it would, since he had no mind to get himself kicked to death by the old fecker if he had to crawl beneath her and show the calf what an udder looked like. So there they were in the dingy shed with the brindled cow and her calf, and the rain beating on the slates above them, and the wind howling through the sacking at the narrow window slits, when there had come to their ears a long, shivering rumble from the direction of Winterbourne House. They had looked among each other. 'Sounds like a chimney stack's gone,' said one of the woodmen. But Amos had known immediately that such a crumbling and crashing was not that of a chimney. To all his other worries, therefore, had been added the collapse of a large section of the roof of the big house.

So when Annie ran up to the gate of his garden where he was sitting in the sun carving a serpent's tongue on to the nose of a new stick, and announced with wide eyes that Mr Horne was even now standing by the well speaking to Davie, he rose only slowly from his bench. His mind, which for thirteen years had been storing up all manner of information concerning storms and droughts, harvests thick and thin, cows died, horses foaled and wonders seen or sensed; which had arranged all these matters meticulously in compartments labelled Livestock Troubles, Harvest Records and Wonderments in preparation for this very moment, now stood on its head. It gripped only that which was closest. He put down his wood chisel and bolster. He brushed the shavings off his lap. He cleared his throat and putting his hands on his knees, stood up with the faltering dignity of an elderly parliamentarian. Mary passed him his hat. With a simple expression in his cloudy blue eyes, he said, 'How shall I tell him –?' There was the sound of footsteps and lively talk. He squared back his shoulders and walked resolutely between his hollyhocks and gillyflowers to the gate.

'Well, Amos, Davie here's been telling me how the devil of a storm fell out of the sky and did for my bedroom. So what I want to know is this: how the deuce do you expect me to play with my soldiers without a roof over my head? Eh, Packy, eh?' Edward stretched out his hand. Amos engulfed it between his two paws and led him into his cottage.

Seven

AT ABOUT the same time as Davie Paxton, lantern in hand, was leading Edward up to the old grooms' quarters in the stables besides the house, Arthur Smith was riding home from Overmoor Grange. Distributed about his person were a golden guinea, a pair of cow's kidneys wrapped in a handkerchief, and what remained after mother nature's ullage of a bottle and a half of Sir Anthony Apreece's claret. How could he and Madge have ever belittled such a clinker of a chap? Frank and grateful, not one suggestion of side the whole evening – it was impossible not to admire so sterling a fellow. Swaying in his saddle and slapping out the rhythm on his muttony thigh as beneath the plum-coloured night he jogged down the faintly limned road, he sang:

> The man at the Grange
> Is not at all strange
> And so I gaily sing!
> He likes his snuff
> And that's quite enough
> for me to name him King!

'What you be after, then?' demanded Mrs Keech, Sir Anthony's cook, standing like a gorgon in the doorway. 'Something for nothing, I'll warrant.' Her daughter, Jessie, had once worked at the Green Man as a maid. She knew all about the Smiths and their goings on.

'Oh, a little matter of words, a few humble words in private with Sir Anthony. Nothing to concern the ladies of the house, you may be sure,' he replied, thinking to himself, Small wonder Obadiah Keech has gone off to be a soldier.

'Well, if it's only words, that's not so bad. Master's down at the kennels with Hucknall. Feeding his hounds.' She gave a flick with her head in the direction of the walled garden and shut the door firmly. From the bull's-eye window to one side she watched Arthur lead his pony off to the stables.

A voice, deep and pleasant in timbre, called out to her from the drawing-room.

'Only Mr Smith from the Green Man, my lady, wanting to see Sir Anthony. Didn't say why and I didn't ask him or else I'd have been on the doorstep until nightfall.'

'Smith? Oh. Well, thank you anyway for seeing to it.'

'Don't think no more of it, ma'am.' Mrs Keech popped her head into the room and seeing that the two ladies were only starting on their afternoon tea went on her way to the kitchen, her strong black boots clicking on the flagstoned corridor.

'Silly old priss,' Arthur said to himself, tying up his pony in an empty stall. A mouse jumped out of the manger and sat on its edge looking at him down its dusty nose. Clayton, the youthful new groom at Overmoor, set down his feed buckets on the cobbles outside and swung on the door as he watched Arthur. He was neat in his ways, proud of his responsibilities, and instinctively averse to a publican making free with his stables.

'Coming down to the inn one night, are you, lad? Always a pleasure to see fresh faces, you know.'

'Waistcoat button's undone, Mr Smith.' He picked up his buckets and went off whistling.

Young whelp, he'd be as bad as mother Keech in a few years. Nevertheless, Arthur glanced down to find the matter was indeed as stated. Not that it made him feel any better inclined towards Clayton. He shot home the bolts and lumbered off past the kitchen garden to find Sir Anthony.

Apreece's fondness for personally trenchering his hounds was considered passing strange by his fellow fox-hunters who, though they knew little else, knew one thing for sure, that a baronet had no business doing the work of a servant. 'How now then, still waiting on the brutes at dinner are you, Anthony?' they chaffed him as they lolled over their port. 'You should get a dog to do a dog's work.'

'But see how they run,' he'd reply. 'Am I not the best prime minister the country has never had? Now hurry up and pass the decanter.'

This reference to the quip of Sir Robert Walpole (the old crook), that it was as difficult to find a perfect huntsman as a good prime minister, never failed to provoke a spirituous warmth of gratitude towards the owner of the hounds. And by the time the company had settled their bets (whose boots were the heaviest: who could hold out the poker with a straight arm for the longest), presented their peony-coloured faces to the night and bawled for their horses, their host's eccentricity had vanished from their minds.

Sir Anthony was forty-five and thus ten years older than his wife, Daisy, and twenty years older than Edward Horne. He was on the taller side of medium, with a strong, well-barrelled chest from which he threw (in fox-hunting parlance) an imposing voice rendered rather pompous and gravelly by port, snuff and the absence of doubt. His neck was powerful and his dark hair thick. On his upper cheeks he sported slivers of stiff black hairs, like an otter's whiskers. His eyes were the faded blue of a showery sky and the skin beneath them pale and lax. His lips were hard from blowing his hunting horn and his teeth in good order. From each nostril protruded a spike of hair yellowed by the snuff that he had sent up from London in waxed packets.

Other things also reached him from London. When there was a scarcity of foxes at Overmoor, he purchased French ones, imported from Boulogne through a dealer in Leadenhall called Hoon. He bought tea, coffee, wine and dentifrice; phials of James's Powder for his gout, and Mr Young's farming surveys from Lackington's, the booksellers in Chiswell Street. Occasionally he ordered a few feminine knick-knacks for Daisy, which he bestowed upon her grudgingly. But his main import from London, more precious perhaps even than Mr Hoon's mangy foxes, was the personal bulletin on the state of the Funds that he received each month from that pillar of London's financial community, Mr Samuel Gomez. Of all the unmoveable feasts in Sir Anthony's calendar, this was the most rock-like. Sunday matins was like a bumble-bee in a gale by comparison. Not that he was a slave to the advice of Mr Gomez. On the contrary. He liked to hear what the other had to say only so that he could take the opposite view, something he did from a conviction that his own opinions were *ex hypothesi* superior to all others.

He enjoyed money. From an early age he had comprehended its power. In due course he made a further discovery: that every penny which accrued to his purse was a penny lost by another. This added a new and combative zest to his dealings. Where before had existed only the pleasure of making money, there was now the additional excitement of the duel. To know that by the operation of his acumen he might not only feather his own nest, but at the same time, like the cuckoo, bundle some less perspicacious fellow out of his, was a rare tonic to him. It was as if he had bought two of something for the price of one.

Life he regarded as a continual tug-of-war. One dug in one's heels, took the strain, gauged the strength of one's opponents – and waited, bracing oneself for the heave and tramp when the condign moment appeared. Of course, mistakes could occur. One might slip, or be distracted by a shout from the crowd of onlookers. It might be advantageous to concede a foot or two, even a matter of yards. But in the end – well, the outcome was beyond doubt. It never struck him as possible that it could be otherwise. It was inconceivable that a man of his intelligence and determination could fail. Fools and losers were what he fed to his dogs.

Nor for a moment did he regard this perception of things as other than wholly normal. It was as banal to him as two times two. Here, life; and there, but a stone's throw away, death. In between but a piddling fragment knapped from the huge block of time, in which to do everything he wanted. So why should he trim and squawk and let his course be perverted by the opinions of others? Every man for himself, *de minimis non curat lex*, he who swims fastest sinks least – these and their like were his mottoes. Had anyone suggested to him that he was a bit of a stickleback or inconsiderate towards Daisy, he would have been genuinely astonished. Me? he would have replied, unrolling his pouchy eyes. Me? stabbing at his chest with an angled index finger. But my dear chap, it is the way I am. It's how I was born. How can I be someone else? And anyway, you mustn't believe everything you hear. You wouldn't credit how jealous some people can be. And at this point he would as likely as not turn on his interlocutor that crinkly, slanting smile that had won him hard-drinking, hard-riding friends throughout his life, winkled Overmoor out of his unmarried aunt, seduced Daisy, and that proclaimed for all to see that here was nothing more complicated than a sympathetic, amusing and good-natured fellow.

'Well, and what brings the innkeeper out here on this fine afternoon?' he said as he stood at his bench, paring the fat off a set of kidneys. 'Been horrid to Madge again have you, Arthur? Catch you having a bit of a scamper in the hayloft, did she?' He laid down his knife and tossed the kidneys to the publican. He wiped his hands on his smock.

'Take 'em for Madge with my compliments, that should help her get over it. You know, Arthur, it's always a problem getting enough fallen stock to keep the dogs going at this time of the year. The cattle are in too good a fettle with all the summer grass around. May have to boil up the wife's horse one day. Can't let hounds starve. No hounds, no hunting. Can't risk that. Course she'd holler like the devil but that's women for you, eh?'

Arthur put back his head and laughed immoderately. He quite believed Sir Anthony could boil up his wife's horse.

'Ever tried horses' kidneys? Sweet as apples, some say, but I don't go for them myself. I give 'em to Hucknall. He'll eat anything from those parts, especially if it's got a touch of green about it. Says it makes him go better. Ain't that so, Hucknall?'

A squat figure with eyes red-rimmed from smoke and a tangle of greying locks came out of the boiler-room. He wedged the door open with the femur of some devoured creature and scowled at the sunlight.

'Ain't that the case, that you and that missus of yours like a touch of green to your tripe? Keeps things moving down below, that's what you once told me. Anyway, hang this up for me. Mr Smith and I are off to discuss the price of coal.' Apreece threw him his smock. His legs were thick, his calves imperious. He was wearing drab whipcord breeches. 'You'll have to trencher the bitch pack by yourself. Don't spare the whip if any of them get too forrard. Now, Arthur, tell me the news from the Green Man . . .'

They set off up the lane that ran from the kennels through the orchard. Hucknall watched their backs recede, their heads turn in question and answer. That Arthur Smith has something to sell, he thought to himself, or I'm a Dutchman. He spat and went back into the boiler-room, leaving the door open.

Apreece gestured encouragingly. Publicans heard things. One ignored them at one's peril.

'It happened this way, Sir Anthony . . .' Deftly Arthur fed him his story.

'No baggage, you say? Not even one small grip? And no one to meet him?' He reached up and plucked an apple. 'Here Arthur, payment on account, as it were. One the wasps haven't touched. Now start again at the beginning, every little thing that you can recall . . .'

On their left was the high wall of the kitchen garden. From its interstices late blooms of valerian were flowering. So, Ned Horne had come into his patrimony. At last, after thirteen years of waiting, the owner of Winterbourne had appeared. Not that he'd been idle in the meantime. Other farms had hove into his sights and he'd pouched them all. Old man Bunn over at Milkwells had woken up one morning and decided, quite simply, that he'd had enough. Only ninety-three acres but each a good one. Johnnie Tytful had been persuaded to sell by the death of his son. Got a pole through the chest when his cart had overturned. Only Hewer at Longbottom had put up a fight. Six years it had taken but he'd sunk him in the end. A fine place, too, three hundred acres of easy ploughing. Or thereby, as the lawyers put it. So how long, he thought, tossing his apple core into the grass and giving Arthur's arm a bit of a squeeze, would it take to get Ned Horne out of Winterbourne? What would it cost? Three thousand acres, begob – but how well it would run with Overmoor . . .

'Dammit, Arthur, but you've done me the best turn a fellow could. Come along in and let's get to the bottom of a glass together. It's not every day a piece of news like this comes my way.'

The sun was starting to dip behind the elms as Apreece lit the candles in his business room. It was a narrow chamber, set apart from the main reception rooms of the Grange and sunken a little below their general level so that from its single Gothic window one could reach out and touch the grass. It faced east, to the front of the house. Only fleetingly in the morning could the sun enter. Under the window was an iron-hooped map chest and standing in the corner next to it a short wooden measuring pole. Against the wall stood a leather-covered sofa. Behind Apreece's chair was an open-fronted bookcase on whose shelves an assortment of agricultural works by Arthur Young and others lay piled on their sides. Beside his pen holder and inkpot and confined within a pair of painted bookends, was an edition of Pope's *Iliad* in twelves in a thumbed black binding. A local gentleman, the same Mr Cryer who had done the portrait of Anthony that adorned the dining-room, had also painted for him wall panels showing half a dozen coarse but effective representations of the more sanguinary incidents in the Trojan War. On the floor were corded bundles of the *Gentleman's Magazine*, their blue wrappers speckled with mouse dirts. An aroma of bachelordom and boot leather mingled with a suggestion of damp.

Arthur Smith sat down gingerly on the edge of his chair. He felt like a sinner who against all the odds has won a seat at the celestial high table. A goblet of wine was placed before him. Glass chinked against glass: a coin slid across the table. It was unbelievable! Just for saying a man had walked up a road!

'Now, Arthur, I've rewarded you generously, have I not?'

'Indeed so, Sir Anthony. Most generously.'

'So you should understand that I expect more good works in the future. You must be vigilant, you and Madge. His comings and goings, the gossip, any little thing, however insignificant it may seem – is my meaning clear?'

Oh yes, swore Arthur, it was ever so clear. Comings and goings. Visitors. Developments. Vigilance at all times. Anything to oblige such a topper of a gentleman. Ladies too? Were they to be included in the inventory? Very good, he'd put them at the head of the list. In fact he'd make a list the instant he got home. Be easier for Madge if she knew precisely what was expected of them. She could be a bit simple at times, ha ha. He'd put it all down in writing so there it would be and no mistake. And no, not a soul to have an inkling. Arthur Smith a blabber-mouth? Never! He leaned across the desk, burrowed his eyes into Sir Anthony's and with his forefinger slowly tapped the side of his potato nose. Honour where honour's due, eh?

63

His host rose to refill their glasses. Then he sat down and with a lazy smile as he placed his hands behind his head and tipped backwards in his chair, said, 'Tell me, Arthur, what really goes on in the Green Man that demands so many people at midnight?'

An hour or so later, Arthur fetched his pony out of its stall, patted his evening's takings, and rode out of Overmoor and down the hill to the turnpike. Anthony listened to his receding warble as he stood peeing on the lawn. Then he tucked his thick swarthy cock back into his breeches, buttoned his flap and went indoors. It had all been well worth the effort.

'Shall we read a little more of Miss Burney before we go to bed?'

'Most willingly, my pet. It's not often we get our hands on a book that sets out so authentically the feelings of our sex. Not often? What am I saying? Miss Burney is the first of her kind. She is a nonpareil. Do you suppose, Miss Daisy, that in years to come, in a century perhaps, we should find at Lackington's nothing but Miss Burneys? It would be strange, but I think rather wonderful.'

Miss Hoole had cared for Daisy Apreece since she was a child and when Daisy was married had come with her to Overmoor. Also in Daisy's dowry had been a middling sum of money and a sloe-eyed milking cow called Sorrel. Anthony had long since quartered Sorrel for his hounds and had many times wished to do the same to Miss Hoole. She was a small, busy, bony woman with views of her own and white hair which she kept in a bun. She drew the candleholder closer to her, tilted her head to one side to catch the light and opened *Evelina*. Daisy put aside her embroidery frame and folded her hands on her lap. The clang of the door bolts rang out down the hall.

'I know it sounds strange to say this,' Daisy said, 'especially as we are deriving such enjoyment from her book, but Miss Burney's writing makes me uneasy. No, uneasy is not the right word. Rather, I feel so removed from the world she describes. She draws a picture in which women have a choice in their fate, a small one, I agree, but nevertheless a choice. Her heroine ponders, decides and acts according to her own decisions, as if she was free from all those powerful influences that men – fathers, guardians, suitors, what have you – bring to bear on women. To me she is like a milliner who sees some naïve miss enter her shop and throws down a bolt of her most dazzling chintz in the hope that the silly girl will be swept off her feet by the effect of the whole and buy it in defiance of the fact that she has always detested its principal colours, its tomato red or sickly yellow. So I think Miss Burney is playing a trick on us. She wishes us to be blinded by a pretty pattern and to ignore what we know unto ourselves to be false. She has put her heroine into an unreal world.'

'You dwell too much on your past, Miss Daisy.' Miss Hoole put down the book and brushed aside a wisp of hair. 'Not all men are like, well, you know whom I mean. How could anyone have been aware of his true inclinations when you gave yourself to him? It was not possible. No one knew, certainly not your mother. If your father had been alive, it would have been different. He was a *man* was Mr Garland. He'd have seen him for what he was. Perhaps the herds knew,' she continued, 'perhaps Hucknall – he's an ugly mind has that one. They're the sort of people who can be counted on to know every smallest thing that happens in a gentleman's house. But none of *us* had any notion. We were all so happy for you after your disillusionment with Mr Trenchard.'

Slippered footsteps sounded in the passage. Miss Hoole quickly began to read aloud: 'Such is the present situation of affairs, I shall excuse myself from seeing the Branghtons this afternoon . . .' The door handle started to turn. Then it fell back with a squeak and the footsteps continued down the corridor towards the kitchen with a new sense of purpose.

'Sir Anthony is off to see if he can worry a plate of victuals out of Mrs Keech, I shouldn't wonder,' said Miss Hoole.

'And she with a headache and long gone to her bed. So he will meet with disappointment. Let us hope he was more rewarded by his conversation with Mr Smith, though what they found to talk to each other about for so long is far beyond my imagination. Now, shall we start again? Despite what I said, I am really most curious to learn whether our heroine will snare his lordship. Mark you, she'll have only herself to blame if she fails, for in my opinion she has set about it very clumsily, forever fainting or being discovered in the wrong sort of company just when he is steadying himself for the leap.' She reached forward and touched Miss Hoole on the sleeve. 'Do, please, if only to humour the romantic in me.'

She picked up her embroidery. 'Now where did I put my scissors?'

Her voice had a sonorous and liquid momentum, like the current of a deep river. It slid gracefully through the candlelight and round the dark corners of the room. It imparted tone and lustre to the heavy oak furniture and the maroon velvet drapes. It was one of those voices that assert its owner's character unaided by gesture, perfume or force of argument. Here, one would say on first catching its echo, is a woman standing four-square on the platform of life. It has swirled her down the rapids, buffeted her against the rocks, sailed her over waterfalls and through spray and thunder, past crocodiles and painted men with blowpipes, and now it carries her at a sedate glide down a stretch where all is understood and surprises are impossible.

Her eyes were rich brown and flecked with tiny mossy points, their brows thin and flexile. From each side radiated a network of wrinkles like forest paths. Her nose, narrow at its bridge, widened over the nostrils into the shape of a bulb, of a tulip, perhaps. When she sensed a jest or uncovered some private irony, it would twitch as if she was on the point of sneezing. It had twitched too, though not for long, when she had fancied herself in love, first with Mr Trenchard and then with her husband. Her chestnut hair she wore pulled back from the temples into a knot that was secured at the back of her head with a silver pin that had belonged to her mother. In the hollow beside her adam's apple was a black mole. Her teeth had lost the eggshell bloom of youth; her skin had an anxious tinge. It was a face that once, when she was plain Daisy Garland and had dreamed of nothing but an inexhaustible cruse of love and the delights of grandchildren, had been bright with optimism. But now it had grown closed, like a flower in drought. Only her voice and her full, childless figure remained from those years of promise.

She rose, austere in her black dress.

'Where can I have put them? They were in my hand only a moment ago.'

'My goodness!' exclaimed Miss Hoole, setting down *Evelina*, 'the things Miss Burney has the lady do! Would you believe she has just persuaded Lord Orville's coachman to drive her round town in his lordship's spanking new chariot with his lordship nowhere in sight? When will she realise –'

'You've been peeping –'

'Only dipping, my pet, only dropping in on them now and again to see they were still in good health. But really, you would have thought she understood that of all the avenues to a man's heart, the one most certain of disappointment is that which risks damaging his toys. What would have happened if a dog had run across the road, or a fly had got in the coachman's eye, at any rate something to cause an upset to the chariot? Upon whom do you suppose Lord Orville would have placed the blame? When will Miss Burney realise that the heart of someone like him –'

'Is probably like that of any man; like an onion, difficult to unwrap and conducive to tears.' Good-temperedly, Anthony stood in the doorway. 'No reason to disturb yourselves, ladies. I have come only for my red crayon, which I recall leaving on the mantelshelf. Smith called on me this afternoon and I find I shall be detained in my business room for a few hours yet on a task for which I have need of this particular pencil. There, I see it, exactly where I thought it would be. And these, my dear, can they be what you are as usual hunting for?' Holding her scissors by the tip of the blades, he handed them to Daisy. He bowed slightly and made as if to leave. Then he stopped and turned back into the room: 'If Miss Burney's constructions so perplex you, may I recommend that you divert yourselves instead with Mr Pope's *Iliad*? You would find it totally free of all such difficulties concerning the hearts of men apropos those of women.'

The door closed. His footsteps retreated once more. Soft nocturnal scents drifted in through the unshuttered windows. A young barn owl essayed a hoot from down by the stables. The September night deepened and grew yet stiller. It hung clammily over the quiet hills, squeezing the air from the narrow-gabled cottages where working people moaned and tossed and prayed for sleep, and children coughed in their crowded beds. For the umpteenth time, Edward Horne cursed the embers of his fire for their too slow dying until he could stand it no longer and dragged his mattress out beneath the horse chestnuts. A bird chirred in the unscythed grass as he fell asleep.

Miss Burney notwithstanding, Daisy and Miss Hoole also soon

went to their beds. Occasionally a howl tapered mournfully from the kennels into the tarry void, but otherwise Overmoor lay silent. It was the hour and the season that Hucknall liked best. For miles he would pelfer on nights like this to check his snares, keeping to the dark side of the hedges if there was a moon and skirting any muddy ground where his footprints might be noticed the next day. He enjoyed the solitude, the night-damp smells and the communion with instincts as feral as his own. It assuaged his feelings of servitude to know that for these short hours he, the common labourer, was the eyes and ears of Overmoor.

He came padding round the corner of the hay barn, an empty sack hanging over one shoulder. Before him the candlelight from Sir Anthony's business room pooled out over the lawn. He put a straw in his mouth and paused. Then he quietly slipped the latch of the barn's double doors and entered. The odour of chaff and rat shite rose to his nostrils. A host of small feet scurried away through the floor litter. 'Ssst, ssst,' he whispered reassuringly, for he counted all animals as his friends and, countryman that he was, saw nothing contradictory in sustaining their lives in order later to encompass their deaths. He waited until his eyes had grown accustomed to the thicker darkness of the barn. Its moist coolth was welcome after the stickiness outside. He climbed cautiously up the ladder to the loft, counting the rungs as he went so that he should not be caught off his guard when he reached the eleventh (which had been broken since springtime). He pulled himself over the coaming of the hatch. Froof! beat the ghostly wings of the barn owl as it dived off its perch and flicked sideways through the gable vent. He crept along the knotty timbers, feeling with his toes for the rotten planks. He relished the musty, tombstone atmosphere of the barn. It was like inhabiting another, more comfortable skin.

He arrived at the entry door in the gable through which they forked up the sheaves of corn. He felt for its snib and eased it open. Then he lay down on his stomach in the dust, cupped his chin in his hands and wondered.

Below him lay the Grange, swaddled in the blanket of night save for the candlelight spilling from Sir Anthony's business room. Its window was open and his view unimpeded. The desk was endways to him. On it stood an empty wine glass, a silver three-candled sconce, from which the buds of flame rose like aconites, and a map weighted down at each corner with a volume of the *Iliad*. Behind it rocked his employer, back and forth like a metronome, his fingers laced across his belly and his profile as sharp as the marble bust of an emperor. Back and forth, back and forth, his slippers rapping rhythmically against his heels . . .

Hucknall's coaly eyes stared down. What was he up to now? What new plot was he manufacturing? Was it not enough to be the most prosperous farmer in the district, to send the fattest cattle to market and have great men visit him for advice? It was not, he thought, as if the man had children to stock up (nor likely to: Hucknall grinned, cat-like, in the gloom). Or that her ladyship had expensive tastes (though she would, given half the chance, he'd wager). So why did he continue to battle so with life? Why had he cosied up to Arthur Smith, when only a fortnight ago he'd called him the grossest blackguard for miles? What was he doing down here after midnight? What was the fox up to now?

With a click that Hucknall heard quite plainly, Anthony let his chair fall forward. He furled the map and tied it with a piece of ribbon. He drew his writing slope towards him. He stroked his nose with the feathers of his pen. Then he dashed off two short letters, one to Mr Samuel Gomez in London requesting by return details of his investments in the three per cents, and the other to Mr Robert Pumfrey, his banker in Buxton, inviting him to luncheon on Sunday. He sanded them and laid them to one side. He kicked off his slippers, put his feet on the desk and picked up a volume of the *Iliad*. It was his favourite bedtime reading. And recently a nice question had occurred to him: had Hector been dead or alive when Achilles dragged him round Troy by the heels? It was hard to be sure. Mr Pope said dead. But Achilles was a violent man, a warrior by nature, and red-haired. There was an implication that he had later decapitated Hector and thrown the trunk to his dogs. So was not the other at least a possibility? He read a couple of pages. He would sleep on it. He stretched and yawned.

But why did the man not keep a dog in the house? wondered Hucknall. Because it might get to understand him too well, that was why.

Anthony lit his night candle from the sconce. He licked his forefinger and snuffed the remaining flames, one by one. Hucknall watched the glow move along the corridor, illuminating each window briefly as it passed. It climbed the staircase and entered his master's solitary bedchamber. The shutters closed with a snap. Thunder rolled in the distance. He pulled the door to and went off to make his rounds.

Eight

THE WEATHER held. Nicholas Hawkesworth proved as good as his word, and ten days after his arrival at Winterbourne a wagon containing Edward Horne's personal possessions came rumbling over Ladysway in the heat of the forenoon. A collie with a blue wall-eye ranged in front, sneering at the farm dogs chained in their hovels.

The carter, a tall, full-bearded prophet of a fellow called Clem Dawkins, began to slacken off the ropes, his bushy fingers teasing at the knots.

'Last time I did a job here, you know, when her ladyship went off to London, you were only so high,' he said to Davie Paxton, making a pincer of his thumb and second finger to indicate a creature the size of a large tadpole. 'And now see what you've grown into. Time she doth atrundle and there's nought a man can do about it. Has but one speed, just like my dobbin here. Ain't that so, Muriel old lady? Same speed for a king as for a beggar. No sense of priorities in that old noddle of yours, eh?' He ruffled the ears of his mare.

'Where'll you be wanting them put, then?' he asked Edward, who at that moment walked into the yard. 'Won't make much of an impression in a place that size, no matter how you space them out. But where's the harm in that if you've a mind to surround yourself with air? Take me, for example. I've spent all my life in God's airy mansion,' he gestured largely with his free hand, 'the sky's been my pillow, the clouds my blankets and more often than I can say, mother earth my four-poster. Am I the worse for it? The wind dries my clothes when I get a soaking, gets a blaze going when I cook my gruel, sings to me when it feels like singing, grumbles at me when it has a mind to grumble, so if it's air you want in that house of yours, Clem Dawkins is not the man to deny it you.

'Course I shouldn't properly be talking like this, seeing how I bakes my bread from folk wanting to suffocate themselves with whatnots . . . Anyway, here we are and a job's a job. And if I mind right, when Jack and me shifted your mammy – beg pardon, her ladyship – we left a fairish few bits and bobs in the old place, so perhaps you'll manage. How long ago was that? Ten year and more, I'll wager. Ten years, what a fancy! Jack was my mate then, Jack Catt. Been dead these four years past, slipped away fearsome quick he did in the end. Showed me the lump one day. Woa, Muriel, woa now. The size of a beetroot, all scaly and cankered and weeping and sort of puffy to look at. Fair made me sick to see it, I tell you . . . It gets to a man when his mate goes. Hard to find anyone to take his place. Too old and they're apt to be particular, too young and they don't know the ins and outs of the shifting business. How to take windows out of their frames if you need to, that sort of thing.

'Anyway, here we are. Mustn't go on like a henwifey. It's the loneliness that does it, not a soul to talk to saving Muriel now that Jack's gone. So where's it to go then, sir? More to follow by and by, is it?' The fringes of his beard fluttered in a puff of wind that came chancing through the yard.

It was a question that went to the very heart of the matter. 'Meal's ready,' shouted Mary Paxton from her doorstep. The sun stared down at the men and the wagon and the patient Muriel.

'I expect so. By and by, like you said.' Edward replied. 'The coach house'll do for the present until things sort themselves out. Davie will show you where. Oh dash –'.

He turned on his heel and walked away urgently, as if he had suddenly remembered something. But the moment he was out of sight, he dropped his pace and finding he was in the lane that led to the churchyard, went up it dispiritedly. Company he would have liked, company of any sort and especially if it brought news from outside. Already London had become as remote to him as Orkney. But he had not cared for the pointedness with which

Clem Dawkins had reminded him of his situation. It had put him on the spot. He had come to accept the rooflessness of Winter-bourne and thus the impossibility of selling the estate for the nabobical price he had hoped for, or even for any price at all. He had stamped and sworn when he had seen its condition. But he had accepted it.

He walked past the row of cottages and up the slope to the church. Bees waggled their furry black bottoms at him as they hunted through the drooping trumpets of the foxgloves. It was all very well to have one possibility dismissed from the roster, but what was he to insert in its place? He was young and healthy. He wanted more from life than a rural exile, much, much more. Oh yes, it was easy now to say he should have rejected his mother's proposal and stayed in London. But it wasn't the point. The point was that he'd done it and was here, at Winterbourne, stumping up the lane to the church behind a gawky little frog with yellow-green legs and in a moment the two of them would be abreast of the parsonage. This was where he was, not at Arthur's with Scrope and Anstruther, or with Caroline Nelson. If he'd had money, it would have been different. At least it was a comfort to know that in Derby the firm of Wiseman & Akers was holding for him the thousand pounds which his mother had given him as part of their bargain. But that wouldn't last for more than a couple of years. And then what? For the present they were his respectful and obedient servants, but when the well ran dry . . . Never mind, he'd get some peacocks and a smart horse: that'd put them off the scent until something else turned up. Everyone knew that a man with peacocks on his lawn had a fortune at his bidding. Thinking of which, and having suddenly a vision of a second Versailles erupting from the soil of Derbyshire, he put his worries behind him and continued up the lane as turrets and campaniles and cloud-piercing pinnacles soared through his mind and his gawky friend led him to the clipped privet hedge of the parsonage. Over it he saw the gaunt figure of the Reverend Digbeth Chiddlestone forking the litter from his runner beans into a wheelbarrow.

'Mr Horne! This is a happy surprise! Elspeth, that is my wife and I were only talking about you over breakfast. She is most anxious to learn whether you have settled into your new home. It worries her constantly. Every day she asks me, "Is he being properly looked after? Is Mrs Paxton giving him the right sort of things to eat?" And with our daughter Eleanor it is just the same. You are an event in their lives, a happening, a bloom in the desert. So come, Mr Horne, come inside and take a dish of something with us. I beg it of you. It will perk them up no end to have a young man to fuss over. And at the same time I would be able to show you the marrows I have been feeding up for our little harvest festival. It is no distance. You can see where I have opened their frame –'

'My mind is rather set on a walk. Perhaps I may be allowed to call on you on my way home?' Edward became aware of Paxton coming up behind him with his scythe. 'And besides, here comes Amos.'

'But I may expect you on Sunday, may I not? All the gentry will be there, the Cuthberts, Mr Quex-Parker, every one of the Scarletts, Sir Anthony and her ladyship. I am certain they will welcome the chance to become reacquainted with you after such a lengthy absence. Your arrival at Winterbourne is much talked about in the parish, you know. People still retain a great fondness in their hearts for your poor departed father. Indeed, if I may say so without presumption, it is the cause of immense sadness to me that he whose ways are impenetrable saw fit to deprive me of the opportunity ...'. He jabbed his fork into the ground and advanced upon Edward. But at that moment Amos drew level and so deflected his purpose.

Together Edward and Amos walked to the church, the scythe hanging over the older man's shoulder like an iron fang.

'Wind's beginning to shift,' Amos said, nodding towards the steeplecock. 'Likely we'll have rain before long. It's wanted.'

They entered through the lych-gate. Amos took the whetstone from his belt, spat on it and, gripping the scythe by its neck, began to strop the blade with long, smooth strokes. The sinews in his forearm bunched and straightened as the stone rasped along the metal. A soft haze had obscured the sun. The afternoon was still and clammy. Edward walked over to his father's grave.

NATHANIEL HORNE

OF

WINTERBOURNE

GENTLEMAN

Taken from this Life and this Parish
On January 18th 1775 AD

So curt, so final and yet so intimate. His father. His only father.
A posy of autumn flowers stood in a bowl at the foot of the
gravestone. He stooped to rearrange them. He went back to Amos,
who was leaning on his scythe watching him.

'It's Mary chiefly who does those,' he said shortly. His face was
clouded and his voice tense. He laid down the scythe and sat with
his arms dangling over his knees, plucking at daisies. Edward
placed himself on the bank beside him.

'Who did the lettering?' he asked.

'That's Tom Glossipp did that. He can do anything with his
hands can that man. We won the stone from the quarry we opened
when we were building the new road, Ladysway as your father
named it. Her ladyship sent the words up from town.'

'I like them. "Gentleman". He'd have appreciated that.'

'Aye, and it's no more than his due. I never knew his equal and
doubt I ever shall.' Amos removed his bonnet and scrumpled it
around in his hands. 'Course, it's not for me to say . . .'

'What isn't, Amos?'

'Well, Mary and I, we sometimes think she should have had
"Father" put on the stone as well. P'raps you didn't see it, p'raps
you never knew how much he cared for you, children often don't.
But I was with him at the end –'. He raised his head and looked at
him with an expression that was flinty and, it seemed to Edward,
accusing, as though he and his mother had been in some way
remiss. 'I was there. I heard what he said, his last words before –'.
With a harsh, twisting movement he began to strip the petals off
another daisy.

'It was terrible, nothing like what folks first thought, nothing
like what her ladyship put out.' Then, staring up at the
steeplecock, he started.

'You remember how he liked his shooting. Another twelve-month and he'd have had you there with him. That was his one idea, to have you at his side and be able to teach you every little thing he knew. Thank the Lord for small mercies you weren't with him *that* night. The ducks were his passion. Partridges, he could take 'em or leave 'em, didn't feel strongly either way – but ducks – all he really lived for, I'd say, was winter and a spell of cold weather on the tail of a flood so he could get down to the Rushes for the evening flight. Bit of frost and the birds'd make for it in their hundreds, literally in their hundreds. It was good sport we had down there together, usually just the two of us, but sometimes with a friend of the master's or a party of them odd folk he was always happening across at market.

'Course if the weather stays hard even the Rushes freeze over in the end, but ducks are like us, I reckon, creatures of habit and not overkeen to take no for an answer. Besides, it's got to be as hard as stone afore they can't find some damp corner to have a feed and a clean-up in. They like oiling themselves, do ducks.

'Any road, this night we went down as usual, your father and I, just as the light was offering to go, all wrapped up in our warmest cloaks with double layers of sacking in our boots. And cold! Couldn't recall anything like it, neither of us. Lasted for weeks, that spell did. And not a good night for the business, not a breath of wind and the moon so bright you could have read a book by it. In came the mallard, first to their feed as usual, greedy beggars, and we got three, I think it was, me pouring in the powder and shot while master picked the birds – never had no fetching dog, only that terrier he called Trump, you'll remember her, I 'xpect. Always said the fetching sort were too soft – "No balls to 'em" were his words. Course Trump wasn't interested in bringing back duck, only wanted to get her snout down a rabbit hole, that's all she was good for, so we did the picking ourselves as we went along.

'Then some snipe came along and he got one to have with his egg for breakfast. Did a bit of a jig when he found it. Flitty little devils they are, difficult to catch up with and hard to pick in all those tufts and tussocks.

'And after that the teal began to arrive, fast and low, whistling like they were out for a walk on a May morning. That's what he used to say, out for a walk with never a care in the world. Prettiest birds in the world he called them and whenever he shot one he'd apologise for it. He meant it, too. I never knew anyone who could get so sentimental about his sport as your father.

'Anyway, in they came, boiling to set down somewhere. Every time we had a shot they just circled around behind us to try from a new angle, like. Four we had before you could so much as blink and then from the corner of my eye I saw a couple swinging round behind us – good testing shots, just what he was always wanting – and I says, "Behind you, Mr Horne", and round he swivelled quick as a flash and bang! down it dropped quite dead and skidded away over the ice. "Quick, man," he says, all excited, "load up while I gets it." And he handed me his gun while he ran out on to the ice. Only fifteen or maybe twenty yards he had to go.

'So I outs with the powder flask and starts to pour the measure. Never looked at him or even thought about him. Had to get the powder just so, you see. He was always on to me about that because of the danger of over-charging the gun.'

He picked up the whetstone and thumped its barrel into the palm of his hand.

'And then the next I knew there was a noise like a tree splintering. "That's a queer go," I said to myself, but still with my mind on getting the powder done properly. Then I thought, No trees in these parts – and I twigged. Master'd gone through the ice. Up I jumped and so did that little devil Trump, dancing around she was and yapping away like anything, and there was your father standing with the water up to his chest, so high', he motioned with his hand, 'and the ice all rucked up around him. Strange thing to remember after all these years, but at the time I thought, Like when you break the crust on the stewpot. It's funny what stays in your mind.

'"Bit of a pother here, I'm afraid, Packy," he called out calmly, for all the world as if he'd only slipped in his bath. "Ice wasn't as thick as I imagined it'd be and now I've got stuck in the damned water lilies. Proper old tangle down there by the feel of it. You stay put while I see what's for the best." And with that he began to pull himself this way and that, but he'd gone in too far, right down among the roots and the more he struggled, the worse it got.

'"Mud's too soft," he said after a minute or so, "Can't find the bottom anywhere."'

Amos stopped and swallowed hard. He stared bleakly at the steeplecock, the veins in his neck quite rigid. Edward could picture it vividly: the harsh winter sky, the pitiless moon hanging above the two men, Trump barking on the edge of the ice and Amos thinking to himself, shall I run back for a ladder? Have I the time? What else can I use to reach him? My God, the cruelty of the choices he'd had. And what of his father, his gentlemanly, doomed father? What must it have felt like for him, that blinding pang as the water rushed up towards his heart? What had gone through his mind as the lilies twined round his legs? Hope, and then less hope, and so on down the scale until the last flicker was itself strangled? Amos wiped his hand across his nose and continued.

'What could I do? What could anyone have done? No one closer than the house, over a mile away. Twenty minutes there and twenty back – at the best. And me in my heaviest boots. No one to hear if I shouted, no rope to throw him, not even any branches or an old tree root to make a platform he could cling to while I went for help. What could I do? It was the most terrible thing I shall ever see, though I live another five lives, to have to stand there and watch him treading in the slime. It was as if he was having a nightmare and trying to escape from a giant or something, but never getting any further away. Know what I mean? Treading at it and getting nowhere and every time he moved, he sank in a little deeper.

'"This is by no means as easy as I first supposed," he said with a croaky sort of laugh, "new measures are called for." And leaning forward, he put his hands into the water and tried to pull himself forward by the roots. But of course they were too greasy and just slid through his hands. Sometimes, though, he'd get a bit of a purchase and sing out, "Hang on, Packy, I'm on the move now" – but nar, it never came to anything. They'd got him all right. His nails were half-ripped off when we fetched him out with the hook the next morning. Course, every time he let go to grip another handful, the mud sucked him down a bit more. And all the time he seemed close enough to touch. The moon was that bright. Twenty yards it may have been, but it seemed like there was no more than a finger's breadth between his eyes and mine. A finger's breadth and no more –

'His face, that was the worst of it, that kind face of his that never spoke ill of no one, never said a harsh word to any of us, never passed judgement on a living soul. I can see him now, chuckling to himself at the beginning with all his favourite oaths, damme this and damme that and mudgy me for an idiot, like it was some everyday pickle in the stable drains but then –'

Edward started to cry, for the first time in his life that he could remember, sitting on a bank among the daisies in the tiny churchyard of Winterbourne. Slowly the tears slipped down his cheeks and into the corners of his mouth. Tears of shame and remorse for what he had earlier failed either to feel or to understand, tears of the profoundest compassion for what his mother must have suffered, and tears of humility on behalf of each of those two hundred people who had journeyed to this very place in order to share with him their love for Nathaniel Horne, his father.

'But then he took to swearing, the vilest tinkers' curses I ever did hear. Blasphemous words they were too, may the Lord have mercy on him for them. And forgive him, as I reckons he should if he's ever had water up to his neck and seen his life's end staring him in the gob.

'And all the time I could do nothing. I'd crawled out on my belly as far as I could, only ten yards away I was, and poked the gun out for him to lay hold of – but then the ice began to crack – I could hear it groaning and chittering around me – and he shouted, "Get back, Packy, get back. I forbid you to come any nearer, I forbid it, do you hear me?" He screamed out more horrible things, hateful horrible things and started to moan and thrash. Then he went all quiet. He'd used up his strength, you see, fighting the mud and the lilies and the cold. All in his heaviest clothes, as well. And then he whispered – I was still lying there on the ice, just *so* far away, no more'n the width of a finger – "Help me. For the love of God do something." But what could I do? All that was left of him was his face, white as a feather under the moonlight saving a long smudge of dirt down one cheek. His head was bent right back, almost floating. He was looking up to the sky, at his Maker I suppose, and I could see him blinking, see the shoulders of his eyeballs glinting in the moon. All around the water was still, like it was waiting, just licking his chin and his ears. Then he rolled his eyes towards me and said, "You've been a good friend, Amos, the best a man could have had. Look after Edward for me. Tell Blanche –". and he was gone. For a moment I thought I could see his face under the water, but maybe it was only the moon.'

For a long time the two men sat and said nothing. Edward trembled with exhaustion. Every particle of emotion had been wrung from him. He thought: but why had his mother told him nothing of this? Why had she disguised the truth with all that talk of guns and accidents? He supposed she had decided to put it off for a year until he was older. One year had grown into a second and so on until – was this what she had been on the point of telling him when they had met at the Cocoa Tree? Had this been the great knot of words he had seen forming in her mouth the second before that waiter had knocked into her chair? My God, but it was no wonder she had fled from Winterbourne. No woman would have been able to live side by side with a death like that, to have looked out of her windows every day and been visited by its awfulness. But could he? He went over and read once more the words on his father's gravestone. Nathaniel Horne, Gentleman. But could he?

The steeplecock had settled into the west. Small frowns of sepia-coloured clouds had gathered over the hills.

'You were right, Amos, we'll get rain tonight,' he said.

'Aye, lad, likely we will,' Amos replied.

Nine

THE ACCOUNT of his father's death stripped Edward to the raw. For two days he sat in his rooms, gazing down at the Rushes with no other company than his emotions.

On the third afternoon Mary Paxton arrived with despairing motherly eyes and a pie, covered in muslin, of turbot cooked in a thick white sauce.

'Amos fetched it this morning from town. Not above four days old, the monger told him. It will be good for you. Fish are placid creatures that are at peace with themselves.'

'Poor turbot', Edward said, picking at the dish with his fork, 'for having both eyes on the left side of its head. How easily it must be surprised. I have often thought that seeing them on the monger's slope. But this is good, this is very good. The meat must have come from near the tail.'

'I would very much hope so. It is what I told Amos to ask for.'

'A curious thing, you know, Mary. There is a gentleman who paints in London who regularly passes a fishmonger when he is walking to his studio. On fish days he makes his choice and has the man turn the creatures about so that their heads hang downwards. Then his sister comes along later, sees what they are to eat and arranges about the price. Is that not a convenient way to do things?'

'Well, I should say it depends on the man and his sister.'

'And I expect that now you're thinking, Since he has no sister, he must be looking for another lady to act for him.'

'It comes to all young men in the end. It came to your father and, from what people said when I moved here to be with Amos, it were a surprise to everyone to see him wed.'

Edward looked sharply at Mary's kindly face. He had not thought he would ever be able to hear his father mentioned without an unsupportable plucking at his heart. But it had happened. He suddenly felt that he could sleep the clock round.

'May the monger be blessed,' he said, pushing his plate away. 'I do not think I have ever tasted so fine a fish. Now, Mary, I shall take a good walk.'

Together they descended the hill between the yew trees. At its foot he handed her the straw basket with the fish pot, and they went their ways, she to her four-square cottage and he to the path that ran alongside the Eve. He understood exactly where he must go, not objectively, but through the operation of some primitive sense. He reached the spot and stood with his hands on his hips, half-listening to the dry shuffle of the flags and the snap, as of a man shutting his watchcase, as the swooping swallows devoured insects. Here my father fought and died. It is here that I, his son, will build him a monument. Tears came to his eyes, the sweet tears of gratitude.

The minute bell clapped its last for the harvest festival. He hurried up to the iron-hinged door of the church. A row of tethered sheepdogs eyed him superciliously down their long noses.

He pushed back the door. The crowd! Every seat was taken, every pew filled by a spreading bustle or a broad-bottomed pair of breeches. He knew immediately that he should have been more forward, that he should have arrived ten minutes earlier so that all these rustling, chattering, gawping people would have discovered him sitting sedately in the family pew as unremarkable and as much of a fixture as the font. The latch clanged as he dropped it in its keeper. He raised his chin and walked up the nave between swivelling tiers of wigs and bonnets and vaporous banks of curiosity. On the altar steps waited Digbeth Chiddlestone, his prayerbook clasped against his snow-white chest.

'Turned out very like his mother,' offered Daphne Cuthbert, adjusting the grip on her stick and leaning towards her daughter-in-law so that their bonnets touched. 'Not much of Jupiter about him from what I can see.'

'She must be a nice woman then,' replied Millie Cuthbert, who was not in the habit of making too decided a pronouncement on any subject without her husband at her shoulder, and whose principal concern at that moment was that her mother-in-law should eat fewer onions for breakfast.

'From what I recall, she was a lot sharper about the face. This young man looks a bit of a rake to me. But . . . well, yes, I see what you mean.' Mr Cuthbert had mellowed with age. Peering and craning, the Cuthberts rose to their feet.

'I like that coat he's wearing. It makes a change to have a splash of colour about the place. Sets the flowers off well,' observed Emily Scarlett to David, her husband.

'I'll remember that, my dear, the next time I visit my tailor,' he replied dryly, thinking to himself what a shock the turnpike company would get if their estimator arrived in anything other than black.

'Who is that man?' asked their daughter, hopping about on top of her double-banked kneelers and trying to see round Mrs Cuthbert's elbow. 'Why are you all talking about him? Is he very important?'

'That's young Mr Horne from Winterbourne House, dear. No, you mustn't do that, it's rude to point. Now quiet, Lucy, the parson's speaking. I'll tell you about him afterwards.'

'But is he very important? Is he like a king or something? Do we have to pay him money?' she whispered, tugging at her mother's sleeve.

'I said hush, Lucy.'

'But that's not fair. Everyone else is talking. You said only holy people were allowed to talk in church.'

'Sometimes we do things differently. It's one of those things you have to accept. Now shush, will you? I said I'd tell you later.'

'Is he married? Why was he late?'

Old Mrs Scarlett stretched across and caught her by the wrist. 'If you don't hold your tongue, child, God will remember and do something horrible to you.'

One day, Lucy thought, she wouldn't need two kneelers to watch him. If she asked Mrs Tomkins nicely and promised not to make fun of her again, perhaps she'd stitch one huge kneeler so that she and Mr Horne could use it together when they got married. Because they would. She knew it.

Not my sort of colour, thought Mrs Gollins as she turned the pages of her prayerbook. Too strong for a country church. Apt enough in London, no doubt. One could wear a horse blanket to church there and be thought proper. But here . . . Anyway, that shade of reddish-brown had never been her favourite. Brought back too many memories of mulligatawny soup in Calcutta. But an interesting face. A shame Mr Gollins didn't have teeth like that. Lively eyes. Mouth something like his father's. (Edward had just exchanged a glance with the Apreeces in the pew opposite him.) Bit of a spark, she wouldn't be surprised. Could be trouble if he cut loose.

Shuffling and wheezing, their immediate curiosity dampened, Digbeth Chiddlestone's flock rose to its feet, slowly except for Lucy Scarlett, who at the words 'Hymn number' bobbed aloft at racing speed; and Elspeth, the parson's wife, who like a plump black crab scuttled round into the space below the pulpit to retrieve the hymnal which she had dropped in her excessive haste to set a good example. She bent to pick it up. Into the narrowing space between her fingers and the book there snaked a cinnamon-coloured sleeve and a white triangle of lace. They straightened simultaneously. 'Your words, m'am,' Edward said gravely. She blushed the shade of sponge cake and darted back into her pew.

Two rows from the back, the Paxton family looked proudly among each other. The honour of Winterbourne was once more in the ascendant. Amos and Davie squared back their shoulders, threw out their considerable chests and with the assistance of Arthur Smith (to whom years of practice in the Green Man had imparted a majestic *basso di taverna*), they fairly gave the roof a fright.

A fright too they gave to Daffie, Tom Glossipp's collie bitch, who put back her head and began to howl so piteously that in the end Tom had to take her out and tie her to the yew tree by Nat's grave. Even so her wailing could still be plainly heard, but no one paid it any heed. Like Mr Cuthbert falling asleep during the sermon or Mr Quex-Parker singing two beats in arrears and prolonging his amens long after their natural season, it was accepted as one of the natural manifestations of Life. Only when Chiddlestone cleared his throat (which he did with a gurgle that sounded like a pail of water being poured down a small funnel) and started to preach, and Daffie, as if on a signal, fell suddenly silent, did anyone think twice about it.

The Apreeces too had observed the incident with Elspeth Chiddlestone's hymnal. Indeed, they could scarcely have failed to, since by custom and social eminence they occupied the pew facing Edward at the foot of the chancel, below the stalls where a choir, had there been one, would have sat.

Daisy enjoyed her church-going. Though by no means devout in the rigorous sense, she was comforted by the ritual. The timelessness of the ideas it provoked, coupled with the wonderfully knobbly complexity of the Christian doctrine as she perceived it, aroused in her an intense awareness of her self. Only in this one place and at this regular hour could she count herself her own mistress. She did not have to consider her husband (except insofar as he sat beside her), the servants, her garden, her brother, Miss Hoole or where she had last put her scissors. The only person to whom she was here answerable was God, and he she was free to deal with on whatever terms she thought fit. Even Time itself, that great despot, seemed to unshackle her in church. The language of the service, the architecture, the sobriety and sameness of the proceedings, the graveyard so adjacent, the very hugeness of the concept by which she was surrounded, elevated her, she felt, on to a new and superior plane. The travails of her earthly existence slipped from her shoulders. She visualised Time seeping like steam from a crater near Lyme Regis and beckoning to her. It invited her to sit by its side in a sort of misty sedan chair, as calmly it travelled hither and anon, knitting the universe together with a seamless girdle. She fed at its table, refreshed herself from the same spring, observed the beauty of the globe spinning beneath her and when (at twelve o'clock) her hour was up and she was lowered gently from its belly, it was into a world that was infinitely more merciful than that which she had left. Then, for another week, Time would curl away until their next rendezvous. Sometimes it was not Time but God whom she imagined in this way. But whichever it was, it made her feel for this portion of this one day that she was part of something noble, gigantic and compassionate and therefore in some modest, but very personal way, important in the scheme of things.

There were more mundane pleasures besides. She could dress

up. Not overly, of course. Anthony would never permit that. But enough to inspire in her a tingle of womanly pride. A dab of perfume on her neck: a splash of sky blue or pink, almost incarnadine, at her throat and wrists. She could meet people and learn how their own little worlds revolved. She could let herself be reminded that there were others much less fortunate than herself. She could prove to herself by this simple intercourse that she was part of a community. All these were dear to her heart.

But today – today was different! For in addition there was to be the appearance of the man who as a boy had stammered and blushed when she gave him her arm at Nat's great party. Any newcomer at church had the allure of novelty, but this one was special. The whole idea of Edward Horne's sudden return had struck her as magnificently romantic. That he should choose to leave London in order to pick up the mantle of his adored father (which was how she supposed it) seemed to her far more than merely estimable. It was knightly, chivalrous and somehow, though she could not say precisely how, voluptuous. She sat quietly in her pew, hands folded upon her prayerbook, and waited as the minute bell tolled.

Another thought came to her, arising from a remark Hucknall had made. 'Nobbut a dainty young Jessie from London town,' he'd said, his eyes gleaming with malice. And then, 'He'd better watch himself or a wolf I knows of 'll put him away for breakfast.' His mouth had snapped shut as tightly as a pair of pliers. Immediately she'd felt sorry for Edward. She knew exactly who Hucknall had meant by the wolf. Only too well could she remember how it had felt to be served up at his breakfast table as innocent and tender as a baby rabbit.

The last ting of the bell faded. The latch rose and fell. She watched him set his coat skirts swinging, walk briskly the few yards down the transept and turn up the nave towards her. But this was not a man to feel sorry for! One might wonder why he carried neither hat nor gloves. One might ask oneself whether nature had made his hair like that or whether his curling tongs were still warm in their bowl. One might even permit oneself the observation that so snapping a coat was not entirely apropos in Winterbourne. But pity – never! It was ridiculous to offer it even the spare room for this lean, dark youth. She smiled at him with the corners of her mouth as he passed and sprang nimbly into his pew. He inclined his head, also with a slight smile, and repeated the gesture to Anthony. He knelt to pray and sat back, spreading out his coat. She watched him lean forward and try the scent from the small vase of flowers that someone, probably one of the Chiddlestone ladies, had placed on his psalter shelf. His nostrils dilated. He stretched his arms along the back of the pew and gazed about him. She saw his dawn-coloured eyes roam inquisitively round the church. His fingers drummed a pensive tattoo as Chiddlestone shuffled through the markers in his prayerbook. Again he bent to smell the posy. Again he smiled to himself. Then abruptly he looked across and directly at her. Not rudely or courteously, neither in meditation nor enquiringly, neither with nor without humour – but directly. Into her skull, her thoughts, and her secret church-going world. She quickly knelt and shielded her face with her hands.

Anthony also found a purpose in matins. Landowners were the guardians of society and it behoved them for one hour a week, starting at eleven o'clock precisely, to be seen acting honourably and responsibly. He therefore attended scrupulously, dressed becomingly in a black coat and breeches, sang lustily, gave adequately and prayed with both eyes closed, kneeling upright, his palms sharp against his nose. Afterwards it was his custom to take Daisy on his arm and circulate promiscuously, enquiring about apiaries, sheep scab, broken limbs, weddings in the offing, deliveries accomplished and the health of his swains. Then he would hand Daisy into his trap, exchange a last jovial sally with this person or that, give a flick of the reins and travel home to luncheon with the scent of roast beef and claret hot in his nostrils and the feeling of a job well done.

Erect and attentive, he watched Digbeth Chiddlestone glide swanlike from the altar to the hymn board to the lectern and back to the altar as he effected the preparations for his divine hour.

'I think I'll begin hunting soon, my dear, now that the rain has softened the ground a little.'

Daisy was annoyed by the intrusion. 'I am sorry Mr Pumfrey is not to bring Constance to lunch. She is young but she means well.'

'You know I cannot abide her. And Robert is much better company when he is by himself.'

'Do you think we should invite Mr Horne also? I believe he is to be here.'

'Then he is taking his time. I wonder we do not start without him.'

The latch rose and fell. Late. The fellow was late for matins. And on his own doorstep too.

In the beginning God created the heaven and the earth. But especially he created the earth, Anthony thought, seeing, as Edward skipped gaily into his pew, none of the things that his wife and the Cuthberts and Mrs Gollins and little Lucy Scarlett had seen, but only a man who possessed what he craved to possess for himself. Like a siege-master, he despatched speculative patrols from behind the shelter of his hymnbook and surveyed Edward for weak spots. And when he had reviewed the youthfulness of his features and the candour of his expression, when he had taken stock of the cinnamon coat with its black braid and cuffs and of the mustard-coloured waistcoat, when he had assured himself that before him there stood only a dandy and a featherweight, a *chocolatier* pure and simple, he was certain that it would take no more than a swift, strong campaign for Winterbourne to be his. He would sweep him off his feet before he knew what was happening. He rubbed his hands together metaphorically, drew a thick red line in his mind round the map of his vastly increased acreage, bellowed the words of the hymns and after the blessing treated Edward to such a rare smile that the other felt quite flattered.

In fact Edward was in a mood to be pleased by anything. He felt bubbly, receptive and alive. The prickle of nervousness that he had experienced on entering church had been overtaken by a sensation of homeliness and of goodwill to all these people, some of whom he recognised. The memory of his father's funeral in this identical place held no devils for him now, but was rich and vibrant. This was where Hornes belonged. It was meet and proper that he should be here too. He listened affably to Digbeth Chiddlestone denouncing the sin of covetousness. He admired the opulent mounds of harvest fruit. He watched Daisy's bosom swell as she sang. With the casual generosity of someone offering to help an old lady with an awkward package, he contemplated her seduction. And when he felt the glow of Anthony's magnificent smile he thought, How lucky I am!

The service ended. Gathering up their skirts and bonnets, the congregation seeped from the church. The sidesmen went around snuffing the candles. A tinkle of conversation broke out. The collies stretched and yawned, their tongues curling like shoehorns.

'Dammit, Ned, but it's capital to see you again,' Anthony said, stepping into the nave and gripping Edward's hand. 'Daisy dear, I'll wager Ned didn't look half so dashing when you took the floor at Jupiter's dance. I'll tell you one thing, I was as jealous as a pig when you got your hands on her.' He punched Edward lightly on the shoulder. 'You've no idea what a pleasure this is for both of us. Eh, Daisy, ain't that so? The place just hasn't been the same without a Horne around. Not half the fun. Now tell me, when can we expect you at Overmoor? Can't be too soon as far as I'm concerned. But first things first. We have duties to perform. Us landowners, y'know. There'll be a few new faces since you were last here. Come, let me take you around. All the main sinners are here today.'

He laughed, a gravelly avuncular rumble, and took Edward by the elbow. They soon found themselves outside the church on the edge of the crowd, the men dressed soberly in fustian, the ladies more striking in their pink or blue ginghams with sprays of vetch and purple cranesbill woven through their Sunday bonnets.

'Now this little lady is Lucy Scarlett, whom I declare you cannot possibly have met before. No call to hide like that behind your mother's skirts, Lucy, it's only Mr Horne from Winterbourne. Six last week, you say? Well, that's something to be going on with . . .

'And these are her parents, Emily and David – do you remember Ned, Ned Horne? Oh yes, not easily forgotten . . . Very apt, I must say . . . and David's mother . . .

'And Mr and Mrs Cuthbert senior with their daughter-in-law Millie, who comes from somewhere in Kent, would you believe. Sam not back yet, do I assume? Tush tush, I shall have to berate him for missing our harvest service. The Lord will get to hear of it. Sam's crops will be blighted, we may be sure . . .

'And Mr Gollins, our resident sea dog. Every parish needs a sea dog . . .

'Ah, vicar, there you are at last. May I present Edward Horne? But you have already had the pleasure – of course you have, you can practically speak to each other from your front doors, I was quite forgetting. Your sermon, let me say, was exemplary, your best for weeks if I may be allowed. You must remind me of your text when we forgather for another of our little discussions. There's a thing, Ned, our vicar is a lively philosopher over a dish of tea and a plate of Mrs Chiddlestone's griddled scones –

'But look, here's a genuine newcomer for you, capital fellow altogether, Fuscus Quex-Parker, lately in His Majesty's employ but too discreet to go into specifics.' He winked at Edward. 'Cipher, actually. Used to intercept the mail to protect us from seditionists and chaps who do nothing but think. So when he retired he came to a place where none of us can either think or write, ain't that so, Fuscus? Lives at the Dell, you know, Ned, that house on the left as you go into town where the Ambrosers were when you were a boy . . .'

Suavely and economically, his hand hovering at Edward's back, Anthony steered him through the shoals. Behind them followed Daisy, smoothing out their exchanges with a flow of more leisured conversation. They reached Nat's grave. Daisy stooped to rearrange the flowers as Edward had done a few days before.

'Fine man, one of the finest,' Anthony said, his hands clasped behind his back, his coat straining at its buttons, his black silk hat tilted forward and his profile very sharp. The three of them looked down in silence. He shook his head. 'Of course, we had our differences, who doesn't with his neighbours, but we were just patching them up and then this had to happen. Fine man. Ghastly business, quite ghastly for you and your dear mother . . .'

'We were all so desperate for her,' Daisy said, 'but she refused to be comforted, just retreated into her grief and closed the door on us all. Those must have been truly dreadful days for you both.' She looked up at Edward, who was some four inches taller. The tail of her blue scarf shivered in the breeze. She tucked it back into her collar.

'Yes, they were not good. But I was too young to understand what it must have meant to her. Only during the last week have I had any real idea of what must have been going through her mind.'

'Tell you what, Ned,' Anthony interrupted, 'why not come to Overmoor for luncheon today? Yes, right now. Put the past behind us over a bottle of wine, repair ancient fences, continue where Nat and I left off. You know, *suaviter in modo, fortiter in re*, as my old schoolmaster used to say. Only the four of us, you and I and Daisy and Robert. Was Robert Pumfrey here in your time or was his Uncle Gilbert still on the throne? I forget. Anyway, the banker from town. Keeps the Bank of Buxton, absolutely tip-top establishment. Could be a useful chap in case you ever need an accommodation in that line of country. What d'ye say then, Ned?'

Sincerity shone from his eyes like a guinea piece. The matter was settled then and there, standing over Nathaniel Horne's grave-stone. Edward would ride over as soon as Davie Paxton had saddled a horse for him.

But as Edward was bidding his farewells, Amos came up to him with a group of men at his heels: Walter Hamilton, the blacksmith at Winterbourne, just back from burying his auntie, a great door of a fellow with a leather belt round his belly as wide as a horse's girth; Tom Glossipp, slim, fair, blue-eyed and with a soft handshake; and a couple of slaters whom Amos fancied might be helpful at the big house. 'From down Forbury way, they be,' he added, contriving by the grandiloquence of his tones to impart to that hamlet an impression of metropolitan importance. Then Arthur and Madge Smith sniffed him up and down, and the parson sidled over to ask if he'd noticed his marrows at the foot of the pulpit, and Lucy Scarlett insisted he accept a posy all of her own picking which *had* to be placed in water instantly or they would die and how could he be so heartless, and Polly, the farm pony, was in hiding at the far end of the field and declared through unequivocally mutinous eyes that riding on a Sunday was something she would not lend herself to for even one moment. So that what with one thing and another, it was considerably later than he would have wished when Edward set out down the Britannia road for his engagement.

Jogging along with his feet almost brushing the ground, he was reminded of another fat pony, the one he'd learned to ride on under the careful eye of Vinson. They'd had only two paces, walking and cantering, since Vinson said trotting was too strong for his piles. Alfred, that had been the pony's name. His stomach had gurgled like a vat when they cantered, but by Jove how they'd flown! Tears coursing down his cheeks, his small heels drumming on Alfred's ribs, by Jove how they'd flown! Like billy-ho!

They reached the ruins of Britannia and turned right-handed. The last of the season's peewits skirmished around them. Slowly they crept down the old green road across the moor. 'Polly, my friend,' he said, wondering if Anthony was the sort of man to hold back lunch, 'ours is not a marriage made in heaven. Do not misconstrue me. The fault is not yours. But if you had my legs and I had yours, we would go faster and the potatoes might still be hot. It is a fact and one can be wrong to deny facts. Parsnips can be eaten when tepid, but potatoes quickly lose their shine. Look at it another way. The only good apple is a good one. Your asking me to reconcile myself to eating second-hand potatoes is like me asking you to eat a rotten apple. So shall you and I learn the art of speedier locomotion . . .?' And chattering in this way to Polly and dreaming about the strapping bay gelding he'd get with sharp black points and a pot of mustard up its fundament, it was not until very much later than the hour for luncheon that he arrived at Overmoor.

Ten

GILBERT PUMFREY is in his counting-room. It has been recently panelled in oak, varnished very dark, and the windows have small leaded lights. The shutters are folded within their boxings. There are no soft furnishings in the room, which as a consequence rings hollow, an effect that Mr Pumfrey favours since he believes it makes his presence more intimidating. There is a deed chest and a tall wooden press, in which he keeps his correspondence and blank bills of exchange. His working capital, all coin, lies in six slotted drawers within a metal safe concealed behind a false section of panelling. On his desk is a set of brass scales.

Prosperity has come to him the hard way. It is evident from the thinness of his lips (which are set across his face like a pair of nails), and the shallow, coppery glaze to his eyes. Also from his clothes, which are those of a poor man. He is sitting at a hard high chair with a gauging rod in his hands.

'Now, Robert, in what year was Pumfrey & Co. commenced?'

'1719, sir, with gifts you received on reaching your majority.'

'Have we ever lent big?'

'No, sir.'

'Have we ever lent poorly?'

'But once, sir, to a Mr Strudwick who defaulted.'

'What lesson did we learn from Mr Strudwick?'

'That credit is suspicion asleep.'

'What is the maximum rate of interest that we may charge without incurring the accusation of usury?'

'Five per cent. But we may also superimpose our own commission.'

'And finally, what do we say, invariably and without exception, when a borrower, known or unknown, enters the house with a proposition?'

'*Amo, amas, amat*, if it's true I'll eat my hat.'

'Very good, Robert, you are learning. Now ride out to Mr Mason's on the Derby road and at midday present yourself to him and request the £25 that falls due at that precise hour. On no account are you to return without the principal and interest in full.'

Thus had Robert served his apprenticeship; thus had he learned to distinguish between the Strudwicks of this world and the local farmers and merchants, from whose business Pumfrey & Co. earned a small but certain percentage every time they entered Gilbert's parlour to turn their bills. In due course he was sent to London, to Mr Andrew Drummond's bank at Angell Court, Charing Cross.

'I cannot trust a man who has not had experience of turpitude at the very highest level,' said Gilbert. 'Take my copy of *Mortimer's Broker* and come back only when you are certain that mankind is essentially foul.'

So Robert sat in a cubbyhole at a high desk (which also contained a mirror in which to adjust his cravat), with a quill in his hand. Some days, for instance when an East India Company fleet had berthed, he would work hard. But many more he spent chatting to Septimus Leftly, who had the desk to his left, behind a pine partition. It was common ground between them that the secret to being a successful banker could never be vouchsafed to an overcrowded mind.

One afternoon they were eating veal cutlets in a chophouse in Exchange Alley. (Ever afterwards Robert would connect the unexpected with cutlets.) It was a strong, gusty day. The door flew open and a short, corpulent man, bundled up in a cloak, entered with a rush. A cabbage stalk entered with him, which he kicked under a table, exclaiming as he did so in a Scottish accent to his two companions.

Robert raised an eyebrow to Septimus.

'Mr Alexander Fordyce, a fellow banker of ours. Made a fortune by getting early news of the peace treaty in 1763. Speculates in East India stock. That's someone we could learn from.'

'I wonder how he started,' Robert said. 'Where does a man like that get the capital from? My uncle would shut the door in his face.'

'Oh, like the rest of them.' Septimus wiped a smear of fat off the table. 'He spun a tale so persistently that in the end someone believed him. They say he began in the hosiery trade, if you can credit such a thing exists in Scotland. Now he's married to an earl's daughter. That shows where a fine tale can get you.'

Covertly Robert devoured him with his eyes: the hogged sandy hair, the glitter from the stone in his cravat pin, the way he spoke from the corner of his mouth, his hot stubbly cheeks, the pimple on one eyelid. A rogue, a sharper, foulness writ large – Strudwick in London! He had found what Uncle Gilbert had sent him to find.

'Wine! A pint of Madeira . . . ! Now tell me everything you can about Mr Fordyce.'

'His family hails from Aberdeen. One brother, a philosopher, was drowned at sea. Another you may hear preaching at the presbyterian church in Monkwell Street on Sunday afternoons. If you remain curious, you may also read his sermons to young ladies, in two volumes. A third, William, is a physician, but it is said that when not so occupied he assists our Mr Fordyce in his dabblings. A family of great talents, but this one has the rest beat for cleverness. His wealth is immense.'

'Oh pray tell, Septimus.'

'He lives out at Roehampton with forty-three servants – that's counting the house and the gardens together. His wife wears *coque de perle* earrings even when taking a walk. Insurers have forbidden her to clap her hands in case the stones fall out of her jewellery. So she has invented a special sign language for the servants. And they burn nothing but wax candles. Imagine it, Robert, nothing but wax! There you have the spoils of banking at the highest level.'

The waiter brought them their cloaks and they made to leave. A hand came out and barred their way.

'Is it the sight of wealth that interests you so, sir, or is there something curious in my appearance that makes you stare?'

'It is the former, Mr Fordyce, for I too am a banker but at a lower scale than yourself. And I wish to better my position.'

'Are you honest? Do you believe the truths of the gospel? Do you have sympathy for the plight of man?'

'Tolerably so, on each count.'

'Then you should find a different profession without delay. There, a quicker apprenticeship you will never receive. Now I wish you goodnight, sir.'

Honoured uncle, wrote Robert, I have at last met a man who answers in every respect to Mr Strudwick. It is my intention to study him until such time as I can recognise his footfall in the blackest night in Tartary.

But then something strange happened to Robert. For when, three months later to the day, on 10 June 1772, Neale, James, Fordyce and Down was hammered and Alexander Fordyce skedaddled, leaving debts of between one and three hundred thousand pounds (in any event a very great sum), Robert found that under the outpourings of horror that he shared with Septimus were hidden a few liquescent drops of admiration mingled with envy. What knavery – but what acumen! So he stayed on for a few months, to think to the end in London what could not be thought to the end in a counting-room in Buxton, and returned only upon the news that Gilbert Pumfrey had died one night in his bed at the age of seventy-four.

His memorial must be the name of Pumfrey & Co. It is what he would have wanted best, said his aunt, wagging the long safe key at his silk-frogged navel. Indeed it will, responded Robert, sinking his youthful but seasoned backside into the proprietor's chair and pondering the resonance of the County Bank against the Bank of Buxton – indeed it will. And it was, for four tiresome years until, at the age of thirty-five, his unsatisfied grey eye met the ambitious, disconcertingly blue eye of young Constance Appleby from Derby. Bachelordom was retired to the attic and with it the weathered oak shingle of Pumfrey & Co.

The Bank of Buxton went off capitally, far better than Robert had expected. The family name, his reassuring embonpoint, his sensible age and his reputation as an honest Jack, all won him trade that had previously grumbled its way down the turnpike to Wiseman & Akers in Derby. He was convenient. He was discreet. He was sound. Furthermore, he had about him a medieval courtliness that stood him well with the gentry and no less with their spouses, who also esteemed his small, narrow feet. It was, in addition, thought most creditable that he should have taken into his house his weak-minded sister, Sophia.

Time passed. The iron law of compound interest went about its grisly business. The bank was in excellent feather. Robert grew plumper, Constance more so. A son, Andrew, was born.

This was in 1780, the year that the Duke of Devonshire commenced building that crescent which was described as possessing 'a style of grandeur as if designed for the residence of a prince'. But who was the prince to be?

'Ah, Mr Pumfrey, I'm glad to have found you at home,' said the duke's agent, Mr Wormald, a short, bustling fox-terrier type of man, as he entered a counting-room now somewhat crowded by the additional presence of a cashier called Jack Long. 'May I invite you to take a walk with me? There is something that I, that is, of course, his Grace and I, have been considering.'

Side by side they sat on a bench and looked down the hill at the spiderwork of scaffolding round the building.

'At each wing will be an hotel. On the west there will be a new Assembly Room. At ground level the front rooms will be shops to provide a diversion for all who come here to take the waters. In due course we shall erect stables behind them with a covered gallery, in which the company may take exercise when the weather is inclement. But what we are seeking at the moment, Mr Pumfrey, is an enterprise to occupy the central position of the Crescent, an enterprise that will be a constant attraction, one that is alluring yet at the same time sober.'

'You flatter me excessively, Mr Wormald,' Robert said, swinging a maidenly toe, 'but I fear that the rent –'

'We have given this much thought. If you will consent to occupy the building before the work is absolutely completed, his Grace is prepared to be most lenient. *Most* lenient.'

'I shall have to consult my wife, Constance. And my partners, Constance's brother Archer Appleby and my cousin William. Mr Appleby in particular can be most fastidious about our business arrangements. Perhaps fastidious is too slight a word ... Oh, partners, Mr Wormald, what a trial they can be ...' murmured Robert. He completed his sentence by inscribing in the air 'etc. etc.' (as between men of the world). As his finger paused, he looked down and saw in an instant what he had not seen before, that a bank in such a tremendous crescent should issue its own banknotes. His heart thumped and across the abdomen of a needy grey cloud he diddled a piece of boilerplate not one whit less heroic than his marriage proposal: 'I Promise to Pay the Bearer on Demand the Sum of . . .' He signed it, Robt. Pumfrey, with a swashing paraph that left the tail of the 'y' coiled round the spire of St Anne's, murmured again 'Oh, partners, Mr Wormald,' and returned his hand to the bull-nosed arm of the bench, which he stroked with lingering relish, as if it were the head of a favourite hound.

'A decision is needed quickly. I fear his Grace is not a patient man,' Mr Wormald said, rising abruptly with a crackle of knee bones.

But you are only his agent and it is not I who do the wooing, thought Robert, but saying gravely as he pinched his dewlap, 'Nevertheless, it is a large undertaking.'

Yet it was accomplished. And one day Temptation, who had known it useless even to try the keyhole in the old counting-room, came snooping along the Crescent. The yew-green portals were agape. She raised her diaphanous chemise, tripped up the three steps, shimmied past Jack Long over the black-and-white tiled floor and without so much as a tap on his new mahogany door, glided into Robert's sanctum. On a pink-braided pearl-grey stool she crouched, hugging her skinny knees and gazing with big round eyes first upon Robert and then upon his broad-chested supplicant.

'He cannot abide his son,' Anthony Apreece said. 'All Mr Bunn can think of is how to spite him. It is anathema to him that a lay about and a spendthrift should reap the rewards of his hard work. So it is to *me* that he would prefer to sell Milkwells, for he knows I would look after the farm. But he must have his money by nightfall so that the sale is done and his family cannot argue. It is not two hours since he told me this. So it was to you, Robert, that I naturally came hotfoot.'

'It seems all very sudden.'

'He awoke this morning and said to himself, I must do it today or never at all. I have had enough.'

'I cannot possibly entertain you without the usual security. This is a bank, Sir Anthony, not a shop. My lawyer, Mr Hodge, will need time to study the documents. You cannot take the risk of receiving a bad title and nor can I.'

'But I appreciate this, indeed I do, and in return I would expect to pay your highest rate of interest. Your highest, Robert. You have but to name it, so long as I can take Mr Bunn his money by tonight. I cannot tell you how perfectly Milkwells will fit with my land – here, let me describe it for you . . .'

Temptation lolled across his desk, tossed her locks, fluttered her lark's wing eyelids, inked his pen and extended it towards him with quick fingers.

Through the tall windows a ray of sunshine spread across Robert's cheek and back a glow of wellbeing. The scent of lilac reached him and the humming of bees.

'It's a rare chance,' Anthony said, 'I shall never have another like it. It's only for me that Mr Bunn will make this price.'

Robert glanced down at the printer's proof of his first banknote. It had been delivered that very morning. He rested his finger pads upon it and moved it an infinitesimal distance so that its edges were in perfect alignment with the tooled leather inlay of his desk. He was champing to get down to work on it. The moment Anthony left he would sign it, as an experiment. His eye told him that the printer had been miserly. His signature would either run off the side of the paper or appear too cramped. People might think, This is a man who gives short change or who clips his coins. Banknotes were a novelty. The smallest hint of parsimony or dishonesty and poof! the thing would go up in smoke. Yes, as soon as Anthony had left, he'd measure the proof against his instructions to the printer. And sign it swiftly, as if there were ninety others to be signed and only five minutes to do it because his horse was saddled at the door and he wanted to go hunting. That would be the test of a well-designed banknote.

And this guilloche – was it not insufficiently distinctive? Might not someone with poor eyesight mistake £10 for £6? And – bless me! if the printer hadn't taken it into his noddle to have him pomise to pay the bearer. As if he were a child trying to disguise a fib! That would never do. He seized his pen.

'Shall we say eight per cent?' said Anthony, inching his chair forward, his forearms resting on his thighs so that only his wheedling face was visible to Robert.

'Very well! Let us say eight per cent and buy Milkwells! Let us make Master Bunn unhappy. You are not Mr Strudwick and I am not my uncle. By Jove I am not!' With a slashing caret he decapitated the unhappy pomise. 'Dear me, I have made a hole in the man's paper,' he said, laughing.

That night, as he lay listening to Constance's whistling snore (which sounded as though she had a starling in her mouth), it worried him that he had taken no security for the loan. But when, not long afterwards, Anthony repaid another debt before it fell due, together with the first instalment of interest on Milkwells, it struck him as pedantic to insist on formalities with a man so solid, a man he would count if not among the first echelon of his friends, at least at the top of the second. Besides, who could quibble with lending at eight per cent what could be borrowed for four?

'You damned usurer, you,' Anthony said playfully, meeting Robert in town on a half-decent morning and dismounting.

'Commission, fees, attendance – the usual outgoings,' Robert replied, his lips quivering at the shared jest. He was holding a pair of candlesticks (pretty but rather provincial) that he thought would go well in his banking parlour.

'There are others, you know, who would be glad to borrow on these terms so long as the lender did not require some cockalorum of a lawyer at his elbow when the deal was struck.'

'Oh?'

'As when you and I made the agreement for Milkwells.'

They fell into step, making their way to the stables behind the Crescent, where Anthony gave up his horse to Melson, Robert's groom.

'I believe that when the building is finished, there are to be three hundred and seventy-eight windows in it.'

'So I have also heard. And each one taxable. His Grace will have to put his hand in his pocket.'

'You mean his tenants, Robert.'

'I mean their customers, Sir Anthony.'

A two-horse carriage was drawn up in front of the bank. Under it the coachman was lying on his back examining the axle-tree for worn timbers. One leg was straight, the other crooked at the knee. His hat lay a few yards off on the pavement. As they climbed the steps, the inner door opened and Jack Long ushered out three generations of Scarletts, Emily, her mother-in-law and her daughter Lucy.

'There must be a collective noun for Scarletts,' laughed Robert, peeling off his gloves as he stepped under the colonnade. 'A tapestry, perhaps? Can I say a tapestry of Scarletts has called on me?' He greeted them in turn, Jack hovering unctuously in the background. He lightly patted Lucy's curly head, enjoying the feel of her soft hair. She coughed with rather theatrical piteousness and silently extended her open palm for a handkerchief.

'Oh, are you poorly, child?'

'But kind Mr Long has given her a slice of pontefract cake,' Emily said, putting an arm round her daughter's shoulder. 'Liquorice is such an excellent emollient.'

'At the Bank of Buxton we attend to all needs, do we not, Jack?'

'And those candlesticks you are holding, Mr Pumfrey, are they for some special occasion?' enquired old Mrs Scarlett. 'Does the bank have cause to celebrate?'

'My goodness, I had quite forgotten them. Come, ladies, come and tell me whether they are the very thing or not to add distinction to my parlour.'

Jack held the door and they all trooped in, Anthony on their heels. After Emily had declared them perfection and her mother, in a reedy but resolute voice, had declared them not a patch on hers, and Lucy had filled her mouth with the last of the pontefract, the Scarletts left and Anthony followed Robert into his office.

'I have been thinking on what you said,' Robert said.

'Your business would increase. There are many sound men in these parts who would gladly borrow at eight per cent to enlarge their trade if they were assured that it would not mean having your Mr Hodge poke his nose into all their little family arrangements. Wives are easily upset by legal enquiries. It makes them afraid. They think something unpleasant is in the offing.'

'But the risk is greater.'

'And the profit also. For my part, I would be quite comfortable to increase my borrowings on those terms.'

'There is more land you have your eye on?'

'Always. Only the sea will stop me.'

'Then you have a way to go, Anthony, a fair distance indeed.

But as to the immediate matter, pray give me time to examine it from all angles.'

'Our corn chandler is such a man as comes to mind. Mr Huggins has more than once remarked to me that it is only the lack of capital that prevents him taking more grain on to his books.' Anthony rose. 'This is a fine door you have. A second Cerberus to guard your privacy, if we are to count Jack Long as the first.' He opened it, permitting a fragment of Jack's chaste repartee to float in. 'You should think about our conversation when your duties permit.'

A narrow, newly gilt mirror hung on Robert's wall. Upon the apex of its swaggy frame libidinous Mercury, god also of thieves and pickpockets, pirouetted on a golden globe. Robert went over to it and inspected his nose. He had become aware (as had Constance) that it was growing more pronounced with age. Fatter, sturdier, spilling out on to his cheeks. He took yet another of the printer's proofs from his desk and bending it round each cheek in turn, measured the distance from the edge of his nostrils to his ear-holes. It was identical on both sides. He recorded it in his notebook, at the same time thinking what a damned good draughtsman God was. He gripped his olive-green lapels and plumped up his broadcloth with an expression that was not humble. He fondly patted his nose, primary organ of the thoroughbred banker, and took it upstairs to share with Constance a luncheon of beef ragout and mashed artichokes, a vegetable of which he was in general wary.

Eleven

THE LOW smoke-stained dining-room at Overmoor was replete with the smugness of the recently holy. A log fire crackled behind the andirons in the wide stone-built hearth. The mask of a painted fox grinned from the bellow-boards. A brace of sconces drew a dull sheen from the green bottles of Muscat. The afternoon was overcast. Sleep was not far away.

'Next time, Elizabeth, you must remind Mrs Keech that on Sundays we use the silver fruit knives,' Daisy said lazily.

Robert Pumfrey twirled his glass between the fingers of a heavily veined hand and sank deeper into his chair. She had done it well, saying what needed to be said without belittling the maid's opinion of herself. He'd like to dance with her, that's what he'd like to do, to squeeze her comfortable waist and read a story from the fireflies in her eyes. She was a good dancer, he knew. She understood how to lend herself to a man, how to make him feel they were sharing a pleasure. Whereas Constance –. He hesitated. The thought was not proper in view of her condition. But she was not there; so he was free to let the raspberries and the Muscat and the thick yellow cream luxuriate in his stomach, and to affirm privately that Daisy was the better dancer. Even, perhaps, the better woman. There was a glitter to Constance that he sometimes found repugnant, an iridescent carapace that enclosed nothing a man would risk being hanged for.

'And how is your sister, Sophia, Mr Pumfrey?'

Robert shook his head. 'She has good days and bad. In general, her behaviour is exemplary and when this is so, no one could be more amenable. She is a picture of lucidity –'

'But the bad days are awful, I suppose.'

'Abominable. I have to lock her into her room until she recovers. There is one man in town, a Mr Please, who was introduced to me by the doctor and who seems able to assist her when she has one of her fits. He is a queer-looking fellow, but once he is with her, the moment almost that he enters her room, she becomes calmer. I really cannot account for it.'

'It cannot be easy for Constance, having Sophia to worry about as well as Andrew and her lying in.'

'No, and here's another thing. You might not believe it, but his Grace's houses are not nearly as substantial within as they appear from the outside. Sophia's room is directly above ours. It is not possible to sleep when she is ill for all the caterwauling that she makes. We have to shift our room. And since Mr and Mrs Appleby have been occupying the guests' quarters for the past two weeks – well, you must excuse me if I look somewhat haggard.'

'You are as speckly as ever, Mr Pumfrey, I assure you. Now what of Constance herself? I have purposely left the subject until we'd finished eating so that you could tell me everything. Is it in a fortnight that the baby is due? Is that the latest opinion of Dr Wood?'

'Ten days is what Constance says. As soon as that. The little fists are like drum beats within her.'

'Oh, how I wish –'

'Now then, Robert, tell me how it goes with your bank-noting business,' Anthony said, returning to the room with a flagon of port, which he proceeded to decant through a square of muslin. 'You have been very quiet about that of late.'

A look of resignation came over Daisy's face, which with the slightest incline of her head she shared with Robert. 'I believe I shall take Miss Hoole and get some vegetables in lest it rain again tonight. The marrows are starting to look a trifle weary. I would so hate to see them spoiled. Will you excuse me, Mr Pumfrey?' She placed her small ivory-handled bell in front of Anthony's fruit plate and, rising, went to the stone-mullioned window.

'I do hope no harm has befallen Mr Horne. Do you think it possible that he misunderstood the invitation and thought it was for another day?'

'His horse has probably cast a shoe. Anyway, the young have no sense of time these days. Don't you find that the case, Robert?'

Anthony placed the decanter on the table and took out his snuffbox, which was made of tortoiseshell and had a brass catch.

'What sort of horse does he have?' pursued Daisy, pressing on the sill with the palms of her hands and thinking still about Constance. 'Hucknall told me that he arrived by post-chaise and then walked up to Winterbourne.'

'Goodness only knows. Some farm hack, I suppose. Nat had the last quad at Winterbourne that was worthy of the name. A dab of Furioso for you, Robert? Capital stuff to top off a meal with. A man I know in London sends me a box every month. Three pounds in weight a month, that's my ration.'

'Oh well, I expect we shall get word of him sooner or later. I'll tell Mrs Keech to keep something back for when he arrives.' Her voice trailed out of the room behind her leaving it, Robert thought, rather cheerless.

'Thank you but no. Constance cannot abide the smell of snuff on my clothes.'

'If you must marry someone half your age . . . now let us discuss the important things in life. These banknotes of yours: have you heard that in town they're already being called Pumfreys? Whatever next! Soon it'll be land at so many Pumfreys an acre, houses at a hundred Pumfreys a bedroom, cabbages at a quarter Pumfrey a gross. Where will it end? Once you can print the stuff everyone's dreams are made of, the world's at your feet. Think of that Scotchman, Mr Law. He got the hang of it so well that the froggies had to throw him out of the country. It's a dangerous business, meddling with things people are used to. D'ye think they'll swallow them here? Not quite the same as a good rattle in one's purse, I'd have thought.'

'Oh, but all the country bankers are doing it these days. It is a simple way of increasing our resources. Gold can be stolen, or hoarded, or debased. It is heavy: you cannot always carry as much as you need. Business suffers when the precious metals are in short supply. And, as I say, they are cumbersome for trade. But with banknotes there can be no such objection. They are in every way more tractable. Mr Law was too impetuous: he let the matter get out of hand and was ruined by the speculators. But in his native land they have been using banknotes since the turn of the century without the smallest mishap. I tell you, it is the way of the future, and as it happens, I have brought with me –'

With a flutter of pride, he drew from his inside pocket a drab, linen-coloured rectangle of paper which he spread out on the table between them. 'The first Pumfrey in the world!'

Anthony cocked his head and fished around for his glass of port.

'Yes, well, but wouldn't something a bit gaudier go down better? Something with some spunk to it?'

'You think so? Come come, surely you would not have me aquatint them? They must be as sober as we who stand security for them. In any case, I would be honoured if you would accept this as a gift. See, it is the first. I have numbered it so and signed it. Jack has it recorded in his ledger so any day that you wish to make Lady Apreece a present, you have only to present it in my counting-room and Jack will hand you five pounds in coin. *Voilà, un cadeau de ma maison.*'

'That is exceedingly generous of you, Robert.' He held it against the candlelight. 'And this watermark you have so ingeniously introduced . . .?'

'Is a pineapple, the traditional symbol of hospitality. Constance thought it most appropriate in view of – well, the relationship between our bank and its customers.'

'Number one, eh! The first Pumfrey known to mankind. I am touched, quite touched . . . But I trust you will not add it to my debt, what!'

'Do you take me for a savage? I assure you that is not my way at all,' Robert replied a little stiffly.

'In any event it is not due for another twelvemonth, by which time you will be engrossed to the exclusion of all else by the addition to your family.'

He filled Robert's glass and took another peck of snuff off the back of his hand. Daisy and Miss Hoole walked past the window, each carrying a long vegetable trug.

'By the way, Robert, I hope you will not be too rigid concerning the exact date of repayment.' His easy smile was replaced by a foxy look of complicity. 'The thing is – and I tell you this in the very strictest confidence, of course – that I have a position in the threes which is not, ahem, not running entirely in my favour. Gomez says that the news from France is unsettling the brokers.

The harvest has been poor and the price of bread has doubled. It has made the citizenry uncommonly restless and if there is one thing the Exchange cannot abide it is restlessness in France. You know how it is. Some peasant in Calais decides to burn his leaf pile and before you know where you are the harbour master in Dover has spied the smoke and is shouting, War! War! The frogs are upon us! Oh it'll come right, Robert, you don't need to worry about that. The rumours will float away, all will be seen to be peaceful and my boat will come rollocking into port.

'But I believed it proper to mention the fact now so that if I am a little behind hand at settlement date, you will not accuse me of acting in bad faith.'

'That is very frank of you, Sir Anthony. Let me be equally frank and say that any delay in repayment would be extremely inconvenient. I have other monies lying out besides yours. It is most necessary that you pay me with timeliness so that I can honour my own commitments. Let that be clearly understood between us.'

'But of course! Short of catastrophe, you may rely on me to be faithful to our agreement, and to demonstrate my good will –'. He moved his chair closer to Robert and swept the cutlery away with his forearm.

'Don't matter how you look at it, Robert, you'll never get another chance like it to do some top-notch lending. Horne'll need the money, I warrant you, what with the roof on the big house, a horse or two, a new carriage, some servants, improvements to the land – you know, all the extravagances that go with a young man's fancies. Bound to add up. Roofs that size don't come cheap. And you can be sure that he'll scarcely have a penny to call his own until the old woman dies.

'Course you'll take a charge on the place, tie him up proper. And when one day he rides in and says, "What about another thousand?" you just say, "Sorry, Ned, the coffers are empty."'

'I don't understand you.'

'Then you reel him in, Robert, reel him in like a chub. Remind him of his failure to comply with the terms of the mortgage (which of course he will have omitted to do), profess the most hideous regret, adduce as the reason for your foreclosure the unfortunate circumstances in which you now find yourself, etc. and so on – and there you are. The owner of a magnificent property. I tell you, it's a rare opportunity for a banker like yourself. Constance will think inordinately well of you.'

'But I have no wish to own Winterbourne. Whatever would I do with it?'

'You would quickly find another to take it off your hands. With not a penny lost from your pocket. And all the time you would have been receiving the interest.'

The two men regarded each other in silence. Robert took from his waistcoat pocket a small pencil tipped with a piece of smoky green agate. He placed it on the table before him and folded one hand over the other.

'The quality of Mr Horne's land, is it something like your own?'

'If it were employed correctly and the necessary improvements effected.'

'But there are improvements and there are improvements,' Robert said discouragingly, out of bankerly habit.

But Anthony was riding high by now, one hand round the neck of the port decanter and the other raised to spiflicate the slightest show of dissent. There was not a man in the county, perhaps not a man in the whole land, who could match his knowledge concerning improvements. And he understood very well how impressionable moneylenders could be when confronted by lengthy technical descriptions of unfamiliar processes.

'Good deep drainage for a start, each drain to be dug to a depth of not less than thirty-two inches, twenty inches wide at ground level tapering to four inches in the bed, stoned for fifteen inches from the bottom. Stones, mark you, not wood. Even birch will have perished within twenty years and when dealing with improvements, Robert, twenty years is like the passage of a moment. Us landowners build for the long haul. Then we must allow for a heavy marl and dunging. Twenty loads of manure to fifty of clay, mixed in a heap and left to rot down for six months, then turned and left for a further six months before being spread. Many's the fool I've known who's ploughed it under too raw. And so, having corrected the imbalance of phlogiston, we can proceed next to refine the system of daily husbandry with the progressive methods now available, to improve the standards by which the breeding livestock are selected . . .'

Phlogiston. The word leapt out at Robert like a clove of garlic in a salad. He instinctively mistrusted it. It was not congruous with *amo, amas, amat*. The scales of his mind, that had been teetering between prudence on the one hand and gain on the other, gave a sudden lurch as, unnoticed by Anthony in the heat of his declamatory fervour, phlogiston was placed on the tray. He must be cautious. Come what might, he must not commit himself further. He heard the hall clock strike four.

'Already?' he exclaimed, putting away his pencil and rising to his feet. 'I regret it, but I must depart or my poor Constance will grow anxious. She has her people all around her but even so . . .'

A watery sun, the colour of an apricot, had come out whilst they spoke and hung a fathom above the hills. Closeted with their private calculations, they waited on the front-door step for Clayton to fetch Robert's horse. The shadow of the stable weathercock straddled the lawn faintly. Woodsmoke tainted the autumn air. They heard the chink of a horse's shoes on cobblestones.

Then from behind the lofty wall of the vegetable garden, perhaps a hundred yards away, there came to their ears a sound as unexpected as that of a waterfall in the desert. It was a man laughing, a rippling bulb of laughter that erupted from the seat of the belly and skipped over the wall and up the lane towards them. Anthony stiffened. Winterbourne or not, this was going too far. A fellow who was late for lunch (and late for matins too), should come and apologise and apologise damned quickly and mean every word of it instead of horsing around in the raspberry canes. Why, he was scarcely known to them. Taking liberties, that's what it was. He set his hands on his hips and glowered at the wall.

'Must be our Mr Horne at last,' chuckled Robert beside him. 'Y'know, it does one no end of good to hear a young man laugh like that. Helps rejuvenate old codgers like us, ain't that so, Sir Anthony?'

Daisy and Miss Hoole came walking up the lane with Edward between them, their heads a-waggle and their faces sparkling with animation. In Edward's hand was Daisy's trug laden with marrows striped green and yellow like a jester's tunic.

'I am so sorry, so abjectly sorry,' Edward said, 'I would have been here hours ago had not Polly sulked the entire way. I swear I would have been quicker walking. We are each of us extremely displeased with the other.'

'But Mr Horne has more than made amends by helping us with the vegetables,' Daisy said, her eyes bright. 'Somehow we began talking about the time we first met at Nat's dance and how he trod on the hem of my dress. All elbows and knees, wasn't that the wording we agreed on, Mr Horne? But the funniest thing was to hear him describe how, after we'd left, his father and Thadie O'Donnell began chasing his tutor round the house with pokers in their hands for having got tipsy with old Mr Cuthbert.' She turned to Edward. 'So like your father, Mr Horne, I can see him now, roaring his head off at poor Mr Dryce and harrying him from room to room like a little foaming barrel –'

'It was no laughing matter at the time. He put Mr Dryce on a coach the next day and within a week had engaged a new tutor for me. As a matter of fact it turned out to be a blessing in disguise. He was a nice man, Mr Morris, a thoroughly decent fellow in every way.' The memory of this conversation and the images that it had provoked was warm in their faces.

'By the way,' he continued, 'is Thadie O'Donnell still in this world?'

'I heard not,' replied Anthony. 'He made the mistake of trusting a bull. Strange for one of his experience.'

'You'd have laughed to hear this young man a moment ago, Sir Anthony,' chipped in Miss Hoole.

'I am sure you are right.'

'And what's more, we were wondering whether Miss Daisy shouldn't ask her brother to find a respectable horse for him. A gentleman like Mr Horne should have something more fitting than a farmer's pony.'

Clayton appeared out of the stableyard leading a nice chestnut with a blaze running down into one nostril. Robert, who had been standing rather in the wings of the conversation, slapped his gloves against his palm to draw attention to his departure.

'How very ill-mannered of me, I do apologise. You must be Robert Pumfrey.' Edward laid down Daisy's trug and put out his hand. 'Edward Horne, Winterbourne. You probably don't remember me, probably never even saw me when you and your uncle – wasn't it? – came to call on father. I expect I was watching you from some hidey-hole. All I can recall is that you both rode huge horses and were quite terrifying.'

'Ah yes, I remember now. Course you've changed a lot since those days. But you must excuse me. I really must be getting home to Constance.' He swung himself into the saddle, an ample, dapper, middle-aged man. 'Come and see me at the bank when you are next in town. We are open only in the mornings. Stop by for a talk once my wife has recovered from her lying in. Just give your card to my cashier. I'll tell Jack to expect you. No need for any formalities.' He thanked his hosts and set off for Buxton at a rising trot.

'But I do not understand why you are so perplexed, my dear,' said Constance Pumfrey from the sofa, stroking her son's hair as he leaned back against her knees with his thumb in his mouth. 'Sir Anthony has set out a way in which our profit may be increased. You have not told me the details and I do not ask for them. It is not I who runs the bank. But in principle this must be to our advantage, must it not? The more we lend, the greater our gain. It cannot be otherwise, surely.'

'Quite so, quite so,' replied Robert, ranging round the perimeter of their drawing-room. 'The greater the lending, the greater the gain. You are absolutely correct. But the greater the gain, the greater the risk. Perhaps you do not see this yet, but it is one of the cardinal rules of our business. If you wished, you could say it is the rule of any business.'

'But a moment ago you said there was no risk. I cannot follow you when you speak in riddles.'

'I was speaking about the generality of things. Consider it, my dear Constance, as if you were studying a portrait. It does not matter whose, any portrait will do. Let us take your father's as an example. Let us imagine before us a portrait of the worthy Mr Appleby. We stand at a distance from it and agree amongst ourselves that it is a fine picture of a much-loved man. We are more than satisfied. It has caught his resemblance more neatly than we would have considered possible. Then we take a step forward and on observing the details more closely, are obliged to conclude that when it came to painting Mr Appleby's hands, Mr Appleby had left the room and a monkey had taken his place. For what do we see? Nothing more than a plate of sausages resting in his lap. The devil lies in the detail, that is all I mean. Taken as a whole, we are a sound business. We can withstand anything. But when it comes to the particular –'. He seated himself and as quickly rose to continue pacing. 'Phlogiston. There, in one ugly word, you have the source of my worries. I have no idea what it means, but I do not trust it.'

'But if you do not trust the word, you cannot trust the man who spoke it. That seems to me logical.'

'It is logical – perhaps.'

'Then you have no need to perplex yourself further. If you cannot trust Sir Anthony, you should not have dealings with him.'

'Easily enough said, but there are other considerations involved. He puts a great deal of business our way. It would be foolish to antagonise him.'

'May I ask if you have already had dealings with him?'

'We have had many discussions over the years. You must realise that I cannot divulge the details without the consent of my partners, of William and your brother Archer. But I can assure you that I have found him invariably honest. I cannot recall one instance where he has not done what he said he'd do.'

'But now you do not trust him.'

'You are putting words into my mouth,' he said irritably, sleeking his greying hair over the dome of his skull. 'What is unusual in this case – and I put it no more firmly than that – is for one man to request that another, not himself but another, be permitted to borrow large. It is as if Sir Anthony were to ask that I go to the fishmonger on behalf of my cashier. Jack should go there for himself. It is not for me to decide whether Jack is in the mood for trout or a pot of jellied eels. By the same token, if Mr Horne wants to borrow money from me, it is he who should present his application and not another man. And it is large that we are talking, Constance, large! We are not paltering about a loan to buy a sack of coals. Do you follow me now?'

'Well, my dear, you are the one who knows best. Just so long as we do not put ourselves in danger.'

Robert took down a piece of blue-john from his collection in the china cupboard and with his head to one side examined it under a wall sconce. 'And when I finally met Mr Horne,' he said ruminatively, 'or rather re-met him, though I hardly recognised a single feature in his face, not the least curious aspect of it all was that he did not strike me as being in any way the borrowing sort. Just a pleasant young man looking forward to a good meal.'

Just then the door opened and Constance's parents entered. Mr Appleby was a dry, calm man, his wife tall and commanding with the same blue eyes and straight nose as her daughter.

'I trust we do not intrude,' she said, bundling Andrew off the sofa and dropping into his place. She kicked off her shoes. 'I find these walks you have round here most fatiguing on a lady's arrangements. We have no hills at all in Derby, you know.'

Robert said nothing. He stared stolidly down upon identical ankles, angular knees and upturned faces, upon twin suits of spiked armour. Ah, but this afternoon he had feasted off a rarer dish. Where his thoughts were invisible, beside a lady who knew how to please a man. He replaced the blue-john and locked the cabinet.

'Now, my boy, what do you say to a quick game of ride-the-tiger before bedtime? Twice round the room and a penny if you don't fall off.'

'I was brought up with the belief that the nursery is intended for games of that nature,' Mrs Appleby said to her son-in-law, placing her bruised feet on a stool.

Twelve

HAVING CAST his bait into the waters, Anthony was content to let it dawdle down the stream. It would not be the end of the world if it were spurned. He had other lures in his creel. But he did not for an instant believe that Robert Pumfrey would turn up his nose at such a succulent, wriggling titbit. And since, through having no children of his own, he took it for granted that all young men were as prodigal as St Luke had them, he was certain that not many months would have to pass before Edward was feeling the breeze. Then it would only be a matter of time.

Thus he reasoned as, with his purplish face sunk in the folds of his riding cloak, he climbed through the mists of autumn to his vantage point among the rocks of Billy Tor. There, on this huge and sprawling hill, he sat for an hour or two on most days with his spyglass on his knees. From time to time he removed it from its leather case and squinnied down at the smoke crawling from the Winterbourne cottages into the flat, grey sky. Such was his confidence that he began to study Winterbourne as if it already belonged to him. Its sour, understocked pastures, the brambles romping out of its hedges, its dockens, ragwort, and jack-thistles, these he would smite hip and thigh. He would tame the land and nourish it. It was not right that God's dowry to the human race should be turned into waste by triflers like the Hornes. It was a form of sacrilege. Heaven alone knew that Nat had been bad enough with all his absurdities – measuring echoes! taming a bat! – but now to have this son of his at Winterbourne . . . Right there! Under his very nose for the remainder of his life. It was too much. No decent man should have to watch land being so abused.

He began to feel frustrated by the waiting. He attended market less often and held himself at a distance from people. He lost his temper at trivial upsets, shouted at Miss Hoole and regarded Daisy with suspicion, as if somehow she was responsible for Robert's tardiness in humbugging Edward. Christmas approached and still no word came from the bank. His foxhounds grew fat from want of sport. When he fed them, they looked up at him with bewildered eyes. Was this not the hunting season?

The frosts of winter arrived. (On New Year's Day he saw Robert talking with Mr Wormald outside the bank, but the man merely raised his hat and continued his conversation.) Now, he thought, Ned will send out his woodmen and his ploughing teams. The ground is hard. The season is ripe. But all at Winterbourne remained as devoid of movement as before, save for Edward flitting darkly between the leafless trees as he came and went on Ladysway, and the broomstick figure of Digbeth Chiddlestone riding errands of mercy round his scattered parish.

Then one January day, when he was sitting in his eyrie in the thin sunshine holding his telescope between mittened fingers, he saw beneath him a single goose beating a late passage southwards. As it flew rhythmically away towards the ruins of Britannia, it uttered at intervals a fluttering, mordant chuckle. Straightway he knew it for a signal. Robert had failed him. The bait had been too insipid. He must move to a different pool. And with that realisation, his spirits began to rise. The forces of his finely meshed brain, which had been demoralised by the rain and the inactivity, regrouped and found for themselves a fresh channel. The smile returned to his mouth. His dogs regarded him with renewed hope. A couple of days later he rode not to Billy Tor but down the Britannia road to Winterbourne.

The air was keen and the hills stark against a sky of egg-shell blue. Priam and Ajax, his favourite hounds, rummaged joyfully through the patches of wayside bracken and, unreproved, chased every rabbit they saw.

He found Walter Hamilton and Davie Paxton moving furniture from the big house into the stable lodgings. Leaning against the door jamb, he scrutinised Edward's sitting-room.

'Very pretty, I do say, and far more spacious than I had ever imagined. Quite the thing for a man while he's single.'

'Tad to the left, Davie, master said to centre it beneath the picture – what's that, Sir Anthony? – a tiddle more, easy now – there!' The men stood back and gauged the position of the sideboard.

'Looks well enough, wouldn't you say? Oh no you don't, my lad, not in here you don't.' (This to Ajax, who was preparing to ease himself in a corner.)

'Mr Horne out for the day, then?' he asked.

'As he usually be,' replied Davie Paxton, kicking off his felt slippers before putting his boots back on, 'getting round the country, him and Sixpence, visiting folk and making himself known. Now if you'll excuse us, Sir Anthony, we've got a job to finish afore he returns. That table next, didn't us think, Walter, the awkward devil from the schoolroom?'

Anthony took from his pocket a book wrapped in cloth, Mr Arthur Young's *Letters on Farming*, and placed it on the sideboard. 'Tell Mr Horne when you next see him there's something here for him to peck at these long winter nights.'

Then he called in his dogs and galloped back to Overmoor, where he bolted a cold game pie, two slices of brawn and a half of burgundy, slapped Miss Hoole on her spiny bottom, told Clayton that he'd 'kick his bollocks to Buxton and back' if he didn't have a fresh horse saddled by the time he'd had a piss, and by one-thirty in the afternoon was leading out his hounds to try a fox which Hucknall had earlier that morning seen entering the Home Gorse.

But he had been mistaken in his belief that Edward had spent the autumn in idleness. It was just that his order of priorities was different. Nothing in his life had prepared him for this moment. He was as green to agriculture as newly felled ash and not eager to be initiated. But in his surroundings and his neighbours, in the sport they could offer, in the figures of their daughters and the quality of their cellars, in their jokes, quirks and tales, he had curiosity in abundance. For was he not a man of Derbyshire now, like his father? Were not these the people he had to live beside?

From Emily Scarlett he bought for the sum of one penny (for the sake of honour), a rough-coated terrier puppy that he named Sixpence. She was rather long in the leg and for a week did nothing but gloom at him from beneath her clumpy eyebrows and snuffle at horse turds through her pepper-and-salt moustaches. 'Never seen the outside of the nursery, that's her problem,' opined

Tom Glossipp when he consulted him. So to show Sixpence how matters should stand between a terrier and the world they took her out with the ferrets one day, by which means she became acquainted with the perfume of rabbit holes and cheered up no end.

With Sixpence balanced like a figurehead on Polly's saddle bow or, if the weather was foul, tucked inside his cloak so that only her button-bright eyes were visible, they soon became a familiar sight in Buxton and around the muddy lanes. People remarked on them. There was something that plucked affectionately at their memories in seeing Nathaniel Horne's boy riding with his arm round a dog on top of a pony shaped like a haycock.

'Grows more like his father every day,' said Johnnie Alcock, the road mender, in the Green Man one night. 'You remember how old Nat was a bit cracked in the pitcher, well I reckons this 'uns going the same way. But a nice man, Arthur, make no mistake about it, a nice man. You can talk to him, you can.' Which coming from Johnnie was praise indeed, for those who mend roads daily are fine judges of the manners of those who pass them at their work.

'Madge and I weren't so struck on him. Could have been animals living here for all the attention he paid us when he arrived. Ain't that so, wife?' Arthur called through to where Madge was slicing turnips.

''Cos he was new to the game, Arthur, not sure of himself to start with,' said Johnnie. 'Three four times now I've seen him on the road and each time he got down (which few of his sort do) and asked me how things were and why I do what I does the way I does. Why I sits down to break up the stones, for instance. Or why I have to get 'em no bigger than pigeons' eggs. Even tried it himself once. There he was this day, sitting on my stool and chattering away and making faces 'cos his hands were oversoft for the job, when what should happen by but a train of packhorses with coal or summat, rumpy-tumpy little beasts with forelocks you could ring a peel of bells on, so up he jumps and starts in on the packmaster – how fast did he go? Why only eighteen animals? How much was he paid? Not a bit of side to him. I tell you, Arthur, he's a curious young beggar.'

And so indeed he had become. Catkins appeared on the bare

wood of his soul. What Nicholas Hawkesworth had described as his enigmatic character turned out to have been nothing more than the natural incoherence of youth. Anthony, brooding in his lair on Billy Tor, had detected only indolence and degeneracy in the plumes of smoke curling skywards from the cottages at Winterbourne. But had it been Edward holding the telescope, he would have seen in their writhing vapours not a sermon on sloth but palm trees, a woman combing her hair or a dancing monkey. Where the older man descried vice and nothing plainer, the youth would have found the excitement of the unknown.

Sometimes, alone at night or when the jackdaws chided him from the naked roofbeams of the big house, he worried about money. His capital was disappearing at a faster rate than he had anticipated. He thought: it may even be that I must discover how to turn a profit from land. Then one morning (the same one upon which Anthony left the book on his sideboard), he snapped his fingers and said to himself, By Jove, what about an heiress instead! He decided to ride into town and take some soundings from Robert Pumfrey.

'The fact is', he said to Daisy, whom he happened across as she came out of the establishment of Kitty Prodger, the seamstress, 'that I feel happier here than I have ever done before. Coming back to Winterbourne has been like putting on a shoe that fits exactly. Do you know what I mean? Neither too tight nor too loose. As if one had been born into it.'

Daisy looked at the sparkle in his eyes and smiled. 'But Mr Horne, what have you done with Sixpence today? How can you be so happy without your friend?'

'She's with Polly in Robert's stable. I have an engagement with him presently, so I left her there while I went to be measured for a new pair of hunting boots.'

'I am glad that you and Mr Pumfrey have struck up a friendship. He is truly one of the most amiable men I know. And as it happens, I have arranged to take tea with Constance and see her baby daughter. They are calling her Julia Henrietta. I am to stand as her godmother. I have just collected a sampler for her from Kitty for when she starts her learning. Do you like those names, Mr Horne?'

On this Edward held no opinion. They began to walk down the hill towards the bank.

'Would you think it very bold if I said that Polly is better suited to a shorter person? My friend Mary Dipple – who incidentally declares herself bowled over by you and wishes to drown poor Dickie without further ado – says the sight of the pair of you remind her of nothing more than a circus act.'

'Oh, but you cannot be so cruel about Polly. It is true we have had some bad moments but now we are perfectly reconciled to each other. It is not her fault that she is so petite. Or that the field mice run away gibbering for fear they will be scraped to death by the passage of her stomach. And in any case, a horse with such a figure has its advantages.'

'Please name me one.'

'I can nearly walk into the saddle. It is a great boon for an idle fellow.'

'But you cannot go hunting on Polly, or at any rate not with any confidence.'

'It is true, I concede it.'

'And I expect she has trouble at narrow gates. You must allow that her girth is against her there.' They stopped outside the bank. Her eyes danced in the crisp afternoon sunlight. 'I mean, she is so broad, and you have your knees to worry about. Unless, of course, you stretch your legs in front of you like a man rowing a boat.'

'It is for this reason that we avoid all narrow gates. It is our firm policy.'

'But the world is full of narrow gates. You cannot elude them for ever. I believe I shall ask my brother James if he cannot procure for you a more elegant specimen so that when you visit us I am not always reminded of Mary's little jest. Will you be long with Mr Pumfrey? After I have visited Constance, I am to meet James at the covered ride behind the Crescent. We could speak to him together, if you wished.'

Edward looked mischievously at her. 'I cannot say how long I shall be. I have a particular question for him that may ramify extensively.'

'Such questions are always the most difficult. But in any event I shall mention your horse to James. It is a business he enjoys. And now, I think, we go our separate ways: I to the nursery and you to

Mr Pumfrey's parlour. Pray remember me to him. Goodbye, Mr Horne.' She extended her hand in a firm, uncomplicated way.

The fire roared. Robert was sitting with his coat off in front of the tea things.

'Do you think a man could get drunk on tea?' he asked.

'If he could, those who govern us would never have removed the tax upon it.'

'An astute reply, Edward. What is physical gratification? Something which is taxed. Do you think we should offer this piece of wisdom to Dr Johnson?'

'But not all of its forms are subject to taxation.'

'Ah yes . . . though as your elder, and that by some years, I must tell you that the pleasure you allude to diminishes with time. You will discover it so for yourself one day,' Robert said with a frown, pouring.

'Then if ever it were to be taxed, it should be done on a sliding scale, with the lady responsible for agreeing the assessment since there are occasions – but this is a silly conversation, Robert. I have a far more ample question for you: how does one acquire money without borrowing it?'

'Unaided by sweat or good fortune? By marriage. Only by marriage or a lottery ticket, which is approximately the same. Mind you, Constance would not like to hear me speak like that. She would say, by love and thus by marriage.'

'Laying to one side the matter of love, and thinking now of money in its generality, local money, mark you, for when it is imported it is apt to be flighty – tell me, where do you suppose it is to be found in its female form?'

Robert put his fingers to his temples and looked steadily at Edward. Then he burst out, 'The roof at Winterbourne! An heiress! I see it all!' He jumped up and put his hand on the bell rope. 'But first we must ask Constance whether you would be a catch. We must get a woman to mark you. Beauty, odour, delicacy of conversation, the quality of skin, the pelt, perfection of limbs – these are all matters that a lady considers most carefully. For example: my feet, Edward, look at them. Unremarkable, are they not? But they are what Constance noticed first. It may be peculiar to look at someone's feet before anything else, but it is what happened. They were small, spruce, moving with a purpose, she said – so she consulted my eyes. They too found favour – so we spake. My voice was agreeable to her . . .' He laughed. 'Women are unaccountable. So we must think of it from their point of view before we start to enumerate heiresses.'

'No, no, Robert, please do not call her,' said Edward. 'It would be a great embarrassment to me. My question was purely one of theory. When I came to Winterbourne, it was with the intention of selling it. Does that surprise you? But it is true. I had hoped for a handsome sale to some wealthy manufacturer wishing to set up a son in style. But now that I have lived here, I wish to make it my home. And so I thought this morning, if I am not to be supported in life by a Master Arkwright, why not by a Miss Arkwright instead? But it was only an impulse.'

'Do you really need an heiress? The Hornes have money behind them, that's what my uncle said whenever Nat called for an accommodation.'

'My father borrowed from you?' Edward said, wryly crinkling his brow.

'Oh yes,' Robert laughed, 'whenever he'd had a falling out with your mother and was short of dust. I remember there was once a piebald horse that caught his fancy. But no, she would not have a piebald near the place. Adamant about it. Said they were unreliable and he'd get himself killed. So he had to keep it in General Scarlett's stable. I don't think he rode it above half a dozen times. Many's the scrape Nat got into like that.' Robert chuckled happily. 'Dear me, yes . . . Did you ever meet that friend of his who wanted him to import German wild pigs to roam loose on the hills . . . ?'

One anecdote led to another. Darkness fell. They went upstairs. Sophia read quietly in a corner, shaping the words with her lips, from time to time raising her eyes to follow the conversation. Matronly Constance bustled between the nursery and the drawing-room. Robert, freed that very morning from Mr and Mrs Appleby, was in a rare humour. They ate a quantity of scollops. In the most sweetly diffident tones, Sophia asked Edward to keep a puppy for her from Sixpence's first litter. No mention was made of heiresses. And the evening ended with a charming rendition by

Constance of 'The Sea Captain's Farewell to His Lady', the tune of which was still on Edward's lips when he rode into Winterbourne.

'What's all this then?' he demanded of Sixpence, picking up the volume that Anthony had left and somewhat falling into his chair. Though the type was generous, Mr Young's style of writing was too ferocious for his mood. And when he reached one of the passages that Anthony had underlined, that 'a net profit is scarcely ever made by gentlemen who farm either for convenience or amusement', he said Pish and went to bed, where he was visited by a sequence of complicated and unpleasant dreams involving pigs and money.

Thirteen

EDWARD WAS an optimist by nature. Disagreeable or depressing information he either erased from his mind or reformulated so that only encouraging aspects were on view. But when he awoke, he found that all he could think of were his horrid dreams and a life hemmed in by poverty and decay.

It was not raining but it might later. Scarves of mist clung to the motionless treetops. He could see from his bed that it was a hateful day. He decided he would stay where he was and read the other chapter Anthony had marked, 'Reasons Why Farming So Often Proves Unprofitable', in case he should spy any loopholes.

But Mr Young's argument was as clear as the weather was not: farming was not a business for amateurs. Edward still could not conceive how this could be true, so contrary was it to common sense. Animals ate grass, grew fat, were sold and thus produced money. The more grass they ate, the more money they fetched. No one could dispute that. Well, he had grass in abundance. In whichever direction he looked, he had grass. He had no idea whether it was the right sort of grass, or how it tasted to a sheep. But he had it and they ate it. It was all they ever did. No time was wasted on frivolities. They rose at dawn, ate grass until nightfall, and went to sleep. So how the deuce could profit elude him?

'It's written here', he said to Davie Paxton when he came in with a new can of hot water, 'that unless a farmer has at least four hundred sheep, it'll *go off very slow*. That's what Mr Young says, that it'll go off very slow. How do you say to that?'

'I'd say it were likely enough, sir.'

'So how many sheep are there at Winterbourne?'

Davie scratched himself. 'Eight hundred or nearby,' he said

slowly, 'that is, it was eight hundred the last time we had a count, but then there's last winter's deaths and what'll die this winter and what we ate and what the foxes ate and what we sold to the Scotchman who comes calling in the summer and the puckle we lost in the snows a little while back and them that'll die at spring lambing –'

'Hold hard, we've got some way to go before spring.'

'Ah yes,' said Davie, giving Edward a pitying look, 'but livestock means deadstock and there's nought we can do about it, so less what we'll lose at lambing, add back the thaives that we kept from last year, less what's gone wandering on other folk's land – so that's more or less how near I mean to eight hundred.'

'That's not much of an answer. If we made cheeses, we could go and count them in the dairy. Three, four, five hundred, it'd make no odds; we'd still be able to count them. So why can't you do the same for sheep?'

'Them's a dying lot, these sheeps are, sir.'

'Piffle, man. Go and saddle Polly for me. I'm going to Overmoor.'

Anthony was spread across the sofa taking a nap when Mrs Keech showed Edward into the drawing-room. A paper was spread across his face. He was still wearing his boots, which rested on the arm of the sofa. On his head was a flat blue-quilted cap.

'Keeps genius warm,' he said cheerfully, jumping up and steering Edward down to his business room, 'prevents it escaping undetected through the integument of the scalp. Only one way out for it, you see, if you wear a thing like this – through the mouth. Deuced good invention, what! Now, Ned, did you find that little book of mine useful?'

Edward tossed it on to the table. He could feel a headache coming on. 'A lot of mumbo-jumbo as far as I could see. And extremely lowering to the spirits.'

Anthony grunted sympathetically. 'Mr Young's a very consider-able authority. There's few farmers of any substance who go against him. But I know what you mean. It's a business, Ned, believe you me. If it isn't one thing in farming, it's another. What bothers you in particular?'

'Take this matter of the sheep. Seemingly you need at least four hundred to make a go of it. So this morning I asked Davie how many I had. I'm damned if I understood more than one word in three of what he said. What the deuce is a puckle? Half a dozen? Two hundred?'

Anthony shrugged. 'Depends on who's speaking.'

'Simplest thing, it occurred to me as I rode over here, would be to go back to London and leave them to puckle away by themselves.'

In fact he had thought no such thing. The remark had come to him on the spur of the moment. It was just that he had felt intimidated by the weight of Anthony's stare and had decided that it was time to show him he had a mind of his own.

'It's certainly a large responsibility for a young man,' Anthony said solemnly, 'drains to be cut, pastures cleaned, hedges planted . . . the roof on the big house, a decent flock of sheep, new cattle sheds . . . It's a lot of spending that you face, Ned, an onerous burden indeed for a young man on his own. And you must think of your own enjoyment too. A fellow like you shouldn't have to worry himself to death about his estate. What you want is a brand-new chariot at the door, a stable full of hunters, a brace of footmen and a manservant who'll jump like mustard when you holler at him. You should leave the hard work to grizzled old warriors like myself.'

He left his chair and perched himself on the front of his desk so that Edward was looking up at him.

'Supposing that you did go back to London, what would you do with Winterbourne?' His hand purred up and down his thigh. The coals shifted in the grate.

'Oh, it was just a notion. Only an idea as I was riding along. You know, one of those silly ideas that comes into one's head.'

'But from the way you spoke, it appeared a very serious idea a few moments ago. The heart never lies, you know how the saying goes. Here's where it counts, here!' He thumped his chest and poured his blue eyes into Edward's. 'I think that if we are to be realistic about it, absolutely realistic and sensible, you would be a much happier man if you were free of the entanglement of Winterbourne. No needs to be coy about it. Nothing to be ashamed of in preferring a city to the land. We all have our ways.'

'But –'

Anthony put a hand on the arm of Edward's chair and leaning

down, said, 'A man I know would give you a good price for Winterbourne. The best. No one would give you more. I know it for a fact.'

'It crossed my mind', Edward said cautiously, 'that perhaps I should make cheese. Or try some German wild pigs. Robert mentioned them yesterday. They could live off the beechmast on Ladysway.'

'But you didn't answer my question, Ned.'

Edward suddenly felt irritated by the man. He disliked being sat over. It was a little fatherly guidance he had come for, nothing more. 'You have a feather on your elbow,' he said.

'A what?'

'A feather. There. On your elbow.'

'What of it?' Anthony rose and twisted himself round.

'A white one. Could be a bantam's.'

'I don't see it.'

'Higher up. Just above the point of the elbow.'

'How do you mean, higher? Towards the wrist' – his hand was pointing at the ceiling – 'or towards the shoulder?'

'How could it be to the wrist? Is not the shoulder always higher than the wrist?'

'Not when you are standing as I am now.'

'Then stand as you would normally. In that way there can be no . mistake.'

'Are you making fun of me?' Anthony removed his coat and inspected the folds round the elbows. He gave it a hefty shake. 'Is this some sort of a joke? Because if it is, I call it a very poor one indeed.'

But just then Edward saw that in fact there was a feather, between his cushion and the side of the chair.

'Not at all. Here it is. It fell off when you shook your coat.' He held it up as evidence.

'That never belonged to a bantam.'

'I only said it could be a bantam's.'

'That's not good enough. You can't expect to be a farmer if you don't know the difference between one feather and another.'

'Please don't shout so, I beg of you. I've got a headache.'

'What were you up to last night?'

'I ate bad scollops. Robert's.'

'So you'll stay clear of them another time. Anyway, you won't make a big cry as a farmer if you can't tell the difference between a hen's feather and a bantam's.'

He went over to the fireplace and released the feather. Edward jumped out of his seat and caught it.

'Whatever made you do that?'

'I'm not sure. I thought it could be useful. For stuffing a pillow, for instance.'

'But nobody uses hens' feathers for pillows, only goose feathers. My brother keeps geese in Lincolnshire, at a place called Holland. He plucks his birds four or five times a year for the feather trade. Hens, my foot.'

'Your brother? You have a brother?' asked Edward, his curiosity instantly aroused. The idea that Anthony should have any immediate family was somehow unbelievable.

'What's so strange about that? Actually, he's only a half-brother. Does that satisfy you? What an extraordinary youth you are!' Perplexed and not a little astonished by this unexpected turn in the conversation, they faced each other in front of the fire, Anthony's coat hanging from the tip of his finger and Edward twirling the stalk of the wispy feather between his thumb and forefinger.

They exchanged a few halting sentences and Edward left.

But he didn't say no, thought Anthony, standing at his window with his hand curled round his chin as he watched Edward amble off on the ludicrous Polly. I offered the notion and he didn't say no.

This one has his farm, the other his bank. Moley Dibdin has a job and so do Johnnie Alcock, Amos, Arthur Smith and the rest of them. They rise in the morning and their duties are straightforward until bedtime. But I am like half-witted Sophia Pumfrey. Nothing is clear to us. We are like drizzle, neither one thing nor another.

So deep was Edward in these thoughts that Daisy and Clayton were almost upon him in the trap before he heard the wheels.

'Did the matter with Mr Pumfrey ramify as successfully as you wished?' she enquired, leaning forward, her oval face pale against the darkness within, her chin level with the windowsill, upon which one hand rested.

'I never knew your husband had a brother.'

'Why should you? He has visited us only once, and that when you were living in London. Anthony does not care for that side of his family.'

'I believe I would have fainted if he had owned up to a sister as well. I just cannot associate him with other family. My mind will not allow it.'

'Is yours a spacious mind, Mr Horne?'

'Infinitely so. But that is not always a blessing. Ideas have too much room in which to flit around. Sometimes I think it would be better to have a tiny cupboard with space for only one thought at a time.'

'I can see you are dispirited.'

'Let us say that I am an optimist who for the moment has lost the scent.'

'An optimist?' Daisy's eyebrows rose. 'I shall have to consider that word. It is a bold flag to fly. I can think of few people round here who would readily own up to the description, and of those who did, I suspect half would be lying. Let me see . . . Mr Quex-Parker, I think he would be our only neighbour I could truthfully call an optimist.'

'Fuscus Quex-Parker?'

'*Ipsissimus*, as you gentlemen say. He is preparing – I do not know when he is actually leaving, but he is certainly preparing to go to the Isle of Wight to learn how to paint in watercolours. Is that not the badge of an optimist in a man of his age?' She put her head out of the window and called up to Clayton, 'Have you heard any recent news about Mr Quex-Parker's plans?'

'I should like to learn how to paint,' Edward said with a rush. It was exactly the sort of enticement he needed on that day and in that mood. His mind flew off to imagine himself beneath an umbrella and the Italian sun . . .

'I spoke to my brother about a new horse for you,' Daisy was saying as she observed his head shoot up and his eyes clear, 'I will ask Clayton to ride over with a note as soon as I have word from him.'

'I am truly obliged. I am sorry to demean Polly in any respect but, yes, you were right. A larger animal would indeed suit me better. Had I still been aged ten –'

He became conscious of her critical eye roaming over Polly and immediately felt ashamed of his gloves, which he knew to be dirty. He had scooped them off the table without a moment's thought. He quickly put both hands into his pockets.

But Daisy guessed why he did it and smiled openly, showing her teeth. 'Let the horse befit the man. James said it might take him the rest of the winter to find the charger you need.'

Fourteen

THE APRIL of 1788 drew to a close. The east winds shrivelled and passed. Frogs began to croak. Thrushes babbled from the tops of thorn trees. Young rooks flopped and stumbled among the early ash leaves. Cherries gripped their flouncy blossoms as scuds of rain drove down from the hills. Chestnut spikelets parted their toffee-coloured sheaths and set out for the sun. Everywhere sharp and slender perfumes rose to the nostrils. From all directions and offering pleasure to each of man's senses spread an English spring, milky, green and glorious.

'Confound it, Ned, I've a mind to have her myself,' Anthony said, standing on his front-door step with his legs astraddle and his hands on his waist. 'What a topper of a quad! Run her out again, Garland, a bit faster this time.'

Daisy's brother, a stocky man of about thirty with a pheasant's tail feather stuck in the band of his hat, made a clucking noise against the roof of his mouth. The mare tossed her head and broke into a trot as he ran alongside her. She was a strong, handsome bay with bold black points except for her muzzle, which was brown.

'Just see how she goes, Daisy,' he called over to his sister, 'just see that action, will you? Clean as a whistle. Straight as a knife from one stride to the next. No risk of brushing with an action like that. Tck tck, old girl, once more . . .'

They circled the lawn again. He eased her off and walked the mare up to the waiting group. She stopped and with molten eyes watched Daisy descending the steps. Her nostrils quivered: she snuffled at Daisy's outstretched hand with whiskery lips. Edward and Anthony clasped their hands behind their backs and, stooping and peering and pointing, set off on a tour of inspection. 'She'll suit our ground all right, Ned, good shoulder to her, not too long in the back. No call for some great brute in these valleys of ours. Lot of short work here, y'know. Clean legs, ample bone, well muscled up . . . Six this autumn, d'ye say, James?'

'Five rising six, I can swear to it, Sir Anthony. I've known of her since she was foaled. Knew her dam, too, a right spunky goer if ever there was one. Reckon this beauty'll be just like her.'

'Seen her out hunting, have you?' asked Edward.

'Better than that, Mr Horne, I had a day on her myself last season. Foot perfect. Never missed a trick. Old Barnaby – you remember, Daisy, that big bugger who used to bring Mother a tray of plums every September – came a cropper only a few yards in front of us. Thought we were for it – and Barnaby too – but this young lady just gave a wiggle of her hips and we landed with air to spare. Not that Jem Barnaby would have noticed if twenty horses had sat down on top of him, the size he is these days. Ain't that so, darling? A flick and a swerve and we were on our way.' He gave her an affectionate smack on her forequarter.

'What do you think?' Edward asked Daisy, coming round to stand beside her.

'I like her. Look at the eye she has. Like an owl's, all wise and unblinking.' She put her mouth to the mare's ear and blew into it, the hairs tickling her nose.

'Well, what do you say, Mr Horne? I know she's not the gelding you were after but she's a good 'un. The best I'll ever find for you.'

'Does she come with her own saddle?' Edward asked.

'Can't rightly say. I never thought to ask Mr Lufkin. Of course, now that you mention it –'

'It'd be better she had one that suited her. Do you remember, Anthony, that tale about the man who went to buy a new horse but could never find one to fit his saddle?'

'I never heard of such a thing. He should have bought the horse he liked and then thought about the saddle, instead of the other way round. That man must have been a hoddydoddy to my way of thinking.'

'Which has precedence, the horse, the man, or the saddle? It sounds like one of those ancient arguments about the nature of the Holy Trinity,' Daisy said. 'Shan't you let Mr Horne take her out for a gallop to see how she feels, James?'

Edward walked over to the mounting block. A gust of wind ruffled the pennon in James Garland's hat. He turned and said to his sister in the artless way that families have, 'Do you think you should go with him then, Daisy? The mare'd go better with another horse upsides of her. It'd give Mr Horne a truer notion of her paces.'

She looked to her husband. 'But not for long, Daisy,' he said, the tip of something poking through his voice like the fin of a prowling shark. 'Here, Clayton, go and saddle up her ladyship's chestnut. Garland, you and I can go in and refresh ourselves while the young people have their sport.'

With short mincing steps the mare coquetted down the lane past the walled garden and the dung heap to the Britannia road. But when they reached the gates, she stood still and alert, her ears questing. Edward felt the tension within her flowing up the reins into his wrists. He leaned over and checked his stirrup leathers.

'Which way shall we go, left to Britannia or right towards Billy Tor?'

She did not care. It was enough that on this perfect spring morning she should be here; that in front of them the moor shimmered, that larks twittered overhead, a pair of peewits piped and somersaulted, their wings brushing the air like feather dusters, and that deep within the sediment of her heart small soft bubbles were bursting. She glanced at him from the corner of her eye, her mouth dimpling. 'Billy Tor!' She sprang her chestnut and was off.

Stride for stride, shoulder to shoulder, shining muscles bunched and driving, the two mares stretched themselves down the old and winding road. Landmarks that once seemed remote – a crab apple beneath its dome of white blossom, an outcrop of rocks, a ewe with a lamb, a bend in the road – raced up and were passed in a spatter of hooves. They came to a stream where the ruins of a wooden bridge still stood and flicked over it without a check, Edward's bay gaining half a length on the jump. He looked across at Daisy and grinned. A skein of her hair had undone itself and was streaming out from under her black riding hat. Helter-skelter they went at it for a mile and a half or two miles until they reached a point where the track disappeared into a blanket of rushes. By mutual agreement they reined in.

'Have you thought what you'll call her?' Daisy asked as she

caught her breath. Beneath her grey habit, her bosom rose and fell, reminding Edward of the time he'd watched her singing in church. How like a woman to ask a question like that! A man would have had quite different considerations: tried to find fault with the mare or gone fishing for the price.

'I hadn't really thought. I'd had it firmly in my mind that she was going to be a he.'

'And then what would you have called him?'

'Oh, something manly, like Saladin or Plantagenet.'

'Pooh, those aren't very nice. I'm glad she's a she. But what's to happen to Polly? Such a homely creature with her droopy eyes and fat little tummy, just the sort of animal you want to tuck up in bed with a cup of warm milk and read a story to. I hope you'll look after her and not send her over to Anthony for his cauldron.'

Edward laughed. His mare lowered her head and rubbed her nose against her cannon bone, jerking him forward in the saddle.

'The last time we were discussing Polly, I have to remind you that you were less than polite about her.'

'But that was months ago! It was the middle of the winter, when a lady may be forgiven for feeling uncharitable. Come the spring and one feels infinitely more sympathetic. It's Nature's way of keeping us interested in life, or so it seems to me. Without spring every year to renew one's sense of hope, life after the age of twenty-five would appear quite purposeless.'

'You truly believe that?'

'Sometimes. But come, Mr Horne, let us ride on a bit so that I can show you my most favourite spot on the whole of Overmoor.'

They turned off the green road and with Daisy in the lead rode up a path in the direction of the hills.

'How does all this strike you after London?' she called back over her shoulder. 'It would interest me to learn how you spend your time. Do you lord it around Winterbourne like a pasha, commanding this and the next from your people? Do you sit with your boots on the table saying things like, "More cream for my rhubarb, Mary", or, "Darn my stockings by Sunday or you leave"? Are you the ferocious lord of all you survey or do you live like a mouse, making little scratching noises in the night?'

Her voice floated pleasantly back to him. He looked at the curve of her waist, saw the tip of her nose wrinkle as she turned her head to inhale the aromas of spring.

'Often I'm out around the county, calling on people, making friends – you can imagine how it is for the new arrival.'

'And how is Amos taking it? Is he upset at having his importance reduced? Does it irk him that he is only *le petit maître* now?'

'If it does, I haven't noticed it. No, I tell a lie. He did give me a very old-fashioned look when I mentioned peacocks to him one day. Didn't take to the notion at all, did Amos.'

They reached a small, flat greensward beside a stream. Scattered coign stones and a rough-hewn lintel lying among the new growth of nettles spoke of a place where a building had once stood; a deeper shade of green where in olden times men had cut out a field and scythed some hay. They halted beside a rowan tree.

'So it's to be peacocks then at Winterbourne, is it?'

'Yes and no. For about half an hour one day, when I was feeling rather down, I was their slave. Then I thought, too messy, too noisy, too like having a lot of children squawking round the garden at first light. What I have in mind now – you know the yew trees on either side of the road leading up to the house.' He stopped. 'Luna, that's what I'll call her, Luna. How do you care for that?'

'Very feminine,' Daisy said with emphasis. 'It sounds like the beating of a bird's wings. Of course you realise that everyone will call her Loonie? But I suppose you men of Winterbourne can stand that.'

'Oh yes, us men of Winterbourne, you know.' He puffed out his chest and beat it with his fist. They both laughed.

'I used to come here in the early days when I was married and had the time to sit and dream. I'm sure the spirits from long ago still inhabit the place, perhaps in little downy nests hidden among the stones. I always felt that if I sat long enough, they'd pop out and talk to me, pixies in long green hoods with a bobble on the end. Silly isn't it, 'cos I expect the people who lived here were no different from ourselves, smaller maybe but just as selfish and worried about everything.'

'I can see you are a romantic at heart,' Edward said, at the same time feeling rather hungry. 'Do you think Anthony would take it amiss if an optimist invited a romantic to share his shortcake? And half an apple apiece? Mary Paxton never allows me to leave without provisions. What would happen if your horse bolted and left you in the middle of nowhere? she says.'

They tied their horses to the rowan tree and spreading Edward's saddle-blanket on the ground, sat down with their backs against a sun-warmed boulder. Above the moor, clouds glided like sails upon an ocean.

A silence fell between them. Then: she was sorry he had not brought Sixpence. She would have so liked it here, woofing at the clouds and exploring in the ruins. But no rabbits, he said, cutting the shortcake into squares. Sixpence would be happy enough with Clayton. And the roof on the big house? She didn't want to pry, but Mary Dipple had been talking about it only last week. Oh, what could she say? She'd had no idea that's how things were. Never mind, something would turn up, the money would come from somewhere. (She leaned back against the boulder more firmly and tilted her face to the sun.) But of course she'd wanted to have children! No, she didn't mind him asking, not at all. Lots of them, and to live in a house with high white ceilings and air and space and happy gurgling noises and sticky fingers pulling her hair. But of course she'd wanted children! Didn't he want a family one day? Men could be so strange. But how did he *really* like it here? Wasn't he lonely? Didn't he miss his friends and the excitement of London? She'd always hankered to go there, just once before she got too old. They chattered on without constraint.

'We should think about returning. Anthony will be getting restless,' he said eventually, rising and walking to the edge of the knoll. He stood there, his arms folded across his chest, gazing out over the amethystine moor across which the shadows boxed and chased.

What a strong, sweet lover he would be! She could not help herself. He turned to watch a curlew, the breeze fretting at his hair. Far away on the horizon, a tiny white cloud was wandering through the sky. It touched the curve of his nose and began to slide behind his head, between his eyebrows and his lips. The moment it appears on the other side, the instant it comes out of the curls on his neck, then we shall go. How long was it since she'd been attracted to a man? How often had she lain in her lonely room and dreamed her hopeless dreams of what might have been?

The cloud sailed out of Edward's hair. Instantly she was ashamed of herself and angry, too. That part of her life was over, finished. She could never give herself to a man again. Anthony had seen to that. It was a man's world into which she had been born and which one day she would leave. Nothing could change that. She was no more at liberty to fall in love with Edward Horne than she had been to control her marriage portion. She swept the crumbs off her habit briskly and got to her feet.

They rode back in silence, Edward wondering as he looked sideways at her what he had done wrong. He concluded it must be on account of what Anthony might say at their too long an absence. They reached the last bend before the park palings came into view.

'The fault is mine,' he said. 'I'll tell Anthony that I couldn't hold Luna, that I was carried away.'

Daisy reined in. 'There are times when we stare out of the window and in our imaginations see not what actually exists in the garden but what we would wish to exist. Then something happens. There is a knock at the door or we sneeze and when we next open our eyes we see things as they really are. I have enjoyed our morning, Edward. May your days at Winterbourne be happy.'

They heard a holler and saw riding towards them Anthony and James Garland amid a pack of dogs.

'My rescue party,' Daisy said flatly. They continued at a walk. Anthony galloped up to them on his heavy grey cob.

'Well, this is a fine thing when a man disappears with another's wife. Eh? Eh? A fine thing, I must say. A canter was what I thought I said, not a tour of the country. The lady's honour –'

'Is uncorrupted, I assure you. The fault is entirely mine. The creature almost pulled my arms from their sockets. Without another horse beside her, I swear she wouldn't have stopped till she reached Buxton. Oh hello, missie, who let you out then?'

'And that Farthing of yours', started Anthony with fresh pugnacity, knowing full well the irritation it causes a man to hear his dog misnamed, 'escaped from the stable and was discovered by me chasing rabbits in the Laurels. Can't have that. Can't have a dog loose in the woods when the birds are nesting. It shames me to think I have a neighbour –'. He remembered how things stood with Winterbourne. His face unbuckled and he waved an arm round cheerfully. 'But it don't signify. No damage done. All's fair between friends, eh? Isn't that so, Daisy? Isn't that what I always say, all's fair between friends? By the way, you've got a piece of dead bracken on your back, dear. Take a fall, did you?'

'I suppose you could say that,' Daisy murmured as she flapped a glove at a cloud of dancing spring gnats. 'Now I am sure you are all eager to discuss Mr Horne's new mare and as I have business with Mrs Keech, I beg that you will excuse me.'

She halted at the park gates to speak to Clayton, who was waiting there with Polly, and turned up the back drive to Overmoor, a trim, circumspect figure in her grey riding habit.

'Ain't she fairly something, Mr Horne? Don't she just stand up and go? Ain't she the best you've ever seen? It's like she had some great –'. James Garland's yellow teeth shone, his eyes popped, his whole rosy face boiled with impatience as he strained for the right word. 'Like some damned great sprocket wheel, that's it, *sprocket wheel*, some perpetual whirly thing inside her that keeps her running.' He clenched his fist and made a thrusting motion with his forearm. 'Or a war galley with hundreds of slaves packed in her innards, a – what do you call 'em, come on, sir, you're the one with the education, try something – small word, had it a moment ago – trireme! That's our beauty, a damned great hairy trireme!'

He leaned out of his saddle and flipped Luna's ears to and fro. 'Ain't she just something? How about a bit of a dash, sir? For old-times' sake, as you might say, something for me to remember her by? What do you say to a couple of furlongs to that oak tree and back?'

Edward grinned and raised his elbows. Go! With a shout and a flurry they pelted off.

Daisy heard the shout as she was passing the walled garden. She had been debating with herself in a disengaged, mathematical way where, in an ideal world, the balance should lie between a person's sense of duty and the tug of all those varied sensations that were compressed into the one word, pleasure. How she would weigh them, what values she would allot to each class of pleasure and what to each consequence. Go! His shout seemed to rebound off the wall beside her, to have been directed at her personally. Go! She rode swiftly to the stables and went upstairs to her room.

She locked the door and sat on the edge of her bed with her hands pressed between her knees. The sun was striking the window at an angle and casting a saffron glow on the wall behind her shoulder. Unsanctioned love: it was like having a rose break loose in the wind. Untidy, carefree people would leave it to flop around and not give twopence when they strolled past. It's a rose, they would say, however you look at it. So enjoy it, worship it, adore it while it lasts. That's what her friend Mary Dipple would probably tell her. But she did not like things that were higgledy-piggledy. It was not in her temperament. Flopping roses were a nuisance and scratched one's legs. She liked things that were secure and orderly. So –

She paused because here, in the privacy of her room and without Edward standing ten yards away, she was able to admit that she had been dishonest with herself on the moor. She had been frightened by the sudden gale of her longing to make love to Edward. She had been reminded in a trice of the impossibility of her situation. Money, honour, and position in society, these were the dictators that must govern her actions and she knew it. There she had been truthful with herself. But as to whether she could again give her body to another man, and not only her body but her entire emotional being; as to whether she could surrender herself without reservation – she had lied. To this man whom she scarcely knew, who was ten years younger than her and who had once trodden on the hem of her russet dress and spoken no more than three words throughout the entire duration of a minuet, she could, she knew with total and unswerving certainty, give everything he asked. Because what he would want to take, she would want to give. She could not say how this had happened. She could account for no part of it whatsoever. She knew only what instinct and the fluttering of previously unknown muscles in her stomach were telling her.

But of course the whole idea was ridiculous. Miss Hoole had been right: she had too much of the romantic in her. So that was the end of it. She would snip off this awkward, ill-advised rose and watch its petals turn brown and drop. Then she would burn it. She found she was still wearing her riding hat and got up to place it on the shelf.

Anthony had gradually dropped behind Edward and James

Garland, the better to be in his own company. That piece of bracken between Daisy's shoulder blades: what exactly had she meant in reply to his question? Go! He looked up briefly, hardly raising his chin. It hadn't flown or sprouted there. No one had placed it there. How could she *suppose* she had fallen from her horse? Either she had or she hadn't. There was no room for *supposing* such a thing. So she and Horne had ridden somewhere. They had dismounted. She had lain on her back. His excuse about being galloped away with had been stuff and nonsense. They had dawdled along side by side, Horne and his wife, enjoying themselves and not giving a straw for his feelings. Not a hoot had they given for propriety, not a hoot. Had Clayton been with them, it would have been a different kettle of fish. But he hadn't been. And the first thing he'd do when he got the chance would be to babble to all his friends how Lady Apreece and Mr Horne had disappeared together and taken three hours to do what could have been done in thirty minutes. And she'd been on her back. Well, as a matter of fact, he couldn't give a damn, not a single damn. She could spread herself beneath the whole county for all the enjoyment they'd get. But they should have thought of his honour first. That was what counted. He'd become a public laughing stock. People would titter behind their hands when he went to church. They'd smack their lips and wink at each other as they sized her up. He would appear a noddy to every jack-the-lad in the neighbourhood. A man stripped of his honour was as humiliated as a man stripped naked in front of strangers. So the sooner he tipped Edward Horne out of Winter-bourne, the better it would be for everyone.

They came racing towards him with shining faces and arms pumping. Thrusting his boots forward in his stirrups and leaning back on a long rein so that he looked as if he was cantering straight out of the frame of one of Mr Stubbs's ducal portraits, he rode to meet them.

'Good show, Ned, damn good show, what! Knew you'd have Garland for beat the moment you kicked off. Now look here, the thought came to me as I watched you frolicking around – I'll be riding out with some of the young dogs for the next few weeks. You know, getting the old-timers to teach the tufters a few manners, so what I thought was, why don't you and I meet up for an hour or two each day and join forces? I can learn you a thing or two about foxhounds and show you some bits of land that p'raps you don't know so much about, and you can settle your new mare and save me from boredom. My God, the fatigue of educating puppies! I'd sooner be a schoolmaster! Say you will, my boy, your company'll make all the difference to my humour. Of course, that's so long as you and Garland don't fall out over the price of that quad of yours.' He winked at James. 'Now then, special terms for the family, eh! Wouldn't want to upset your sister by being unkind to her friend, would you?'

So until the third week in May Sir Anthony Apreece made a daily excursion to Winterbourne in order, little by little, to apprise his pupil in the most unclesome way of the urgent necessity (if he wished to enhance his income) of installing so many miles of land drains, building so many miles of walls, planting so many chains of quick-set hedges, buying this number of sheep and that number of prime shorthorn cattle; of the imperative need to invest in ploughing oxen, threshing implements, wagons, dung carts, a seed drill, ventilated housing for his livestock and such a multitude of unequivocally desirable and vital gadgets, each of which he described with punctilious exactitude both as to purpose and cost, that by the end of this period, and with only the slightest gilding of the figures, a provisional sum had been reached as the price of Edward's daily betterment that was larger than could safely have been carried in Cleopatra's barge. There, he thought, capping the list with a stone-built dovecote, that'll sink him.

To Edward, of course, all these marvellous things were no more intelligible than Hottentot language. But the weather was fine, Luna a challenge, and since he had nothing better to do, he listened with varying degrees of attention to the older man's lectures. But for Anthony, these daily expeditions provided the same reassurance that a man gets from tapping the side of his goldfish bowl and seeing his captive circle without any other hope of escape than into his cat's breakfast dish. So when, on a drizzly, rather humid, morning, he arrived as usual and rapped with his knuckle on the glass, he was very far from pleased to find that this time the bowl contained nothing but water.

Fifteen

'GONE? GONE? He said nothing yesterday of going. How do you mean? Gone where?' He towered over Davie Paxton, the tassel of his whip jiggling like a black spider on the grass.

'To London, we suppose, sir. Leastwise that's what Arthur Smith said.'

'Arthur Smith said that? How the devil does he know and not I?'

'Well, sir, seemingly old Clem – Clem Dawkins, the carrier – had a letter for the master which he left with Arthur. So when Arthur saw Mr Horne a-passing by yesterday in the forenoon – after he returned from riding with you – he went out and gave it him.'

'What sort of letter? Fat, thin, official-looking, what sort of letter?'

'Arthur said the writing was very small and particular, lots of it, went across the page in straight lines. Like soldiers out marching was how he told it. Master looked proper shaken up, Arthur said, when he came up to tell us someone was to go to Derby to fetch Loonie home. Like he'd seen a ghost. Just told Arthur he was riding for the Derby coach and could Arthur see his horse was got home, and then upped and was off, the letter sticking out of his pocket.'

Anthony's young hounds had found a hen on the dung heap and with huge gangling strides were chasing it across the farmyard.

'What did Mr Horne say when he read the letter?'

'Nobbut bollocks according to Arthur.'

'Nobbut bollocks? I don't believe it. No one says bollocks when he sees a ghost and leaves it at that. He must have said something else. Think, man, think.'

Davie looked down and worked a sliver of mud off one boot with the toe of his spade. He'd better watch points. A right stew the fecker was boiling up to. No knowing which direction he'd take off in.

'Weren't anything much. But Arthur thought he said – couldn't be sure of it, mind you, sir, as master was really speaking only to himself – but he thought he said, "Has she, by God?"'

'Ha! "Has she, by God?" Well, that's not the same as bollocks, is it, you little lobcock?' He leaned down and thrust his face into Davie's. 'Is it? Anyone with a barleycorn of sense would know that. "Has she, by God?" puts quite a different shine on the leather. Quite different. Pah! you people here, no wonder the place is going to the dogs.'

He exhumed from his adenoids a snort of unutterable contempt and for a moment sat still, his eyes flickering vacantly round the yard. Of course that must be it. The old woman had died. What else could it mean? Why else would he bolt for London but to count out his inheritance? He snatched up the thong of his whip and shortened his reins. His cob skittered back a few paces.

'That Arthur Smith, I'll teach him a lesson, I'll make him dance on coals for this, I'll . . . I'll . . . out of my way –'. He slashed at his horse. The spurt of hooves rang on the cobbles. His hounds peered guiltily out of a cowshed, their mouths full of feathers.

'Vermin! Filth! Muck-worms! I'll learn you, by heavens –'. He uncoiled his whip. Spangs of fur flew from their rumps as he pursued them howling through the stack yard and past the Paxtons' cottage and the granary and out of Winterbourne on to Ladysway.

Davie scratched himself in his habitual way. Well he never did, what a letter could do to a gentleman. He stood his spade against the wall of the cowshed and, seeing the bird had retired to the rafters only a little plucked, walked to the cottage, where his mother and Annie were standing on the doorstep. Together they listened to the hullaballoo climbing up Ladysway.

'There's a to-do and no mistake,' said Mary Paxton phlegmatically, dabbing with her besom at the dust gathered under the lip of the threshold. 'Quite takes me back to when old Mr Horne was alive.'

'Oh no, Mother, you'd never have heard Mr Horne carrying on like that. The most he'd have done would have been to puff out his cheeks and go pop-pop-pop you dogs, you really shouldn't do that sort of thing, you know by Jove.'

Davie chuckled and laid his hand on his mother's shoulder. 'Next time parson starts to tell us about the pit of Gomorrah and the fate that's in store for us sinners, I won't need any pictures to tell me what he's on about. You should have seen his face when he started laying into those hounds of his. Made Satan look like a dormouse. Tell you one thing though, old Arthur's in for a drubbing, that's for sure.'

It was Madge Smith who opened the door of the Green Man. She had been rolling out pastry when she saw him gallop up.

'First thing I says to myself,' she reported to Tom Glossipp when he happened by in the evening, 'there's trouble in this, Madge me girl. You could tell by the look on him. Didn't call for no more'n a glance to see something was eating at his guts. So I think to myself, best try to keep the old mackerel at bay till Arthur's up and about again. 'Cos there is something of the mackerel about him, you know Tom, something in those wishy-washy eyes of his that reminds one of a mackerel losing its colour.

'Anyway, the thought had scarcely gone through my mind as I was unbarring the door than he kicks it clean out of hand and there he is, him in his boots, whip in one hand, face as black as night saving for those fishy eyes of his. And do you know what he says? No fine morning Madge or with your leave or anything else you'd expect from a gentleman. "Get him," he says. That's all. "Get him." Like he owned the place and us with it. Oh, I says, I can't do that, he's been in his bed with a migraine these two days past. Course, looking back on it, that's where I went wrong. Made a mistake there, I did. What a mop-head! Lord only knows what made me say it was two days when in fact he'd only been caught with it yesterday after supper. And naturally the beggar knew it weren't two days 'cos it was only yesterday forenoon that Arthur gave Mr Horne that letter.

'But Tom, you wouldn't have believed what it did to him. It was like I'd tipped a wasp down his breeches. Next I knew he'd pushed me against the wall and was screaming and hollering about all the tricks people were playing on him and you couldn't trust a soul any longer, and then he throws me to one side and up the stairs he goes and into the bedroom, where Arthur's lying with the shutters drawn, and grabs his nightshirt at the throat and shakes him like a sack of oats. "You've cheated me! You've let him escape! You've cheated me!"'

'Whatever did he mean by that, Madge?' enquired Tom Glossipp in his mild-mannered way. 'Who'd escaped him?'

'Mr Horne, of course, young Mr Horne getting that letter and rushing off to Derby, that's what he meant. Anyway. Course the din he was making was going through Arthur's head as if someone was banging nails into it and all he was wanting was to bury himself in a hole somewhere, but he couldn't as the beggar had a grip on him like a bear with a bale of sugar, shaking him up and down and shouting over and over again, 'You've cheated me! You've broken your word! You've cheated me!'

'Well, fair sick with fright I was in case he killed my man and eventually I pulled him off – you'd be surprised at the strength a woman can find when she has to. Yes, Thomas Glossipp, it'd surprise you no end so there's no needs to look at me like that. So I got him to give over. Tossed Arthur away into the corner like he was flicking a ladybird off his sleeve – and he's not a small man is my Arthur so you can imagine the paddy Sir Anthony was in – and then when Arthur starts to vomit, he just stands there wiping the spittle off his mouth on the corner of the sheet, and do you know what he said, Tom? Cool as a cucumber, just like you and me talking here, he says, "Fancy a grown man not being able to control himself." Just like that! After what he'd done to Arthur and him choking to death with his head under the pillow, he had the nerve to say that.

'Oh, I was mad, I tell you, mad as anything. "You can't do that," I says, "You can't come into another man's house and half kill him, there's a law against that. I've a mind to ride over and get the magistrate out from town. You wouldn't be acting so brave if it was Mr Pumfrey standing here with his book of laws instead of a woman like me."

'Then he sticks his face up against mine and says, "You ever threaten me with the law again, Madge bloody Smith, and I'll burn this place of yours round your ears. I'm the law in these parts and you'd best not forget it." And with that he marched down the stairs with his spurs thumping behind him, calls his dogs and rides off whistling "Lilliburlero" as if the whole thing had gone clean out of his mind.

'One thing's for sure: that's the last time Arthur does any favours for that man. He'll be scared witless to go within a hundred miles of Overmoor. What a morning that was, I'm telling you.'

A donkey cart drew up and in stumped Moley Dibdin wanting to get his hand seen to on account of having had it nipped by a rat. Then Johnnie Alcock stopped by on his way home, and a couple of travellers making for Buxton. By and by more arrived and to each, as he sipped Arthur Smith's small beer, Madge related the story with relish. Within a day there was hardly a person for miles around who had not heard how Sir Anthony Apreece of Overmoor had gone to the Green Man and thrashed old Arthur to within an inch of his life.

Few had been the mourners' carriages following the night-black plumes of the hearse up the rise and through the cypresses of the English Cemetery. But the day had been fresh, clean, and *gioconda* ('to use Mr Orsino's redolent word', Hawkesworth said with a smile): the sky had been a painter's blue, the olives plump in bud and the cruelty of a Florentine winter forgotten. Only an ironical god could have paired such a day with such a purpose.

Edward turned away from the window. The coach had been full. He'd had to pay an outlandish sum to another man to buy his seat, and an outside one at that. Then they'd broken an axle. It had taken two days in the end to get to London. His face was stained by fatigue, his eyes dull with pain.

'But I thought she had friends in Florence. Don't you remember it was one of the main reasons she wanted to go there?'

'They did not exist. It transpires she knew practically no one there. You and I believed what she said because we wanted to. We were wrong.

'Mr Spratchett called on me. He sent a note round first to prepare me and then came over himself the next morning. I wrote to you immediately after our conversation.'

Nicholas Hawkesworth was a sensitive man and fond of Edward. He wished now that he had given more consideration to Lady Blanche's state of mind at the time the bargain was being negotiated and had understood something of her real motives in acting as she had. Things could have been managed differently, nudged along in the same direction but by other means. Both she, and now Edward, could have been spared much suffering.

'I withdraw everything I may have said about Augustus Spratchett. He is not the rough and ready lawyer I took him for. No man could have displayed more delicacy over your mother. I believe there must have existed between them a very real affection, certainly more than mere professional sympathy. I had him in the chair where you are now sitting for virtually the entire morning and I have to say that it is rare in my business to hear a lawyer speak so movingly about a client . . .

'So you see we were mistaken on both counts. Not only had she no friends to mention waiting for her in Florence but there was never the slightest need for her to worry about her financial affairs. It is all here, in the depositions made by Spratchett and Orsino, her man of affairs in Italy. No, don't make a face like that, Edward, Signor Orsino is entirely reliable. All the English in Florence use him as their banker.'

'But why did she go there? Why didn't she stay here where she had people to help her?' He had been sitting with his head bowed between his hands. Suddenly he crashed his fist on to the table.

'That's both of them who've done it to me. Both of them who've gone and died without letting me know. Oh God, you've no idea –'. He wrenched at his hair. 'That last time I saw her – you cannot imagine how it felt. My mother – a few scraps of skin and bone stuffed into a dress. It was horrible. Awful beyond description. Why – why did it have to happen like this?'

'I believe it's very simple, judging by what Spratchett told me. She was consumed, he said, by a profound – ineradicable was actually the word he used – sense of remorse over the death of your father. Not so much for the way he died, though heaven alone knows how many hideous nights she must have spent dwelling upon it, as to the life they had failed to share. The wife she thought she could have been but wasn't; her failure as a mother, companion and helpmeet. There was absolutely no question of sin, according to Spratchett. There was only ever one man that she loved. And once your father went she let herself be overwhelmed by this conviction that she had failed everyone from the day she was born. You, your father, Winterbourne, even her parents – she was certain she had failed you all. The guilt lay in her like an anchor plate chained to her heart.

'So when her illness came along, she determined to use it as the instrument of her redemption. To understand your father's death, you had to be persuaded to return to Winterbourne. You had to be plunged into it, not as part of your inheritance but as something you'd earned. As a commercial bargain, if you like. It was no good her telling you about it, you had to be forced to feel it for yourself, to let it grow from within you. Then in time you would come to terms with it and not suffer as she had. The problem, of course, was how to get you there of your own free will.'

'It's strange to think that the mother of whom I knew so little knew *me* well enough. For she got me there, didn't she?'

'You should have heard Spratchett on the subject. "Now," she'd say, "we mustn't make it too easy for him. He must taste the gall for himself. So hide the hook well. My son may be idle but he has good eyesight." So Spratchett would run up a few ideas while she took a dose of powders and pottered coughing round his office, poking through his piles of documents and making remarks like, "My goodness, old so-and-so can't still be alive, he's been around since the Flood. Surely you mean his son, young whatsisname." Or "D'ye know, this man's brother once proposed marriage to me? Fellow was as drunk as an owl. Went down on bended knee – and fell over. At least he was tight enough to speak the truth. Said the best part of me was my marriage portion." And so on. Then when Spratchett had sketched out a plan of campaign, she'd rap on the table with her cane and say, "No no, dear man, he'll never swallow that. Ever known a horse eat a lemon? Think of something better." She could be so gay, Spratchett said, almost as if she realised that at last she was free to be happy. She'd done all she could do to atone for what she saw as her sins. You were going to sign the deed and she was going to join Nat. She wanted no tears, no fuss, no deathbed scenes. Only to suffer and die by herself. I believe she saw it as her final act of penance.'

'Perhaps, then, it was one of the few occasions in her life when she was truly at peace with herself.'

'We must hope so.'

They sat and looked across the desk at each other as a soothing calmness floated down from the bookcases and the Hawkesworth family portraits and settled round them, like dust after a storm. A tortoiseshell pit-pattered in a warm corner of the window. No more could be said for the present.

'She's left you a very wealthy young man, you know,' Hawkesworth said, rising to his feet, 'Eximiously wealthy, as one of my colleagues calls this happy condition. But we can speak of that later.'

It was while they were thus engaged a couple of days later, on a squally, fizzing May morning with wads of cherry blossom pelting at the windows, that a curious incident occurred.

Hawkesworth was in full flow concerning the merits of the New River Company (in which concern Edward now found himself a shareholder) when he broke off in confusion. He had quite forgotten. A provincial client had written a few weeks earlier to say he would be in town that day and wished to call at eleven o'clock to discuss his son's debts. There had been no opportunity to put him off. Would Edward excuse him for fifteen or perhaps twenty minutes? So he put on his coat and went out to buy flowers for Letitia Hawkesworth.

As he was returning, he met coming down the stairs a stout, squabby man of about sixty with a high colour to his cheeks, a pitted nose and a black wig that sprouted from each side of his head like a pair of wings. Edward stepped to one side on the half-landing and waited for him. The other arrived slowly, breathing stertorously, taking the stair treads sideways and always leading with the same foot. He surveyed Edward with curranty eyes. 'Gomez. Your servant.' He waddled on downwards.

'Oh, the damned fellow never arrived,' Hawkesworth said, stalking animatedly round his chamber. 'But instead I had a call from Gomez, the broker.' Edward said yes, he'd met him on the stairs. 'Turned up quite out of the blue. Bit of luck as it happens, as I was able to sweat him for an opinion on your three per cents.'

'And?'

'Avoid 'em like the plague. Sell at best. Only one way they'll go.

So that was a useful piece of information. Then we talked on a bit. And just when I was going to show him out, he wedged himself into that chair of yours, looked me square between the eyes and said; "I'm not sleeping too good these days, Mr Hawkesvorth."

"'However can that be, Mr Gomez?" I said, wondering what was coming next. And dammit if it doesn't turn out the fellow has agents in every major city in Europe. Agents or family, one or the other. And they're all telling him the same thing: there's a stink on the way. Yes, I know we hear this sort of thing every six months, but this time Gomez says it's different. His men are like musicians and can detect a false note with their eyes closed. The marketplace, the council chambers, the king's bed, there's not a place but they don't know what's being said there. He sees trouble and plenty of it – which is why he advises us to sell the threes. But now this is the intriguing bit.

"'So I look through my ledgers", Gomez said, "to see what's what. You know how it is, Mr Hawkesvorth, when a tempest is brewing, one doesn't want to be caught in the same boat as chentlemen who cannot swim. My clients are very fine chentlemen, some of the finest in the kingdom, but there is only one thing I want to know in times like these – can they swim? Sinking clients are bad for one's health. Their arms can be vairy strong. They could pull Gomez down with them. So I go through my ledgers and prick off all the gamblers and the butterflies one gets near a sugarbowl and send them ever such a nice letter saying please would they do their sinking somewhere other than with Gomez. Of course, not in a manner that is so frightening as to put them off sailing for ever. But firmly and politely, like the good captain Gomez is.

"'Now this is what makes me sleep so bad. For I have one client, a nobleman, who I just don't twig at all. He insists that every month I write and tell him how the bowling green is playing. You know what I mean by this, Mr Hawkesvorth? Good. So I tell him this is happening and that is happening, but what does he do? Whenever I say to him sell, he buys. And whenever I say buy, he sells. Is he mad, I ask myself, this bold chentleman who believes he can play the three per cents better than Samuel Gomez? But sometimes he makes a little money. I have to be truthful. It is my nature. Sometimes he strikes a profit. And when he does I see him spit and say to himself, Gomez is a fool: why should I ever do what he says?

'"And there is another thing. When I see his name, my friend up here" – by which he meant his great beacon of a nose – "begins to wiffle around like a dog. Borrowed money, your honour, the chentleman is playing with someone else's blunt, that's what my friend tells me. A man in your profession, Mr Hawkesvorth, can sense it and it is the same with us. But this nobleman – well, sir, since we are not great fools like he is, you and I know that buying long with borrowed money never answers in a falling market. And I think that my fine friend who understands everything so much better than Gomez is a dangerous companion in a storm. He pretends he has been swimming all his life, but has he? And then this morning I thought, that nice Mr Hawkesvorth who is so familiar with noblemen, he is sure to know more about this strange chentleman . . ."'

'I need scarcely say who Gomez was referring to, Edward. Your neighbour –'

'But it was only the other day that he more or less offered to buy Winterbourne from me.'

'Then it's all very queer, just as I told you it would be nine months ago.'

Hawkesworth fished the key out of his drawer and they passed through the scarlet baize door with Gomez's tale rumbling around in their minds.

But extraordinary events soon lose their glitter. Our brains are too concerned with picking their way through the petty chaos of existence to be impressed for long by the bizarre or by what is plainly grotesque. So as the coach jolted him northwards some days later, it was not the waywardness of Anthony Apreece that chiefly occupied Edward's mind but the death of his mother. And when, jammed bodkin in his corner seat by a coal merchant who overlapped him at every point of convergence, he gazed out at the countryside and considered how he should employ his inheritance, he did not gloat or gasp at its extent but cautiously and primly, like a man who would save a feather from being burnt, reflected that now he could afford to pay James Garland for the other half of Luna.

Sixteen

SMALL COMMUNITIES beget large ears. The scandal of Sir Anthony Apreece's treatment of Arthur Smith had scarcely dried on people's lips than it was replaced by information that was infinitely more succulent. The old lady had gone aloft: young Mr Horne was in possession of her immense fortune. Of course none could be certain it was immense. It was only the innkeeper's word they had for it. But hope admits to no boundaries where money is concerned, and since the very word inheritance breeds hope faster than a rat does fleas, a warm and universal expectation arose that Edward Horne would return to Winterbourne like Clive of India, bringing in his groaning panniers work and wealth for all.

Digbeth Chiddlestone plumped in advance for a new altar cloth. The roofers let Amos know they were available at short notice. Robert Pumfrey cracked his knuckles. Maidens buffed their shoe buckles. Horse copers, loriners, joiners, gilders, upholsterers and every artisan around Buxton fretted with anticipation as they awaited the return of Croesus. Only Amos was unimpressed. 'Maybe, but then again, maybe not. How shall we know for sure? He's not going to make a proclamation in the town square, is he?' he said to Bill Whitehead, the slater, as together they poked among the roof timbers of the big house. 'And in any event, I don't see a man who'd rather have peacocks clipped from yew trees than the real article as one who's going to go wild with his money. I grant you that a new roof's in a different class. That's the sort of work that has a purpose. But fancy goods? Nar, Bill, not at Winterbourne.'

Elsewhere, which is to say in the halls of society, the approach of loose capital was viewed from a contrary angle. They were indifferent to it, men assured each other as they jostled round the billiard table at the Assembly Room. His wine cellar, yes, that was fair game. Also his croquet lawn, his splendid duck shooting and the occasional loan of a hunter. But money? Never give it a second thought, my dear fellow. Leave it to my man of business every time. And then they galloped furiously home to scrub their gelding-like daughters and consign to the attics, the mice and the cobwebs, any portraits that hinted by even the tiniest slur of an eyelid at the deformities of their ancestors.

Over and above these varied ranks of aspirants and distinguishable as sharply from them as gamblers are from the motley of spectators who observe the play from the sidelines, were Daisy Apreece and her husband. For Anthony, the news was calamitous. He had understood this immediately. What use would Edward Horne have now for his money? He would be immune to all threats on this front. He could do as he pleased. He could fribble away the remainder of his days stretched in a curule chair with a lace scarf round his neck while the place went to pieces around him.

Withdrawn and short-tempered, sitting lumpishly on his bob-tailed cob, he resumed his journeys to Billy Tor and there ploughed his brains for a fresh device.

But to Daisy there was no such difficulty. Pure, clean and crystal clear, like a liquid bubble of glass, the thought had formed in her mind the instant she heard the report: why, the poor soul has lost his mother, what can we do to prevent him from getting lonely? She was glad about the money if it meant Edward could repair his roof, but what was money compared to the death of one's mother?

It was on the third day of June, a warm, soft day beneath mounds of gently chugging clouds, that Daisy and Mary Dipple set out in the dog cart for a spin. At the same time as they tittupped decorously down the hill towards the Green Man, Edward was approaching from the south in a cloud of dust. He had breakfasted well in Derby and felt full of himself.

'Good lord, Arthur, what the devil's happened to you?' he exclaimed as he paid off his chaise and, turning, saw the publican's bruised throat. 'Madge been pestering you for favours again?'

Arthur was skimming the slime off the horse trough with a rake.

He scowled at Edward from beneath his armpit, for he was still half-inclined to blame his woes on him. 'Tweren't no quimmy sprig of lavender that did it, that's for sure.'

The sound of pacing hooves and the skitter of wheels in gravel reached Edward's ears. He stepped out on to the turnpike and seeing who it was, waved his hat. In a matter of moments he was perched on the back bench of the dog cart with his arms folded along its top and his curly head poking between the ladies' bonnets. The three of them began to speak simultaneously. With a twist of her wrists, Daisy turned Tib up Ladysway.

'So you see, that's how it was. Poor Arthur! Needless to say, my husband has not thought fit to say one word on the subject. All I know is what everyone else has told me. It really wouldn't surprise me if one day he killed someone in one of his rages.'

Perhaps that had been rather indiscreet, Daisy thought immediately. (Edward's beaky nose kept popping into the corner of her vision and distracting her.) But the weather was so marvellous! She felt so free, somehow electrified and hare-brained, as if she'd been let out of school for the day.

Slowly they toiled up the hill.

'Come on, Daisy, give her a bit of a tickle,' Edward said, 'or it'll be night before we get to Winterbourne. Anyone know if Luna came home in one piece?' His hands began to inch towards the reins.

'Oh no you don't, sir! This is a ladies' outing and you but a guest. Pray keep your hands to yourself!' Daisy giggled and held the reins over the side of the dog cart, out of Edward's reach.

'La, but sir is very fresh this morning.' Mary Dipple had taken off her shawl and laid it across her lap. She was a broad, comfortable, untidy woman of about forty. The breeze ruffled the downy blonde hairs on her forearms. 'Very fresh indeed! The young master departs, leaving misery in his wake. He grieves. He laments. The cark of anguish is his. But then lo! he is come amongst us again like a skipping colt. What are we to make of it, Daisy my dear?'

'I believe it must be because he anticipates great pamperings and feasts from all the ladies in the neighbourhood. Do you remember what it was like when your mother died?' she said, turning to Mary.

'Far too well. It was as if I'd been left on a deserted rock somewhere and the last ship in the world had just sailed away over the horizon. The death of a parent is not something anyone can easily forget. But we all have to endure it at some stage. Perhaps it strikes a man differently . . .' Their heads turned expectantly on Edward like a pair of feathery pincers. Daisy released the reins. Tib took advantage of the pause to start grazing.

With an explosion of laughter, Edward lunged forwards and seized the reins.

'Women!' he cried, thrashing at the startled horse, 'Lord, but the demands you make on a fellow! Hah! Hah! Giddy up, you great fool! Hah! Hah! You're like a pair of village matrons, the two of you, discussing the new vicar over toast and a pot of strawberry jam, spreading his character very thin the better to see what sort of pips he's got to him. Hah! Hah! Get forrard, my fat beauty! And let me just say this: my mother is happier now than she ever has been. There, my very last word on the subject.'

Daisy leaned back and folded her hands. His shoulder was pressing against hers. She watched the play of tendons in his wrists and the curl of his fingers as he joggled the reins. The sun was warm. Little birds sang from the bushes. The green leaves of the beech trees danced in front of them. She glanced over at Mary and smiled. A feeling of rare contentment possessed her.

They topped the crest of the hill and bowled down the descent to Winterbourne, the ladies clutching their hats as the old mare put her best foot forward and Edward regaled them in a tumble of words with his youthful adventures on Ladysway.

There, by the beech tree with a fork, that had been where he'd had his first fall. Vinson had been taking him to join his father out hunting. His first day with the hounds! Six or seven he'd been and as hot as mustard. Too hot, alas, for Alfred, who'd whipped him off his back before you could say cock robin. He'd cried. Vinson had knelt and wiped his face for him. Vinson? Had either of them ever heard what happened to him?

And there, that's where the man his father had had from the assizes had broken his leg. He'd seen it happen and, heavens, the caterwauling the chap had sent up. Drunk? He'd say! Drunk as a bucket with a hole in it!

And that's where he and Vinson had built a treehouse. Well, it was mostly Vinson who'd done the work but he'd done his bit as well. Look, Daisy, you can still see some of the timbers. Used to be an old track up the hill before father built Ladysway. Ran like a waterfall when it rained. Funny, isn't it, how things change?

Look, over there to the left. Do you see that mossy sort of tump in the clearing? That's where I tried to smoke out a wasps' nest. Never tried that trick again. Did they chase me? Dear ladies, I fled faster than an arrow with a gale behind it. And here . . .

Their cheeks flushed and each a little giddy with pleasure, they emerged from the beech hanger and drove at a good clip past the farm buildings and up the rise to Winterbourne. They halted. For a moment they sat unmoving in the sudden silence. Then a dog barked. A man shouted. The magic faded. They grew aware that during the excitement of the drive their bodies had become rather over-involved with each other.

'Must I?' Edward said, the reins slack in his hands, his nose close to Daisy's ear, which he looked into. Then, wriggling backwards and jumping to the ground, he said impetuously, 'Come and see my house, my country temple. And the ballroom where we danced, do you remember, Daisy? And the roof, I insist you inspect the roof with me. It no longer embarrasses me now that I can do something about it. You will be my first guests.'

A volley of barks broke out from Paxton's cottage and in a few moments Sixpence came charging up the hill grinning like a lunatic. Behind her followed Amos, puffing. Together they set out on a tour.

'You'll have a lot of furniture to buy,' Mary said, listening to the echo of her voice, 'and curtains do not come cheaply for rooms this size. Or are you thinking of hiring?' Spears of sunlight invaded the gloom as Amos unfolded the shutters.

'I have my mother's. She didn't take a single stick to Italy.'

'Or you could use all the rooms as ballrooms,' Daisy said, standing with her arms folded on its threshold, hearing the sound of fiddles and seeing, as if in a dream, the pulse of dancing bodies and Nat bowing to his waist before her: 'Just once, my dear, or twice. At any rate not more than three times round the floor with my darling boy. A boon, I prithee a boon, O lady fair.'

'I did the petronella with your mother-in-law that night,' Amos said proudly to Mary as he joined them. 'Ever so light on her feet she was.'

'So my husband has told me. I believe he could say who was with whom for every single dance . . . Do you suppose, Mr Paxton – it is mad, I agree with you in advance – that if Daisy and Mr Horne were to improvise a little music, you could show me how that petronella went? I was not there that night. But I too would like a memory of it. I would count it a very great honour. No more than a step or two.'

'In my boots, Mrs Dipple?' Amos said, blushing in the mote-speckled sunlight.

'In *our* boots, Mr Paxton,' she replied, extending her hand.

What a queerness, thought Daisy, for two ladies who set out for a spin in the countryside. Ta-rumple-tumple-tumple she sang, laughing and sneezing. Then Edward was speaking and, still singing, she took his arm and went whirling down the floor as Sixpence snuffled through the jackdaw nests that had fallen down the chimney.

'Now you must visit my temple,' Edward said, as Amos locked the front door.

'I believe we should learn to call it the temple of optimism,' Daisy said to Mary. 'Edward avows himself an optimist in all things.'

'So I perceive. A man who has his lawns cut clearly expects to see tomorrow at least.'

'Wait!' Edward ran back a few paces and jangled the great iron bell. 'That's what you'll hear next time you call. When I have finished the roof, I shall hold a party to match my father's. But – oh my goddy god, the guests are arriving already.'

Out of the yew-lined drive rode Fuscus Quex-Parker, startling in a suit of straw-coloured dimity and a grey wide-brimmed hat with a light blue band.

He was a little to the right of middle age. He had a sage, pleasant face peppered with the stains of advancing years. His ears were lined with a fog of curly hair like birds' nests. His eyebrows were bushy and his teeth white.

'Forgive me – but the day, ah! this English weather. When it puts its mind to it, it can be the greatest joy of the creation. I could not resist an adventure. I have called on Mr Cuthbert – *young* Mr

Cuthbert, let us be clear about that – and been educated in matters bovine. I have enjoyed a thimbleful of spirits with Sir Anthony, learned from Dibdin that moles can swim, and from the vicar that he expects a Visitation from the archdeacon very shortly (which by the way is troubling him), and then I said to myself, I wonder if nice Mr Horne is at home yet. We may not be neighbours, but we have it in common that we are both bachelors. So I thought I would continue down the road and see if I could not lay the foundations of a friendship.'

'But we thought you were going to become a watercolourist, in the Isle of Wight,' Daisy said.

'Next week. I depart on Thursday, travelling at my leisure via my sister in Kent and a nephew in Petersfield. Then I shall spend two months as a guest of my Lady Marchant in the company of other aspiring amateurs. Both ladies and gentlemen, I am informed.'

'At any rate you could not have come at a better time,' Edward said. 'And you are right; it is the weather that affects us all. This morning, when I awoke on the stagecoach –'

'You slept on a stagecoach, Mr Horne?'

'When I opened my eyes then, I was returning to my home and nothing more. But now', he spread his arms wide to the sun, 'everything is transformed. By courtesy of the ladies, my dwelling has become the Temple of Optimism and thus it will be marked in the next edition of Paterson. "Ashbourn: to Buxton $20\frac{1}{2}$ miles. Left at the Green Man for the Temple of Optimism, seat of Edward Horne, Esq. Four tickets daily.' As he spoke, the notion flew through his head in increasingly dizzy circles. He flung his arms around and made a leg to Daisy. 'I shall be the Horace Walpole of the shires. My temple will be a bolus upon which the faint-hearted may revive themselves. People will visit me from miles around, from London itself. The printer must cut a new symbol to distinguish it from the mausoleums of other gentry –'

'How is he to symbolise optimism?' Daisy asked. 'By a god gambolling in the firmament?'

'Or do you see him as someone like Noah, white-robed, resting on a cloud?' Fuscus said.

'My dear sir, that is for puritans. That is the personification of gloomth. The man I have in mind is short and swarthy, naked to the waist, with a grizzled chest and a huge drum between his knees.'

'He is not a woman?' Mary said, pulling a face.

'He is sitting on a lionskin, Mr Horne,' Fuscus said. 'You omitted that. A magnificent pelt with a mask snarling down the staircase up which sinners must approach for an audience.'

They had reached Edward's door. Daisy stopped, tapping her teeth thoughtfully: 'I cannot easily come to terms with the image of sin bending its knee to optimism. I think sin will always be superior.'

'We must consult the vicar,' Fuscus said. 'This is a matter on which we need professional guidance. Shall we go as a delegation or elect a spokesman?'

'I cannot be party to this,' Mary said. 'The god of optimism is a woman. It cannot possibly be otherwise. All the evidence points to the gender that understands about the renewal of life, that has known the miracle of childbirth.'

'And I think its travails, also?' Fuscus said, the tendrils of his eyebrows twitching. 'Women . . . ach, it is so difficult for a man to pronounce upon an ordeal that he cannot himself experience. Are you saying, Mrs Dipple, that it is impossible for a man to be a full-blooded optimist?'

'I believe I must have been making my way to that position.'

'I cannot but disagree,' Edward said. 'All that I might concede is that whoever is by nature happy feels the slings and arrows of misfortune more keenly than those who are by nature melancholic. But let us discuss it more fully in the temple itself. Why do I not leave you to make an inspection while I run down and borrow a cold pie from Mrs Paxton?'

But this had the opposite effect to that which he had desired, for it reminded the ladies of their duties at home. Mary put on her shawl. Daisy fluffed out her little green cape. The dog cart circled the chestnut trees and rattled down the hill, leaving to Edward and Fuscus an afternoon of great splendour, which they spent touring the sites of Nat's follies and debating the morality of Fuscus's previous occupation, that of opening other people's letters in defence of the realm.

'There is a word for it we used in the office which is so much more dignified than eavesdropping,' he said, 'but I forget what it was.'

Thus commenced the summer of 1788, a summer long remembered for its unpitying heat. For week upon week, month after month, the sky was a thin hazy blue. Deep cracks appeared in the pastures; the turf rippled and split. Sheep herds had to drive their flocks for miles to water them. Only the fruit trees prospered.

In August Mr Wormald bumped into Robert Pumfrey at York Races and told him that without an autumn deluge they would record less than twenty inches for the year at Chatsworth, the driest, he said, since 1780 (19.4 inches).

At the same meeting a Mr George Baker, sometime Member for Durham, staked a hundred guineas that his grey horse would beat Mr Maynard's bay mare: the distance, one mile; the weight to be carried by each horse, thirty stones. The betting was two to one on the horse, but the mare won. Afterwards Mr Baker complained to the stewards that Mr Maynard had bribed the man who watered the course not to remove the bungs in alternate barrels so that his hard-loving mare would be favoured. The stewards said that a man who had sat in parliament should certainly know about bribery and showed him the door.

Robert missed the race (he had found a fellow banknoter), but Constance watched every inch of it, from its galumphing start (one of the jockeys was a coachman) to its tawdry finish. On her return to Buxton she buttonholed even strangers and with angry blue eyes told them exactly how repulsive the spectacle had been. The memory had seemingly effaced that of all the grandees who had spoken to her during the meeting, a fact which impressed people far more than her description of the race.

Events were more mundane in Derbyshire. The hay was gathered, a few small fields here and there. At Overmoor the wheat ripened and fell in fan-shaped poppy-strewn swathes under the flashing blades of the harvestmen. Expressionlessly, Anthony rode through his stubbles and tallied the sheaves into his notebook.

Daisy and Mary Dipple continued to go jaunting in the dog cart, but though Daisy always made a point of passing the Green Man at the same time in the morning as they had done before, no lean figure again jumped out into the turnpike and waved his hat at her.

And Edward travelled to and from London, cursing lawyers and stuffy coaches alike. On one of his visits he persuaded Nicholas Hawkesworth to send money for deposit at the Bank of Buxton. It was rather more than was needed to repair his roof, even though he were to use the finest slates. It was certainly more than Nicholas counselled.

'Oh, but let's do it,' Edward retorted, 'so it is there, on my doorstep, where I can lay my hands on it, instead of having it cooped up in a London bank. How can I enjoy it if I cannot touch it?'

'A small sum would be very well, I could not argue with that. But the figure you have mentioned – it is not a risk that I would sleep easily with.'

'I consider Robert an honest man,' Edward said, choosing his words carefully. 'I would have nothing to do with him otherwise.'

'And his partners, what of them? For if one falls, usually they all fall.'

'It is true that I have not met them. But they enjoy a very pleasant reputation. They are men of probity, people say, of good birth.'

'Of course they are. All scoundrels are upright men until they are discovered not to be. And I note also that you are fond of Mr Pumfrey. It is another disadvantage. One is always reluctant to go against a friend.'

'But I would. Without compunction, without mercy. If the choice lay between my money and my friendship for Robert –'. Edward leaned across the table, his eyes very dark. 'Listen: Winterbourne is only six miles from Buxton, less than an hour's hard riding. If only one small whimper were to reach me about the bank, I'd horse into town – day or night, it'd make no difference – and then –'. He lunged forward, seized Nicholas by his hair, and with a sideways cut of his hand gestured as if to slice his head from his shoulders. 'That is what I would do to Robert,' he said softly. 'Believe me, that is what I would do. I have no wish to be poor again.'

'You have changed,' Nicholas said, ruefully rubbing his scalp. 'Let us hope it does not come to it, but if it did, I should not care to be Mr Pumfrey. Now, let me take the arrangements forward –'. He removed his coat and hung it beside his wig. 'A plaguey affair, London in an August like this.' He eased his neckband, shook out his capacious lawn sleeves and sat down again. 'I expect you cannot wait to get back to your hills. Oh, what would I not give to have a gentle breeze blowing around my ears. You know, my friend, I sometimes envy you for the life you chose.'

At last, towards the middle of September, just when people were asking themselves if it would ever end, the weather began to change. The sun still glowed like a copper discus, but for the first time there was a smell of autumn in the air. Dews started to fall. Moths came out in great numbers in the evenings. Spiders foraged among the rafters. Rickles of tired leaves spun down from the beeches. Sleep came more easily at night. Daisy and Mary took one last turn in the dog cart.

By the time she had left Mary at Michaelmas Farm, it was past forenoon when Daisy drove into the stableyard at Overmoor. Mrs Keech and Miss Hoole had had Hucknall put a table on the lawn and were sitting side by side topping blackcurrants. They were wearing plaited straw hats, Mrs Keech's very round and formal, like the cakes she baked, Miss Hoole's bursting in the crown and tilted over one eye. Leaving Clayton to back the dog cart into its hovel when he had finished watering the dust, Daisy walked across to the house. She was carrying a bunch of wild flowers and grasses at her breast.

'Sir Anthony's been looking for you, Miss Daisy,' Miss Hoole said, her stained fingers snipping away like locusts. 'Has some notion about giving a party for Mr Horne when he's finished with all his Londoning.'

'Came out and discussed it with us proper, he did. Quite his old self again. I dare say it's the relief of seeing his harvest brought in,' Mrs Keech said, not looking up.

'A party, did you say? Well, that shouldn't be difficult.' She went round to the kitchen entrance and through to the scullery, where she set about her flowers.

'Oh I think so, I'm sure he would appreciate it greatly,' she said as they sat across the table from each other at luncheon. 'But do you know when he's expected back from London? Mary told me this morning that according to Arthur Smith – to whom everything is according, it seems – this was to be positively his final visit to his lawyer. Who else had you thought of asking?'

Anthony carved himself another slice of brawn. His knuckles gleamed like ivory. The weeks he had spent ferreting through his loamy brain had paid off. The way forward was as pellucid to him as if it had been inscribed in capital letters.

'It would be nice if we could have the Dipples,' Daisy said demurely.

'But of course we shall have the Dipples, my dear! And Robert and Constance Pumfrey – I rather think Ned has taken a liking to Robert and my aversion to Constance is not insuperable. And Fuscus – there's another one. Oh, leave it to me. I'll think of a few more by and by. The thing is to discover when Ned'll be at home. Tell you what, I'll ride over to Winterbourne this afternoon and leave him a note so that when he returns from town we can make a definite arrangement.'

He emptied his glass, threw his napkin down and went over to the window. Then he spun on his heel, clapped his hands and rubbed them together with a brisk, washing movement.

'A party eh! Just like the old days!' His portentous eyes looked straight into her.

Yes, by God, he thought a little later as he jogged down the road to Britannia, still clapping and rubbing his hands, the old woman's death had thrown him and no mistake. Blown the coals clean from his hearth. Quite testicled him. But where there's a will there's a way . . . What an incredible day it was! How splendid to be alive! And the harvest secure! A cracker, too. Sometimes happened like that in a really hot summer. One never could tell. And, like a bolt from the blue, the answer had come to him only the other evening as he was riding into the stack yard behind the last of the wagons. The plaited straw ropes had not been properly secured. It was always the same with hired men, always leaving a little something to chance in the hope there'd be a spill so they could quickly glean a couple of bushels of corn for themselves. 'Watch for the branches now,' he'd growled to the lads riding on top. That was one of their favourite excuses. 'No more'n a damned twig but it just caught that sheaf on the side and the whole lot came tumbling down. T'weren't our fault, Sir Anthony, t'were the fault of that carter fellow of your'n for driving too close to the trees.' But today they hadn't strained the ropes well enough, or had left a knot undone, so that the topmost layer of sheaves was beginning to bulge outwards. And he was on the point of riding forward to tell the carter to halt while the load was re-roped, when suddenly there it had been. From nowhere! From absolutely nowhere! One moment his head had been as empty as a scraped plate and the next – plop! there it had been, gleaming in his brainpan like a shiny white hen's egg. Of course, of course! The key to Winterbourne wasn't in the duck-fucker's purse but in his character. Yes, his character! Nothing would ever come of a direct assault on so spongy a man. He had to be undermined. Struck from below. Piff! Like a pin into a pancake. Into his underbelly. Piff piff piff! He'd never stand it. Didn't have the bottom. He saw that quite perfectly now. Ned would be glad enough to take the first decent offer for Winterbourne by the time he'd finished with him. And then? No point in false modesty. Winterbourne would be his.

In rampageous good humour, chuckling and grimacing and plucking at the snuff-stained hairs in his nose, Anthony crossed the bridge over the Eve and rode up the hill to Winterbourne. He found Mary Paxton at home and left with her his invitation to Edward. Then he made for the parsonage and Digbeth Chiddle-stone, itching for an argument.

Elspeth was airing the vicar's nether woollens in preparation for winter. All baggy at the knees and freckled with archipelagos of small rust-coloured spots, they flapped on the clothes line like plucked chickens.

'I expect so, Sir Anthony. He's been busy working up his sermon most of the day but I'm sure he'll be finished by now. Wait while I give him a shout. Ooh-ho, Digbeth dear, it's Sir Anthony. He says would you care for a visitor with your tea?'

Chiddlestone's mop of white hair shot out of his library window. Elspeth laid out their tea on the terrace. And within minutes they were at it hammer and tongs, trident versus net, as the seed cake dwindled and they carved into the dark, gamey meat of metaphysics.

The subject of the day was Reason and Death. It was Anthony's opinion that because we are all fated to die, therefore we need to assign to ourselves a reason for living. We cannot bring ourselves to bobble aimlessly to the grave like corks. We are too noble and destiny too pressing. So we seek out a purpose to justify our existence. So far as women were concerned, that purpose was directed primarily towards procreation and the preservation of her family. Hers, argued Anthony, was the reasoning of an insect and he bid Chiddlestone observe the host of caterpillars which, having stripped the vicar's nasturtiums of their leaves, was marching on the parsonage to pupate within its warmth.

'Women, we may be sure, every man jack of 'em, born into this world solely to reproduce and die. And mark 'ee, vicar, without the stimulant of death beckoning to them, they'd never have had the nous to fathom out all those tricks they're up to.'

Men, on the other hand, uncovered reasons for living in the defence of their possessions, in manufacturing things, in making money – in short, in accomplishments. They dug gardens, ploughed fields, built boats – did anything to lend meaning to what would otherwise be a void.

'And so, my dear Chiddlestone, that is why we have – to give but a few examples – the compass, toothpicks, marmalade, saddles, calculus, buttons. Are we the worse for them? Would our lives be improved if some fellow had not been bored to distraction one day and invented the shoe? Everything has a cause, and where there is causality, reason is not far behind. Reason is sovereign. We shall one day be able to control everything through its exercise. Those with the most powerful reason will prevail over those with the weakest. And it all stems from the fact that we die. Death is the mother of reason. It is the imperative that drives us all.'

But Digbeth Chiddlestone saw things in a softer light. For a start, he could not accept the other's view of death for even a single moment. It was naïve, not to say heretical, to think of death so crudely, as if it were a spade blocking a rabbit hole. If anything, it was more like a spade unblocking a rabbit hole. But leaving that aside, he was aware that as he'd grown older he'd become increasingly distrustful of the untempered application of reason. It was too brutish and indiscriminate a tool for everyday use. To prostrate oneself uncritically before its altar was narrow-minded. Our emotions, the eye of the artist, the feel of a musician for his work, were these not matters in which reason occupied the lower berth?

So for Scipio Africanus one could have nothing but the warmest feelings, for where would life be without the toothpick? Marmalade came from heaven, everyone knew that. So no tampering with marmalade. Without the compasses to guide the ships that carried them, one would be without either tea or coffee. And that would not be easily endurable. But gunpowder and the muzzle-loader, the pike, the pistol and the poniard, could he really accept that by inventing these terrible instruments reason had been acting for the best? He did not think so. If that was the crop that sprang from reason, then let reason be extirpated, he said gruffly to Anthony.

They stood up and set out for a walk. By the time they had settled themselves on a bench facing the church, a fresh twist had been added to their discussion: is it reason or the absence of reason that most influences people's lives?

Anthony contentedly took a pinch of snuff. This was an old chestnut. His attention wandered. He gazed upon the church. Piff! Like a pin into a pancake. Piff! And lo, the day came to pass when Edward Horne, gentleman, no longer attended services at Winterbourne . . .

'But what if, out of the blue, the branch of a chestnut tree falls on you as you are riding beneath it?' Chiddlestone was saying. 'Is that not the operation of chance? They are the least predictable of our trees. You cannot say what a chestnut will do next.'

'It will have a reason. Canker, some deficiency of structure – there will be a reason somewhere.'

'Or if you slip on a rock and are drowned in the river?'

'It is my poor judgement that is to blame, that is all.'

'Or if the bank gives way, consequence ditto?'

'It has been eroded by the stream. Faugh! I call these very piddling arguments.'

'Then let us instead imagine that you are walking one afternoon through a pasture. The air is heavy. Your bullocks are flicking their tails in apprehension. Gnats are dancing in your face. The bombilation of the bees is unnaturally loud.'

'In short, my dear reverend, we are talking of thunder.'

'The sky darkens. The cloud is above your head. Suddenly there descends from it a black snake like a tentacle: a whirlwind.'

'I see it in my mind. It is not difficult.'

'Which with a violence that is unholy plucks you off your feet, dashes you to the ground and kills you. It happens, not frequently I am sorry to concede, but it happens. You cannot deny it. It is like being killed by lightning.'

'But what are we talking of here? One chance in a million?'

'But what a chance! We are not speaking of some twopenny misadventure that has made you miss a shot at croquet, but of death itself. This tiny chance has killed you, Sir Anthony! Reason has been baffled and chance has put you under the sod.'

'You are splitting hairs. It is absurd to base an entire argument on a footle.'

'All I wish to establish is that the important things in our lives are as likely to be determined by chance as by reason, that they occur accidentally, "whatever the pompous history in octavo says".'

'So it was by chance that you learned how to speak, was it? Chance that caused you to apply for the vicarship at Winterbourne? Unpremeditated and by its own volition, your pen picked itself up and wrote a pleasing letter – was that how it was? Poppycock, Mr Chiddlestone, poppycock!'

But Chiddlestone was not to be bullied. He knitted his fingers round a bony kneecap. His tongue flickered over his lower lip. He said slyly, 'The accident of love, how then do you account for that?'

'Love is a form of madness, a temporary derangement of the senses. The ancients knew this and so do all persons of intelligence. It does not endure. It has no weight, no substance. Madness can have no place in our discussions.'

'But its accidentalness, Sir Anthony: you have not answered me on that. Strangers meet, their eyes cry out to each other – and the thing is done. Reason has played not the slightest part in it. And, what is more, this madness, as you call it, is the foundation of matrimony and thus of society. Without it, neither of us would be here today.'

Like blind windows, Anthony's pale eyes engulfed the vicar. 'I am astonished to hear someone of your years arguing out of such bare-faced sentimentality. The decision by a man to take a particular woman as his wife is governed solely by reason. Solely! Her looks, character, expectations, her suitability in society – these are matters for the brain and nothing else. Marriage is a contract dictated by reason at its most cogent.'

'You are going out of your way to misunderstand me. I am not referring to reason but to its absence. To love, to magic, to lust, jealousy and suspicion. To all those times when reason quits and madness reigns. Surely you are aware of what I am talking about?'

'What is this I hear? Magic and madness conquering all? Come come, vicar, I think you have got a little over-excited.' He eased his buttocks and gathered himself to leave. He had had enough argufying for the day. Then he added with a smirk, 'And do I detect in your reasoning a denial of His all-powerful intelligence? Can it be that you are saying that His purpose is inferior to that of mere chance? Tush now, that is scarcely what we expect to hear from our ministers. But you must excuse me. A few harvest duties still await me at Overmoor. And besides, I have a wife to consider, you know.'

Seventeen

WHILE HE was in London, Edward had sought out Caroline Nelson. But he had increasingly come to feel that there was something missing, or at any rate incomplete. His dissatisfaction was not physical. It came instead from emotional pulses deep within him, from an insistent grumbly voice speaking a language he could not decipher. A new face, a new body, new sensations: these were what he needed, he thought, not realising that he had reached that state of ripeness where a man starts to seek more from an engagement than a warm platform upon which to exercise. To him it would have appeared extraordinary, but to his grumbly assistant it was clearer than spring water that his employer was on the lookout for magic.

It was a warm forenoon at the end of September when he set out from Winterbourne with Sixpence. His purpose was to call upon Robert Pumfrey to ensure that the money he had sent for deposit was secure. It was not what he'd say. But it was very much at the front of his mind. He had gone no great distance when Luna overreached and cut into herself. So he was leading her down the hill to the bank for Melson to put a salve on, worried about the injury, unsettled by the murmurs within him, glad to be home at last, baked by the heat yet stimulated by all the little welcoming conversations that had been had for nothing as he and Luna walked through town; in short, he was alive with a full complement of human contradictions when he saw a solitary woman ascending the hill towards him.

Not another soul was on the road, only this small strong reddish woman waddling up the hill towards him on out-turned feet. Everything was silent save for the rhythmic clop behind him of

Luna's hooves. Gradually their paths converged, his and that of this unknown, ordinary woman. He casually absorbed the details of her clothing, her duck-like gait and the round straw-plaited basket on her arm. He decided from the evidence of the green fronds hanging limply over the side that it held carrots. Soon only twenty yards separated them. She was walking more slowly now, her chest heaving. Still in the same negligent way, he began to inspect her face. Suddenly it became fuzzy and blurred. He wiped the sweat from his eyes with the back of his hand – and found imposed upon this sallow throat in front of him not the face of a small reddish woman but that of Daisy Apreece. He halted transfixed. With the clarity of an etching, as bright as a figure in a stained-glass window, he saw Daisy's neat oval head, her laughing brown eyes, the dimpling round her cheeks and her twitching nose. She came closer, lips parted, her mouth and eyes smiling in a shared joke. Slowly the image thinned and faded into the sunlight.

The woman drew level and climbed on up the hill without a word. Kitty Prodger came out of her shop and said something to him through a mouthful of pins. He went quickly over to her.

'We, I, Daisy – I mean – is Lady Apreece with you?' The words rushed out willy-nilly. Kitty removed the pins and eyed him curiously.

'It's my horse, you see, I'm taking her to the bank.' What on earth was making him talk like this? 'But nothing too serious, nothing a salve won't cure,' he said, collecting himself and retreating into the road.

He went on a little and stopped a second time. He ran his fingers through his hair and squinted into the sun. Something that was not hunger bubbled in his stomach. He looked around. Yes, this was where they'd stood in that slip of January sunshine, he and she together, opposite one another, as close as he and Luna were now. They'd joked about Polly. He'd said she was so small he could walk into the saddle. She'd laughed. Her teeth were uneven. And then she'd said, 'But the world is full of narrow gates. You cannot elude them for ever.' Mr Horne, she'd called him Mr Horne.

Sixpence was sitting on his foot, examining from under her eyebrows a beetle out on an errand. A cheerful, gappy-toothed flower girl appeared from somewhere and walking round them went into Kitty Prodger's with a bunch of hollyhocks trailing over her arm. He searched her face eagerly. She caught his glance and said something to Kitty. They both stared at him. It was here they'd talked that day, at this very place. She'd been carrying a box, no, two flat boxes tied together with a blue ribbon done in a bow. A sampler for Miss Pumfrey, that's what she had said. So what had the other one contained? She'd put her hand into his to say goodbye. Had done it firmly, as a man might have. The veins had stood out like the chart of a river system. He should have bought her some gloves from Kitty. Then and there. But perhaps it had been a new pair in the other box? Such *womanliness*, he thought. Such a depth of smile, such tenderness, such sympathy welling out of those soft eyes. A woman for a man to go with and come home to. A woman to guard over. A woman who was the wife of another –

'Counting moonbeams are we, Mr Horne?' He started. It was old Mrs Scarlett, who had glided up beside him in her town coach. Her minute face, as ancient and wrinkled as a lizard's, peered out at him unwinking.

'Just giving the mare a breather, ma'am. You know how it is when one stops on an afternoon like this. Thoughts arrive unexpectedly. Odd little thoughts from nowhere . . .'

Her groom came round and lowered the steps for her. She put her hand on his forearm as she descended.

'My sunshade, if you please, Peterford. Well, young man, weather like this is no time to be without a hat. Make a habit of it and you'll go the same colour as your father did. I always told him he'd end up looking like an Abyssinian. Getting over your mother all right, are you, Mr Horne? Poor girl, she was always a bit lost up here. Never should have left London.' She made a little jabbing movement with her cane as Sixpence snuffled round her ankles. 'Cats and ladies make poor travellers. You remember that when your time comes, young man. Cats and ladies and – there was another one too. It was one of the general's favourite expressions. Now off with you, I'm not a pretty sight walking. Hold it over my head, Peterford, not between us. Towels, spouses and umbrellas should never be shared. That was another of his sayings. I'm glad I don't have to listen to them any more. Peonies, Mr Horne, that was the other one. Cats, ladies and peonies. Come on then, Peterford, give me your arm . . .'

Edward left her, a gnarled old lady crabbing her way to the dressmaker, and with Luna and Sixpence following him, continued down the hill to the bank. His senses were on tiptoe, tingling as if someone had been flicking him with damp flannel.

Nothing could have been more conspicuous or more convenient in town than the Bank of Buxton. No one on his way to market, visiting the baths, attending the Assembly Room or even simply taking a promenade could avoid seeing the pale of gold-tipped iron railings that, alone among the buildings on the Crescent, the bank possessed. Irresistibly the eye was drawn under the colonnade to its dark green, six-panelled doors, its refulgent leonine knocker (polished first thing every morning), its arched windows (polished weekly), and its two gleaming boot scrapers. Should its purpose still be obscure, immediate clarification was provided by the words THE BANK OF BUXTON chased across its upper windows in Mr Baskerville's new capitals, two foot six inches high. When it snowed or there was a frost the rime would hang on the ledges of the horizontal strokes or gather in the feet of the Os and the U so that, with the light from Mrs Pumfrey's candles shining behind them, the whole place took on from outside the appearance of Aladdin's cave. And it was proper that it did so, for the entire thrust of the façade was to proclaim the existence of an enterprise that combined olympian sagacity with all the properties of a jewel box. Of course there had been doubters and scoffers when Robert had started. But once they had stepped into his parlour and allowed themselves to dwell upon the pomp of the oak wainscot and the solidity of the candlestands; and once they had observed the trusting manner in which (for instance) Leonard Huggins the corn chandler made a deposit, there were few who did not emerge with total confidence in the steadiness of the operation.

'Here you are then, Jack,' Mr Huggins would say to Jack Long as he thumped a purse on to the counter. 'Better by far Mr Pumfrey had the caring of these than Mrs Huggins.' They'd chat about men's whatnots, Leonard leaning on his elbow and fingering his moustaches, while Jack's pink skull bobbed up and down as he talked and simultaneously tallied the coins and entered them in his ledger. Then he'd sign the ledger, give Leonard a receipt, which he put in his purse for Mrs Huggins to look after when he got home, and everyone could see that doing business at the Bank of Buxton was honest and courteous, and that when the corn chandler came out and paused on the steps of the bank, the furrows of worry had quite vanished from his face.

And if yet more was needed to settle the nerves of the doubters or to put gristle into the timid, they would find on application the counter smoothly opened and Jack's silken hand on their elbow as he nursed them across the black-and-white tiled floor to the office of the proprietor himself.

No no, of course it was no trouble! Nothing could be more agreeable to him than company at this precise instant. You know how it is, sir, when one steers a mighty vessel. A man cries out for a friendly word or two to get him through his watch. A seat, sir, I beg you! And as a matter of fact, it was the very time when he liked to have his coffee. No, he would not hear of it, he positively insisted. He had but to ring that little bell and Jack would ask that Mrs Pumfrey place an extra cup on the tray. And now, perhaps, he could learn in what manner he might be of assistance . . . Or while they waited for the coffee to arrive, might he be permitted to explain how his banknotes were manufactured . . . ?

'Can you believe it, sir, even a bush, a humble bush, can be turned into a Pumfrey?' he would say, his eyes out on stalks. 'You have only to bring me that lilac on your lawn and after a few weeks of whirring and chopping – now sir, there is no cause to look so pained. It is an old tree. I look at it every time I ride past your house and I say to myself, It is an old tree, it has seen the best of its life. Look upon it as God's mulching, that is the best way to come to terms with death, I do feel this most strongly – now where was I? – ah yes, whirring and chopping, and then you can walk out of this room with a Pumfrey in your pocket and with it buy yourself a yard of cloth, a saucepan or a five-bar gate. Is that not an achievement, turning a lilac tree into a five-bar gate?'

There were some among his visitors who were frankly uninterested in this part of Robert's recital. All that concerned them was the security he required and the rates at which he lent and borrowed. Ladies especially tended to become a touch restless. His talk of turning their well-tended gardens into gates and kettles and the like made them nervous, for what if their husbands took him at his word? So they let Robert's enthusiasm whistle round their ears while they admired the appointments in his office: the blue-john in the dresser, the fine pieces from Etruria, the china firedogs on the hearth, his lapis pen holder, the sconces with their bold wax candles that drew such an agreeable glow from his green velvet curtains – are these not, they would ask themselves, of the very same shade as the paintwork on his outer door? What a considering man Mr Pumfrey must be, how attentive to detail – from which it was but a tiny step to thinking: how scrupulously will he inscribe my name in one of those plump ledgers on his desk.

But Robert was a banker. He had witnessed at first hand the fall of Neale, James, Fordyce and Down. He had seen fear in the face of Mr Drummond, had heard fear in his voice. He had learned how rapidly trust could curl into suspicion. Rumour, fraud, miscalculation – any one of these, he knew, could devour his business within a matter of days. In no time a mob could be at his door. Oh yes, they'd all be there, from his friend Leonard Huggins to that God-fearing parson from Winterbourne. In fact he wouldn't be surprised if the parson was first in the line. Even Edward Horne would be there. On this score he had no illusions. So he kept his calculations to himself. When he balanced his books, which he did every Friday evening, he did so with his office door locked. When he met with his partners, his cousin William and Archer Appleby, he kept the proceedings as swampy as he could, describing their affairs with an opacity worthy of a somnambulist. Sometimes Archer questioned him too closely for his liking. 'Dammit, Robert, what is happening? We have a right to know. Remember that if there are losses, we too have a share in them.' Then Robert felt like a huntsman who has cast his hounds on a spec and hears behind him the growl of his critics. Trust me, he'd reply, have faith: there is room for only one man in this saddle and I am he.

He sat behind his desk and waited for Edward. He was nervous. Beneath his sober broadcloth with its green lapels, there was a chafing flutter in his breast that had nothing to do with the coffee he had drunk or with the consignment of banknotes that was late arriving from the printer. In a week's time the first of Anthony's loans was due. The interest had been delightful. Oh yes, Constance had enjoyed every penny of that eight per cent. But now he wanted his capital back. He had borrowings to repay. Mr Wormald had increased his rent. Almost six months would elapse before those other loans he had made came to hand. The security he had taken had been less than copper-bottomed. What if the price of land dropped in the meantime? What if someone defaulted . . . ?

Anthony had been very quiet of late. This invitation he had received for dinner, what was he to make of it? Of course Constance had let out a great squawk and almost run up the road to Kitty's. All she could think of was what to wear and whom she'd be wearing it for. But how was he to take it? Was Anthony powdering him up for another cock and bull story about Gomez and the woeful state of the Funds?

He pared a speck of dirt from beneath one fingernail. Of course, now that he had Edward Horne's deposit, matters were less immediately pressing. And in any case banking would not be what it was without an alarum now and again.

Jack Long knocked on the door. 'Mr Horne coming up the steps now. Shall I lock up behind him? It's long past our usual hours.'

Jauntily and with a flush to his cheeks, Edward bounced into Robert's office. He apologised for being so late. He had been delayed by Luna's injury, no other reason. You really can't be too careful with a horse that's cut into itself. Actually, the slower one walks the better. Robert snapped his fingers. Ffft! It hadn't bothered him a jot. He'd written some letters, taken the air, gone to the fishmonger, chatted with friends. Yes, he'd really passed a most relaxing afternoon for a change. In fact, when he returned he'd nearly nodded off in his chair, would you believe!

The spectacle of two men lying to each other is not unlike that of a pair of clowns inside a circus horse where everything goes off very clumsily and the show is only kept going by astonishing contortions at each end. So it was with Edward and Robert. The former insisted that his high colour was due solely to the heat of the sun, and that if he preferred to pace around with an air of distraction it was only because of his anxiety for Luna. Robert swore that it was of absolutely no consequence to him at all that

Edward might soon have to draw down some of his deposit in order to make a payment for the roof at Winterbourne.

'In point of fact,' he said with a well-struck laugh, 'you are doing me a good turn. A banker with too much money to lend invariably makes an ass of himself.'

No sooner had he made this remark than he was struck to the marrow by its all too horrible truth. The tappings and knockings started afresh in his stomach.

'Surely it's rather late in the year to begin work on a roof that size?' he said. 'Are you certain it wouldn't be more sensible to wait until the spring?'

'You may well be right, but Bill Whitehead assures me it is vital at least to get it covered over before the bad weather sets in. Now tell me, what is the easiest way for you to deal with his payment? He started last week . . .'

Their conversation stumbled to a halt. Neither had any intention of admitting it, but both men were anxious to be, if not somewhere else, then at least alone.

Robert saw his guest to the door. They stood for a moment looking up at the evening sky. There was a hint of frost in it. They touched upon the state of business in Buxton, exchanged some perfunctory words about the dinner at Overmoor – and parted.

He shot home the bolts. On the counter was Jack's summary of the morning's transactions. He glanced at it as he passed. No miracle there. He went into his office and stood beside the curtains. In the courtyard below him, Edward was saying goodnight to Melson. They held a lantern to Luna's injured fetlock, which now had a bandage round it. Edward gave the man a coin. Robert waited until he saw him ride out into the street. Then he locked his door and drew up his chair.

His features were hooded in the candlelight, his eye sockets like black discs. He pulled his ledgers in front of him and removed those on top until only a common daybook remained. He took a tiny silver key from his waistcoat pocket and undid its clasp. His eyes flickered to the door and back. He hurried through its pages until he reached an empty chamber, a coffin, in its centre. He extracted a small notebook bound in worn shagreen and put on his spectacles. His gaze flowed down the columns of figures and halted at the last balance he'd struck, only three days before. He picked up a pencil and ran through them again, placing a small tick against each as he went. He retallied them. No, there had been no mistake. One squall, that's all that would be needed if Anthony was false. He leaned back in his chair and brushed a speck of fluff off his sleeve. He rolled the pencil between his lips. His eyes glittered in the dingy light. So fine a balance, the thickness of a few roof slates between night and day. Pray God that it was a hard winter and Edward had to abandon his work. Pray God Whitehead slipped off his ladder and broke a leg. Pray God Sir Anthony was in funds.

Eighteen

HUCKNALL BLEW into his lumpy hands and shuffled them together as if he were rubbing out a twist of tobacco. Jiggery but it was cold in the hall tonight. Damned if he wouldn't be warmer outside with Clayton. It'd freeze, he was sure of it.

Voices trilled and boomed, diminished and advanced from behind him in the drawing-room. He went over to the tiled stove and pressed the backs of his knees against it. Gentry! Never any call for them to suffer like ordinary folks had to. Just flounced out of their carriages, tossed him their furs and what have you (thinking to themselves, That Hucknall looks a right monkey prinked up in his serving costume. Didn't say as much but he knew that look in their faces, oh yes, he knew it well enough), and before you could say dandipratt it was 'By Jove, Sir Anthony, stuff and bollocks' and 'Oh my lady, let me slide my tongue up your charming cleft', and there they'd be bowing and pawing and stroking each other like they were head over heels in love. Which he knew damned well was shite as they'd only come to criticise each other and have a free guzzle. But good actors, he'd say that much for them. Then the drawing-room door'd close in his face and while he half-froze to death, what did they do next, these pellet-headed nobs? Did they have great speech and plot the betterment of people like him? Nar, not for a second. All they could think of was jostling round the fire like animals and braying about their sport while they toasted their furry little orifices. Oh yes, he'd caught them at it often enough, he knew what they got up to. A flip of the coat-tails and off with a good fart. So who was the shitty monkey in the house? that's what he'd like to know.

He tipped the gloves out of the glove basket and laid them out in their pairs on the console table beside the silver card tray. Only two to come now, Scrawny and Queer-Parker. Pigs'd fly sooner than Scrawny arrived on time. He'd probably got half-way and found he'd forgotten to dabble some perfume in his oxters. Perfoom, he said to himself, puffing the word like pipe smoke through his rounded lips. The sound pleased him. He walked up to the picture outside the drawing-room. Two women were depicted squatting beside a stream while they beat out their laundry with wooden bats. Perfoom, he said, you'll need lots of perfoom before you're through with that caper. He went back to the mirror and straightened his neckcloth. Perhaps the nobs had a point. But it wasn't a monkey he looked like in his black waistcoat with yellow piping. It was a wasp. That's what he was, Overmoor's resident wasp. He bared his rotten teeth. Zzzz. Good for the wasp. Saw everything. Didn't stand for any arrogance. Pricked the nobs and made them cross. Packed up and went to sleep when it got too cold. Zzzz. He slapped his arms round his shoulders. God alone knew why anyone'd want to live in a barn like this if they had the money to do otherwise. What it needed was a foot of straw and a few farrowing sows to make it comfy.

There was a tap on the bull's-eye window beside the front door. Haloed against the gleam of the outside lantern was Clayton's head. He gestured into the night, his lips moving wordlessly. Hucknall opened the door a fraction.

'Dog cart coming up the front drive,' Clayton said. 'Think it'll be Queer-Parker?'

'None of your cheek, boy. You've got a few years to go before you can –'

'What's that, men? Another of our guests?' Anthony was wearing dark grey stockings, a lighter grey waistcoat and a suit of ox-blood red with large silver buttons. Hucknall could smell the drink on his breath. He thought of the heel-taps that would come his way later in his pantry. Perhaps there was something to be said for these occasions after all. Once they'd got going and one's blood was on the move.

'Be a frost tonight, I'll wager,' Anthony said, glancing at the steel-bright sky. 'Early enough for it. Could be a hard winter ahead of us.'

'Just what we was thinking, Sir Anthony. Early frosts means

early flakes, my father always said.' Clayton too gazed up at the stars.

Like glow-worms, the lamps of the dog cart approached down the front drive. Without a check the vehicle swung round the corner between the stone pillars. The spinning wheels slowed and halted in the penumbra of lantern light. At the reins was Fuscus Quex-Parker wrapped in a full-length coachman's benjamin. The collar was turned up round his ears. On his head was a wide brown beaver. Clayton darted forward and caught the bridle. With his right hand he unlatched the door. Fuscus descended, the folds of his cloak unfurling like curtains around his travelling boots. He peeled off a glove and started up the steps to where Anthony was waiting.

'My dear Fuscus –'

'Heavens but you're in a fever tonight, Anthony. Your hand's as hot as a kettle.'

'And yours like a block of ice. You should have brought your carriage, you know.' Anthony waved at the dog cart, which Clayton was leading off to the stables. 'These toys are all very well in the summer, but once autumn starts to bite it's as if one was driving a burial chamber. Now come along in before we all freeze. Give your gloves to Hucknall. Here, Hucknall, take Mr Quex-Parker's gloves for him.'

'Yes, Sir Anthony.' Do this, do that, always the same when there were guests around, always treated the servants like muck.

'Just Mr Horne to come now, sir?' he asked as he closed the front door and helped Quex-Parker out of his cloak.

'Yes, yes. Now for his boots, Hucknall. Can't have Mr Quex-Parker clumping round in front of the ladies like a bear.'

From the depths of the armchair beside the stove, Fuscus elevated a portly leg for Hucknall to straddle.

'Thank 'ee, Hucknall, thank 'ee kindly. Pumps in me pocket yonder.' Hucknall went to fetch them. The smell of roasting meats was wafting down the corridor from the kitchen. To the heel-taps he added a basin of broad beans with white parsley sauce. Maybe he'd get his hands on some trimmings of fat if he treated Ma Keech well. Crisp brown fat, the colour of a fox.

'There we are then,' said Fuscus, standing up and giving his coat a few tugs and pats. 'All snug and shipshape, as much as an old dog ever will be.'

Hucknall threw the door open for the two men. He saw Fuscus bow to the waist and raise Daisy's hand to his lips. 'Ah, my dear Lady Apreece, how ravishing you look this evening, how positively ravishing . . .' Hucknall smirked. Just like he'd said. He picked up Fuscus's boots and lined them neatly alongside Mr Dipple's and Mr Cuthbert's. That one on the right'd need its seam stitched soon. But good quality leather. Robert Pumfrey's wig was askew on its nail. He squared it up, blew out his cheeks and rubbed his hands. Only Scrawny to come now. He wondered if any of the guests would souvenir him when they left. Some evenings they did and some they didn't. Once he'd collected threepence for his efforts. You never could tell. The more they had, the less they gave. At any rate that was his experience.

The sound of raised voices reached him from the kitchen. Mrs Keech was putting Elizabeth and Agatha through their paces. These girls, it didn't matter how often they'd helped at table before, they always panicked on a big night like this. He leaned against the wall with his shins crossed and his arms folded. Better not let his head touch it in case he left a spot of grease. Her ladyship wouldn't fuss, she was understanding about that sort of thing. Poor woman, you had to have pity on someone in her situation. But Sir Anthony, he'd only have to find a dab of something and he'd chase him quicker than a terrier after a rat. In the distance he heard Mrs Keech's voice rumbling away like a pot full of boiling potatoes. Now whatever did Miss Hoole do on nights like this, the old busybody?

Suddenly Mrs Keech's sharpest tones came flying down the flagstoned corridor. 'You horrible creature, Agatha! How dare you do that! If I've told you once, I've told you a thousand times . . .' He chuckled to himself. Poor Aggie, been caught picking her nose again, he'd warrant. Hardly a day went by but she wasn't in trouble with the vulture for it. But you slip along to my pantry later, my dear, and you can pick your nose to your heart's content, just as long as you let me squeeze up behind you and feel those juicy diddies of yours. Whoppers they were, nothing like them for miles around, all pink and flobby with nipples like raspberries. He rummaged his groin thoughtfully.

Again there was a tap on the window. Clayton beckoned to him. He pushed himself off the wall and went to the door. It was good to know that there existed someone even colder and more menial than himself; that he had the power, if he wished to use it, to tell Clayton to roger off. That's authority for you, he thought, that's what it's all about. He stuck his nose out a couple of inches.

'Think I should ride out Britannia way in case Mr Horne's had an accident? You know how the master doesn't like to be kept waiting.'

'Give him a few more minutes. You know what an idle beggar he is.'

No one can say I never offered, thought Clayton, tucking his hands into his armpits and drawing his head down into the armature of his leather jerkin. No one can blame me if he's lying out there with a broken leg. It wouldn't be his fault. 'It's him,' he could say, nodding at Hucknall, 'he's the one who was giving the orders.' But it was queer a man didn't turn up on time for a meal. If it had been him, he'd have been back home already with a full belly and all. He stamped up and down the terrace swinging his arms and feeling his nose grow more like a small blue pebble with every minute that passed.

The trouble with Horne, reflected Hucknall as he watched Clayton through the window, was that he thought too much. You could tell it by his forehead. Like a wheel of cheese, all smooth and white, an upper-class forehead if ever he knew one. Wasn't his fault, of course. It wasn't as if he'd asked his old lady to put his head in a jelly mould when she was carrying him. Still . . . No, he couldn't say he was struck on Scrawny, not one little bit. Anyway, what did he care. He shrugged and set off prowling round the hall again.

'I know, I know, late as usual. My apologies to you all –'. Of a sudden it seemed that the doorway was full of Edward Horne. The conversation faltered, heads turned towards the slim figure who stood on the threshold wearing a coat the colour of greengages. With quick eyes, he sought out Daisy. She was standing in the centre of the room, at an angle away from him, speaking to Dickie Dipple. Her hand described a quickening loop as she elaborated upon a point in their discussion. The hairs tingled up the nape of her neck. Without looking round, she continued with her sentence and only when she had reached a natural breathing space did she say to Dickie, 'So now we are complete.' Then she wheeled and crossed the room to Edward. His coat swung open as he bent to take her hand. Its silk lining, the luscious pink of a magnolia bloom, shimmered and rippled before her. His lips touched her knuckles. He raised his head and their eyes met.

The certainty that Daisy was the most wonderful woman in the world had been marinading inside him for the past fortnight, steeping in the hot juices in which his grumbly assistant special-ised. His concern about the Bank of Buxton had passed clean out of his mind. All he could think of was that he loved Daisy. He had tried to consider it rationally. He had gone for long rides with Sixpence and told himself time and again that she was a woman bespoken for, the wife of a friend and neighbour. He had lectured himself about honour and duty and informed himself repeatedly that he had only to be patient and a more suitable engagement would come his way. He had reminded himself until he was blue in the face that he really knew nothing about Daisy, that he might as well declare a passion for a total stranger. More often than he could say, he'd convinced himself upon each and all of these points and washed his hands of her for a few hours while he threw himself into some task with Amos. But no sooner had he sat down to a meal, opened a book or let his dreams roam across the brown-tinted moor, than in a flash his pretences had crumbled like a sandcastle before the waves of love for this woman whose small hand now rested in his. He did not care that she was ten years older, that she was married, or a single thing about her husband. Boldly his eyes asked the question that she had longed for – and feared. Her hand trembled in his.

Then Anthony was standing beside them. She took her lace-fringed handkerchief from her left cuff and tucked it busily into her right cuff. He looked from her hand to her face, uncertain whether he'd just seen what he thought he'd seen.

'We might have got worried had you been much later,' he said to Edward.

'I'm most damnably sorry. I would have been here on time, truly, bang on the hour, if I hadn't pulled a button off my coat.

Then Mrs Paxton couldn't lay her hands on the right coloured thread. And so . . . but here I am at last. Have I kept you all back?'

His eyes, which, during the intensity of that exchange with Daisy had turned almost green, hardened and bored into Anthony's face as he spoke. What they saw now was a quite different man from previously, an obstacle, an opponent, a challenge. They flickered up and down him, searching for defects. For the first time they noticed his lumpy feet and the ridiculous angle at which his ears stuck out from his head. They saw his knee buckles did not match, and a tiny black stain on his grey waistcoat. Then into the corner of his vision the lilac cloud that was Daisy turned as Robert Pumfrey spoke to her. Edward became conscious there were others in the room.

'I'm sure you've met all these people a hundred times already,' Anthony was saying. 'Anyway, this is Sam Cuthbert, one of the county's finest graziers. He hires his rams from Mr Bakewell. He is even a member of the Dishley Society . . . What? See that, Sam, he has never heard of the Society.' Hunching his shoulders, he turned down the corners of his mouth and extended his arms in a deprecatory semicircle as if to say, What an ignoramus we have here.

A short square bull of a man in a plain black suit made a slight bow to Edward. He had a brick-red neck and stocky calves whose veins stood out like whipcord under his white stockings.

'It's a pleasure to put a face to a name, Mr Horne. Your parents were good friends of mine. Nat was a man in a million and I'm right glad to meet his son. Don't you pay any heed to what Sir Anthony says about the Society. Nothing more than a lot of old droops talking up the price of their livestock. It'd fair bore you to death to listen to them. Not a man like your father among them – takes after old Nat, don't you think, Millie?' He stepped back and bestowed on Edward the careful scrutiny of a farmer, that mixture of suspicion and contempt that he reserves for all living creatures not born smack-dab under his nose. Tarnation but that coat lining'd fairly give his cows a move on. Make 'em milk like the clappers. But an honest-looking fellow, too honest to make a good farmer. Buying or selling, he'd likely be at the losing end of the trade.

'See here, Millie my love, just the same set to his phiz as Nat.

183

Don't mind me speaking like this, I hope, Mr Horne. Only it fairly gives me a turn to see the resemblance.'

'I do believe you're right,' said his wife, a timid body who had no intention of saying anything erect in such company. Sam gave her bluish arm a squeeze.

'Must be coming up fifteen years since Nat passed on,' he continued. A tall man with a crooked, purple-veined nose poked his head over Millie's shoulder.

'Fifteen years this winter it'll be, Sam. I can remember the day as if it were yesterday 'cos when I was riding home from the funeral I grew that cold – I tell you, Edward, me cods were practically frozen to the saddle – pardon me French, Millie – that I'd have been lost if I hadn't stopped off on the way for a noggin of Freddie Bissett's brandy. Did I ever tell you that's how me and Mary got to be man and wife, all on account of the weather at Nat's funeral? Hang on, better if I get Mary to tell it. Mightn't get it off right by myself.'

'But Dickie, we all know what happened. You've told it more often than a cow farts.' Sam nudged Edward in the ribs. 'Only got to mention Nat and he starts up about him and Mary like it was the only tune he'd ever learned. You'd think he'd have got over it after fifteen years in the same bed.'

Hearing her name mentioned, Mary disengaged herself from Anthony and Constance and trundled over in her flagship style of going, treading on the outside of her slippers, her beige dress already sloppy round her shoulders.

'You are discussing me, gentlemen. I detect it from the way you are smiling. Now don't try to deny it. I have yet to meet the man who can smile and lie at the same time.'

'At which women are expert, are they then?'

'But of course, Mr Cuthbert, of course! From the very first time they wake up beside their husbands and say, "Good morning, dearest heart." Oh, aren't I awful, Edward? I really can't think where these dreadful ideas spring from. Now tell me, what repulsive things has Dickie been saying about me behind my back? But first, Edward' – she put her hand on his arm, her mouth twitched conspiratorially – 'tell me frankly – that is, do not for a second hesitate to agree with me if you wish to – do you not share my opinion that Mr Dipple resembles an alligator, all bone and gristle, scaly and fearsome?'

In an instant the subject of the Dipples' betrothal, which but a few seconds earlier had stretched as drearily as a Siberian plain, was transformed into a fizz-pot.

'An alligator, indeed! Very apt, Mrs Dipple, very apt I do say. How do you reply to that then, Dickie? But hold on – don't alligators have green teeth?' Sam Cuthbert handed his glass to his wife and going up on tiptoes made a performance of examining Dickie Dipple's stained teeth.

'Is it possible you're confusing them with foxes?' ventured Millie, 'I've seen their teeth in the coach lights looking as bright as emeralds.'

'More like cooked spinach than emeralds, dear,' Sam said. 'Any road, how do you say to being an alligator, Dickie? Fancy lying round on a sandbank all day, do you?'

'I only wished to say, before my wife loosed on us this absurd *canard* –'

'No more foreign words, Dickie. We've had enough froggy from you already – a proper shocker it was too, Mrs Dipple, goodness knows where he picked up that sort of language. We be simple folks in these parts, don't we, Mr Horne?' He winked ferociously at Edward.

'As I was saying, I was riding home from Nat's funeral with me aforementioned frozen to the saddle and I took an oath –'

'A proper lardy one, I'll be bound,' shouted Sam, jiggling his hands in his breeches pockets like castanets.

'That never again would I leave Michaelmas Farm in such weather without a warm wife and bed to return to. Never again I said and by jiminy! I never have. I took one look at Mary Bissett as was, downed a jigger of Freddie's brandy in a oner and asked her if she'd have me. Kept me riding crop handy in case she gave me any trouble. (From behind his hand: 'Always a good idea when you're doing business with a woman, y'know, Edward . . . ') And so here we are, the pair of us as happy as sandpipers. And that's how I know Nat died fifteen years ago,' he concluded with a triumphant snort.

Mary went and put her arm through his.

'I can see you now, my dear, stalking into our drawing-room as though you were a heron, the snow lying in teeny-weeny drifts in the folds of your riding cloak. Oh, you were so manly and romantic that I wanted to jump up and hug you like mad only –'

'Only what, Mrs Dipple? Come on now, lass, tell it us as it was,' roared Sam, snatching back his glass and holding it out to Hucknall. Mary looked impishly around and let her voice fall away to a trickle.

'Only he was that stiff and blue round the gills and his eyes that glassy after father's brandy that for a moment I thought it was a dying pike I had promised myself to. I swear it! A dying pike! But I love my little pike, I do! I do!' And with that she rose on her toes and landed on the slopes of his rubescent beak a kiss like a water bomb.

'Steady on, Mary,' exclaimed Edward, glimpsing Daisy out of the corner of his eye, 'or you'll have us all in a lather.'

Suddenly Millie Cuthbert piped up, 'I like the notion of you on a sandbank, Mr Dipple. But somehow I think I'd like it more if you weren't there.' A blush rose immediately to her cheeks. The image of some solitary sea-lapped isle *sans* mud, sheep and cattle had sprung into her mind so abruptly and enticingly that the remark had just popped out like a cork from a bottle.

'I assume that you are speaking alligatorally, madam, and that your objection is not to Mr Dipple himself but to his reptilian *alter ego*,' Fuscus said.

'But of course that's what I meant . . . I mean . . . I mean, if Mr Dipple wasn't an alligator, nothing would please me more than to be on a sandbank with him. So long as Mary was there with us . . . Oh Sam, what am I saying?' The laughter fell around her ears. She wished the floor would swallow her up. They should never have come, should never have left Larkhill. She'd known all along they'd be out of their depth. With little sobs, she buried her face on Sam's shoulder.

Well, whatever next. Grown people acting like children, tears to fill a saucer and the evening only just started. Hucknall smoothed a napkin round the neck of the next bottle. He had thawed out and his night-loving soul felt almost cheerful. He gloatingly imagined Clayton crouched over his fire in the icy saddle-room, the draughts whistling round his feet. No fat little Aggie to roger in the pantry, no diddies to squidge between his fingers, no gossip to snigger at, in fact not one decent expectation the whole night long except Sir Anthony La-di-da shouting for the carriages at God knows what hour. Probably when he was just falling asleep. Poor sod. Well, he shouldn't have chosen to be a groom, should he? How would it be, he mused, to be someone like Queer-Parker and have the money to do as he pleased? To lie in a four-poster of a morning with his hands behind his head and listen to Clayton go arsy-versy when he slipped on a frozen puddle. To dabble with the hem of a snow-white sheet as he planned the littleness of his day. To pull the bell rope and command his varlet, 'Take away the pot', or 'Fetch my chocolate' . . .

'I think we're ready now,' Daisy was saying to him.

'Sorry, m'lady, just wondering if the gentlemen's horses were lacking anything.' He stole through the guests to where Anthony was talking to Robert and Constance Pumfrey.

Ting-ting! Ting-ting! Anthony tapped his glass with the edge of his snuffbox. 'Everyone, we are bidden to table! Now', he looked down at Daisy, 'will you, my dear, lead in our guest of honour and will you, let me see, will you take in Mrs Pumfrey, Fuscus? And Robert, Mrs Dipple? Sam and Dickie you must go it alone while I make up the rearguard with Mrs Cuthbert. That should at least get us as far as the table. As for how we leave it –'

'If we can leave it –'

'Quite so, Sam. But there's always Hucknall to help if our legs should fail us. Won't be the first time. Now look sharp, Ned, my belly's as empty as one of Dickie's woolsacks.'

Edward smiled at Daisy and made an arm for her. His heart was pounding like anything. She took a pinch of her dress between the fingers of her right hand. Her left she slid lightly up his forearm towards his elbow. The cloth was coarser than she had expected.

'Shall we?' he asked – and they started to walk towards the door, Edward in his swinging greengage-coloured coat and Daisy in a flowing gown that was a little more than lilac and a little less than lavender. From the peeping tips of her oatmeal slippers, up her satiny calves and her thighs to the wine-dark sash that circled her waist, it rustled with the faint susurrus of bulrushes stirring in a breeze.

Behind them Sam and Dickie Dipple formed up with boyish raillery.

'Now, Dickie, is it I who take your arm or you who takes mine? I'm the shorter but you're the more slender. So which of us should be the lady? I say, ain't life a puzzle and a half?'

'But some things in it are clear enough,' Edward said quietly, looking straight in front of him. Her hand dimpled his sleeve with the gossamer impress of a ladybird alighting on a leaf.

Hucknall was holding the door for them. She avoided his eyes and stared at the picture of the two washerwomen that hung on the far side of the corridor. She didn't trust that animal instinct of his. If their eyes met for only a second he would ferret out her secret.

'My lady,' he murmured, thinking to himself, oh-ho, so that's how matters lie. Then good luck to her. She deserved it. But it'd mean trouble.

They passed into the hall. At its far end, by the entrance to the dining-room, stood Agatha, her eyes large and nervous beneath her white mob cap. She brushed a slick of hair off her cheek and made a bob as Edward and Daisy appeared. They came abreast of the console table. Hucknall's neat line of gloves reminded her of the empty bodies of small animals. In a matter of fact way she said, 'It worries me that the Pumfreys do not seem to be entering into the spirit of the evening. They appear so tense. I overheard Robert speaking to Anthony with a most uncharacteristic snap in his voice. It's not like him. I've never known him to be other than the most amiable of souls. I do hope Anthony isn't up to something with him.' They were walking rather deliberately, the length of their paces matching each other exactly. The fancy came to him that it was not her dress he could feel beside him but her naked flesh. 'You know, Edward, he can be a hard man, as hard as flint. There are moments when he hates me. Heaven knows I have done nothing to deserve it, but I can see it in his eyes. I think hate is the most odious feeling in the world. Once it is out, it never leaves but clings to everything like the smell of a fox. There are times when I wonder how I have lived with it for so long.'

Her features tightened. Mrs Keech called out and they saw Agatha scuttle away down the corridor. Edward reached across and covered her hand with his. With a jerk of her head, she looked behind them. But on account of an argument between Sam and Dickie over who should take precedence at the doorway, only now was the rest of the party beginning to spill into the hall. Her fingers closed on his arm.

They reached the door to the dining-room. By rights he should have disengaged her arm and held back. But they looked at each other. Without a check in their step, they looked at each other, gauged the width of the doorway, found it wanting – and advanced. She angled her body into his. Her breast pushed against his wrist as they slid through. Their shoulders and hips melted into each other. Her dress might have been made of cobwebs so little did it count for. She led him to one side, into a shallow alcove. From his portrait at the far end of the room, Anthony regarded them down his ochred nose. She removed her hand. He took it and ran the tip of a fingernail down the grooves between its bones. He traced out the line of her jaw. He kissed her tulip-shaped nose on its bud and on its wings, and her lips, softly.

She felt tears at the back of her eyes. What a *good* man he was, this man she loved. How happy they could have been at a different time, in a different place. What a miracle they could have wrought together, Mr Horne and Miss Garland. But was it still possible? Did she dare? Had she the strength? She raised her hazel eyes to his and searched them for a sign. Her eyebrows were level and unmoving. A frown wrinkled her forehead as joy struggled against duty and elation against a foolish vow taken sixteen years before.

It seemed to Edward her eyes were burrowing into his skull. She put her hand to her throat and touched her necklace. Her wedding band winked at him malignly. And suddenly there exploded within him a torment of lust. On the floor, under the table, on top of the table among the jumping, jangling knives and spoons, the spinning bowls of flowers, the quivering candlesticks, the demented bonbon saucers, the little hopping salt cellars – anywhere, he didn't give a straw where they did it so long as he possessed her. To hell with hooks and laces, to hell with Kitty Prodger's tailoring, to hell with words, he just wanted to throw her down, to crumple her buttocks within his hands and steep himself inside her –

Footsteps and the coarse rumble of men's laughter approached the door. Daisy pushed him away.

'Just remember, he can be dangerous, dangerous do you hear? Think what happened to Arthur Smith.'

Then with a swirl of her lilac dress, as pale as a wraith against the dark oak panelling, she went dancing down the length of the table, firing words over her shoulder in a voice as taut as a bowstring, waving her arms, squaring up the chairs, plucking at napkins, marrying the knives more perfectly. 'Just look at this, will you? Is it a picnic I asked for? Do they think we should eat like donkeys? And the flowers, just look at them will you, Mr Horne – do you have flowers at Winterbourne? Are you good with a spade? Do you prune as you ought? And mulching – what have you to say about mulching? It was the storm last week. Everything was wrecked. Did you get it at Larkhill, Mr Cuthbert? Nor you, Mr Dipple? Only at Overmoor then. How odd and perverse. So the flowers are all of my own devising. And the blame is all mine as well. They are nothing. Everything is nothing.'

'Fiddlesticks! Whatever do you mean by blame?' Edward said quickly. 'I only wish I could have done them half so prettily. Dickie, Sam, support me. Look at that great tufty clump of purple in the middle. Don't you call that original? And with that moss all around it – never in a month of Sundays would any of this have occurred to me. Had this been my dinner and a storm come along and destroyed every bloom in the place, I'd just have shrugged and left you all to imagine what the flowers might have looked like.'

'By Jove you're right, Edward,' Dickie Dipple said, bending down and lifting a spray of tiny orange seed-heads on the back of his finger. 'Only someone who really cared for her friends would have gone out and picked wild flowers. Look at all these different shades of yellow she's found, hawkbit and nipplewort and flowering ivy. And look, Edward, damme if she hasn't given us each a posy of cranesbill. I'll wager she had to walk a fair distance for those at this time of the year. And then she talks about blame! Come on, Daisy, let's see if we haven't put a blush on your cheeks!'

She had turned her back on them while they spoke. She could feel the perspiration on her forehead. A strand of hair had worked itself loose. Surreptitiously she repaired herself, her eyes fixed on the flap of Anthony's pocket and the gritty swirl of black paint on which Mr Cryer had scratched his minuscule initials. The very idea of having to continue to sit three times a day in the shadow of the man to whom she had had to submit in so many other ways struck her as too abhorrent for words, and the prospect of liberty as sweet beyond measure. But she needed help. Life was asking too much of her if it thought she could break the mould unaided. She heard Mary enter the room. She swung round and in a voice that was only a little shrill said, 'At last! Whatever has kept you all?'

Nineteen

THE UNIVERSE was Mary Dipple's parish. Not only individuals but the whole human concept she visualised as her personal responsibility. Class, creed and sex were as meaningless in the glass-walled globe of her philosophy as birthmarks. She accorded all whom she met her genuine interest and sympathy. Each was somewhere between those immutable distance-posts, life and death. No one knew exactly where, any more than she did. All deserved a helping hand, a pat on the rump, a ripe red apple to cheer them down the course. Emotions of all moods and conjugations registered themselves in her sensitive mind with the same unerring clarity as a bat discerns a moth at dusk. And now, as she unhanded the fretful Mr Pumfrey, as she lifted the hem of her beige dress and placed the toe of her fat fawn slipper upon the tongue-and-groove floor of the Overmoor dining-room, as she saw before her the anxious faces of Daisy and Edward, and as she caught the tinge of hysteria in that 'At last!', she understood everything that had puzzled her during the summer. Her entire stock of womanly sympathy rushed out to embrace her friend.

'Humph. You might have made more of an effort with the flowers, Daisy. It is not every night we have a dinner like this, you know,' Anthony said as he surveyed the table.

'Pish and nonsense, Sir Anthony, how can you say such a thing? After a storm like the one Daisy had in her garden? I think what she has done is a miracle. Loaves and small fishes are nothing compared to finding ten cranesbills blooming in October.' She picked up one of Daisy's slender china flutes and held it between them.

'See, the common cranesbill. Unworthy of a place in a

gentleman's garden, you will say. Too vulgar, too blowsy, too like Mrs Dipple. But look at the richness of that colour, think of the imagination nature must possess. You could not copy it in a thousand years. Look at these veins racing down each petal. Such delicacy and yet such simplicity. So shame on you! You should be grateful to Daisy that we have any flowers at all instead of grumbling like an old bear. Now speaking of gardens, did I tell you that since we last met, Mr Dipple and I have paid a visit to Chatsworth to inspect His Grace's latest improvements . . . ?'

Replacing the flute on the table, she slipped an arm through his and in a manner of speaking, held him captive. Cuckoldry *après le façon de tout le monde* happened every day and if the rumours she had heard were true, he would be a cuckold in name alone, a cuckold *blanc*. So considered superficially, as a diversion enjoyed by mature people, it need not be the end of the world so long as Daisy and Edward were discreet. But in her heart she knew that nothing could ever be considered superficially where Anthony was concerned. His nature was too intricate and jealous. His brooding physicality frightened her. Whenever she looked closely into those puffy blue eyes of his, she felt as though she was peering into a dim, crypt-like laboratory full of ropes and pulleys and hissing instruments. But for Daisy's sake she must humour him. He must be distracted from what was happening between her and Edward. She pressed his arm against her ribs and gazing up at him, said, 'I hope you will not place a chasm between us when you send us to our seats.'

The evening had not commenced as Anthony had planned. Edward's tardiness, the look-who's-here contrival of his entrance, the grossness of his costume, the way he had looked at Daisy, all of these things had discountenanced him. And then Mary Dipple's claptrap about pikes and alligators and Millie Cuthbert's blubbering. His thunder had been stolen, the wind plucked from his sails even before he'd cleared harbour. Whose house did they think they were in? Who had invited whom?

With a wave of his hand he despatched Edward to the chair on Daisy's right. On her left he placed Fuscus and beside him Sam and Dickie. Robert Pumfrey he sat two seats to the right of Edward; and to the vacancy in between them he assigned Mary Dipple with a contemptuous flick of his forefinger that indicated only too clearly the extent of the chasm by which he wished to be separated from her. Then he sat down heavily between mousy Mrs Cuthbert and tart Mrs Pumfrey and signalled to Hucknall to charge the glasses.

So he thought he could silence her with a seat in no man's land! The Dipple nostrils flared. Even as Edward was easing the chair beneath her rumpled backside, she was pawing at the ground. And when she had shaken herself down and settled her napkin, she went at it as only she could until Hucknall, who was helping with the side dishes, could not believe that a single thought in existence remained unexpressed. Her eyes flashing, her earrings swinging, the opal brooch glittering at her throat and her tawny mound of hair quivering like a caramel pudding, she sprayed her squibs, conceits and anecdotes relentlessly around her as course followed course and she exchanged the baton of her marrow spoon for the baton of a soup spoon and the baton of her soup spoon for a baked onion on the baton of a three-tined fork which, leaning on her elbow, she flourished like a pompom in the vanguard of her sallies. She lobbed them over the nipplewort at Fuscus Quex-Parker, skimmed them through the crystalware into the parsleyed teeth of Sam Cuthbert, and bowled them to left and right so that they spun like marbles amid a dazzling trail of sparks and before long convinced even Daisy that life had its funny side as well.

Sam swore he would choke to death if she continued and threw off his coat. Fuscus lost control of himself over her story concerning the habits of a goat she had once kept and cried so much with laughter that Hucknall had to put his handkerchief by the fire to dry. Robert was wooed from his despondent cave, Edward was folded beneath her wing and Daisy was apprised that in Mary Dipple she had the staunchest ally in the world. As if some great sea battle was taking place, the shouts and exclamations reverberated round Daisy's end of the table, amongst the yellow nipplewort, the hawkbit and the tiny buds of trailing ivy. Diminishing waves broke upon the plumes of purple hair-grass in the centre. But no such merriment was heard around the bowl of livid hips and guelder berries that separated Mrs Cuthbert from Mrs Pumfrey and into which Anthony Apreece frowned with increasing disapproval.

Millie Cuthbert's chirrups went unheard as he mined his

marrow bones and drank his watercress soup. In vain did Constance blacken the characters of Mr Baker and Mr Maynard.

'I cannot think why you are telling me all this. It is not my affair if they wish to saddle their horses with thirty stones apiece,' he said curtly, glancing down the table at Daisy, wishing to surprise her in some intimate passage with Edward and give himself the pleasure of seeing guilt in her face. But she was talking to Fuscus; and Edward was laughing at some inanity of the old rhino with his head thrown back and his mouth open. How long could she keep it up? Suppose she talked them all under the table and never let him get off the mark? Well, he'd just have to shut her up. It was high time someone put her in her place. He scraped up the dregs of his soup and wiped a crust of bread round his plate. His coat of arms appeared, a stag's head picked out in gold, and beneath it, within a scroll, the motto of the Apreeces: *Nemo me deridet.* 'No one makes a monkey of me.' Ha! Very apt. So was he going to let himself be dispurposed by a lot of womanish prattle?

'And what is more,' Constance was insisting in clarion tones, 'the saddles were so heavy that five people were needed to place them on the horses' backs. Is that not conclusive evidence of the barbarity of the proceedings? Barbarity, Sir Anthony, wholesale barbarity is what I call it.'

'Never! Not for a moment!' he shouted. Heads turned. Mary skipped a bar. It felt as if a tourniquet somewhere inside him had been loosened. He sat up straighter and slid his eyes round the table like a fox sizing up a hen-roost.

'There's my answer for you. Does it fit your question, madam?'

But it was Fuscus who instead replied, 'Us philosophers here, that's to say Dickie and myself, find we have got ourselves stuck in something of a ditch. And the question that's concerning us is this – correct me if I am wrong, Dickie – does money have any moral weight, any significance over and above –'

'The moral weight of money? Good heavens, Fuscus, what a thing to talk about at dinner. Can't say I've ever thought about it. All I know for certain is that its absence is damnably bad for morale, like the absence of food or water –'

'Or fox-hunting!' tinkled Constance, who in response to a frown from Robert, now laid her conversation on a fresh tack. 'Life without fox-hunting? Unimaginable, you'll say, Sir Anthony, and I am with you every inch of the way. It may make me wet myself with fright, but without it winter would be a complete misery. It is an essential. You and I could no more exist without it than Robert could forgo counting his money.'

'Oh,' said Anthony, cocking his head, 'Robert does that often, does he?'

'He must, alas, or we sink. The poor man, you've no idea how consternated he gets when he tallies his figures. First they won't balance, and then it turns out that some scoundrel hasn't repaid what he should – which of course worries him *sick*. Really, Sir Anthony, you cannot conceive what a botheration it is owning a bank, how positively anxious-making it is for my dear husband and me. You go out of your way to be kind to people and tide them over a bad spot and then all they do is try to take advantage of you. I do think it *frightfully* unfair, don't you?'

Her words dropped like a stone into a rare pool of silence. Robert's chin shot up. A flake of partridge meat paused between his lips. He swallowed it without chewing and waggled the drumstick at his host.

'How do you say to that then, Sir Anthony? How say you to my Constance?'

'My dear fellow, I say anything's better than the sight of you sitting there with a face like a wet week.'

Just then Agatha pushed open the serving door for Hucknall, who marched in bearing a silver salver on which rested a sizzling carbonado of beef, slit and scored like a courtier's doublet and exuding the pungent smell of nutmeg. Behind him followed Elizabeth with a dish of roasted capon, which she set in front of Daisy.

Anthony jumped up. 'And now to the serious business of the evening!' He snatched the whetstone from Hucknall and began to sharpen the carving knife with long, even strokes.

'Come, Robert, I beg you to appear less sunken. All things come to those who wait: beef, capon, the devil – and who knows what else? But meanwhile we must feed you like a prince, for according to what your dear lady says, you bankers lead nervous lives and so require large ingestions of food and drink else you faint clean away and become vapour. Can't have a guest of mine turn to vapour. No room for vapour at Overmoor, is there, Daisy?'

Faster now he whistled the blade along the stone, flicking his wrist over with a twirl of lace at the end of each stroke.

'Where shall I start? Mrs Cuthbert, you have been very silent of late, so let the first choice be yours. Which shall it be, the roast buttock of old England or some dainty pale meat from the hand of my dainty pale wife?'

He bounced the tip of the blade on the glazed slope of the joint. Gad what an evening this was turning into! But would Ned ever understand how passionately he interpreted the duties of a landowner? Did he even know what the word duty meant?

'A capital choice! Do you prefer rouge or noir or somewhere in between? A slice of mulatto, perhaps? And some adipose tissue to go with it, crisp on one side only and guaranteed safe on the teeth? There! As you commanded, so it is done. Wait – I insist you have a spoonful or two of the juices to boost your fortitude during the marital procedures. What now, there is no call to blush like a maiden merely because – surely you cannot be thinking – Oh la! Mrs Cuthbert, you quite take my breath away . . .'

Playfully he engaged the table with his moist smile. And they all thought they were here to fill their bellies at his expense and provide company for a poor mite who'd lost his mummy. Hunting might be the sport of kings, but this – this was the sport of gods. His teeth gleamed. Again there was a hiss of steel on stone.

'Parsnips for Mrs Cuthbert, if you please, Agatha. Elizabeth, the condiment dish when the lady is ready. Fresh wine glasses for those drinking burgundy, Hucknall. Don't just stand there looking at me, man.'

He drew his thumb across the edge of the blade.

'Buttock for you also, Mrs Dipple? Grazed on clover, smooth as soap, firm as marble. Better you could not find in Valhalla. Assured to bring new-found joy to old loins and all adjoining departments. It is my particular recommendation for artistes requiring a post-recital rejuvenation. You are in a post-recital condition, may I hope?'

But Mary was having none of it. The idea of accepting food from him was as odious as the thought of being touched by him. She batted her eyelids demurely. If he didn't mind, she'd prefer a slice or two of Daisy's capon. Dickie provided quite enough excitement for the whatsits of an old trout like her.

The meats were carved and the wines poured. Anthony and Daisy sat down. Soon there were no sounds other than those of knives scraping on plates, the chink of glasses, logs toppling in the fireplace, the click of jaws, the creak of a chair leg; and flowing beneath it all a gurgling tide of gravy slurped, finger bowls splashed, burgundy slithered, 'More leeks, Mrs Cuthbert?', 'The horseradish, Sir Anthony?', tongues licking at fatty lips and the flutter of small belches.

Then it was done. The men groaned and wiped the grease from their cheeks. Limp and unprotesting, they fell back and stroked their stomachs as the white hands of Agatha and Elizabeth stole the plates from before them. Edward's stockinged foot nuzzled against Daisy's. Theirs had been a largely silent conversation; an affair of the eyes, a clandestine trade in unspoken questions and answers. He looked at her as she pensively dribbled the loops of her plain gold necklace through her fingers. She felt his toes on her instep, felt his foot glide between her oatmeal slippers and part her legs. Adultery! it whispered, and the tips of her ears grew pink.

Adultery! Was there no other word for it, nothing in the language that was less rancid? She disliked problems with hard edges. She ranked their gravity as a weather prophet does clouds. A decision on the sort of cake that old Mrs Scarlett should have for tea was a meagre puffy affair that no sooner showed on the horizon than it vanished. Engaging a new maid was a middling cloud, piebald in colour, that hovered pregnantly above the elm trees in the garden. But adultery was a thunder bag of unrelenting menace and negritude, and it frightened her. She shrank from its biblical harshness. She felt guilty merely by admitting the word into her thoughts. She considered it vindictive and inequitable that her passion for Edward, the first of such pure intensity that she had experienced for any man throughout her entire existence, should be rendered unclean by this bristling handful of syllables. It was not adultery that she wished to commit but love. But adultery was how the world would see it. Adultery and not love was the word from which people would wring every drop of malicious pleasure of which they were capable: the adultery of a woman. But how could she have love without it? How could she scale the wall of the forbidden garden without cutting herself to ribbons on the spikes of that hateful word?

This was what she had been thinking about during the meal. Anthony's sudden ebullience did not deceive her for a moment. She knew that mood of old. She was sure that he had something disagreeable up his sleeve. For a minute or two, as he drenched them with his charm, she wished that a good fairy would wave its wand and spirit her back to the safety of her room, to its calm, its dreams and solitary regrets. But then, as she carved the fowl for Mary, she was struck by a thought: what on earth was the point of having solitary regrets? (The slice of meat dangled mutely on her carving fork.) There was time enough for that when she was dead. She should take the corn in its fullness and repine, if she had to, for what had been done and not for what had been left undone. Why avoid the issue? She was thirty-six. Such lightning would never strike again. Was it sinful to escape from an unnatural husband? Was love so ignoble, so injurious to others, that it had to be quarantined like a disease? If love for another man was the only means of escape from such a grotesque union, could any reproach her for taking it? No one, not one person, could lay a finger of blame on her once they heard the truth of what she'd endured.

Of course Anthony would call it adultery and so would his friends. And their wives would have no choice but to agree with them. In private they might sympathise with her, might even be jealous of her happiness, but they would never dare show it and in time they too would attach themselves to the party of opprobrium. Moreover there were practical considerations involved of no small importance. But in general, insofar as the specific question of guilt versus justification was concerned, it was not, she assured herself as she watched Edward's fingers curl round the stem of his wineglass, his body that she ached for. Neither his body, nor his love, nor his protection. Neither revenge for the past, nor a deposit against the future. What she sought was escape. And since when had escape been a sin?

She pushed her sliver of capon around in the gravy and examined her reasoning with something of the awe that an explorer feels on striding out of a dense stand of timber and perceiving beneath him a valley of breathtaking fecundity. She held it against the light. She twisted it this way and that. From all angles it appeared healthy and sufficient. Two hours earlier, when Edward had declared himself so violently with his eyes, she had known fear. The realisation of a dream, which up to that very moment had occupied a pinnacle of impossibility in her mind, had taken her by surprise. It was as though a bomb had been thrust into her hands, a bomb crammed with razor-sharp words like adultery, dishonour, scandal, shame and humiliation, any one of which could disfigure her for the rest of her life. But now she saw it was not so. What his look had contained was nothing more sinful than the ladder down which she might scramble to the freedom that she deserved. And so the inky-purple cloud of adultery sailed out of her mind and was replaced by the crocus tints of rightfulness.

The tip of her nose began to twitch. 'So that's how it appears to me,' she said to Edward in a low voice and with a smile of great tenderness. Then she turned happily to Fuscus Quex-Parker on her left.

'What I cannot understand', he said, 'is why my own house-keeper is unable to produce meals like this. Is it because she is ignorant of her job and careless of my needs? Or is it because I do not make enough fuss of her? Anyway, it is neither here nor there, for I swear I shall not touch a morsel of food for a fortnight. I am positively engorged.'

'Oh but you cannot be! We are nowhere near finished. We still have Mrs Keech's burbage pudding before us. She has been steaming it since three in the afternoon. We cannot disappoint her. I beg of you to look around for an empty cranny.'

'*Prodigious!*' he murmured twenty minutes later as he slumped in his seat with his waistcoat bulging like a mainsail with a gale behind it. 'Prodigious! I'd horse to the end of the world for a pudding like that. Yes, madam, to the end of the world, wherever that might be. What a feast to remember!'

'And I'll tell you something else,' put in Edward, 'if I hear even a whisper that St Peter doesn't serve us burbage at least once a week, then I'm taking my business downstairs. So long as old Harry signs up to give me burbage and all the trimmings, he can pour molten lava down my ears until the crack of doom.'

'I did not think the devil was recognised at the temple,' Daisy said.

'So we return there again – what an invigorating morning that was! Far more so than anything I did on the Isle of Wight. I discover that Nature did not intend me for a painter. By the way, Edward, the word I was searching for was perlustration.'

Edward smiled at him and said, 'Of course we recognise the devil. But he is a rather weary old gentleman who spends his time playing chess against himself. He has long since lost interest in the world. It was too much of a struggle.'

'I think he also plays the clarinet, rather badly, on winter evenings,' Mary said.

'What is all this nonsense?' interrupted her husband. 'I thought we were discussing the burbage.'

'We are corrected, Daisy. We must leave the temple until our next visit. Tell me, Sir Anthony,' she said, raising her voice, 'what are the names of your milking cows? It is most agreeable to know we have enjoyed the produce of something still living.'

'Jonquil and Toplady, but I'm damned if I know which was responsible.'

'Excusing me, Sir Anthony, but I know something of that,' offered Hucknall unexpectedly from the sideboard, where he was buffing up the port glasses. 'See, it's always said by folks that the cow that's milked last gives the best cream. Now Mother Keech believes Toplady creams best, but Billy – he's the man who mostly does the milking – Billy and I knows otherwise. So when there's quality in for dinner', he hesitated, pinched between his natural curmudgeonliness and an urge to excite the souveniring spirit, 'when there's *real* quality in, like tonight for instance, we fetch her Jonquil's and tell her it's Toplady's. Then everyone's happy.'

'Hang on a moment,' said Sam Cuthbert, throwing down his napkin and struggling to his feet, 'hang on, everyone. You'd think we were having a tea party from all this talk about strawberries and cream. Now this was a noble pudding and no mistake but 'tweren't all that fancy stuff that's making us lick our chops. I'll tell you what it was. Suet! Yes, common suet! So enough about Tadpole and Daffodil or whatever their bloomin' names were – what was that? Oh all right, Tophole and Tranquil, makes no difference to me – get off, Millie will you? No need to look at me like that and spoil a man's fun just when he's getting going – and what I say is this: three cheers for the cow that gave us the suet and five for the farmer that gave us the cow!'

His face shone like a ripening mulberry. His gravy-speckled

stock was half-way round his neck. He thumped his glass on the table.

'Charge it, man, up to the brim! A toast! A toast to our hostess for being more lovely tonight than ever I did see her' – he fumbled a bow towards Daisy – 'and to Sir Anthony' – he swayed round – 'for his, dammit, what's a good word? For his beefery! That's it, beefery! Ladies and gentlemen, I give you beauty and beefery!'

He upended his glass. A trickle of wine glided out of the corner of his mouth. 'Pfah!' he said, wiping it away with his loosely buttoned shirtsleeve. Like a rosy-red angel he fell back into his seat and lay there, his arms dangling above the floor. He belched repletely. Millie clasped her hands and looked away. Daisy returned to fingering her necklace. Robert, who had drunk very little, eyed him pursily across the table. But the others chortled with the easy temper of satiety. Good old Sam, just the chap to set an evening alight!

Anthony flicked the crumbs off his coat. Hucknall placed the port decanter on the table and slipped out of the room.

'No, no, my dear,' he said, rising to his feet as Daisy gathered herself to take the ladies away, 'what I have to say concerns you as much as anyone. Now Sam here, a man I know to be a fine farmer and a fine judge of farming, was good enough a few moments back to comment favourably on my beefery, as he called it. He is someone who understands these things and I am sensible of his praise. But there is more to farming than feeding a cow, more than just hay or turnips. At heart it is the *land* that feeds our cattle. Yes, my friends, the land. It is this that produces the crops that fill their bellies and swells their flanks. Therefore I ask you to join me in a toast to the doctor whose philosophy contains it all. I give you John Locke!

'Now: you'll be asking yourselves what I'm getting at. It is this. The good doctor (may his memory be forever green), states that property is the mortar of civilisation. Unless we respect it and define its ownership by a code of laws we are no better than savages. Can anyone dispute this?'

He paused, one hand flat on the table, the other extended before him in an oratorical flourish. Constance and Millie folded their hands on their laps and gazed out to sea. Mary Dipple studied the ceiling. Robert looked into the depths of the purple hair-grass and rotated his thumbs.

'The spectacle of Sir Anthony Apreece as philosopher is an engaging one,' Fuscus said, arching his eyebrows.

'Thank you. Allow me then to develop my point. Property is the foundation upon which our world rests. Our civilisation, everything. On this, we are at one. But if this code of laws is to be upheld by all classes of men, then those without property must be able to see for themselves that those with it are treating it conscientiously and not in a manner likely to disadvantage them.'

'How so?' demanded Dickie. 'Are you saying that we should have our morals audited by the vicar before we can own a house?'

'Or before we take on a farm?' joined in Sam. 'The way I look at it, you either make the rent or get thrown out. Wherever would I be if my virtues were rung like a horseshoe? Out of the back door and pretty smartish, eh Millie, my love!'

'Ah yes, Sam, but there you're talking about a man who farms as a tenant. I was looking at it from the angle of a landowner, like Ned there at Winterbourne.'

'That's very decent of you to look over Winterbourne for me,' Edward said affably, licking a splash of port off one finger. 'Saves me the bother. Did you see anything you thought I should know about?'

Anthony turned pointedly to Fuscus. 'Consider this. Suppose some tramp is passing down a road and glancing over the wall, espies a fine herd of beeves or a bunchy crop of oats. He'll say to himself, "One day I'll get to eat those", and so walks on. This is a world he can accept. But if he looks over another wall and sees nought but thistles – if he were walking round Winterbourne, for example – he'll likely say, "Damned if I can eat those. Pish on this fellow, he stays in his bed all day, let another take his place who can manage things better." Now do you see my logic?'

'Poo, Sir Anthony, you can be a frightful bore when you put your mind to it. Do you suppose Edward grows thistles solely to annoy you?' Mary laid a sympathetic hand on Edward's arm. 'He's only been at Winterbourne a twelvemonth. It's Amos you should be growling at, not him. But if it so irritates you, I'll lend him my goats to chew them down. Mr Dipple will be in raptures. He can't stand them. Says they smell as bad as Mrs – no, I shall not speak ill of her. I owe her my recipe for gooseberry jam. Would you like to borrow Marigold and some of her friends, Edward?'

Edward laughed, the comfortable, honey-flavoured laugh of a man astride a fortune, a man in good health, a man who has invented love.

'I hope they also have a taste for docks and brambles,' he said into Mary's ear with a sort of faux confidentiality that was inexpressibly annoying to Anthony.

They were baiting him. No one had ever called him a bore. He had more intelligence in his little toe than the lot of them put together. Real intelligence. He had read his Locke. He knew his way round the three per cents as well as his own farmyard. His opinions on agricultural matters were solicited by famous people. No one mocked Anthony Apreece of Overmoor. He knocked back his port and scraped his sleeve across his mouth. The fibrils in his brain began to squirm like maggots in a jar.

'You're not listening to what I say. Laws are the very warp of our society. The life that we enjoy would not be possible without them. When they're abused, they fall into disrepute. And when they are no longer respected, what happens next? Ha! Now I have your ears. So listen well. What we shall get is not the rule of honest, decent people such as those we have now, but the rule of the mob, of the basest elements of society. Imagine them, ladies, open your lily-white minds to your fates as they creep through the night to our lonely farms. Their eyeballs glint in the moonlight. Torches are thrown, our barns go up in flames, singeing horses scream. The servants fly. Your man, your Amos Paxton, goes out to parley on the lawn where but a few hours earlier you tapped a croquet ball. He falls. Your husbands and sons are done to death as you watch. Then you are alone, pink and mewling in your nightgowns. You scream for the magistrate. The law, where is the law? But Mr Pumfrey cannot help you. Him they have hanged first. And now the vermin start to climb the stairs towards you –'

'What tosh –'

'It is not a dream, Mrs Dipple. It is the fate that awaits us inescapably unless we who own the land tend it in a manner that is respected by those who do not. Land that is not productive is an evil. That is why I say that the thistles at Winterbourne, and all the other filth that Ned Horne lets sprout beneath his nose, are a threat not only to our property but to our very lives. To our lives, Mrs Dipple. Are you such a fool that you do not understand me now?'

He's mad, Robert thought, in a moment he will become violent like Sophia. Fearfully he cast his memory down his balance sheet.

'It's all far too deep for me,' Sam Cuthbert said with a yawn. 'Come on, squire, let's talk about things a simple fellow like me can twig. Fox-hunting, women, politics, something uncomplicated.'

'Well spoken, Mr Cuthbert. Mary, Constance, Millie, when men have reached the stage of believing that women are uncomplicated, it is the signal for us to retire.' Daisy stood up firmly. She understood enough of what was happening to know that nothing would stop him so long as he had an audience. 'Do not linger, Anthony. Constance has promised to sing for us.'

'Stop! Does your husband so embarrass you that you must scuttle for the door if he speaks his mind? Do you think I've lost my reason?'

'Why, yes,' Mary murmured without causing herself surprise. She too stood up.

'That I do this out of pleasure? I tell you all, I say it to your faces, property is – a – sacred – trust.' Between each word he crashed his fist on to the table. Spittle flew from his mouth. Daisy looked helplessly at Edward. His elbow rested on the table. His head, angled quizzically to one side, lay in the cup of one palm. His first thought had been: he has guessed, it is jealousy that speaks. But now he thought: can he really want my land so badly?

'And you, Ned Horne, are not fit to hold it. Not fit, d'ye hear? You are a leper among us. I have tried to befriend you, God alone knows how much I have tried these past months – but you have no interest. A century will not be time enough to put Winterbourne to rights. And while you wamble in your pleasure grounds and bring shame on us all, we go trembling in dread of our lives.' He speared a finger down the table. 'Only one person will be to blame if we all fall with pitchforks through our bellies: Ned Horne, the feckless lord of Winterbourne. I tell you straight, you have but one choice unless you wish to take us all down with you.'

'And what might my only choice be, Anthony?' he asked emolliently. Come the morning he'd probably have forgotten all about this outburst, like when he'd laid into Arthur Smith and ridden off whistling.

'You must sell Winterbourne.'

'But what if I don't wish to sell?'

'There is no alternative. As a man of honour, you are obliged to sell.'

'And if I have no honour?'

'It don't signify. You must sell so that we may live. We have been through all that. It is your duty to sell.'

'But Anthony, where shall I find a man to buy thistles?'

'You are looking at him. I am your buyer. As you have a duty, so do I. It is at our peril that we shirk our responsibilities.'

Anthony kicked back his chair and strode round the table. His hands dug into Edward's shoulders. His voice was silky in his ear. 'I asked it before and you declined. Now I ask it again and I ask it before witnesses. Your price, Ned, you have but to name it and you shall have it tomorrow. Winterbourne is no place for you. Your friends are in London. Sell it to me and go.'

Robert could restrain himself no longer. He shot to his feet, oblivious to everything except the crisis at hand. His skin hung grey and loose upon his face.

'How can you say such a thing? It is not Edward but I who should be paid tomorrow. It is the date we agreed. By the last stroke of midday and not a minute later.' He flung off Mary's hand and seizing Anthony by the shoulder, shook him violently. 'It is me you must pay first, me, unless you wish to have your name posted among the defaulters on the Exchange with all the common mountebanks of London. It is I who have the first claim –'

'Tomorrow, in a month, in a year, it makes no odds, Robert,' Edward said, forcing the two men apart as he pushed back his chair. 'You must believe me, Anthony, that when I say I have no wish to sell Winterbourne now or at any time, to you or to another, I am speaking without guile or equivocation. My husbandry can only improve. The mob will not invade and I shall not sell.' He touched him lightly on his upper arm. 'So why do we not all retire to the drawing-room? Mrs Pumfrey has an excellent voice. Then Robert need not do further injury to his temper and when we go to our beds we shall be able to dream in peace about Mrs Keech's burbage pudding.'

A murmur of agreement wafted round the room. Enough is enough, it said.

Anthony stared glassily around at the bobbing heads. His cheeks were the colour of old snow. His brain felt as thick as midnight. Swarms of coal-red insects were racing round the convex slopes of his skull, scratching and squeaking and jabbering with impatience. His mouth opened and shut. He flexed his fingers.

'You shan't leave,' he shouted, 'I won't let you,' and he ran stumbling to the door, hurling the chairs aside. He crouched with his back against it. His chest was heaving. A drizzle of sweat stood out on his forehead.

'Do I have to say it all again? Has not one of you understood? It's Ned's duty to sell to me, his *duty*, do you hear? Does the word mean nothing to any of you? Fail me in this and the rabble will be on us before we know it. You know I'm right. I've always been right. Look at Overmoor, look at the prices my animals fetch at market. Look at them. Huge. Huger than the sky. What more do you want for proof? Come on, let's get it over with so Ned and I can settle up. I can't go through the whole thing again. I'm not strong enough. God knows but I support the world as it is.

'Here, Sam, come and stand at my side. You are my friend. Now's the time to show your colours. What's that you say? Too fuddled? Well, pish on the Cuthberts and their house. Pish on every one of you. But it's all one in the end. I'm not short of friends.'

His eyes trawled round the room, lingering on each face in turn.

'I have Robert there for instance. Robert wants something from me. So speak up, man. Tell Ned loud and clear where his duty lies.'

Robert had known all along it would come to this; that before the night was out he would be forced to choose between a debtor he would alienate at his peril and a depositor whose faithfulness was imperative. On the one hand, Scylla: on the other, Charybdis. Reefs and a boiling tide whichever way he steered. He reviewed his balance sheet for the last time. He looked across at Edward, young, constant and wealthy. He looked at his wife. He looked at Anthony crouching at the door – and made his judgement.

'Give me my money by midday tomorrow or I shall have you

posted at the Exchange. The choice is yours.' He bowed to Daisy. 'Come, Constance, it is time we returned to our children.'

Arm in arm they marched on the door. They reached it and stood breast to breast against Anthony. A pin could have been heard to drop. For long seconds they stared at each other. Anthony blinked hard, twice. He shook his head rapidly from side to side as if to dislodge something. He put one finger to his eye and wiped it around the eyelid. He touched each of his silver coat buttons in turn. Then he unwrapped his face and with a familiar smile said, 'So soon, Robert? Must you really go so soon?' He flung open the door and shouted for Hucknall. 'Now on no account are you to forget your wig, Robert. On a night like this, a chap could catch his death without a wig.' He clapped him on the back. He pressed Constance's hand to his dry lips. Then he whirled round. 'Shall we settle down for a nightcap or play a charade? What do you all say?'

Twenty

THE HOUSE was quiet. Daisy was nowhere to be seen. He drank a cup of chocolate and went down to his business room. On the desk was his map, in the same position as he had left it the night before. He pulled up his chair and glowered at it. He felt crabby. He had a headache. This red line round the boundaries of Winterbourne, did that now represent a fact of ownership or did it not?

(He looked out of the window as Clayton rode past, coming in from exercising his grey cob. He was sorry that it showed no signs of lathering. He felt in a mood to shout at somebody.)

No, he had to say that he did not think it did. That would have been something that surely he would have remembered. He would not have forgotten buying Winterbourne, by God he would not. And then, with a jolt as if he'd been stung by a wasp, he remembered why he had failed: because Pumfrey – out of nothing but personal animus against him, there could be no other reason – had cut him short at the very moment of truth. The man was muck. God, his head hurt. No one makes a monkey of me, that was the motto of the Apreeces. But Pumfrey had. He swept the map to the floor. There was gratitude for you. After all he'd done for him, after all the business he'd put his way – and now this. Well, he'd teach him a lesson. He'd remind him who was who around Buxton. He'd show him who was cock of the heap. Today, while he still felt ill. That'd be the tonic for him.

He ran upstairs, shouted to Mrs Keech for a pitcher of water, drank it at a go and went to the hall to put his boots on. He sat in the armchair by the stove and, resting his ankle on his knee, kneaded his toes. But that would be comical, to put the parson up to it, to send in the man who believed emotion mightier than reason. What delicious irony! It'd be around the town in a flash. Robert wouldn't make the same mistake twice, no by Harry he would not. He jumped up with one boot on and hopped to the front door, where he yelled for Clayton to get the saddle back on his horse that instant.

It was a calm, cold, autumnal morning. He found Chiddlestone exactly where he had expected, sauntering home for his midday meal. The lane was deep in leaf-wrack, the hedges afire with hawthorn berries. Jackdaws were clamouring in the thin air. A chalky veil hung over the land.

'Oh and by the way,' he said after a bit, thinking to himself how abjectly the vicar sat his horse, 'I don't know if you've heard the rumour –'

'What rumour's that, Sir Anthony?' asked Chiddlestone, poking out his neck. He liked to bring home the odd morsel of gossip for Elspeth.

'Well, nothing is proven, you understand. I want that to be quite clear. There is no hard evidence. But I hear –'. Anthony nudged his cob forward so they were knee to knee. He looked guardedly up and down the lane. His voice dropped. 'But I hear in town – well, people are saying that the bank's having trouble meeting its obligations.' He watched the parson's adam's apple bobble like a mouse beneath a piece of sacking. 'Not that one should pay too much attention to what people say. And of course Robert is an old, old friend of mine. But a man like yourself, Digbeth, who has only his stipend to live off and must lay down a provision for his old age . . . Anyway, I just thought you should be aware of the rumour in case it affects you.'

Chiddlestone deliberated. If he rode into Buxton immediately . . . But Mrs Tangly clearly had not long to live; he had promised he would call on her again within the hour. It would bring comfort to her family. It was his Christian duty. Mammon should wait on man, not man on mammon. Tomorrow would be soon enough so long as no one else knew. They talked on for a few minutes.

Then Anthony turned for home, lying back in his saddle, hump-shouldered. Sprawling white towers of travellers' joy passed slowly by. A flock of redwing chattered among themselves as they flew diagonally across the lane between two elm trees. He heard the thump of a billhook and a couple of fields away saw a spiral of smoke rising where hedge-layers were burning elder lop. Of course Chiddlestone would horse it back like Jehu to his wife and confessional. He'd blabber everything before he even had his boots off. Would they keep it secret? At least until they'd got their money out. Then Robert would come running, full of bluster about having him posted at the Exchange. Which he never would, not unless he wanted to forgo all chance of being repaid. He decided to go and inspect his new plantation to see if the rabbits had caused much damage in the summer.

Daisy was in the kitchen when Anthony rode off.

'That pudding last night –' she said.

'Not a bit came back –'

'Not a bit of your cooking *ever* comes back, Mrs Keech.'

'Gentlemen like that sort of thing. They can't be doing with them fancy items.'

He trotted past, suddenly huge outside the window. The road being a little high at that point, he could have looked down into the kitchen and waved, or tipped his hat. But he didn't. His nose remained triangular, a dark fin guiding him to she knew not what destination. She was glad he was out of the way.

She left Mrs Keech and walked through the house, singing to herself in a low, smooth, rich voice. Elizabeth, who was doing the drawing-room, sat back on her heels and smiled as Daisy passed the door. Miss Hoole heard her climbing the stairs. She too smiled, as from her lookout point in her narrow attic chamber, she sipped her mid-morning chocolate and watched Sir Anthony kick his horse into a canter.

But when she got there, Daisy forgot why she had gone to her room. Imperturbably, holding up her cream woollen dress in both hands, pointing her slippered toes like a dancer, humming a tune that was full of soft, carefree mounds of notes, she descended the stairs and entered the drawing-room.

'Mr Horne left last night without taking his slippers. If he should call before I return, pray tell him that I can be found in the garden.' Again Elizabeth smiled to herself.

Daisy repinned her hair in the hall mirror and, putting on a coat and her overboots, went out.

She was sitting in the gazebo when Edward arrived. She heard the sound of voices in the drawing-room. Elizabeth threw open the window and called to her, laughing as Sixpence tried to wriggle under her arm. Daisy rose and went to the wicket gate.

With a careful distance between them, they walked round inspecting shrubberies which neither could see distinctly. He kept his hands behind his back. She was hatless. Her cheeks were flushed below the white hummocks of a sleepless night, and her eyes larger than usual, or so it seemed to Edward.

'There is something about you this morning that convinces me you have Russian blood. I cannot be particular. It may be your costume, or the slant of your cheekbones. It may only be the smell of autumn around us, but there is something foreign and romantic that I detect in you, a dash of Prince Thiski or Thatski showing itself in the Garland blood.'

'That is not very flattering. All the Russian women I have seen in pictures have been fat and ugly. They have large feet.'

'Ah, but this is a picture from a different book altogether. It shows you speeding over a snowy plain in a little hooded sleigh, a pack of wolves snapping at your heels, a crow crouching atop a fingerpost –'

'What does it say?'

'On the weather side, which I can scarcely read it is so caked in ice, it says Moscow 304. And on the other, burnt into the wood in black capitals, it says, The Temple: No Distance.'

'That is strange, to find it so accounted on a Russian steppe. But tell me, what of the wolves? Are they shaggy and fearsome with eyes like hot coals? Is their breath warm on my neck?'

'They are licking their lips. None of them can remember such a toothsome traveller. They cannot believe their luck.'

She pushed her lips up at him in a little pout. 'Shall I be eaten, then? Is that what it must come to?'

'A man is riding hard to your rescue. He is on the other side of the slope from you, out of your sight. If you stood up in the sleigh and waved a handkerchief tied to your whip, he would probably just be able to see it.'

'But will he reach me in time? Do you think I should scream?'

'It is not easy to scream sitting down. Besides a wind has got up. He might not hear you.'

She ran the tip of her forefinger down the shiny groove of a laurel leaf. 'So what must I do?'

'You must be bold. It will be horrible. It will be the worst time in your life. Only if you have faith –'

'We must go where people can see us.' She studied her brown boots as they strolled up the lawn. To their right, so temptingly, the gazebo beckoned in the corner of her eye. But it would never do, not with all the servants watching. 'I agree. But do we mean the same thing by faith?' They halted in the centre of the lawn.

'For my part I mean a certainty, an omnipotent conviction that something which cannot be seen, which cannot be touched, which has no concrete presence, is so vital to one's life that one would go to the stake for it. That one would sooner die than be without it.'

'Would you go to the stake for me, Edward?'

'Yes.' Yes, he wanted to shout, I would go barefoot among cobras to have your nose twitching beside me for the remainder of my life.

Elizabeth pulled up the window and knocked the broom against the sill more vigorously, perhaps, than was warranted.

'We must walk forward. Point at your feet. Pretend you are making a joke about your slippers. Laugh, wave your arms around. What colour is your faith?'

'It is not blue or red. It is quiet. It does not argue or raise its voice. But it is everywhere, like the air. I do not think it has any colour.'

'Can it live anywhere?'

'It can live wherever its owner lives. No, I do not mean owner, I mean some other word. I do not think one can own faith. But it cannot live in two places at once, at the temple and here – do you trust me, Daisy?'

'Sixteen years ago I gave my trust to a man. I have regretted it ever since.'

Again they halted. Her eyes held his, searching them. Then, with the poignancy of a woman who is not afraid to know that within the petals of love there lies, coiled like an asp, the certainty of pain, loneliness and misery at some point before the final one, she smiled, hesitantly at first, and then with a brimming surge that swept up to and into his very core.

'I will take you away. We shall live as man and wife in London, abroad, wherever you say –'. He seized her arm just above the wrist. His taut face was inches from hers –

Anthony rounded the corner of the plantation and sitting very still on his horse stared down at the figures on the lawn below him.

When he left Overmoor, Edward rode to the Scarletts to look at their new litter of puppies and to show Sixpence to Lucy. David had returned the night before from a turnpike mission.

Afterward the two of them lay on the drawing-room floor with Lucy and her crayons and played a game that involved drawing the likenesses of the queens regnant of England and then guessing which was which. Since the supply was quickly exhausted and Lucy was not, they set their hands to Eleanor of Aquitaine and Catherine II of Russia.

'That's not Eleanor,' Lucy cried, snatching Edward's sheet of paper and scornfully perusing the oval head, the pinned-back hair and the wide-winged nose. 'She was poky and spiteful. Mummy, look, Mr Horne's drawn a picture of Lady Apreece.'

Old Mrs Scarlett placed her embroidery frame on her knees and looked speculatively at Edward over lowered glasses.

'Oh, I don't think there's at all a resemblance,' Edward said uncomfortably.

'Oh yes there is,' Lucy said, jumping up and carrying her trophy to Emily. 'Look, Mummy –'

'Shall you and I go and shoot some wood pigeons?' David said tactfully.

'Absolutely not,' barked Mrs Scarlett, 'they'll have been feeding on Anthony's turnips. It gives them a taste I find positively revolting. We have perfectly good food in the house without them, is that not so, Emily?'

Indeed it was. Emily spoke to Lucy (who for the rest of the afternoon would not even as much as look at Edward); the men went off to play billiards; and over an excellent meal Edward stoutly resisted their efforts to prise from him any details as to what had happened at Anthony's dinner. All he would allow was that he had been so fuzzled by the brilliance of the evening as to leave his slippers behind.

David said he needed the exercise and so accompanied him back to Winterbourne. But he wouldn't come in. 'I think you have someone already waiting for you. I see young Paxton over there trying to pretend it isn't urgent.'

'Great God alive!' Edward exclaimed, staring open-mouthed at Davie. 'Pumfrey? The Bank of Buxton? I don't believe a word of it.'

'Father said for me to tell you as soon as you got home. Parson's wife's full of it. Been in and out of mother's all afternoon like a housefly.'

'But Robert Pumfrey? Pumfrey of all people? I don't believe it. I just don't believe it.'

'That's what Mother told Father and what I was to tell you.'

'Then we'll go and see him ourselves.' They walked down the hill.

'It's not possible, Amos. Someone must have confused the names. It must have been old Humphrey, the candlemaker next to Kitty Prodger.'

'T'aint the name Mrs Chiddlestone gave.' Amos's rheumy eyes looked obstinately into Edward's. 'And anyway, who'd care if Andrew Humphrey had run out of blunt?'

'It was Mr Pumfrey all right,' affirmed Mary Paxton, putting the kettle on the trivet. 'She must have said his name a dozen times or more. Pumfrey this, Pumfrey that, Pumfrey the other. And my! was she in a state, eyes jumping out of her head, wouldn't sit down but had to go to the window every second minute as if she expected the gentleman himself to ride past.'

Up and down the small, square, dark-beamed room Edward paced, dodging the bundles of herbs that hung from the rafters. The fire popped and spat. The kettle came to the boil. One by one he searched the stolid faces of the Paxtons. Sympathy he saw but not doubt. They knew well enough what they had heard.

'But where did Mrs Chiddlestone get the information? We must look at it from all sides.'

'It was the parson himself who told her,' Amos said.

'And he had it direct from a local gentleman,' Mary added.

'Who? Which gentleman?' (Though he knew the answer beyond a shadow of doubt.)

'Wouldn't say. Only that he was one of the best thought of in the county. Said the parson had been sworn to secrecy.'

The prospect of being parted from a substantial slice of his inheritance before he had touched a groat of it struck Edward to the quick. Anthony out rumour-mongering was a deep business. A trickle of people after their money could soon become a rush in a small place like Buxton. It didn't matter whether the rumour was true or not: it would still be believed.

It was obvious after last night why Anthony had done it. It was so obvious it was ridiculous. But outsiders would know nothing of his motive. All they'd hear was the scurrying footfall of rumour, exaggerated by a thousand echoes along the way. They wouldn't care where it came from or about the small, mean purpose for which it had been conceived. They'd reason as he was doing and slink to the bank as fast as they could. No warning shots, no alarums, just a prayer they got there before their neighbours heard, before the money ran out.

Constance could please herself: his good nature had its limits. But what of Robert? He was a friend and with friendship went obligations. The instant he thought this, it struck him as false. Friendship was a condition entered into freely: obligations smacked of a contract, of duties. If Robert had been imprudent in his lending, if he was unable to repay him, would he remain his friend? Of course not. And if he did repay him? It would be grudgingly, suspiciously, in bad faith. It was the way of mankind with money. And anyway, what obligation would Robert feel towards *him*? None. All that would concern him was saving his own skin. The words of warning of Nicholas Hawkesworth returned to stab him.

'I have money with Mr Pumfrey, Amos old friend, and I do not choose to be parted from it. This is what we shall do . . .'

At dawn the next morning, beneath a cold but open sky, the smaller of the two farm wagons rumbled out of Winterbourne yard. The lanthorn stuttered in its bracket as the horses took the bit. Amos walked alongside them until they reached the foot of Ladysway.

'Remember now, son, you're to wait at the Green Man until Mr Horne arrives with Bill Whitehead. If Arthur comes out and asks what you're up to, tell him you're on the way to fetch a load of roof slates. Now off with you and mind you bring the horses back safe.' He clapped the nearest one on the rump. Far out in the valley an owl cried. Davie raised a gloved hand in salute and clicked his tongue. The swingle bar tensed. The horses leaned into their harness and began to ascend Ladysway.

Twenty-one

IT WAS Jack Long's plump black posterior, straining at the seat of his breeches as he rattled up the fire, that Edward saw first. His topcoat was still folded across the counter. He looked over his shoulder and straightened, the poker in his hand. His face was pink from the heat. His few strands of hair lay flat across his skull like seaweed upon a boulder.

'Winterbourne's early on the road, Mr Horne! Why, it's only a few seconds since I opened the doors.' He replaced the poker in the hearth and hung up his coat. 'Now, that looks more businesslike, don't it? One can never be too tidy in an occupation such as this, I always think, or folks may get the wrong impression. No one cares for slapdash near their money. So I like to keep things just so from the very start. Only this morning you've been and caught me out. Now, if you'll just give me a moment, I'll tell Mr Pumfrey you're here. Oh, hello Bill . . .'

'A seat by the fire and he'll be happy enough till I'm finished,' Edward said.

'Just as you say, Mr Horne.'

On his pear-shaped legs, his buckled shoes clacking on the tiles, Jack opened the counter gate and disappeared into Robert's office. Edward leaned on the counter and dibbled at the balance of the set of coin scales beside him. He read the table of weights that was pinned to the lid of their box. For use with gold coins only. Excellent. So there'd be no nonsense about saying he didn't keep any.

'Edward! The gate for Mr Horne please, Jack. His hat and gloves too. Then send word to Mrs Pumfrey to lay one extra for coffee. Come along in, Edward.'

Robert stood dangling his spectacles by his office door. His eyes were smudged and wary. The two settled themselves, Edward rather upon the edge of his chair. He was wearing a plain buff coat and drab breeches. A boil was forming in one nostril.

The opening gambits were exchanged. The weather, that dinner at Overmoor ('extraordinary performance, can't think what came over the man,' Robert said, testing the water), Sixpence, Constance, young Andrew Pumfrey and the tribulations of learning ... Like sentries they circled their ramparts, cocking an ear whenever an unusual sound emerged from the conversation. Does he come as friend or foe? Robert asked himself, peering into the shadows. Has he an argument that I have not anticipated? Edward wondered. With fumbles and feints from both sides, the conversation was manoeuvred into a defile from which only one road debouched.

'The fact is', Edward said, 'that I recently deposited some money with you.'

Ah-ha, thought Robert, uncrossing his ankles and wincing. It was his experience that the word deposit was only ever used by his clients when they wished to withdraw their money. When they placed it with him, it was always a loan.

'Indeed you did, Edward, and it caused no small gratification to Constance and myself that you should find the Bank of Buxton worthy of your confidence. Let us see now –'. He flicked open a ledger. 'H for Handyman, Harris, Hewer, Hodberry – not one of my most reliable customers let me say, quite *entre nous* – Hodgkinson – now there's a different kettle of fish for you. Farms out on the Bakewell road, big belly, laughs a lot, wife has a fine singing voice, something similar to my Constance's but with a rather affected vibrato and less finesse in the lower registers, even though I say it myself – no? don't know him? Then I shall effect an introduction. We'll get you both over one Sunday ... Hopkins, Horne. Here we are. Horne, Edward, Winterbourne House. Principal plus sixty-two pounds, thirteen shillings and fivepence accrued in interest, make-up day Friday last. Have a look if you wish, I believe you will find it all in order.' He tapped the page with authority and sat back with his hands folded across his stomach.

'I'm sure that it is exactly as it should be. But it is not to check your arithmetic that I am here.'

'Oh?'

'It is to make a withdrawal.'

'But of course. I understand perfectly. Your roofers cannot live off fresh air. They have families to feed like all of us. Ten pounds in mixed coin, something of that order?'

'I have not explained myself, I fear. I have come to withdraw it all.'

'All of it? You mean . . . well, that's rather different.' Robert shifted in his chair. He picked up a stick of red sealing wax and twirled it between his fingers. 'Decidedly different. Is there some aspect of our service that has caused you dissatisfaction? Has Mr Wiseman been courting you, may I enquire? You'll find it a plaguey business traipsing down to Derby every time you need a few pennies. Tell me about it, Edward, as between friends.'

'There is really nothing to say, only that my situation demands that I must withdraw my capital from your firm immediately. It is the sole purpose of my visit.'

'But you must have a reason. I cannot believe that you got out of bed and said, Oh, I've got nothing better to do so I think I'll take my money out of the bank this morning.'

'It is for personal reasons. I really cannot add anything more.'

'I see. Well, this is a surprise, I must say. And by no means an agreeable one. No banker enjoys having a client remove his money without knowing why. Least of all a friend. For I count you as such, you know, Edward. Remember that at Overmoor I had the chance to take Anthony's side against you – but did not. I had the choice – but I spurned him. And now you wish to be unfaithful, is that it?'

'You are making it sound as though I had come with the intention of ruining you. It is not so, I assure you.'

'So you say. But Buxton is a small town. Fewer than a thousand people live here. They will soon get to hear of this. They will talk. They will tell all the farmers around. Nothing in the world will prevent people talking about other people's money. They will ask, Why has Mr Horne thought fit to lift his money from the Bank of Buxton? What does he know that I do not? Should I not do likewise? You must realise that there is more to it than perhaps you had allowed.'

'They will hear nothing from me. You have my word for it.'

'You are kind. But you have more faith in the human race than I.'

Robert went to the window. He had expected some form of reprisal from Anthony, some further intransigence over his debts. But this was a stab in the back that he had never dreamed of. The entire deposit. He did not have it. He knew exactly what sums he had left and this was not among them. In March, when Hodgkinson's loan became repayable, things would be different. But today his vaults did not contain what Edward Horne was demanding.

In the stable courtyard below him, a boy with a grazed knee was playing hopscotch with three friends. He could hear them shouting and arguing. A red-hatted flower vendor was going through her blooms, tying the fresh ones with twine and dropping those that were spent in front of her dog, a white bull terrier with a pirate's patch round one eye. Melson, his groom, led out Luna. He was in his shirtsleeves. He placed a hand on her forequarter and began to curry-comb her with a long, raking movement of his hairy forearm. The horse's skin flickered with pleasure. He saw her eyes start to close, her head move slightly to catch the full warmth of the early sun.

'It is scarcely believable –'. He wanted to make some sarcastic remark about Edward continuing to use the services of Melson.

'That I should be doing this?'

Robert wheeled and turned on Edward the glittering eye of a fishwife. Was he callous enough to see it through? What could he threaten him with?

'Yes, that a friend should enter my office and declare he has no confidence in me.'

'That is how it must seem, I suppose.'

'Does friendship mean nothing to you then?'

'It's no use, Robert, my mind is made up.'

'So you are fixed in your determination to withdraw?'

'Yes.'

'There is nothing I can say that will persuade you otherwise?'

'Nothing. I am sorry, but it has gone beyond that point.'

'Very well. I see I have no alternative but to accept it as one of the knocks of the trade. As someone once said to me, Life can be a hard turnip.' He took up his pen. 'I shall mark your account "Notice of withdrawal given October the 24th" – I think that is the date – and if you present yourself at the counter in exactly six months, my cashier will have it ready for you.'

'Six months? What is this about six months?'

'It is the customary period for notice of withdrawal.'

'But you said nothing of this when you took my money. The conditions were quite clear. Repayment of capital on demand was what you said and that is what I am doing, presenting my demand. It is today that I must have it, not in six months.'

'Come now, there is no need to flash your eyes at me as though I were a common thief. Six months is the standard practice for sums of this magnitude, I assure you. Ask your Mr Hawkesworth if my word is not sufficient. Six months and in banknotes is the best I can do for you.' Robert leaned back, watchfully.

'Banknotes? Banknotes be damned. Gold is my entitlement and that is what I shall leave with. What good are your notes to me? How can I know that you won't cancel them the instant I have left? Who will I find to give me value for Bank of Buxton notes?'

'Ah, do we draw a little closer to the truth? Do I detect the stink of rumour-mongering? It's Apreece who's behind this, isn't it? I suppose the two of you have cobbled up some arrangement whereby I'm to be brought to my knees so that he can buy my bank cheaply and then exchange it for your land. Is that what all this is about? Don't answer me, I can see through you as easily as a pane of glass . . . Well, you can wish for whatever you like. Wish to fly to the moon if it pleases you. But it's banknotes you'll get in six months and nothing else.'

'Then why do you keep gold scales on your counter?'

'Why do you think?'

'To weigh gold for your customers, why else?'

'Ha! A fine banker you'd make . . . I'll tell you why, because there are always young fools like you who need to be impressed. For the same reason I have oak wainscoting and all the other bottles of smoke that go with being a moneylender.'

Immediately he regretted the remark. Both men sat down again, their faces suffused with blood, of a sudden aware they had been shouting at each other.

'I apologise, Edward. I should not have said that. The fact is that Sir Anthony did not make the repayment that was due yesterday and after his unpleasantness to me at dinner, I find myself somewhat overwrought.'

There was a knock on the door and Jack Long stuck his head into the room. 'The Reverend Chiddlestone is here to see you, sir. Say's it's on a matter of the greatest urgency.'

There were footsteps behind him and in bustled Constance Pumfrey with the coffee tray.

'Coffee, gentlemen,' she chirped, placing it on a side table. 'I know how you working men must have a little stimulant to get you through to luncheon. Shall I pour for you, my dear? Oh, but how serious you both look – is anything amiss? Would you like me to retire?'

Robert put an arm round his wife's shoulder.

'On the contrary, you could scarcely have arrived at a more opportune moment. Edward and I have just completed our business – is that not so, Edward? We have inspected our affairs and find they are concluded. Of course you must stay. See, Edward, she expects it: she has placed a third cup on the tray. It is the prospect of our company that draws her. Is that not flattering?'

A mulish look settled on Edward's face. No, he would not be seduced by a lady's chatter. He would not let them burden him with guilt by talking up the sweetness of their children, by reminding him of their blue eyes, their fluffy hair, their innocence. What was the expression that Robert had just used? Life was a hard turnip. And well it might be. But he was damned if he was going to be the one to eat it.

'I regret infinitely to be obliged to say so, madam, but your continued presence would be malapropos in the extreme. Despite what your husband has told you, our business is far from complete.' He crossed the room and with a cursory bow, opened the door for her.

She set down the coffee pot. Slowly she straightened her back, presenting to him in turn her curving eyebrows, the fine-boned nose that she had from her mother, and her powerful chin. She flexed her fingers and placed them round her waist, thumbs to the fore. He bowed again. 'If you please, Mrs Pumfrey.'

'If you please . . . la, such politesse I am granted now.' Tartly, throwing out her feet, swinging her new bustle from the hips, she stepped with deliberation across the floor and halted, less than a yard in front of him. The stir of her dress, which was a strong pink with a thick grey stripe, ceased. Robert sat down heavily, his coffee cup chattering to its saucer.

'Is my dress not charming?' she said, so unexpectedly that Edward, who had been bracing himself for a broadside, let go of the door handle and took a pace backwards. His shoulder brushed the swaggery of Robert's wall mirror. The door swung to with a click. 'Is it not charming?' she repeated, extending the folds gracefully. 'Or do you have eyes only for those milder shades such as I recall Lady Apreece was wearing the other night? I declare the colour suited her admirably. It took years off her age, whole years. Why, she looked almost sprightly in that dress of hers, would you not say that too, Mr Horne, that she looked like someone who has rediscovered her youth? Perhaps – this is what I thought – her air is that of a woman who is readying herself –'. She advanced a step, pinning him more firmly in the corner. 'One gets to recognise the expression after a while. But for whom? Oh, I searched and I searched that table for her suitor. Could it be Mr Quex-Parker? But he is so retiring in his ways and, to be frank, I could not see him as my lady's gallant. Or could it be, I asked myself –'. Her eyes grew bold. She lined up a jabbing forefinger beside her nose and aimed it at him. 'Or could it just be –'

With an angry flush on his cheeks, Edward knocked down her hand. 'Enough of your hints and winks. I love Daisy Apreece. She is worth twenty of your sort. There, I have said it. Are you satisfied? Now go, and leave us to our business.'

He pushed past her and flung back the door.

'Well, this is most piquant, I do say.' She walked up to him and snapped her fingers in his face. 'Most piquant indeed.' With her nose cocked, she swished out of the room as Robert came swiftly behind her, calling out her name.

'But of course, Mr Chiddlestone, of course I shall not keep you waiting a moment longer than I need,' he tossed smoothly into the banking parlour. Then he closed the door and leaning against it, turned on Edward.

'That was not necessary. That was not the behaviour of a gentleman. You arrive unannounced, hector me about how I should run my bank, and then insult my wife as brazenly as a tinker – your manners leave me speechless. A minute or two of your time, a few comfortable words, that's all she was asking for. Is your money so precious that you cannot hold off for five minutes? Do you suppose I would have escaped out of the window? Half an hour ago I took you for a friend, someone I would have been proud to call my son. But now I see that you are no better than a cad. Your father would be turning in his grave if he knew how you behaved.'

'I wonder what the vicar can want so urgently. Perhaps there are more to follow him. Perhaps by tomorrow you'll be done for,' Edward said brutally.

'Six months and in banknotes. Not a day less.'

'Now and in gold coin.'

'As you wish. It occurs to me, however, that should you insist I could be tempted to repeat to Sir Anthony what a moment ago you said to my wife.'

Edward pulled back his shoulders. 'It is the truth. I am proud of it. But you will not tell him.'

'How can you be so sure?'

'Because you are afraid of him. I too used my eyes at dinner. You would never dare because you are afraid of what he might do to you in return.' Edward went over and sat on the edge of the banker's desk. But suppose Bill had tired of waiting and left? He picked up the sealing wax and tossed it from hand to hand.

'Tell me,' he said conversationally, 'do you recall the man I entered the bank with, the one with a canvas sack who looked rather out of place?'

Robert looked at him for a second. Then he rolled his eyes and laughed. Skirting Edward's legs he went over and stretched himself out in his chair with the thankful expression of a man who has just survived a fall from a great height.

'Oh I see, you are going to call him in and have him threaten me if you don't get your way. Make him wave his huge paws at me until I see sense, is that it? Ha ha ha. Dear me, young man, you really will have to sharpen your wits if you believe that is how to succeed. Now you tell me' – he sat up with a rush and jabbed his pencil into Edward's thigh – 'have you given the slightest thought as to how public opinion will value your reputation when it gets to hear of this? Have you considered how such an assault could be represented in a court of law? An assault in a bank, mark you sir, not in a bootmaker's but in a bank where there are monies stored which it is your avowed intention to depart with. Shall we reflect for a moment on the penalty that the law exacts for attempting to rob a bank? Is it not transportation for life that we are talking of? Dear me, what a very wooden imagination you possess. Six months. I have nothing further to say.'

'And has it ever occurred to you how you would fare without this elegant door to your office? Answer me that before you laugh yourself into a state.'

'My door?' Instinctively Robert glanced at it. Resplendently, its every tawny-grained inch throbbing with the dignity of ancientness, the bevelled mahogany threw back at him its gleaming lustre. 'My door? What foolery is this now?'

'Only that you ask yourself how you would transact your daily business lacking a door to your office. Your private affairs, all the secrets of the sorcerer exposed to the world. The great man and his – what did you call them? – bottles of smoke sitting there as naked as daylight. Imagine it, Robert, just imagine it for a moment. Whatever would your clients think of a banker who could not afford to have a door? They'd say, This is a sorry ship when one can't have a quiet word with the captain: I must have been mistaken when I chose the Bank of Buxton . . . Think of it, the breezes wafting in and out' – he motioned with his hand – 'free to come and go as they please, along with the chatter of Mr Huggins and the yapping of Emily Scarlett's terrier, and everyone peeking in to say how-do-you-do just when you're adding up a column of figures, or to see who's on their knees before you begging for a loan. I suppose you could always hang a blanket in its place –'

'What pish is this? What is all this bladdery nonsense you're talking about? Take my door off its hinges, is that what you mean? Make off with my property in front of all the people outside? Walk away with my door under your arm? Ha ha. What an infantile jest. You are no more grown up than a schoolboy.

Enough, Mr Horne. You know my terms. Take 'em – or go to the devil. *Now* let us agree that our business is at an end.'

Without looking up, Edward began to riffle through the pages of one of Robert's ledgers.

'Go and have a look into your parlour if you don't believe me. Bill Whitehead, that's his name. Get him to open his bag and show you what's inside. Wedges, claw-hammers, pincers, all the things a man needs to remove a door. Wouldn't take him long. Two three minutes was what he reckoned. Davie'll help hand it on to the wagon.' He pushed the ledger away and opened the next one. 'So you see it's you who has the choice. You can give me my money now or you can lose your door today. Choose the latter and within ten minutes I'll have every man, woman and dog in Buxton queuing up for the peepshow. The bank will be a public joke by midday. And don't think I wouldn't do it. Or that you and Jack could stop me. I have Amos and two more of my men waiting in the wagon. It's up to you, Robert. Unless –'

A thought had come to him as he turned over the ledger. 'All I can find are the details of your customers' deposits. Why don't we get out your loan book and consider it from a fresh angle, eh? I'll be bound you keep a record of your lending somewhere close by.' He parted his fingers. The stiff marbled cover fell with a plump thud on the matching endpaper. 'Shall we do that, Robert?' He flicked open the next one.

They all heard the church bells strike eleven: Jack Long, who was stacking coin when Edward came out; Bill Whitehead as he picked up his tools; Digbeth Chiddlestone as he leapt to his feet and darted into the banker's sanctum; Constance Pumfrey lying upstairs with a compress of spirit of lavender on her forehead; her husband sitting bowed at his desk; and Edward Horne as he stood in a daze on the bank steps. The last vowel of the chime tapered into the October stillness. It was life, it was a hard turnip. He put his hand into his pocket and touched Robert's little shagreen loan book. Goodness knows whether he'd ever recoup his capital from it. Robert had said it was his all. He had sworn, had pleaded, had invoked the spirit of friendship past, present and future until Edward could stand no more. He had taken a chance, snatched up the book and stumbled out on legs as weak as cotton wool.

His boil felt the size of an acorn. He became aware of Bill Whitehead standing beside him. 'Come on,' he said roughly, 'let's go and have a drink.'

Twenty-two

'DAISY, LOOK who's over there, standing outside the bank.' The two women, each carrying a box of coloured threads, tapes and whatnot which they had that morning purchased from Mr Jolly, the haberdasher, stopped abruptly in the middle of the street. A coal-heaver growled at them from beneath his sack as he was forced to mend his path.

'Very sorry, I'm sure . . . There, right in front of the bank. He's got someone with him. He's speaking to him. They're walking away. He looks very serious.'

'Where, where, Mary? I can't see him.' She went up on tiptoes and peered through the momentary intervals in the market-day throng. 'I do wish all these people weren't so tall.'

'There he is, I can see the top of his hat, not fifty yards away. Shall we go and meet him, would you like that? It'd cheer him up. The poor soul, ever so sorry for himself he looked standing outside the bank.'

'Oh, did he not look well? Do you suppose he's caught something? There's a lot of it around, Miss Hoole was telling me the other evening. We thought it must be the change in the seasons. Do you still see him?'

'Not for the moment,' replied Mary, her bonneted head weaving back and forth, 'he must have turned up the hill. No, there he is, outside the inn. To your left, Daisy – there, he's turned to say something to that man of his – surely you can see him now?'

Daisy hopped up and down like a wagtail snapping at an insect. Her breath came in soft bumps. 'Oh, *there* you mean. But he looks quite dreadful. Whatever can he have been doing? We can't go up to him if he's in that sort of mood, it'd be, well, too much as if we were intruding. Anyway, he's gone into the inn, so that deals with that. Perhaps he's been buying things for the new roof. And there's Davie with the wagon. That's what they must have been doing.'

They walked on, each swinging a ribboned box in one hand and a parasol in the other.

Mr Short, the butcher, passed them wearing a full-length brown leather apron that came down to his shins. He was followed by a lad with the pink-striped carcass of a piglet balanced on his shoulder. 'And a good forenoon to you, my ladies, a topper for the season, I'm sure,' he called over to them, going to raise his hat and making a mocking grimace when he found he'd left that article in his shop. A horseman clattered up behind, dashing sparks from the cobbles. The crowd parted to let him through and then re-formed in his wake, a bright, noisy, good-tempered hodge-podge of citizenry going about their business.

'Did you ever see quite so many people in town? It feels as though the whole county is at my heels. Dear me, but they are rather tiring. It's my age, Daisy, I'm becoming like an old woman . . . Why don't we pay a visit on Constance Pumfrey? I think she would be glad of a little encouragement after that scene at dinner. Poor Robert, what a position to have been placed in. Shall we do that?'

They pensively eyed the augustan splendour of the Bank of Buxton. But Daisy preferred to keep the sweetness of what she remembered best from that evening unsullied by Constance's prattle. What had happened between Robert and Anthony was no more than what had happened between Anthony and her ever since she had been married. Roundshot screamed through the sky; then the battlefield fell quiet and the survivors limped off to bandage their wounds. Constance was old enough to look after herself. So she wondered to Mary whether this might not be the hour when Constance was feeding, and after completing their calls, they made their way to where Clayton was waiting with the dog cart.

'Flickery-flackery, flickery-flackery, a little flick here and a bit of polish there, that's what I does while I waits for my ladies,' he said jauntily as he stowed a large chequered duster beneath his seat and took their boxes from them, 'until such time as I can count every eyelash in its reflection.' A hoverfly threatened to besmirch his housework and he whished it away with an exclamation of 'Get off, you beastie, go to Hindustani land and bother them there.' Then the three of them piled aboard, Clayton on the front bench with Daisy and Mary sitting with their backs to him. He had spent the summer repainting the dog cart, in black with vermilion wheelspokes and a thick vermilion stripe all around the body, and was as proudly conscious as any young groom should be of its dusky conceit. He plucked at his hat to give it a bit of a buccaneering rake and shook up Tib. He enjoyed taking his ladies to town. It made a pleasant change from stable duties. And while they did their rounds, he had the chance to glean a small harvest of gossip, which he would squirt over his shoulder with just enough impertinence to make Daisy and Mary giggle.

But when, as today, they had something private to discuss, viz. Edward Horne, the intimacy of the dog cart lost its allure. So they sat together with a rug over their knees, watched Buxton slip out of sight and, alone with their separate reflections, contemplated in silence the flurries of yellow autumn leaves that came spinning past them. Soon Clayton sensed that his morsels were falling upon barren ground and began instead a muttered confabulation with Tib, whose woolly ears quivered receptively. Their road took them down a wooded valley where the leaves were so deep that it seemed they were running on a carpet of moss. Sometimes a wheel would creak as it bounced over a tree root growing out from the verge, but otherwise they heard nothing but the rushing of air and the murmur of the river alongside. What serenity lives outside us and what turmoil within! Daisy sighed, a soft exhalation from deep within her lungs, and looked tenderly at Mary. Instinctively they moved closer to each other, their tall bonnets converging like lovesick owls sidling along a branch.

They reached the humpbacked bridge from which led the driveway to Michaelmas Farm. They crossed it and Clayton reined in. Usually his orders were to take Mrs Dipple straight home, but just once in a while they decided to go to Overmoor first.

'My lady?' he enquired, turning on his bench.

'What would you like to do, Mary? Will you come and have something light with us at Overmoor?'

'Not today, my dear. Mr Dipple will be back from market

presently and he likes to have me waiting so that he can tell me his news while it's still fresh in his mind.'

She put her head to one side. 'What is it then, Tib? What do you hear?' The pony, which a few seconds before had been pulling at a clump of grass, now stood erect with her ears pricked, staring back up the way they had just travelled.

Clayton made a sign to them and cupped his ear. 'Someone riding hard from town. A single man, by the sounds of it. Hard to be certain with all them leaves on the road.'

'Quick, Clayton,' Daisy said, 'drive on a few yards and pull into that quarry on the left. It'll be interesting to see who's following us in such a hurry.'

In a trice they were hidden. Now they could plainly hear the beat of hooves and the altered rhythm as the horse changed legs coming down the hill. There was a patter of drum taps as it crossed the bridge. Mary Dipple put her hand on Daisy's. Then it raced past the turning to Michaelmas, a pounding, lathered chestnut with outstretched neck and desperate eyes, and in its saddle the crouching figure of Robert Pumfrey. In a flash he was gone. They heard a whip strike flesh, a cry and then nothing but the pulse of hooves receding up the hill in the direction of Overmoor.

'He'll founder the bugger if he goes on like that, beg pardon for the language, my lady.'

'Spend the night with us, Daisy, please do,' Mary said urgently. 'There's something about seeing Mr Pumfrey like that which frightens me. I can't explain. I just feel it – here.'

'Oh, I don't know . . . you may be right . . . but –'. She gave a joyless laugh. 'He probably only wants to ask Anthony if he's taking the hounds out tomorrow. Yes, yes I think I will come after all, but only for the afternoon.'

'Mr Pumfrey! Whatever have you been doing? You look like – well, I can't rightly say what you look like,' exclaimed Miss Hoole, holding the door and running her governessy eyes over him. His chest was heaving, his face livid and running with sweat.

'I must see Sir Anthony immediately. It's imperative.'

Miss Hoole looked him over with mounting disapproval. He might own the Bank of Buxton and be the magistrate, and his business might be every bit as vital as he said – but, really, Overmoor was the residence of a baronet, not a gamekeeper. There were procedures to be followed, the customs of society to be observed. She kept her hand on the door latch, neither opening nor closing it.

'This is not an inn, you know, Mr Pumfrey,' she said with all the tartness that her four-foot something could command. 'May I ask that you give me your card while I enquire –'

'My card, Miss Hoole? Do you think I have galloped my horse to a jelly to have you ask for my card?' He kicked the door open and strode past her into the hall. 'Where is he then? Skulking in his dungeon as usual? We'll soon see about that. My God, I can't wait –. No, Miss Hoole, I will not remove my boots, I will not leave my gloves in the tray and I will not give you my card. If the sight of a man in a hurry is insupportable to you, I have only one piece of advice: smelling salts, Miss Hoole, smelling salts and plenty of them. Now out of my way, woman. Apreece, Apreece, I know you're hiding down there somewhere . . .' He ran shouting along the corridor and took the steps down to Anthony's business room two at a time.

Anthony had been selling cattle and had drunk too well. With his feet on his desk and his cerise face flopping over the side of his chair, he was peacefully refurbishing his liver when Robert arrived. Huge bullocks were ambling through his dreams, veritable aurochs with pendulous dewlaps and muscles as polished as glass. The sun was setting in a shoal of pink and cucumber. He was young again, striding through a Winterbourne meadow of unimaginable lushness. He recognised the river Eve lapping at his feet, saw albescent moths dancing beneath the alders. He owned all the Winterbourne meadows now . . .

At a great distance he heard the crash of boots, insistent and obnoxious. He squeezed open a pouchy eye. A spasm of irritation screwed across his face. He snorted and slid deeper into his chair. He waggled his riding boots tauntingly at Robert. One of them had a hole in its toe.

'God, I could kick you to London and back, you unprincipled monster. Get up!'

Anthony yawned. 'Piss, but you can be a nuisance, Robert.'

'Get up, I said.'

Again he yawned, this time putting his hand over his mouth. 'So what is it now, some farty nonsense about the bank, I suppose. Unless you've come for a lock of my hair to put under your pillow.' He rubbed his eyes. 'Oh for God's sake sit down, Robert, and stop behaving like a housemaid who's wet her bed. It gives me a headache just to look at you.'

'Oh, very humorous. What a little wit our Sir Anthony is today.' He pranced around in imitation of a discomfited housemaid. 'Please, sir, I know I've got the fires to do but I've had an accident so may we play a parlour game instead –'. He lunged across the desk and pitched Anthony's legs to the floor. 'Get up, I said.'

'For a housemaid? Not until you can fetch me a parrot that says, "Robert Pumfrey is a mannerless ass."'

'Manners? You have the nerve to talk to me about manners?'

Anthony gathered himself together and sat up. 'Why ever not? You rush in here without so much as an if-you-please, shout at me, manhandle my person, and then expect me to lie there like a spaniel? If you have some business that you wish to discuss, then kindly present it with the normal courtesies.'

Robert planted himself in front of the fire and folded his arms across his chest.

'Very well then. This is not a game. I have no time for games after what happened at the bank this morning. Who do you think came to see me, one after the other?'

'I have no idea.'

'Horne and the parson, that's who. And what do you suppose was on their minds? Seed cake and coffee? They were after their money, that's what they wanted. Every last farthing of it.'

'Yes, I do see that would be upsetting. But Robert, you're a banker. It's all part of the risk if some of your customers leave you. Has Mr Wiseman baited them down the road? Did you say something injudicious, something to antagonise them?'

'I? It is not I who has said anything. What sort of a fool do you take me for? Yesterday you failed to pay me my money and today they call in their deposits. And now you ask if *I* have said anything. But someone has, and if it is not I, then who, pray, can it be? ... You make my blood boil. The last time I was at your house, it was as your guest. Guest? What am I talking about? If that's how you treat your guests, then God have mercy on your enemies. But now it's as a dun I'm here.'

He took three quick strides to the table. Leaning on his knuckles, he thrust his face at Anthony and said quietly, 'I want my money back, Sir Anthony, and I want it now.'

'Tell me, as a matter of interest, what reason did Ned give for wanting to take his money out?'

'Rumours. Said there were rumours going round about the soundness of the bank. Nasty things, rumours, wouldn't you say?'

'It's no good your looking at me like that. If Ned's been accusing me of rumour-mongering, then he's an out-and-out liar. I haven't uttered a word to him about the bank. In fact I haven't laid eyes on him since the other night.'

'And the parson, what of him? Do you expect me to believe they arrived on each other's heels by a fluke? That they were sitting at their breakfast and all of a sudden had the identical thought, Yes, dash it, that's what I'll do today, I'll go and open Robert Pumfrey's scuppers?'

'You must believe what you want. Chiddlestone had probably had a vision. The clergy are like that. Comes from all the fairy tales they have to swallow in their line of business. You can't argue with fellows who've had visions. So then what happened?'

Robert sat down. Tersely, angrily, preserving always in the needle-hole of his mind the image of Constance sobbing hysterically on her divan, of his bold Andrew clattering his hoop-stick against the railings of the Crescent, and the terror of bankruptcy, he related all the events of the morning.

'Remember how you pleaded with me? How you begged me? Milkwells was the chance of a lifetime, you said. No time for lawyers and security and all that nonsense – the money was the thing – on the nail, or all would be lost. Trust me, you said, you can always trust the word of a gentleman. Your word – I spit on it. Pah! Your word is not worth a sausage skin of pus. What prevented you bringing my money yesterday? What is it that you want: to condemn us all to the gutter for the rest of our lives?'

'Desist, I beg you, or you'll have me in blubbers.' Anthony took out his handkerchief and feathered it ironically round the corners of his eyes.

'Very well then. I shall take it to the courts.'

'But why should I pay you anything, Robert?'

'Why? You ask why? My God, I must be dead and living in a cemetery. So it wasn't you who borrowed money from me and signed my loan book to prove it. It was another man altogether who by coincidence shares your name. Forgive me, dear sir, it seems I have been living under a misapprehension all these years. You should have informed me before. God, you deserve to have your tongue ripped out for all these lies. Ay, and be castrated . . . Look, I make one last appeal to you. You have investments in the Funds, moneys lying with Mr Gomez in London. You told me so over lunch last autumn. And I, without the bank, I have nothing in the world except my family. No land. No house save that which I rent. Nothing. I am a ruined man without my bank. So give me your note of hand for the debt and let me depart. Here –'. He pushed the inkstand across the table.

But Anthony only tipped back his chair and laced his hands behind his head. 'Look 'ee, Robert,' he said slowly, 'there exist no papers, no securities, nothing to prove I owe you a penny except for your private loan book, the one that you kept secret, the one that you preserved for your most intimate transactions. It is true that I signed it. I do not deny it for an instant. But now you've given it away, traded it with Ned. So is it not the case that I am his creditor and not yours? Is this not so?'

'Enough. It is not becoming to a man in your position to play tricks on a man before whom an abyss yawns. Pray sign me a note unless you wish to cross swords with Mr Hodge.'

'Mr Hodge can have at me until the world ends. It will change nothing. So long as Ned has your loan book, you possess not one iota of evidence to support your tale. Not one iota, not one speck of ant shit to lay before a judge. Had you kept your nerve, my obligation would indeed be to you. But you did not and so it is not.'

Robert stared at the puffy face opposite him, at the thick fingers clasped on the table, at the calmly nodding head, into the awful needle-eye of ruin. He had been improvident and foolish. He had done what he should not have done. For Constance's sake he had taken his eight per cent each quarter day. For his own, because it pleased him to be well thought of, he had lent a friendly ear to all the hobbling waifs with a story to tell. *Amo, amas, amat*: he had believed it a caution that applied to other men only. And now it had come to this.

'You should have told him to go to hell. Take the damned door then, you should have said. I would have. The man has no bottom. It was all bluster.'

'It was not you who was there. And that book,' he burst out, 'it was not only your debts that were in it. There were others –'

'Others that you wanted to conceal from your partners, let us be blunt about it. All those sums of eight and ten and even twelve per cent, or so I hear, flowing doucely into your private pocket. I dare say you'll have some explaining to do when Mr Appleby and your cousin William get to hear about it.'

'You'll live to regret this. You'll rue this day when you have not only Mr Hodge but also Edward Horne to deal with.'

Anthony rose and stood looking out across the lawn. 'You have a squint that is unfortunate for one in your profession. You can see in two directions at the same time. Bankers should be one-eyed and keep that eye strained on their ledgers. As it is, you have become too interested in the colouration of mankind. You have let your attention wander and allowed your customers to lure you into their pavilions to view the fine mirages hanging on their walls.' He turned back into the room. 'It was the very first thing I remarked on when we were discussing the purchase of Milkwells. Ha, I thought, this man is as interested in the place as I am myself. As I described it, I saw your banker's eye calculating the terms and your squinty one go striding across the fields thinking to itself about the sport to be had from the coverts, of the trout waiting in its little stream, of a book of poetry, perhaps, lying beside you on a tussock while overhead –'

Yap! Yap Yap!

'God's boots!' he exclaimed, whirling round and throwing open the casement, 'if it isn't that bloody bitch of Ned's again. I swear I'll hang it from the weathercock one of these days. Scarcely a week goes by –. Hucknall! Hucknall! Come on, Robert, let's go and catch the brute and give it a good thrashing. It'll take your mind off things.'

But when he looked back, the door stood open and he was alone. The banker's chair remained at the same angle. The crumpled green cushion still showed the impress of his back. His whip lay on the floor. But of the man himself there remained not a whisker. Robert Pumfrey had gone.

Good God! He heard the front door close and craned out of the window. 'Robert! Stop!' Hooves sounded in the gravel. Good God almighty! He surveyed the room in disbelief, half-expecting him to crawl out from under his desk. He jiggled the whip in his hand and laid it along the mantelshelf. He picked up the tinderbox; lit the candle stubs; pinched his jowls; sat on the edge of his chair and changed into his slippers. He gazed through steepled fingers at the picture of Achilles dragging Hector round Troy. Well he never did! What an extraordinary thing to have done. Extraordinary! Had he taken his congé for ever? Was this finis to the Bank of Buxton? It must be. What else could it mean? And with this thought came a twitch of annoyance. It was as if he had been deprived of the company of an old tame bear that had broken its chain and shambled sulkily away into the woods. A landmark as certain as a compass point had disappeared. The butt into which he had pinged so many arrows over the years had grown legs and stalked off in a huff. This was not what he'd intended. By no means. Shake him up a bit, give him a fright – but not this. You knew where you were with Robert. But Horne, who could say what the little earwig would do now that he had Robert's loan book? He'd be cock-a-hoop. Come and strut around in some ghastly coat, shouting the odds and demanding his money. Yes, *his* money. He'd worsted Robert. He'd come for him next. And what had he got to give him?

He pulled out of his desk the letter he had received from Samuel Gomez's margin clerk: '13 July 1788. Unimaginable hailstorms in the centre of France wiped out the crops. August, the market in government bonds dissolved in panic; the Caisse d'Escompte besieged for three days and two nights. 25 August the resignation of Brienne, the Finance Minister, was announced . . . In the circumstances, Sir, I am requested by Mr Gomez that you arrange with all possible expedition for a further sum of six thousand pounds to be sent to your account with us. Should this not be convenient and should you wish to liquidate your position in the three per cents, we calculate that your loss would not be in excess of . . . We remain, esteemed Sir, etc, etc, etc.'

The cowards! Did none of them have any balls down there? Did they think a few hailstones were going to lead to war? In a month it would have blown over. The threes would be back on their feet and his losses recovered. As for six thousand pounds, did they take him for Croesus? Or the golden thigh of Pythagoras?

He flung the letter aside. So what now? Gomez in London was as distant as a planet. Let him yammer away until he tired of writing. But Horne – the man lived only a few miles away. Within a day – or an hour, or five minutes – he might be banging on the door. Perhaps as he sat there. Perhaps not in five minutes but in one. Perhaps before ten beats of his heart. He had the loan book. He had the proof. And if Gomez pressed him too – sent up that gallows-faced clerk of his to say what about it then, cut your losses or pay up. Then where would he be? Well, he wasn't just going to sit there and wait like that blockhead Cicero to have his topknot lopped off, was he? He stood up and tugged squelchily at his nose.

In a corner by the window leaned the cylindrical wooden pole, about a yard in length, which he used to measure the spacing between his seed drills. He picked it up by its leather thong and set off up and down the frayed blue runner that stretched from the door to the window. He thumped it rhythmically into his cupped palm as he arranged the problem in its compartments. Seventeen paces there, pivot, seventeen paces back staring at the diamond-leaded window panes. He looked at Achilles, at the ceiling, at the carpet, at his scuffed slippers advancing mechanically beneath his knees. And wherever he looked, he saw the dapper and detestable figure of Edward Horne. Pumfrey's loan book? In his pocket. Winterbourne? He still owned it. Daisy? Ah yes, now Daisy . . . He paused, the point of the measuring pole resting at an angle on his desk. Had he had her that day they had gone riding together? She had gone very quiet afterwards. But what did it matter where they had started? He had caught them again, yesterday, on his own front lawn, in full view of the servants. Arguing, by the look of it. So if they'd reached that stage –

But what did he care? What was at stake was his honour and not hers. The honour of the Apreeces. His dignity. His reputation in the county. By God, cuckolded by a youth. He put his hand to his forehead. It was on fire. A colony of ants was humming inside his brain. It was unspeakable. It was worse than unspeakable. It was the foulest, most odious crime a man could commit, to lie with his neighbour's wife.

Thwacking and thumping, each foot descending with the precision of a tightrope walker, his eyes rigid and unblinking, he patrolled the narrow border of fleurs-de-lis. Somewhere lay the solution. Everything had a solution. Horne with the loan book must become Horne without it. Horne and Daisy must be separated. He sat down. He stood up. He toed the fire, trimmed a candle, worried at his nose. Two distinct problems, requiring two distinct answers. Or – he stopped dead. The pole trembled. Or could – or could they be conflated into one? From layer to layer, this new configuration trickled through his mind, expanding, ripening, growing limbs, sinews, flesh and an expression of goat-like malignancy. He ran his tongue round his lips. His temples began to throb. Horne, Daisy, the money – by God! Even Winterbourne itself if his luck held.

Faster now he began to pace, more furiously to thrash his pole. Sweat glittered on his brow. Images that were at the same time fantastic and wonderful descended from nowhere and spun through his vision like showers of coloured glass. Voices whispered to him and he called back. Words and half-words and fragments of words; hopes, caveats, imprecations and remonstrances, all rushed incoherently from his mouth. He wagged his finger at Achilles, shook his fist at Hector, struck his forehead, dashed his sleeve at his spittle and at last threw himself into his chair and closed his eyes. All of them, all in one fell swoop.

Twenty-three

I SHOULD HAVE been a rougher diamond, Robert thought, have stood my ground and fought until I dropped. I should have hewn and cudgelled, nailed him as a man without honour, as a common sharper, a Strudwick with a title. I could have answered deceit with deceit and bribed him with the tinsel of a partnership. 'Ho now, Anthony,' I could have said, 'I perceive a difference between us where there was never one before. This is not the way for friends to behave one to another. Constance and I have sufficient money for ourselves. Friendships are what count in life. So if there is a profit to be made, why do we not share it and rejoice, like two soldiers of fortune who happen across a chicken ripe enough for plucking?' Or I could have been a lickspittle and sugared him like an almond.

But he had done none of these things. He had had it easy for too long. He had enjoyed too many years grazing on the finest cuts of clover; the iron had been leached from his soul. He had suddenly felt intolerably weary, depressed and middle-aged. And when Sir Anthony had made his last and most telling challenge, he had not had the resilience even to raise his lance.

It was the end, the end of everything. With limp reins and his head sunk upon his chest, he let his horse pick its own way through the gathering dusk to Buxton.

Melson was waiting for him, leaning against the stable door and chuckling with a friend as he smoked a stubby clay pipe. He told him to ease off his horse's girths and give it a good feed, and then to come in and get a meal from Cook. There was work to be done that night, vital messages to be carried on bank business.

He entered the house by the kitchen door, quietly removed his boots and coat and went immediately upstairs to his office, carrying his slippers. He placed them on his desk and sat down. Before him the hollowed-out daybook lay where Edward had left it in the morning. He looked at it, squeezing the sides of his lower lip into a bunch. Six hours ago, no more than one quarter of one day among all the days that his life would contain, he had been the envy of the county. Robert Pumfrey, king of kings, lion of lions, beloved of his family, adored by the gods. And then – then nemesis had rapped on that panelled mahogany door and within this tiny space of time he had sunk to being nothing. To less than nothing, to a minus quantity. Even a pauper had a sense of dignity, threadbare though it might be. God gave me these poor brains or paltry muscles, he could say, and I did my best with them. I tried; they were insufficient; I failed. The fault was not mine but that of a greater being. But a rich man reduced by his own folly had no such excuse. When he fell, stripped of his fame, it was into the nethermost depths of rancour and self-contempt. He could expect neither sympathy nor pity from his friends. Constance would hate him. His children would despise him as soon as they were old enough, and disown his name. The autumn of his life would be joyless and his grave unmarked. Because he had once thought too favourably of a man and had been mistaken, he would be alone for the remainder of his days.

With a grimace, he closed the daybook and locked it. For a moment he sat quite still, pondering over the small silver key that lay in his palm. He rose and stood over the fire, letting the key swing by its tassel. His features were cold and graven. He parted his fingers. The cord flared and shrivelled among the coals. He released a long breath through his nose and returned to his chair.

He drew his writing slope towards him and scratched a terse note to each of his partners. He sanded them and tipped the sand back into its box, spilling some on his desk. He folded them into quarters, held them in turn to the candlelight to ensure that Melson should not be able to decipher anything of their contents, and waxed them heavily, baring his teeth as he impressed his seal with a vicious screwing motion.

The rope shivered beside the fireplace, its bell strident and unwelcome in the silence of his thoughts. He ignored it, took his slippers down and shuffled out of his office and across the black-

and-white tiled floor of the banking parlour until he reached a point that he adjudged to be its centre. He could not say what impelled him towards this one black tile. He had not previously been aware of its individuality. So far as he knew, it had been living quietly among its friends, touching them with its fingertips and sharing amicably the chalky veins that spidered across their gloomy surface. But now it called to him and he went. The moment it had encompassed his small feet, a feeling of calmness came over him. His view was unimpeded on all sides. Here, in this one spot at least, no bogles could surprise him, neither trap nor quicksand engulf him, neither treachery nor disappointment diminish him. It was a modest kingdom, but he was master of it.

Presently he went over and fetched Jack's stool from behind the counter. The wood was warm and smooth to his touch, another comfort to him. Carefully, making sure that none of it impinged upon another tile, he positioned it in the centre of his square. He hoisted himself up, put his feet on the rungs, cupped his cheek in his hand, and let his gaze come to rest on the yew-green doors through which, one morning, Temptation had scampered and no one had noticed her.

An hour passed, a misty circuit dense with memories that were both sunny and sad. He thought of how it had all begun, of his weekly catechism in front of Uncle Gilbert, of his first cautious forays into the towns and dales to transact those minuscule portions of business from which Pumfrey & Co. had earned its daily bread. He heard the grating of seldom-opened cashboxes and, peering over a burly shoulder, saw again the pitiful treasures that a farmer ranked worthy of being stored with his money: a legal scroll – a title deed, or perhaps some family settlement – a loved one's curl of hair in a tortoiseshell clip, a memory ring. So little for such awful labour . . . He passed by the pretentious white villa of Mr Strudwick, Uncle Gilbert digging him in the ribs, and remarked to himself upon the singularity of the fact that neither his uncle nor he had ever again done business with the occupants of that house. It had been tainted for ever by Strudwick. It was as if the house, instead of the person living within it, had acquired the stain of the default. (Was that what people would say about his own house? In years to come, would they point to it and, as they crossed to the other side of the Crescent, say, That was where Pumfrey did his fiddling, do you remember?)

He took the coach to London (so young, so tender, so dewy-eyed!) and found himself once more in Mr Drummond's bank in Charing Cross, with Septimus Leftly chortling on the other side of the partition. The grease glinted on Septimus's chin as he leaned over that chophouse table to tell him about Alexander Fordyce. That he remembered especially, not only on account of what followed with Mr Fordyce, but because Septimus had had, in the very centre of his chin, a dimple like a woman's navel that his barber's razor could never adequately deal with, so that on this evening the sight of a slender pillar of ginger stubble arising from the middle of a greasy moat had been irresistibly comical. But oh, Mr Fordyce, it was wrong of you to have fled the country when you were wrecked. I know, I know, your feelings are an open book to me tonight; the spear thrusts of shame, dishonour and fear. But you should have held firm, cried *mea culpa* and bared your neck with seemliness. It would have stood you in good stead later. It is what I shall do when my time comes.

The curtains of his life swished and parted, and a new set of actors took up their positions. The crackle of frost in the hinges as Jack threw open the doors, the thump of leather pouches on the counter, men's voices loud and true, jokes and good cheer, the sweet trickle of gossip like a waterfall in summer, the rumble of a lady's carriage drawing up outside, pretty words and pretty manners, fans and sunshades, borrowing at four per cent to lend at eight and still being stroked and courted . . . Ah, even in his misery there were good memories to be had. Toppers! Real clinkers! A rosy-cheeked footman, not a bit censorious, on every step of the long, long staircase down to the watergate of oblivion . . . A guard of honour at his beck and call until the day he died . . . The pressure eased in his chest. He felt his pulse: it was quick, small and hard. He sat up and spread his hands across his thighs. And it was he who had done it all! They had called him a fool, a dreamer, the most hopeless optimist who had ever lived. They had scoffed at his banknotes, but a month later had gratefully christened them Pumfreys. Who else had lent his surname to posterity? Who else? All right, there was Dr Cocker. For sure he'd been a fine mathematician in his day, but who ever did anything useful with a Cocker? Who ever heard anyone say, 'A Cocker for your thoughts'? Whereas he, Robert Donnybrook Pumfrey, would be remembered for as long as people found a reason to use his banknotes, for as long as they had anything to buy or sell. So in a way he had already achieved a sort of immortality. Was that not something to be proud of?

He saw that a few ashes had crept out of the hearth. He rose awkwardly, for during his musing his legs had become rather entangled in the rungs of the stool, and went down on his knees to sweep them back in. Every successful man had at least one good upset in his life. It was not human to be otherwise. It was a necessary part of genius. It primed the spark of inventiveness and set the gilded wheels rolling again. Yes, that was how he should look on this day. As an upset, an interregnum, a partial eclipse of a mighty sun. He would sell off his blue-john and pay back his creditors – Constance's parents would help him, they had more than enough for their own needs – take his household to London, find a partner who would value his experience in banknoting – start afresh – put his bad luck behind him –

'Must I shout to attract your attention?'

With the smile still warm on his face, he turned to the door that led from the banking parlour to their rooms above.

'I never heard you come in,' he said, putting down the hearth brush and cumbersomely levering himself upright with one hand on his knee.

'Nor did you hear me ring your bell, which I did twice, nor did you hear Melson when he knocked to ask if the letters were ready to go out yet. And all the time you have been cleaning the fireplace like a housemaid. You really have behaved most inconsiderately to me today. You let me be insulted by Mr Horne, you rode off to goodness knows where without saying a word to anyone, and now you keep us all waiting for our supper. I sometimes think it is not a wife you need but a mistress.'

'Constance –'

'So I shall take the letters down to Melson myself. And I shall tell Cook to serve the food in ten minutes exactly. Does that give you time enough to finish whatever it is you were doing? Incidentally, you have no idea how silly you looked when I came in.' Without pausing for a reply, she walked briskly through into his office.

Robert drew himself up. It seemed he had spent too much of his life apologising to Constance. And this time, he was aware, it was no ordinary apology that he had to deliver. But do it he must, and do it now. He pulled down his waistcoat, rubbed his index finger to and fro beneath his nose as if addressing a billiard ball, took a deep breath and followed. He would have preferred a moment of his own choosing and a different confessor. To Daisy he would have abased himself and implored her forgiveness in the certainty that the frailty of his human clay would be received with all the womanly compassion that she possessed. But of Constance he was afraid. He stood in the doorway and studied the stitching on his slippers.

'Why do you keep this book locked, Robert? I don't think I've ever noticed this one before . . . Now, just the two letters are there?'

He raised sad eyes to her. 'Constance, my dear, I am afraid there is something I must say to you –'

'How strange to correspond with your partners by night,' she said, glancing at the inscriptions. 'I do declare that most remarkable. What can be so urgent that it will not wait until morning? I am sure my brother will not thank you for being roused from his sleep . . . What is it that you wish to say to me? Is it . . .?' A note of alarm entered her voice. She snatched up the letter to Archer and peered at it against the candlelight. 'Is it about what happened this morning? Is that why you're writing to them at this hour? Did something occur between you and Mr Horne that you haven't told me about? Is it – has he taken his money away from us? Oh Robert, say it is not so, I beg you, I beg you –' The paper knife trembled as she attacked the seals. 'Say that it cannot be –'

'I am warning you, Constance, that you will not find it pleasant reading. It would be better if you were to sit down and compose yourself.'

But by now she had the letter opened. Her eyes swept across the page. Her hand went to her bosom and up to her mouth. She lifted a pale slack face to him. 'Dear God, we are broken,' she whispered. The paper fell from her hand; splinters of wax flew across the desk. Her eyes widened and turned bluer than he had ever seen them. Her knees began to buckle. She swayed, drooped and slid to the floor, where she lay with her legs in a huddle and her dress pulled up almost to the middle of one thigh.

Robert stared down at her. Daisy would not have done that. Without hurrying, he went upstairs to the children's room. Susan, the housemaid, was putting little Ettie to bed. There was nothing to be disturbed about, only Mrs Pumfrey had suddenly been taken poorly ... He returned to his office and resealed the letter to Archer, standing on the opposite side of the desk from where Constance was lying so that he would not need to think about her. He shouted down the backstairs for Melson. Then, while he waited for Susan, he rammed the daybook into the heart of the fire and broke it up with great stabbing thrusts of the poker which he held in both hands, as if it were a sword and he gory Brutus.

Later that night he told Sophia everything. There would have to be changes and he could not pretend they would be for the better. Their situation was quite altered. Money would be less plentiful. There might be times when they must deny themselves what hitherto they had regarded as essentials. Mr Please, for instance, the man who came to see her when she was ill: the expense was not great, but she would have to manage without him.

'We should move,' Sophia said. 'We cannot stay here now. So the matter of Mr Please will find its own solution. Though where we should go and who will lend us a kindly roof until you have established yourself anew – oh, Robert dear, you look so worried that it frightens me. I am sure it will come right in the end. It is not as if you have committed a sin.'

She licked her fingertips and, taking her brother's hand, moistened the mound at the base of his thumb and began to knead it, pressing her thumbs side by side into his soft flesh.

'Our parents would be happy if they could see how we care for each other in our adversity,' he murmured.

'Our parents will be happy, you mean,' she corrected him.

'Of course it is so. You are right. There is nothing conditional about the Christian faith. It is only because everything is so heavy upon me that I spoke in that way.'

'I shall always be at your side,' she said simply, her grey eyes steady on his, his hand between hers.

'And I at yours, flesh and blood of our mother's rib.'

Silence fell between them. Through the wall, they heard the sound of Constance moving around.

'Where will you sleep?'

'Here, on the floor. I'll take the cushions off the chairs, comfort myself with a measure of brandy and do the best that I can.'

The night was thin when he awoke, abruptly and with the hooves of fear pawing in his stomach. Outside, riding atop the crest of the hill amid a fleece of skimpy clouds, was a sulphurous moon that appeared to be sneering at him. He lit his night candle, dressed and went down to his office. He saw that the lanthorn which Melson had left hanging outside the stable had been extinguished. The man had returned. The letters had been delivered. By breakfast his partners would have arrived. Then his trial would begin.

Backwards and forwards he paced. He wanted to have someone beside him whom he could tell what had happened, a man who would not faint but listen intelligently. He wanted to say this happened, and this and this and this until he reached the end; to receive sturdy sensible questions that he could answer in his own time. He would not flinch from the blame. In fact he looked forward to it, as a means of cauterising the wound. But above all he wanted someone who would listen to him.

Then there were the arrangements that had to be made, the obsequies. Mr Wormald must be told; and in eight long pages, as dawn inched its bleary way up the window panes, he told him everything, omitting nothing by which he could lacerate himself and concluding with the request that his lease be terminated at the Christmas quarter day. Notice, too, must be given to the public. By the grace of God today was a Saturday and the bank therefore closed. Nevertheless, it was better done sooner rather than later. For ten or perhaps fifteen minutes he deliberated over the wording until, in a hand so misshapen by the turbulence within him that he scarcely recognised it as his own, he settled on:

THE BANK OF BUXTON
Payment is suspended from this date.

GOD SAVE KING GEORGE

Robt. Pumfrey, 25th inst. October 1788

He found a tack in Jack's desk, went out into the Crescent and
nailed the paper to the door with a lump of coal. Smoke was
unfurling from a few chimneys. The morning was dry and cold. It
would be ironic if it rained and the ink ran so that no one could
read what he'd written and people had to come in and ask. But he
did not think it would rain. He went inside and bolted the door.
He wiped his hands on the back of the sofa and, as an
afterthought, wedged it against the door with the heavy iron
fireguard. Then he dozed in his chair until Archer Appleby arrived.

The coals burned dingily in the drawing-room upstairs. On a side
table a cold repast lay neglected. On the principal table the bank
ledgers had been neatly stacked. At its head presided Constance.
Robert and his partners sat around her. His cousin William was
reading the partnership deed intently, his fingers travelling down
the margin as his lips moved wordlessly. Andrew Pumfrey was
playing on the floor with his toys, Sophia reading in a corner.

Of a sudden the low muttering of the crowd on the hill outside
picked itself up and broke into a roar of renewed taunts and
threats. A missile, the lump of coal that Robert had used in the
morning, struck the wall and rattled down into the street.

'How can you possibly say such a thing? A year ago, in this very
room, you swore we were a solid concern, that we could withstand
anything. I asked if you trusted Sir Anthony, do you remember? A
man of his word, you said, the sort of man who'd never let you
down. So why hasn't he paid us back our money? Why didn't you
take any security for all these loans you made him? You must be
an imbecile, you and that Sophia together . . . Your little book, the
one you kept locked up and that none of us knew about, you sit
there and tell us you thought it sufficient? Well, where is its
sufficiency this morning, then?' Constance's lips curled. 'Gone!
Taken from under our noses by that so-called friend of yours . . .

What do you mean, you had no alternative? Would he have killed you? How *could* you have been taken in by such a preposterous threat? You a grown man and he little more than a youth – and what if he had taken the door? Anything would have been better than giving him that book. There is no other record of these debts – not one! We are lost without it, done for as surely as if we'd been drowned in a barrel ... Oh, the degradation of it all, the humiliation, the stigma on a name that is not even my own – how shall I be able to look myself in the face again?'

She flung herself into a chair and let the skeins of unmade hair hang across her face as if, by concealing it, she could conceal her shame also.

'Give us back our money or we'll come in and get it ourselves,' shouted a man outside who had found a bucket lacking its bottom and was using it as a speaking-trumpet. The sudden boom made William jump. 'And Pumfrey with it,' added another in a no less menacing voice.

'Listen to them, it's not just Robert they're after, it's me, the children, anyone they can get their hands on. We'll be mincemeat if we leave the house. That's what you and your trickery have done to us, you've made mincemeat of us all.'

'Calm yourself, sister,' Archer Appleby said. 'Mr Wormald has placed constables at back and front. None of us is in danger. But I incline to think we should be more private if they could not see everything we do.' He motioned to William to draw the shutters and bar them. 'And you can light the candles,' he said brusquely to Robert, 'seeing as how there are no servants left in the house.'

'What? You mean Susan has gone as well? She said –'

'An hour ago. I let her out myself. In a fair state of distress too, I may add, which is scarcely surprising since her father had placed his little all with the bank for safe-keeping. These people trusted you, you know, Robert. They are not great swells from London who are accustomed to stake thousands on the turn of a card. They put their faith in you and you deceived them. It will go hard on many of them, I fear.' He took a drink of water.

'I cannot bear it ... All of us ruined, *ruined* by Robert's stupidity ... Go away, you horrible child, and you too, Sophia, I cannot *stand* it when you look at me like that. And what are we to do with *her*, may I ask,' Constance broke out afresh. 'Did you think of your sister when you threw away the bank? Did you stop to ask yourself where we would find the money to pay for her lodging and medicines? One thing's for certain, she won't be coming with us when we leave –'

'Sophia comes with us. Though I have to sell fish from a barrow to keep us alive, she comes with us,' Robert said, looking straight at his wife.

'And I say not. If we cannot find someone to take her, she must go into a house of charity. My mother will not tolerate a lunatic as well as a family of paupers. Dear God, what are we to do? What have you done to us, Robert, what have you done?'

'Come, William, let us go through the books once more. We must be prepared for when the examiners search them.' Archer hung his coat over the back of his chair. He was a heavy, sweating man with strong dark features, quite the opposite in build and colour to his sister. 'If you please, William. We are both partners in the bank. It is our duty.'

'I really don't see why I have to be involved in any of this. I have scarcely put a foot inside the bank since the day it opened. I may be a partner in name but –' The sound of Henrietta squalling in the nursery made everyone look up guiltily.

'The poor little mite,' Sophia said, 'all by herself and seeing goojoos coming down the chimney.'

Constance gave her a glance to curdle and hurried from the room. Returning, she gave the pacified, gurgling Ettie into Robert's arms. 'There, you care for her for a change. It is something you must get used to. No servant will ever want to work for us again.'

'I very much doubt there will be anyone to work for,' Archer said with an air of finality. 'It does not matter how William and I construe the figures –'

'But there may still be something we've missed. Jack Long may have kept a secret drawer. Or the vaults –'

'Will you stop harping on about what plainly does not exist, William? How many times have we been through the counting-room since we arrived?'

'That's Jack outside in the crowd,' Andrew Pumfrey piped up, running over and trying to lift the shutter bar from its socket. 'I've heard him ever so often, telling them all to be patient, that Father will give them their money back as soon as he can. I'd know his voice anywhere.'

'Don't do that, Andrew,' Constance screamed, jumping up and pushing him back. 'There's people with stones outside, you could get yourself hurt.' A handful of pebbles spattered against the window panes.

'Come on out and show yourself. Put your face where I can hit it.'

'Thief! Coward!'

'Oppressor of the poor!'

'I'll catch up with you somewhere, Robert Pumfrey, even if I have to follow you down to hell. You *bastard*, Robert.'

'Leonard Huggins,' whispered Robert. 'He gave me everything he'd ever earned.'

'But I could ask Jack if he had a secret drawer,' insisted Andrew, beating his small fists against the shutters. 'I know he'd tell me. He always told me everything I wanted to know.'

Archer thumped his fist on the table. 'Will you stop all this? Stop it, I tell you, stop it. The bank's broken, can you not get it into your heads? Done for, finished, dead.' He took hold of Constance by the elbow and propelled her roughly to the table. 'Look, here are the figures. On the left are our assets, our cash and the loans to customers that we can prove, and on the right our debts and when we have to pay them. Can you not see which is the larger? I agree, if we had Robert's private book, if we had any other legal evidence of the sums he's lent to his friends, it'd be different. But we don't. And the reason we don't is because Robert saw fit to trade it with someone his partners had never heard of before this morning.'

'But we know who these friends are. Why do not you and William ride out and force them to repay us?'

Archer wearily rubbed his eyes. 'Because they'll disown their debts. They'll say, I never borrowed a penny from your bank. Where is Mr Pumfrey's book? Show me your proof, show me where I signed for the money. And we can't. Mr Horne has the proof and we don't and that's the fact of it.'

'But if we did have it . . . Wait, why don't we get some more banknotes sent up from Derby? William could ride down there tonight –'

'Are you mad? Do you think the rabble out there'll go home happy with bits of paper in their pockets? Do you think they'll say, By Jove, this is just what I had in mind? They'd spit on them. It's not a nice piece of engraving they want, it's hard, tested coin they can bite on . . . Oh Robert, Robert, what have you done? We are beggared, every one of us in this room. How your Uncle Gilbert must be writhing.' He spread his forearms on the table and buried his head in them.

The sound of someone hammering on the door reached them distantly.

'You go, Robert, you go and get yourself killed. You're the cause of all this,' Constance said spitefully, screwing her eyes tight so that their pouches resembled bladders of wrinkled grey paint. He handed Ettie over to her and left the room.

'Well, I'm not going to pay,' William said, nervously flicking back his hair and looking defiantly from Archer to Constance. 'I was never a party to any of this. I knew nothing of what was happening. You, Archer, you were the one who said he understood banking. It was you who should have kept Robert in check, you who should have asked him all the proper questions. The only reason I became a partner was because you said you needed three partners for a bank and I was convenient, being a relative. Not a single farthing will I pay, not one farthing.'

'But you shall, William. You signed the partnership deed; you took your share of the profits. It is the law. The examiners will see to it that you pay every penny you should. And if you can't pay, or you can't find someone who'll pay it for you, there's always Newgate waiting,' Archer said grimly.

'But I have just read the deed again. It says each of the partners is also entitled to a salary. I have received no salary. Therefore I have not had the status of a partner and am absolved from their obligations.'

'You're whistling in the wind.'

'Only a lawyer can determine that and you are no lawyer.'

'Poor William, he's younger than all of us,' Sophia said, going up to him and stroking the hairs on his neck so that he felt more uncomfortable than ever. 'Why should William have to do something he doesn't want to?'

'Go to your room this instant, Sophia. I cannot abide your nonsense a moment longer.'

Sophia stepped resolutely up to Constance. 'You have no authority over me, madam. I am not a servant to be commanded. Only my brother has that right. Besides, the candle behind you has gone out. You are a poor mistress of the house on all fronts.'

Long slow footsteps dragged themselves up the stairs. Robert opened the door, further disaster written clearly in his face. Andrew ran to his side; Robert clasped his son to him. From behind them emerged the terrier-like figure of Mr Wormald. He stepped into the room and surveyed it with the quick eye of a man accustomed to the embarrassments of tenants. Without ado he took the seat at the head of the table.

'Mrs Pumfrey, Miss Pumfrey, gentlemen, please. I shall take only a few minutes of your time. I have been made aware of what has taken place. You have my personal sympathy, all of you, and I offer it with total sincerity. But I am employed by another man and must be dispassionate. His Grace was spending last night in town and I have spoken to him. He pointed out to me the clause in your lease which forbids the use of the premises for immoral activity. It is his opinion that the refusal, or inability – His Grace is not minded to distinguish between them – of Mr Pumfrey timeously to meet his obligations *to these poor people* (those were his words) is an act of the most wanton immorality. He therefore wishes to withdraw from his association with you immediately.'

'Immediately, Mr Wormald? Surely he cannot expect us –'

'I regret so. Initially his Grace said today, but after I received your husband's letter in the middle of the morning, I was able to persuade him to grant a deferment until tomorrow at midnight. It was all that was possible. His Grace was in no mood to be merciful. The constables will remain at their posts until you leave. You are in no danger. The crowd will disperse as soon as it gets cold. I have seen something similar once before in my life. Let me reiterate my sympathy and bid you all goodnight.' He departed as briskly as he had entered.

'So what did my clever husband who is so skilled in lies write to Mr Wormald in the middle of the morning? Was it that your wife had a migraine? Or that the axle on the carriage was being repaired?' Constance sneered across the table. 'In any case he has been despatched to join the rest of the gulls . . . Yet he still expects us to pack every possession we own within a day, without a single servant to help us – can you do nothing but sit there and stare at me like a half-wit, Robert?'

'What do you expect me to do, woman?' he suddenly shouted, jumping to his feet. 'I've made you all my apologies. I've admitted everything. If I could erase the past, I would. *Mea culpa, mea culpa, mea culpa*, how many more times do you want me to say it? What else do you want? That I ride out and steal the book back? That I beat Edward Horne senseless?'

'Yes, do exactly that. Do what any other man would do who's worthy of the name.'

'Then I shall. I'll do what you say and the devil take the risk. And when justice uncovers me, I'll say I did it so that my wife could fill her wardrobes with Kitty Prodger's dresses and stuff her belly with plovers' eggs. And that, gentlemen, is the truth of the matter. All the wrongs that I have done have been for the sake of a woman and her luxury. Now are you proud of yourself, Constance?'

'There is another way I have thought of,' she said slowly, 'one that need involve neither injury nor lie. For it is what Mr Horne told us himself. Do you remember that I taxed him in your office with the tenth commandment, Thou shalt not covet –'

'You would not! No gentleman could use such a weapon against another.'

'La, what a pretty conscience you have of a sudden, husband. But I know why you are so vehement. It is because you are afraid. You think that if you told Sir Anthony he was a cuckold, he might do to you what he did to Mr Smith at the Green Man. But it is not you who will have to do it. It is I, and I am no gentleman. Coming from the mouth of a woman, it will win more credence and be sharper off the tongue than anything you would say. Then we may marvel at the speed with which Sir Anthony can repay his debts. And I beg you not to bring Lady Apreece into the discussion. If she must suffer so that we do not, it is a price I can tolerate.'

Archer and William looked greedily at her.

'An amour between Mr Horne and Lady Apreece, is that what you are speaking of, sister?'

'It is. Sir Anthony has a name to uphold in the county and a character that is jealous.'

'But it is Mr Horne who has our book. And forgive me if I lack in sophistication, but it occurs to me, who is also a man, that if Sir Anthony is as you say, Mr Horne might pay us more to keep the affair hidden. The book, Constance, the book is the thing.'

For the first time that day, the clouds began to lift at the Bank of Buxton. With the exception of Robert, who was thinking about Daisy, they looked at each other with new hope.

'But what if you are not successful?' William asked. 'Will Robert still consent to go after Mr Horne?'

'He will,' Constance replied. 'If I cannot get it back, then he must. Our very futures depend on it.'

Twenty-four

STRAIGHT AS a pin she sat in Edward's pew. The coat and her spine within it, the body and her heart within it, her falcon's nose and jay-blue eyes, all were rigid and without mercy. On a shelf in her brain, pat and black as the type in a printer's galley, lay her text from Job 24.

'Some remove the landmarks; they violently take away flocks, and feed thereof. They drive away the ass of the fatherless, they take the widow's ox for a pledge.' This she would declaim publicly, from the chancel steps. Then she would walk down to wherever Edward was sitting and for his ear only, invite him to listen to verse 15: 'The eye also of the adulterer waiteth for the twilight.' He would have seen what she was capable of. He would know what she wanted from him. He would be a stronger man than she thought if he did not concede. 'And if it be not so now, who will make me a liar, and make my speech nothing worth?'

She waited, her eyes fixed on a knot of pine above the heads of Daisy and Anthony Apreece, her breath motionless.

In the body of the church the unusually large congregation watched her keenly. Some knew more than others, but all had come to matins hoping that through the operation of their individual instincts, or through the pooling of their information, they would reach the truth of what had happened. The vicar had been seen speaking closely to Sir Anthony only two days before the bank closed its doors. Edward Horne had been closeted with Mr Pumfrey for nearly the whole of that morning. Jack Long had been heard to call him 'an out-and-out highwayman'. But then Mr Pumfrey had galloped to *Overmoor*. Whyever would he do that? And what was there for Digbeth Chiddlestone to be so cheerful about? So they pondered as they made their way to Winterbourne, and when they entered and saw Mrs Pumfrey ensconced in the pew that for generations had been occupied solely by the Hornes, they were certain they would depart edified.

The thoughts that were driving Edward to distraction as he walked up the nave were two: what was he to do now that he had Robert's loan book, and was Anthony mad? But from each, like long scarves of sea mist, trailed a whole series of subordinate questions that he could couch in only the vaguest terms; and in the space between them was a problem he could well have done without – how was he to think what he wanted to think when the man was standing directly opposite him?

'My goodness – Mrs Pumfrey!' he said, surfacing from his reverie. He withdrew his hand from the poppy head and took a pace back. 'I beg your pardon. I did not expect . . .'

Instinctively, he made a half-turn towards Daisy. There'd be room for him there if she moved up a bit . . .

But though she understood immediately what he wanted, she would not accommodate him. She did not like herself for this. But she wished him to know as clearly as looks could convey that she disapproved of what he had done to Robert. She had heard as soon as she returned from Mary Dipple's that Robert had had words with Anthony (warm ones according to Mrs Keech, roasting by Miss Hoole's scale). She did not understand how this was connected to the collapse of the bank. But the fact was that the Pumfreys were being driven from Buxton and Edward was responsible. A part of her was agreeably surprised by his boldness, but in general, as a statement of how she viewed the world, she abhorred the destruction of anything that was not demonstrably evil – and she wanted to make the point. Imperfect Robert might be – and of course she could not answer for the way he conducted his business – but she was sure he deserved better than this. So she made no attempt to find room for Edward and looked instead to the hymn board.

Reddening, Edward walked back down the aisle, conscious of a host of prying eyes upon him. At the far end of the church, sitting by himself – the rest of the family had colds – was David Scarlett. He stepped out and funnelled Edward into the pew. Edward pushed his hat out of the way and arranged himself.

'What is she up to?' he whispered.

'What are *you* up to?'

'No more than any other man would have done in my position.'

'Nothing, then, that you are ashamed of?'

'No! I would do the same tomorrow.'

'Then you have nothing to be worried about. She has occupied your pew; she has discomfited you in public; she has done what she set out to do. People will talk about it for a few days. That is the worst that can happen.'

'But she knows something. I spoke too strongly. I said that which should not have been said, least of all to her.'

'But words that are exchanged in the heat of the moment have no power.'

'They were not heated. I was speaking quite calmly. I meant what I said – and she knows it.'

'And you think she may use them against you, here, in church?'

'It was what I thought the instant I saw her.'

David looked up at Constance with his estimator's eye, and then back at Edward. 'You need to have the passion of someone like Luther publicly to denounce another person in church. And I do not see Mrs Pumfrey as a Luther.' He opened his hymnal. 'I should dearly like to know what it was that you revealed to her. I suspect that Eleanor of Aquitaine could tell me.' But when Edward made no reply, he said with a sigh of disappointment, 'No, Constance Pumfrey is no Luther, you may be assured.'

And so it was. The solemnity of the language, the dignity of the ritual, the repeated invocation of an Almighty and Merciful being, all those things about matins that so affected Daisy also laid their invisible weight upon Constance. Her hatred for Edward did not falter, but her courage did. At first, when she looked across at Daisy and saw a body so homely, so honest, so openly unadventurous, she thought: Edward was lying. It was his imagination that was at work. But later, when she happened to catch Daisy's eye, she glimpsed for a moment something in her expression that was imbued with such serenity and such heart-rending helplessness that even though she knew immediately that Edward had told no lie, the resolve within her began to trickle slowly away. A harridan from London or some frothy local wench, these she would gladly have torn limb from limb. But this small woman opposite, she could not, she would not injure. At least, she told herself, I kept Edward Horne out of his family pew and everyone saw it. He will think: This is an ugly turn to events; what plague will she visit on me next? I must seek an arrangement with the Pumfreys. Then it would be up to Robert.

The service ended. Daisy and Sir Anthony remained in their pew and she followed the shuffling worm of her fellow worshippers out of the church. All contrived to avoid speaking to her. Digbeth Chiddlestone pretended not to see her when she reached the door, but she waited so long that he was finally obliged to acknowledge her. And then she cut him dead, which gave her no little pleasure. A small part of her expected that Edward would be outside to draw her away and, were she ever so lucky, make a full restitution. But he had disappeared by the time she got out and more than ever she felt she was being hounded by circumstances she could not control.

That weekend the Indian summer had come abruptly to a close and a blanket of iron-grey cloud now lay over the hills. The rawness of the air prickled in her throat as Melson drove her back to Buxton.

As Mr Wormald had predicted, the determination of yesterday's crowd had proved inconstant and only a handful of men and women were there to jeer at her as the trap rattled into the yard at the back of the building.

Her brother was in the drawing-room. She frowned in reply to his expectant look and tossed her gloves on to a corded chest. Against one wall lay their rugs, rolled and bound. Two men of Mr Wormald's had that moment finished taking down the curtains and were carrying them out of the room. Archer closed the door behind them. Her words echoed off the denuded walls: 'The proper occasion did not arise. I took his pew. I embarrassed him greatly. But in the end' – she hesitated – 'it was not appropriate.'

'So in that case it is Robert who must do it. But we must ask ourselves' – he drew her into a corner – 'whether Robert is a man who can be relied upon in the situation one might envisage. I do not say that he is incapable, only that our prosperity, our entire way of life is at stake. It is imperative that we regain the book. Everything hangs upon it. And even if this is not our last chance, it is certainly our best one. We cannot afford a bungle now.'

'What are you suggesting?'

'Only that, with your consent, William and I accompany Robert. No more than that. It is not difficult to foresee a situation where six hands will be better than two.'

'I am relieved that I have at least one astute member of my family. But –'. She laid a hand on his sleeve. 'The connection should not be obvious, in case questions come to be asked – you understand what I mean. Robert has proposed that we spend tonight at the Green Man. He heard someone say it looked very like snow and he does not want to be caught out on the Derby road in the middle of nowhere.' She gave a brittle laugh. 'It is a pity he is not so careful in all things ... But you must not accompany us. You and William must find somewhere else to spend the night. Then tomorrow we can see about Mr Horne.'

To think he'd once called it the temple of optimism. It was the most hateful house he knew. He kicked open the door and threw himself into the first chair he came to. It stank, the whole place, inside and outside, not of fish-heads but of the feelings that came from within him, of rejection, despondency and solitariness. Happiness had been his, spurts of the most violent joy he could imagine – but now life was rushing at him with its dagger drawn.

Mary Paxton had left a cold meal for him. He ate it quickly and without relish. Then he called Sixpence and set out for a walk.

Was this what he should expect from loving a woman ten years older than himself? Did the scars of what had gone before fester for ever in a woman's mind and sprout fur, like old bread? Were they like the upas tree, which people said blighted everything for fifteen miles around? Or could one strong gust of youth blow them clean out of the window? How was he to know? One just had to have faith in the idea. They had touched upon faith, that day on the lawn at Overmoor. He had done most of the talking. In fact, he now realised, she had given away almost nothing. But he thought – at the time he had had the firm impression – that they understood each other. So why had she snubbed him in church? Of course she could not have offered him a seat, things being how they were, but the quiver of an *œillade*, a flicker of eyelashes, the dusty beat of moths' wings, that was all he'd been looking for. A gesture of love to defend him against Constance Pumfrey. She could have done it – but she had chosen not to. She had looked away and scorned him. It was not his fault alone that Robert was in difficulties. Anthony was out of sight in blame. But that was how she was interpreting it. Oh Robert, Robert, what have you done to us all?

And there it was. He had been looking in the wrong direction and while his back was turned truth had stumbled through the door on its own two feet.

'Well, my dear chap, it seems that you are the Bank of Buxton now. Let us see if you can play the hand better than Robert.' That was what David Scarlett had said as they parted, with his arch smile; and that, he now saw, was the precise cause of his dejection.

He skirted Bill Whitehead's debris and folding his coat skirts beneath him, sat on the terrace wall overlooking the Eve. Its slatey waters flowed silently down to the Rushes. The Paxtons and Tom Glossipp were herding the cattle up from the Out Ground to bring them into shelter. Cows halted to bellow for their calves and tossed their lowered heads at the dogs that circled them. The sounds echoed through the dismal afternoon.

For the umpteenth time he took Robert's loan book from his pocket. Was Anthony trying to buy the whole county? Women, horses, gambling – these were weaknesses he could understand. These were the stuff of life. No one should go to their grave without knowing something of vice. To assemble cases of enamels, or books, or Roman coins, these too were passions that had their place. But land! Where was the pleasure in beggaring oneself for the sake of rabbit warrens and wormcasts and things that bleated and died as soon as say good morning to you?

He flicked the book open with its pale green marker. And beggared himself Anthony most certainly had. Milkwells, the Tor, High Hill, Upward – every debt, every pustule of greed was chronicled in Robert's looping, generous hand. What possessed the man? What had possessed Robert to accommodate him? Eight per cent. There it was, eight per cent in black and white.

He turned more pages. Who were all these others? Hodberry – that had been the man Robert had called unreliable: he was paying ten per cent. Cutler – never heard of him – twelve per cent. Hodgkinson, the man whose wife had such a fine voice – he was ticketed at only seven. Each loan had been signed for. So if he wanted to, he could become a rural Shylock and on quarter days ride round the county collecting his interest. The capital, too, as it became payable. The moment he concerned himself with one he could not avoid the other. He didn't need a yard of brain between his ears to foresee all the entanglements he would encounter, the hostility, the whining, the excuses, the lawyers' fees. And Daisy, the lover of a debt-collector?

No! He thumped his fist into his palm. No, he would not be the Bank of Buxton. He would not be trapped in its sordid wrangling, his life consumed by endless dickering with farmers and merchants. He wanted – how should he phrase it? He rubbed his chin against his collarbone. How to pluck from such a boiling the words that would convey to Daisy exactly how he imagined their world?

He rose and set off along the terrace with his hands behind his back. This, he recalled with a casual nod to the past, was the route along which Digworth had patrolled when his father had vanished to further his private enquiries. Bong! bong! 'Mr Horne, Mr Horne, beetroot soup today, kidneys' – bong! – 'Cutlets' – bong! How clearly he could still hear those lugubrious incantations which had seemed, whenever it was foggy, to resonate up the drainpipe and into his schoolroom. He wondered what had happened to that set of dimpled gongs that were a daily temptation to a boy who had just slid down the banisters into the hall. He would have liked to be striking one now with its white, padded mallet to see if it could summon for him the word he was seeking.

How could he draw a picture for Daisy that had no lines? How could he explain to her all the hope and excitement that the word tomorrow conveyed to him? For this, at last, as he kicked a pebble at the door of his house and Sixpence came thundering out of the bushes, was the symbol that seemed clearest to him. Tomorrow was a splash of pink between half-opened curtains, snowdrops in their three-petalled hats, the song of small birds; it was rainbows arching through thunderclouds, the peal of church bells, the play of shadows on Daisy's instep, the crease of silk at her knee. It was the nip of expectation, the joy of discovery. It was life in a nutshell.

He had erred. It was as simple as that. He ought to have

abandoned his money at the bank, written it off to experience and left Robert and Anthony to come to blows or not. And now? He would get rid of the book and the slavery that went with it. He would return it to Robert first thing in the morning. It was for the best. It was the only way to free himself from the chains. And then –

He paused, the door ajar, Sixpence's nose pushing at the slit. He would take the tide in its fullness. Would she consent? Who could say? It would depend on the balance of faith. He ran down in the gathering dark to give his instructions to Davie.

Twenty-five

Amos did not like it. Edward could see that as soon as the gist of what he wanted from Davie became clear. He pecked at a callus on his thumb, several times made as if to speak and harrumphed noisily whenever Edward paused. But since the carriage could be arranged in no other way and since he was set on it, Edward paid him little attention and continued with his sketchmap of Derby on the scrubbed planks of the table.

'Now, Davie, where these streets join, this is the inn where the landlord always has two carriages for hire. Not post-chaises, mark you, but four-wheeled carriages. Leave Winterbourne at first light and unless you want your skin sent down to the tannery, return with one of them no later than the time the hens go to roost. Feel the axles and tap the felloes. Remove any old straw. Scrub out any marks of livestock. Look for hoppers under the cushions and down the sides and slay them to the last man. Give the coachman a half-guinea down with the promise of another half if he arrives here sober. And Amos, please do not grind your stumps like that. I know four-wheelers are expensive.'

It occurred to him as he left that perhaps there had been more to Amos's objection than mere cost. These country folk, nothing escaped them. A sparrow had only to cough and they'd discuss it for months. Well, that was their business and not his.

Sixpence pricked her ears and growled. He stopped, half-way up the hill, and listened. A horseman was crossing the bridge over the Eve. At a walk, at his leisure, and therefore most certainly not Robert, who would have been charging like a paynim. Even so there was something unsettling, something suggestive to his mind of the arras and dark deeds about the cadaverous echo of hoof on wood as it pingled through the dusk and among the boles of the still trees.

Anthony was wearing a brown woollen cap with a small shaggy peak and earflaps that were tied beneath his chin in a bow. He unfastened them and dropped the cap on to a chair. He undid his cloak at the throat-latch and laid it, rather studiously, over the back of the same chair. His boots were dry but dirty.

'I'm not disturbing you, am I? . . . I'm afraid I forgot to bring my slippers,' he said, looking down.

'Would you care for some spirits?' Edward asked.

'I would and that most readily,' he answered. His voice was more nasal than usual, his whole bearing unnaturally subdued.

'I think –'. He sat down and tugged his boots off. He stood them neatly under the arm of his chair.

'I've been thinking –'. Though by themselves so banal, the choice of these words and the docility with which he spoke them seemed quite extraordinary to Edward. He could so easily have said, It crossed my mind – a phrase much more in keeping with the assertive Anthony that he knew. Edward handed him his glass. He sniffed it and placed it untouched on the table beside him. He smoothed back Sixpence's scalp so that her eyes became yellowish chinks.

'I've come to apologise,' he said. 'My behaviour –'. He raised his hand. 'No, please say nothing for the moment. Just hear me out, I beg of you. Afterwards you can say what you want. This has not been an easy decision, as well you can imagine.

'Until you came home last year I was a peaceable, conscientious fellow going methodically about my business, improving my livestock, playing the squire, hunting my hounds, dancing at the Assembly Room; all the things a gentleman must do in the country. I did them very ably. With pride and a sense of accomplishment. No one bothered me. My word went uncontested. Yes, I was a sort of monarch, a hard-working monarch who dispensed justice and moderation with an even hand. That's who I was. From time to time I was able to add a few acres here and there – you know how it is with land. When the opportunity arises, you must drop on it like a hatchet, *coûte que coûte*. You must always think: I'll farm it better, prices'll go up, I'll pay for it somehow. Dally and you're lost. There's never a second chance with land. You must sever it from its owner the instant you see the way the wind's blowing. I don't think your brain cogs in quite the same way as mine in this respect.

'Oh yes, it has always been my dream to own Winterbourne. I'm not ashamed to admit it. Can I explain how it's felt? Somewhere between hunger, jealousy and love – yes, even love. Whenever I look at its fields and woods and the happy little Eve, whenever I think of its beauty, my heart gives a bounce. Isn't that what happens when you're in love? A jarring bounce that fills you with an ache to possess a thing? In the early days, when your parents were at Winterbourne, it didn't trouble me. It can wait, my time will come, I said to myself. I lay low and held my tongue. Nat died. Your mother took you off to London. An agent began to oversee it. And still I waited. Patience, I counselled – and I was patient. Unpassion yourself – and I did.

'And then you arrived from London, just when I was beginning to think your family had given up on the place. Just when I was beginning to hope. One day there was no other noise than the beating of my heart, and the next – there you were. I can still see you swaggering up the aisle that Sunday.

'I wanted to say, Get out, go away and leave us alone, go back to where you belong. And from that very day, I was a lost soul. Everything I had dreamed of was shattered. All my work was ruined. All the farms I'd bought, all the parcels of land I'd collected so carefully so that when the time came and Winterbourne was at last mine, I could close the ring on my map and say to myself, It's mine, all this land is mine for ever and no one can steal it from me – it all collapsed the morning I saw you in church. My blood boiled. I was like Prometheus with the crows pecking at my liver.

'So I had to start all over again. And I did. It's the kind of person I am. Nothing stops me once a notion has entered my head. At first I thought that if I was kind to you, and explained all the problems you'd inherited, you'd see sense and sell up. Reason must out in the end, that was how I calculated it. But you never listened.

'And then I could stand it no longer. What I couldn't achieve openly, I tried to achieve by stealth. I decided to shame you into selling. That was my purpose behind that dinner, my only

267

purpose. It was cheap, bombastic and selfish. I admit to each. You would have been perfectly within your rights to break my crown for what I said that night. Robert, too.'

Again he held up his hand. 'We shall come to Robert presently. But in respect to Winterbourne, I have acted grossly and unnaturally and I apologise to you and your father, of whom I also thought ill. That is what I have come here to say.'

His shadow, which Edward had been half-watching as it nodded and gesticulated on the wall behind him, thickened and spread across the ceiling. Anthony winced as his heel touched the floor. He sat down again.

'A touch of gout,' he said morosely. 'One's thoughts always turn downhill when one's poorly.'

'I'm sorry you thought ill of my father. You are the only person I have met who did not love him.'

'I spoke too loosely. It was not a personal animosity but a professional one, on account of his disdain for perfection. It was the same as I felt for you – until this morning.'

'What happened this morning?'

'You blushed. Your mind was elsewhere as you came up the nave. You saw Robert's wife in your pew. You looked to Daisy for support, you looked to me. Then you turned, and turning you blushed.'

'It is true. I cannot remember –'

'And I felt so envious of you, Edward. Yes, envy!' His face filled out. His eyes grew quite fresh and shining. 'I looked at myself and for the first time, yes, for the first time in my life, I saw who I was, a grumpy selfish man who had time only for *things*, whereas you – here was someone who spent his days laughing and waving his arms around, who could take a joke against himself (I was thinking of Polly), make friends, someone who could actually blush and then – I looked across at Constance –'

'Whom I believe you do not greatly care for –'

'Whom I have detested – but why? What has she ever done to harm me? I looked at her, I thought of Robert and their children and half-witted Sophia, I looked at you blushing – and I thought, God, what a beast I am.' He drained his glass and held it towards Edward.

'Why did you do it to Robert?'

'Two reasons. One, that it suited me not to have to repay him at that particular moment. And here's another thing . . . God, I wish I could walk properly. Pass me that stool would you? Ah, that's better . . . Anyway, you'll have learned from Robert about the scrape I was in with Gomez and the Funds. Well, yesterday morning what do you think happened? Clem Dawkins drove up with a letter from London. And here was that ass Gomez, only a month after he'd told me the world was coming to an end, writing to say the threes had gone up by eight points and a profit was in sight. The little man, all those threats – for nothing! I'd scallywagged Robert needlessly! But the other reason –'. His face grew serious again.

'I saw him refuse his horse a drink. Just when the weather was at its hottest this summer, I saw him ride up to the Green Man, his horse perishing of thirst – I tell you, when it smelled the water trough it pulled its lips half-way up its jaws: you could see every tooth in its mangy head it was that desperate. And all Robert did was tie it up and go in and have a drink himself. I can't abide a man who'd do that to a horse.'

'You astonish me.' It was true. He could think of nothing else to say. In fact, he felt quite moved. This handsome, and he believed sincere, apology showed a degree of humility in Anthony he had not thought possible. His dissatisfaction with himself, the yearning for a different skin in which to do business with the world, reminded him of his own mood earlier in the day, when he had returned from church.

'Yes, that's what I am,' Anthony was saying. 'I've been a beast to Daisy, to you, to Robert, to my brother and I am truly penitent. I'm not taking up too much of your time, am I?'

Edward went into the hall to fetch another coal scuttle. He undid his knee buckles so that his stockings hung in rumples down his shanks.

'How boyish you look! Just like Nat! Exactly the same impish expression, as though you had a frog in one of your pockets.' He took his feet off the stool and rested his forearms on his knees. He made a loose juggling motion with his hands. 'Do you know what else I thought this morning? I thought, if only I'd had children – sons, of course – I should never have been so driven by this desire to own land. They would have ruined me, that goes without saying –'

'You seem to have got yourself in a fair state without a family.'

'Maybe, but the cause would have been nobler. When I die, my name will die with me. 1674 was when we got our title and one day soon it'll be gone – pfft. Struck from the record, buried in clay with these horrible bones of mine. How sad is our mortality, how fatuous our efforts to leave some monument behind to show we have existed.'

'But you have a brother –'

'A half-brother. The same mother, that is all we have in common. But had Daisy been able to bear my children – I should not be here now, Winterbourne would not have become my passion, all this land I have fought for, it would have meant nothing to me. I should have had my children instead. Ach, but it is a dream, the bitterness of someone who finds that many miles ago he took the wrong turning.'

He looked intently at Edward: 'It did not have to be Daisy, you know. I could have had any woman in the county without leaving my chair. Believe you me, any woman I chose. And then how different my life would have been. But that's by the by. It can't be mended now.' He dabbled his hands around again.

'Look, Edward, one of my tenant farmers from out Billy Tor way came to the house yesterday. There's an old dog fox killing his lambs left and right and he wants it dealt with. The sooner the better. A big ginger bugger with a lop ear. Said he'd withhold his rent unless I took Priam and the rest of the hounds over. So why don't you and I take the pack out tomorrow, give our livers a good shake-up and then – then I'll give you the money I owe Robert.'

He leaned back with a chuckle.

'I thought that would surprise you. But I've got to start somewhere and Robert's is the neediest case. What you do with it then is up to you. At least my conscience will be clear –'

The hall door burst open, there was a rush of feet and in a second Davie Paxton was crumpling his bonnet before them, his face running with sweat.

'It's Madge Smith, sir, she's been and had an accident and they need help. Arthur and Mr Pumfrey can't do it by themselves, there's no one else in, no man that is, Miss Pumfrey's been taken queer like and –'

'Calm yourself, Davie, and tell us what's happened. Slowly, now.'

But the dew of his gallop was still fresh on him and Davie was in no mood for slowness. 'Fizzy-tizzy wasn't half the word for Father when you left. Them four-wheel carriages are a spenny piece of work at the best of times, he says. Master'll soon be clean out of blunt at this rate. Now if he had someone to share the cost – so off he sends me to Arthur's to see if there'd be other folk thinking on going down to Derby tomorrow night – well and well, I'm coming to it at any moment, sir – but when I got there – Mrs Pumfrey, now there's a hedgehog in petticoats if ever I saw one –'

'The Pumfreys are at the Green Man?' Edward asked.

'Oh yes, sir, all of them. Their big travelling coach is at the door. Seemingly they're waiting to see what the weather does before setting out for Derby. Didn't want to be caught in any snow, I expect. And that Mrs Pumfrey – Fetch me this, Mr Innkeeper, fetch me that. It was a treat to see Arthur jump.'

'I'll wager that's the truth of it,' Edward said with a portion of a smile. 'But Madge, what of her?' he continued, wishing to hasten Davie into safer waters.

'Can't say for sure how it happened, only that she was out in the shed with a troubled cow and it had a sort of seizure, leastways that's how it seemed to us, and fell on Madge and the two of them are lying there in ever such a tangle, and Arthur told me to ride up here as fast as I could.'

'Come along, Anthony, let you and I go down to the Green Man.'

But Anthony did not move. He joggled his leg and pointed to his foot. 'Mustn't overdo it or I'll be no good for hunting tomorrow.'

'Sorry, Davie. Sir Anthony has the gout. You'll have to get Amos to help you. And Tom and Walter. That should be enough to get a sling under the animal. Put the wagon to and take a length of rope with you.'

The door closed. Sixpence yawned and spread herself across the hearthstone. A raffle of soot plunged down the chimney, half-smothering the coals. Anthony fixed Edward with a slow stare.

'A four-wheeler, eh ... Now that's a most superior sort of

271

vehicle. What can it be for? Why not a humble trap like the rest of us? I shall have to consider what sort of purpose a single gentleman can have with a carriage like that during the night. Let it pass as a ball. You are going to a ball tomorrow near Derby and wish to think well of yourself.' He bent down to put on his boots. Sixpence came over and burrowed her nose into his doings. 'Yes, little doggie, your master is going to a ball which no one has told me about. Donning his alderman's coat and going far, far away, across moors and dales and rivers, through peaks and high places, and for this he needs a four-wheeled carriage, like a banker we know who is also going far, far away. So only you and I will be left, little doggie, only you and I to wuffle at the clouds.' He slid his hand under Sixpence's jaw and, shaking it softly, gazed into her eyes. 'Only you and I, little whatsyourname . . .'

He stood up, swirled his cloak round his shoulders, and pulled down the peak of his woollen cap. On his way through the hall, he stopped to tap the Dollond.

'Humph. It's strange that a barometer should rise before snow. You know, I think I'll buy Daisy a new dress. It's high time I did something for her. That thing she wore the other night – grey was never my colour. It reminds me of – oh well. It doesn't matter for now. Tomorrow morning then, are we agreed?'

'But no banknotes, Anthony. London bills only, if you please.'

Edward set the candle on the ground and helped him on to his horse. For a few moments he lingered on the step, listening to the hooves clopping down the hill. Then he went in and started to pack a trunk.

Twenty-six

EDWARD SUPPOSED he had slept, though for the life of him he couldn't imagine when. It seemed when he awoke that it had been only a minute ago he had last looked at his night clock. But he felt sharp and limber. He lay in bed for a few minutes and then remembered Davie would be on the road for Derby, so there'd be no hot water for him this morning.

He dressed quickly: a greyish flannel undershirt, a pair of thick yarn stockings to go with socks over, his best tan buckskins (a colour they called London style), an overshirt and a clean white stock. He picked out of the box his favourite stockpin, one with a round pink knob like a baby radish, and slid it at an angle through the heavy folds of cloth. He tilted his nose with a forefinger and clipped its hairs. He put on a heavy woollen waistcoat of his father's and sat down to latch up his boots.

He had thought at length about Anthony's conversion during the long night hours. He did not disbelieve it now any more than he had the previous evening. But he was warier. He saw no reason to involve himself further with a man whom he would shortly see the last of. The moment he accepted a penny of Anthony's money, he would be stepping straight into Robert's shoes. So he would return the book to Robert as he had originally planned, and have done with it.

He fastened the straps of his boot garters and tried a few steps. Though he had made Davie oil them every day for a month, and had even had him walk the farm in them, his new hunting boots were still far from supple and cut into his instep. He put on his coat, an old-fashioned knee-length frock coat that once had been scarlet but which after three generations had weathered to the pink of a half-ripe cherry. He picked his riding cap and gloves off the table; and glanced around. Everything was packed and roped. Davie could take it down in the wagon. Davie, he would say, I want you to look after this place if it starts to crowd on Amos. Mr Wiseman will deal with the money. Keep an eye on Bill and the roof, for one day I wish to live here with my family. Be kind to Sixpence and do not let another soul on Luna.

The autumn air smelt of frosted nettles. He inhaled deeply. Then he walked down the hill with Sixpence to see if Mary Paxton had breakfast on the go.

When he came out, he found Amos smearing tallow grease on Luna's hooves. This displeased him for he had expected to find her hooves blacked and gleaming like coal.

'There's snow around,' Amos said shortly. His scarf tail unwound itself and obscured his vision. He put down the tallow brush, laid Luna's fetlock across his knee, and tucked it back into the top of his smock. His face was pinched and poorly slept in.

'T'ain't none of my business and I know that. I know that so it's no good telling me it ain't. And it's not the cost of a four-wheeler I'm speaking of. You know well enough what I mean, just the same as I know what you're up to. But it'll go hard on us who's left if you ups and down the road not alone like. I'm not saying you aren't a free man to do as you pleases, but there's others besides yourself in the world. There'll be a rare hugaboo, I'm telling you, Mr Edward –'

Edward stepped off the mounting block. Luna shook her head and snortled knowingly through her velvety nostrils. A wisp of foam showed white at the sides of her mouth as she played with her bit.

'– there'll be such a song and dance as I expect we'll never hear the end of.'

He patted his pockets: knife, string, flask, Robert's book. He took the flask out and shook it against his ear. He checked inside his saddlebag: three apples, a large piece of Mary's gingerbread wrapped in a greasy paper, a spare girth, a small hammer, a hoofpick and a pair of pliers. He wriggled into his gloves (which were the colour of a beech tree's bark in winter), stowed a second pair under his saddle flap, and standing up in his stirrups, eased his crutch.

'My whip, please, Amos. And you're right, it's none of your business. If you didn't want to hear the answer, you shouldn't have asked the question. Tell Davie when he gets back that I want to leave here no later than five.'

He tapped his cap down, turned the mare's head and set off up Ladysway to the Green Man.

'About an hour ago,' Arthur Smith replied, his frowzy head protruding sideways from the small kitchen window. 'And it's not a blind bit of good asking me where he went. Wait. I'll go round to the door. Everything's very slow this morning without Madge.'

'What of Madge, then?' Edward asked a few moments later.

'Twas only a scraping she got, so it turned out when we got the cow off. All that straw and muck in the shed, that's what saved her. Gave her a good squashing, that's for sure. But the cow's dead, no mistake about that, deader than justice. Have a slice with your breakfast, I says to Mr Pumfrey, but he wasn't overkeen at all. I read him as a man with something on his mind. So it'll be a week of ragout for everybody.'

'Did Mr Pumfrey give you no idea at all where he was going?'

'Nary an inkling. Said he had some business to deal with and rode off. I just wish the whole lot of them had gone with him. Phah! We'd be better off with a plague of grasshoppers. You could tell they were at loggerheads as soon as they arrived. Yap yap yap, I could see them at it as they sat in their coach.' Arthur made a parrot's beak imitation of Robert and Constance arguing. 'Place wasn't fine enough for her, any fool could see that. But in the end he got her out and in she stalks as if she was carrying a sceptre in her pudsy white hand. Eyes like thorns. "Best watch our step here," I says to Madge. First she had to inspect the rooms. Sniffs. "Are you sure I'll be warm enough here, Mr Innkeeper?" she says. "Madam," I says, "you'll be warmer'n a finger up a duck, I give you my word for it." "Oooh," goes the batty one and tipping askew in the makings of a faint, catches her head on the edge of the stairs, whereupon she wakes up smartish and starts bawling, and madam gives her a clip round the ear and Mr Pumfrey says, "You can do that to your family but I'm damned if you'll do it to mine," and grabbing her by the nose – which is a bit of an invitation, the length it has to it – gives it a good tweak, so of course she starts up too – and then her trunk wouldn't go up the stairs without that I take off the newel head – I'm telling you . . .'

'I think Mrs Pumfrey is accustomed to a better class of accommodation.'

'It's not us who asked them to stay at the Green Man.' Arthur peered up at the sky. 'It'd be just my luck if she was to get herself snowed in. The way they were talking last night, she's of a mind to reach her father's by this evening. Let's hope for it, Mr Horne, let's hope for it . . . This carriage that Davie was to get for you – quite between ourselves – anything a man should read into it?' His eyes darted up and down Edward.

'Was Mrs Pumfrey going down to Derby by herself?'

'You mean was Mr Pumfrey going with her? So far as I can make it out, he's going to follow her tomorrow morning. Leastwise he's brought his riding horse with him, so I expect that's what he intends. But where he's gone today, I really can't be saying.'

They heard Constance calling for her chocolate and Edward quickly remounted. He had no wish to encounter her and certainly did not propose to leave Robert's book with her.

He rode up the turnpike until he reached the top of the hill, where he branched left for Overmoor. He met Moley Dibdin scratching along in his donkey cart, Johnnie Alcock sitting on his stool breaking stones, and a train of wool carters who stank of mutton grease and spoke anxiously of the snow they could smell in the wind. He would miss them, he thought, he would miss all these familiar characters with their unmannered ways and odd snippets of information. Even Arthur Smith, the old gossip.

The oval pate of Billy Tor loomed slowly into view. Behind it the bland grey sky was scored by horizontal bands of darker clouds. Smoothly and sullenly it flowed over the heathland. As he descended to Overmoor, the sun broke through and spread across the shoulder of the hill a smear of corpselike yellow. Then the clouds closed in again.

Clayton was unrugging Anthony's cob as Edward rode into the stableyard.

'No one else to come?' he asked.

'Nobbut the two of you, sir, and master's proper done up this morning with the gout, so it's Fulke who'll be hunting the hounds by my way of thinking. Nine and a half inches across the root of his toes, that's what Mrs Keech told Hucknall.' He finished folding the rug over his arm and gestured in wonderment with his fingers. 'Nine and a half inches, would you credit it?'

But already Edward was half-way out of the yard. He was thinking: Has Davie found a carriage; and what if she wasn't complaisant, if their passions were agley, if she wanted a discussion, for which there was no time. He took out his handkerchief and, leaning down, flicked it over his boots. He wished Amos had polished Luna's hooves.

The front door was open. He halted, facing up the steps and into the dark recess of the hall. The pontifical ticking of the big clock was plainly audible. With each stroke, another fraction of his life was unpeeled. Down these steps she had walked, only six months ago, to greet Luna – and of a sudden down them she was walking again, gravely, firmly, her eyes fixed on his, each shining leather foot carrying her, it seemed to him, one more pace towards a carriage waiting with doused lights.

'So,' she said quietly, running her forefinger down the arch of the rein, 'how is Luna this morning? How is her master?'

She was wearing a long, wide-pleated coat of titmouse blue. It was fastened at the neck with a silver button, had narrow lapels, and on each side of her chest a triangle of three more silver buttons. Its cuffs and hems were trimmed with beaver fur, as was its collar which she'd turned up round her ears. A belt of a much darker blue with a figure-of-eight buckle gathered it at the waist. Her wide hat was black, to match her boots, its brow pulled down so that her eyes peeped out like a forest creature from its lair.

'Last night', she said, 'I arrived in my dreams at an unwalled place, alone. The air was hazy and the ground was carpeted in thick, gritty sand. It looked like a desert, but I could sense the presence of people around me. There was nothing hostile about it. I felt perfectly comfortable in myself. Antioch was the word that came to me, I cannot say why. A distance away – you know how difficult it is to judge distances in a dream – was a town with ramparts made of mud, with narrow alleys and poplars growing on the banks of tiny rippling streams –'

Hucknall came carefully down the steps, watching his feet round the corner of the tray he was holding. Edward frowned at

Daisy and said loudly, 'Nine and a half inches is what Clayton told me.'

'Master's just putting on his boots,' Hucknall said. 'We had to rip them or he'd never have managed it.' He proffered the tray to Edward, watched as he took a tankard and walked off across the lawn.

Edward flicked up the lid of the negus with his thumb and regarded Daisy through a cloud of spice-flavoured steam.

'He has brought me a genie,' he said in a low voice. 'Did your dream have an end?'

'Not really. I wanted to get to that city. I *had* to. There were people there in bright-coloured robes who kept waving me towards a particular place by the stream. I could see donkeys walking away from it, tied head to tail, with full panniers and scarlet cockades in their headbands. I expected to find a bridge, but when I got to the edge of the bank there was nothing but the water and swirling skeins of watercress. Then I woke up.'

There was a gleeful roar from the kennels and the repeated crack of a whip. Luna took a half pace backwards.

'Come with me, Daisy, come to this place and let me be your bridge.' His voice was urgent, his eyes plunged into hers. 'By ourselves we are nothing in this world. I need you, Daisy, I *need* you.'

The mingled cries of the hounds drew closer.

'This evening there will be a carriage waiting in the quarry a mile this side of the Green Man. It will take us to Derby. There we can catch the night coach to London. By this time tomorrow – come with me, Daisy, by the splendour of God I beg it of you.'

Her eyebrows rose like a pair of leaping fish. She glanced behind her, towards the head of the lane from which the hounds were starting to pour. She looked back at Edward. She ran her gloved palm up Luna's muzzle and teased a sprig of hair out of her headband. 'Is it a command your master is giving me, or an invitation? These things are important to ladies.' Then: 'I shall think about it. If you find on your return that Clayton and the trap are gone, you will know that I am waiting for you. If you do not –'

Skirling with joy, their sterns curling over their backs like scimitars, the dogs fanned out across the lawn. Behind rode Anthony, enormous in a blistering scarlet coat, and at his shoulder

Fulke, his terrier man, a sparse, ageless figure with a face as wrinkled as a walnut.

'But sir,' Daisy said with a brisk laugh, 'you cannot go hunting with a cup in your hand.' He passed it to her and rode over to join Anthony.

His face was furrowed with pain. His eyes glared crabbily out of their dark-rimmed sockets. He pointed at his boots with his whipstock. They had been slit along the side of each foot and tied loosely around with twine. Clayton had fashioned for him a pair of padded rope stirrups through which his heels could hang. He took the tankard that Hucknall was holding and emptied it at a draught.

'Should you wish to know what purgatory is,' he said to Edward, 'it is having to chase someone else's fox with one's feet in buckets of red-hot nails. I shall not love this day. I shall hate it. Be careful I do not hate you with it. Now we shall go.'

His eye fell upon Daisy standing with her arms folded. 'To think I could have had any of them in the county . . .' He suddenly whirled round and threw his tankard at Hucknall, catching him in the middle of the ribs so that he gasped. 'Take it, you damned cheeser, and get out of my sight,' he shouted, 'and don't come near me again until I need you.'

His hands were shaking as he picked up the reins. 'And where the devil do you think you're going, Horne? Not over the lawn, man, not on the lawn. Oh God, the lawn . . . What are you standing there for, Hucknall? Can't you remember what a roller looks like? Have those hoof prints taken out by the time I get back or I'll roll you in with them. Fools! Fools! Around me everywhere . . .' He dug in his spurs and cantered heavily out of the gate that Clayton was holding.

'If you see Robert before I do, give this to him with my compliments.' Edward fished Robert's book out of his pocket and bundled it into Daisy's two hands. 'Your husband is mad. Yesterday I thought not, but this morning I am sure of it. And what worries me is that to every lunatic is given an allowance of sanity. I am fearful, Daisy my love, fearful on all sides.'

She watched them depart, two red splashes amid a rippling pool of white and tan. A little behind rode Fulke. Thus do men leave for war, she thought, thus the Scots left their homes to die on Flodden hill. She closed the door and sat in the chair beside the stove, drumming her fingers on its arms. Miss Hoole passed by on her way upstairs, holding a pot of negus. They exchanged a few words. Presently Daisy took the book from her pocket and started to read.

Twenty-seven

IT FELT to Edward as if he were riding into a world upon which the dust of creation had only lately settled. The trim fields of Overmoor slipped away. Its green and rounded vales became tangled banks of thorns. Each coomb seemed deeper and harsher than its predecessor. Remorselessly the hills crowded in on them. Soon they were riding in single file along a sheep path that straggled through a jumble of gorse and boulders. Above them the hounds worked busily through the scree, their white rumps flickering like handkerchiefs. Below oozed a dark brook criss-crossed by the skeletons of dead trees from which swags of lichen hung like rotting cerements.

Daisy and Winterbourne were suddenly very distant. There was something about the savageness of their surroundings that frightened him. It was all so bleak, so primeval. This was how it must have been thousands of years ago when every step a man took was a duel against the power of nature. Here, perhaps along this same path, men in skins with spears in their hands had once prowled, and stopped and grunted as they bent to examine a muddy spoor. How little things had really changed. Those people would have understood without a word of explanation the tingle of fear at the base of his neck, his feeling of helplessness among these brutal manifestations of a force unimaginably greater than his own. He was a pigmy, a tiny and ephemeral speck by comparison.

Occasionally Fulke let fly a whoop of encouragement to the dogs, but otherwise it was in silence that they rode. They came to a cliff jutting out into the brook and rounded it, their coats brushing against the dripping rock. Now the terrain took a change for the better. The hills opened up and they found themselves in a sort of basin, with gentler slopes and a floor of pasture shaped like the head of a spoon. The atmosphere was less oppressive to Edward. The stream had come to life and was babbling in his ear. He cantered forward to where Anthony was waiting.

'Hill Brake,' he said brusquely, pointing to a newly planted covert on the opposite bank that was thick with brambles and the shabby grey flags of autumn willow herb. Fulke trotted off to make an uphill cast with the hounds.

'Toasty-looking place,' Edward said amenably. 'If I was Charlie, it's here I'd come to lie up.' He leaned forward, his hands folded over the pommel. 'How d'ye think he'll run, over the hill or out down the valley?'

Luna stared into the hillside with her ears pricked, her head as vigilant as the beak of a Viking galley. A few small flakes of snow fell.

'As a fox usually does, where he pleases. As doubtless you will also. It appears to be the way you lead your life.'

'Last night you did not have these bees in your breeches.'

'Then I was not thinking what I am now. Do you expect me to pat you on the head every time we meet?'

Of a sudden they heard the tremulous whimper of a bitch hound running a solitary line at the top of the wood. For a moment it hung in the windless valley. It was repeated, sharper and more confidently. Luna took a step forward. Then there rose from the heart of the brake an exultant roar as the pack hit off the scent, a sound as vibrant as a peal of cathedral bells, as spine tingling as the rumble of war drums. Fulke blew half a dozen staccato notes on his horn.

'Go. Follow Fulke. Follow any damned thing you please so long as you leave me to myself.'

Edward looked at the sky. Five hours he had, or perhaps six, before the rendezvous. Had they agreed a definite time? No, he had only to see if Clayton and the trap were still there. In the answer to that lay the answer to everything. So meanwhile –

He unleashed Luna and like a chamois she scrambled up the hillside in pursuit of Fulke's russet, faunlike figure.

They reached the top. Head low, eyes slitted, calves gripping Luna's ribs like staves round a barrel, he settled to his task. A wall:

they topped it with a clink of iron on stone. Another wall and a third, strong black walls with never a gap to fiddle through. Over they sailed, as smoothly as thistledown. The ground tipped sharply away below him. Down they slithered as hounds streamed up the opposite bank, arrowing slips of cream and brindle. The rant of tongues, Priam's booming cry: the valley echoed with their tumult. A loop right-handed along a meadow bottom, a set of roughly hewn rails, a double bank with a bushy ditch between – Gad what a horse! Pegasus was not her equal! Up a slope in Fulke's hoof prints, over its brow by a single oak, past a knot of staring sheep, another leap, another downward plunge, divots spattering to right and left . . . 'Rocks, 'ware rocks,' came a shout from Fulke somewhere in front of him, but he saw no rocks, only a drizzle of thorns rushing towards him. He glanced left, he glanced right. No room for a sparrow, oh Jesus Christ, god and mortal rolled into one, oblige a sinner and send him a path – and there it was, and down the tunnel they went, twigs thrumming on his coat and snapping at his cap. Off it flew, but what did he care? Less than a peppercorn. Like a bung from a bottle they burst from the spinney. Peppercorn peppercorn peppercorn he sang to match Luna's stride. A grassy glade, an open gate, the rattle of hooves on stone, a sheep pond with two mallard (the drake very green), apples bouncing in his saddlebag, a crow floating through the pancaked sky. But *oiseau oiseau* we too can fly and over the stream they went, an absolute piddle they both agreed, looked this way, looked that way, peered, listened, wondered – and halted.

So where was Fulke? Where the hounds? Where Anthony? Silence. Everywhere silence.

He trotted on down the valley. God, but this was a miserable part of the world. Dense, dark, spiky undergrowth pressed in on him from both sides, tortuous alleys that led nowhere, the snow rising at his back. A man could get lost in country like this, lost until his bones were bleached to ivory . . .

He rounded an elbow and saw in front of him Fulke drawing a steep, gorsey bank and below him Anthony, watching. How the devil –? A babble of triumph broke out afresh from the hounds. He put his head down and went in pursuit as Anthony swung sharply uphill into a curling sadsome wood of yews and box.

He found the woodcutters' track by which Anthony had

entered. The sky vanished. Silence descended like a blanket. He felt as if he was trespassing in the abode of wood goblins. After a few hundred yards, he reached a fork in the way. He strained his eyes for the glimpse of a scarlet coat: listened for the snap of twigs. But it was as quiet as the grave. How could the man have disappeared so quickly? He dismounted and examined the ground. But it was too hard and the light too dim beneath the yews to make out any hoof prints. He squeezed his nose pensively. The upper road looked the more used. It was always preferable to have the advantage of height . . .

A woodcock came swinging down it, low and deft. Its liquid eye quizzed him as it passed. Then it banked and flipped like a wraith through the inky canopy. He climbed back into the saddle and turned Luna up the slope.

He rode with his left hand flat on his thigh. From time to time he spoke a few words towards the back of Luna's nodding head. He came to a gap and looked up. The sky was the colour of pewter. The wind had risen and was soughing through the trees. A snowflake landed on the coarse sprig of hair between Luna's mane and her forelock. He shivered and continued more rapidly.

He fetched Daisy out of his thoughts and set her on his saddle bow. What was she doing? Pacing before her drawing-room windows, one small foot behind the other, a finger tapping against her teeth? Was she thinking of him, could she see him riding up this dark tunnel, could she feel him reaching out for her? Had she decided? Had she done her packing? How many trunks would she bring? What would Clayton think? She would have to say she was going to stay with the Dipples, or with her brother.

He took out Mary Paxton's gingerbread and ate half of it. Luna's ears twitched at the sound. The other half he put back in his bag. One could never tell. He might not get a decent meal before Derby. He took a pull at his flask.

Then there were welcome portholes of daylight in front of him. The yews ceased and he found himself riding on the top side of a steep bank of sycamores and ash poles (which his woodmen called whistlers). He came to a clearing where the tree-fellers had been working. In its centre was a mound of ash, its crust tinged in places with a rusty colour. A few yards away stood a crude shelter of branches laced through a framework of ash stakes. A number of tracks radiated from the clearing. He studied them carefully. Hoof prints there were in numbers, but none of them were fresh; and he could tell by their size they had been made by draught horses and not by Anthony's cob. He stopped. It was later than he supposed. Dark would come early on a day like this. Already the bramble leaves were speckled with snow. His forehead was cold now that the sweat had dried on him. He should have had more sense. It would have cost him only a couple of minutes to go back for his cap.

He tried to read the land, to imagine how this wilderness connected to the great lump of Billy Tor, which he could now see plainly in front of him. It was obvious that he had taken the wrong turn at the fork. Somewhere he would have seen Anthony's marks by now. Therefore there must exist below him another and probably easier route. He peered down the hill. It would be a sore piece of work. Plenty of places a horse could break a leg. And to what advantage? He looked back at the yews and the path by which he'd come. He could not deny it. Retreat was the more inviting prospect.

But at the same time he knew he would not. There was business to be finished with Anthony that could perforce be done in this place and no other. From the moment that Davie had unwittingly disclosed the arrangement with the carriage, he had been conscious of the inevitability of a confrontation. It would not be a pleasure. No, not for either of them. But now that matters had progressed in the way they had, he saw it as a natural and necessary conclusion to this part of his life. The medicine had to be swallowed: one day he would feel a better man for it. He fastened his collar button.

Tk! Tk! He flung out an arm to keep his balance and pushed Luna down a slick, clayey bank which she took sitting almost on her hocks.

Down they went, lurching and slithering and picking their catlike way round tree roots and trembling green mosses, through scrub oaks and screes and slabs of rock the size of billiard tables, down they went through the lightly falling snow to he knew not where with the sole intent of telling a man he was going to take his wife. Could there be, he wondered, a stupider thing in the world? And this was the thought that was still rolling round his mind as the ground levelled off and with one arm thrown up to protect his face, he plunged through the spikes of a blackthorn thicket and emerged into a narrow grassy bottom.

'Good God!'

'Poorish road you've come by, sir.' Fulke said impassively, looking up at Edward from under his eyebrows as he lit a stumpy clay pipe.

'I thought . . . Where's . . . ?'

'Sir Anthony decided that seeing as how the dogs were his, they'd answer better to him than to me. Charlie diddled him for a while back there, but not two minutes ago I heard them strike his line again, so if you ride on smartish, sir, you should still get a peck at the business.' He nipped a thorn out of Luna's shoulder. 'We was watching thee, you know. Only a good 'un could have carried thee through that lot. Now as I said, sir, if you press on fairish . . .' He put his tinderbox away.

He was waiting for Edward, sitting squarely on his horse in the centre of the glade, a scarlet giant amid white petals of falling snow. Around him the defeated hounds lay panting, licking their paws. Priam snuffled round a soily maze of holes, his torn ears brushing the ground.

Edward dismounted and walked round flexing his legs. He took an apple out of his saddlebag and offered it to Luna. Her rubbery lips whickered over the mound of his thumb. He wiped his sleeve across his forehead. He remounted and looked Anthony in his grey, crumpled face.

'Well then . . . there is a tide in the affairs of all men and it is to here that it has brought us.'

'I shall not give you what I owe Robert. I've changed my mind.'

'I never thought you would. You do not have the money. It is all around us, in the land, the trees and the cattle, but it is not in your pocket. I did not think so yesterday and I do not think so now. In any case I am leaving Winterbourne tonight and I wish to be free of all your petty snares.'

From out of the trees on the edge of the glade rode Fulke. He tapped the dottle from his pipe and nodding, began to count the hounds.

'Only Ajax and Oarsman missing – no, there you be, you devil.

So it's only Oarsman to account for. Do you want that I take them home when I've found him, Sir Anthony? T'aint a night for a man in your condition to be out, begging your pardon.'

'As you like.'

He caught up his whip and led the way back into the wood, down a dark track. Sparrow flocks of leaves danced along in front of them. The crowns of ashes clattered against each other like sabres in the rising wind. After about fifteen minutes they reached a piece of open ground where the track forked. A snow-rimmed pole stuck in a pile of boulders marked the divergence of the ways, downwards to Buxton after many a mile, upwards to the pass over the shoulder of Billy Tor. On the top side of this small plateau stood the carcass of an ancient ash tree. For thirty or forty feet its massive warty stump rose straight and true. But there it ended and now only one limb remained of its former pride, a single branch that it had nurtured through the slow ebb of its life. Under it they halted.

Anthony pointed to Billy Tor. 'There lies your way to the Britannia road. As you pass along it, you will recognise the place where you first lay with my wife. I think you would both find it too inhospitable today. It concerns me that your carriage may be impeded by the snow. I expect it worries you too. It would me if I was in your situation, no end.' His tone was even and agreeable. He tapped a few grains of snuff into the hollow at the back of his thumb. A sudden gust blew it off and his sneezing horse skittered away, brushing his foot against the ash stump. He grimaced with pain.

'A few days ago I made a plan to kill you just along there. A few hundred yards on there's a gorge with a bridge across it, none too safe at the best of times. It would not have been difficult to lure you into crossing it. The hounds would have been on the other side, hot on the scent of the aniseed bag that I'd have trailed along the ground. We'd have galloped towards the bridge like madmen – and it's nothing but a rickety thing of sticks nailed to a couple of poles, truly it is. "After you," I'd have shouted, or I'd have taken a little fall, it wouldn't have mattered which. Down you'd have gone and I'd have trotted woefully home and said to everyone, I shouted but he wouldn't stop. Damnedest piece of bad luck you ever did hear of. Poor Ned, unlucky just like his father. And do you know what I'd have done next? I'd have bought Winter-bourne and moved in there myself. Probably without Daisy. Yes, on reflection I'd have left Daisy at Overmoor.'

'Why are you telling me this? Do you want to hear how grateful I am that you've changed your mind again?'

'Don't treat me like a child, Edward. I am quite serious about this. When I came to see you last night, it was to offer you a sort of *farewell* apology. I meant everything that I said. I was never more sincere in my life. I *am* a beast. It is exactly how I see myself when I am being candid. But then your man let slip about the four-wheeler and I suddenly thought: death is too easy for you. Dead men can't feel a thing. I want you alive so that you know what it's like when men spit at you, when you hear them say – not so loud that you can be certain, but loud enough – "That's him, that's the man who stole Sir Anthony's wife." I want you to feel every insult, every cut, jibe and poke that's in store for you.'

'Good. I hoped you'd say something like this. I could have cut and run hours ago but I said, no, Anthony wants to feel wronged; I shall not disappoint him.'

'It'll go on for years. The pair of you will be marked until you die. And if Daisy tries to divorce me, there's first the ecclesiastical court, then an action in the courts of common law and if and when she obtains her decrees there, she'll have to approach the House of Lords and sue for an Act of Parliament. A pretty penny it'll cost, and all the time you'll be branded as the paramour. Paramour Horne! I declare it would suit you very well.'

'And in the meantime you can pass yourself off as the innocent dupe. You should be careful. You have a peculiarity that few people care for.'

'Do I? If you say so, I suppose I must, for you are demonstrably well learned on the subject of sin . . . Of course, you must realise that you can never live at Winterbourne with Daisy. Even you would not have the gall for that. And Daisy is completely devoid of that sort of courage. In fact it surprises me that you have managed to wind her up to the pitch that you have. It must be a very great passion indeed. You will have to live abroad, you know, and Daisy is quite provincial in her ways. I really can't answer how she'll take to it. A few times to York for the races, and once to Bath. I can't recall that she has ever been further. Still, the chalice is yours and the wine that goeth in it.' He took off his cap and began to catch snowflakes in it. There was a purple welt across his forehead where it had fitted.

'Do you know nothing at all of passion?' Edward asked quietly, watching his cap swoop through the speckled air beneath the bough of ash.

'Fifty, fifty-one . . . Oh yes, a very great deal. But whereas yours are the passions of an animal, mine are church honest. The passions of a gentleman. Loyalty, honour, duty: things of which you are quite ignorant.' He replaced his cap with a flourish.

'There! A little dampness for the straining cerebellum. I wonder – I wonder, Edward, if you'd sell me that mare of yours. I'm awfully taken with her. And seeing as how you'll not be needing her when you leave in your barouche . . .'

'I'm surprised you don't ask that I sell you Winterbourne as well.'

'Oh no, that'd strike people as too much like a trade, Daisy in return for the land. That would give quite the wrong impression. I would have appeared acquiescent. I may be. As a matter of fact I am. Personally I couldn't give a fig whether Daisy is at Overmoor or Timbuktoo. But that's not what I shall say. Thinking and saying live on opposite sides of the moon. So do what you want with her as long as it is clear beyond any shadow of doubt that it is I who am the injured party. There must be no question of my being at fault, of my having driven her out. In that way it will be only you who will suffer, which is as it should be.'

'This is the absurdest conversation I ever knew,' Edward cried. 'A man comes to you and says he intends to elope with your wife. You do not abuse or threaten, you do not even try to dissuade him. Instead you catch snowflakes and ask if you can buy his horse from him. All that concerns you is how you will appear afterwards. What you said last night was a sham. You wish only to feel lonely and wretched and hear everyone say, there there, Anthony, how rottenly you've been treated. Now I am going. I will take Daisy if she will have me and you will be free to be as miserable as you like.'

'What do you care how I feel?' He pushed his horse up to Edward's so that their legs were touching. 'I have been wronged throughout my life – the father that I never saw – not once, do you hear, not once – the children I never had –'

'That you never wanted, that you were never inclined to have. I do not think I have ever heard one sentence from you that did not contain a lie.'

'The land that should have been mine –'

'What are you talking about? There was never any question of *should* where Winterbourne was concerned.'

'Even now you refuse to understand me. Don't you see? With Winterbourne, I'd have owned everything around me. I'd have been safe.' His eyes grew round. 'Safe at last. No one could have touched me. Land, land, and everywhere my own.'

'You're mad, Anthony. You have blockaded yourself within yourself. You're like a mine that's full of rotten air. I am truly sorry for you. Goodbye.' He touched Luna with his heels. Like a snake, Anthony's hand shot out and gripped his rein.

'You must leave me a letter. I'll wait here so the two of you can escape. I could not control myself if I had to watch – but you must write something. Go to my study. There's ink and paper on the table. Write: I took her against her husband's wishes –'

'I shall then. I'll head it, How I stole Daisy Apreece from her lawful husband in October 1788, and sign it. Now –'. He chopped his hand away and without a backward glance galloped out of the clearing.

Twenty-eight

THE CARILLON played its dainty jingle; the mechanism whirred; hounds and horses jerked through the enamelled landscape; the fox went down its hole; the clock chimed three. Daisy laid down her book and looked out of the window. Where were they now? What was happening in the hills?

Only one corner of the drawing-room at Overmoor admitted much natural light at this time of the year and into it, exercising the privilege of age, Miss Hoole had insinuated herself. She had heard talk of fox-hunting and had believed that as was customary, there would be stirrup cups, and a meet attended by a swarm of the county's worthiest. If not by His Grace (that would be asking too much), then at least by lords and ladies and all the understrapping of the aristocracy. The sight of Daisy swishing along the landing in her coat of titmouse blue only served to encourage this belief. But when, as she prettified herself in her attic bedroom, she looked out and saw the solitary figure of Edward Horne, she thought twice about exposing herself. She would get chilled. Her old (but lately re-plumed) hat would not receive the appreciation that was its due. There would be no possibility for the sort of nostalgic conversation with twinkle-eyed noblemen that she adored. So she nipped down to the kitchen for a pot of negus and returned upstairs to discuss it as she sat with her elbows on the window sill. Now, after a strong luncheon on leftover pies, she was enjoying an afternoon nap.

Her head had fallen against the wing of her chair. On its brink her hat, a black satin dome inflamed by a spray of quivering scarlet feathers that kind-hearted Kitty Prodger had given her, teetered in defiance of every law of gravity. Her blotchy hands twitched in her sleep. A shadow lay across her nose and cast dark pools beneath the veined pouches of her cheeks that to Daisy, sitting opposite, resembled segments of withered apples. Small bubbles formed between her lips as she snored. What would she think, wondered Daisy, if she awoke to find I'd gone?

Daisy had been up and stirring for a good hour before Elizabeth arrived to make her fire. She had pulled back the curtain, opened the shutters, seen the angry clouds spilling across the horizon, and ever since had been conscious of a premonition, instinct, call it what you will, that this day carried in its seed the resolution of her unhappy existence. She was certain that something was afoot. After sixteen years of marriage, she knew well enough what Anthony's creaking silences portended.

Last night he had ridden to Winterbourne. He had been gone – what, for three hours? – had returned with a face like stone, and had not addressed her since, either then or at breakfast. She had dreamed she was on the threshold of Antioch. And this morning Edward had said, come, let us go there, you and I.

She tiptoed to the door. The smell of Mrs Keech's baking wafted down the corridor. She turned towards the hall. There was the picture of the two washerwomen pounding at their laundry. This was the way she had walked to dinner on Edward's arm. He had dabbled his clothes with attar of roses. Its scent floated through her memory. She would go to the stables. Perhaps there would be movement there, word of the hunters, some reverberation from the field of chase. She put on her gloves and blue coat and took her muff out of the tall oak press.

But of course she had chosen her costume for Edward! Normally she would not have given much thought to her appearance. But this morning – ah, this morning was not like others. She had lain back against her pillows while she listened to the scrape of Elizabeth's shovel in the drawing-room fireplace below. She had felt the flutter of nerves in her stomach. It had excited her. It was as if she had found within herself a secret chamber piled to the ceiling with a musty profusion of musical instruments that offered, at no more than a touch, to play every note a heart could dance to. She listened rejoicing to the pings and tings and squeaks of love; and with foreboding to the growls of affronted masculinity. Then one by one she reviewed her clothes, hanging them on the wardrobe door and jumping back into bed whenever something caught her eye. The blue! It could only be the saucy blue. Perhaps the cut was a little severe. But the colour! It would proclaim to Edward exactly the sort of woman she found herself to be that morning.

Had she given the impression of being a flirt? It was conceivable. (She put on her hat and walked over to the mirror.) People always found something to disapprove of in the unexpected. How much did she care? It was stupid to say one didn't mind what others thought about one. Everybody had a streak of vanity in them somewhere. And if they didn't, more fool them. Especially a woman. A woman who possessed no opinion about herself, no opinion at all, neither good nor bad, was in a poor way. Yet was that not exactly how she had been before she met Edward? She smiled at herself in the mirror. Never a truth but a lie dozing beside it.

Anyway, the fact was – and it was worth repeating – that the moment she slipped the blue coat on over her nightdress, spanned her waist with splayed fingers and did a twirl or two round the room, she had felt, well, precisely as she wanted to feel. Attractive, womanly, sentient. No longer as a household effect, or as some candle stub that Anthony was free to discard as soon as she gave insufficient light, but as Daisy Garland, comely, loved by a man, herself. It had taken her breath away. Daisy Garland metamorphosed from leaf mould! A mouse setting off to examine the battlements of life – fancy it!

She opened the front door and made for the stables with a firm stride. Of course there had been the additional pleasure that is attached to mutiny. The underdog's glee at getting his hands on the tiller ropes, the sensation of revenge at subverting the given order of things. She had acknowledged the strength of this feeling with surprise. Mutiny, like adultery, was an activity reserved to the male of the species. It was not a subject that featured on a lady's curriculum, except in invisible handwriting. But why ever not? She too had a claim on the consequences of this day, whatever they might be. So wasn't she also entitled to dress as a principal? And as for whether she cared what other people thought, what she chiefly remembered was worrying lest Edward should smell the camphor on her coat.

But only Clayton was in the yard, bent beneath a yoke of dripping water buckets as he prepared for Anthony's return. She spoke a few words with him and passed through the wicket gate into the pleasure grounds. The gardeners were in their shed mixing loam. She told them to go home once they'd wrapped some sacking round her young laurels, the weather being as it seemed to be. Fleecy snowflakes settled like moths on her coat as she walked across the lawn to the summerhouse. She placed herself in the centre of the curved wooden bench, between two white streaks from the swallows' nests. In front rose a quincunx of elms that were beginning to sway in the wind. Beyond stretched the hills. She sat hunched, with her hands cupped over her knees.

It was not as easy as she had expected. One could look a memory in the eye, greet it gladly, embrace it, exclaim at the shimmering vista of eternity that it proposed and say to oneself, Yes, I will place my hand in yours, enter the carriage and travel to Antioch and the furthest ends of the world. For the sake of love, I will surrender all that has been familiar to me since I was a child, be patient with your strangenesses, hold my head up when times are bad and suffer all that a mortal must. All this could be said with total sincerity to a memory, to someone who was not standing in front of you, asking yea or nay. But now the moment of decision had arrived. The clock had struck three. The afternoon had reached a point where nightfall had ceased to be a contingency. Soon she must pack. Soon she must uproot all of her that belonged to a life with one man in order to bestow it upon another.

She could feel the cold water of the Rubicon lapping round her ankles and was afraid.

Fingers would be pointed. She would see them wherever she went. Lust, they would say, whatever could be plainer than the lust of a middle-aged woman for a man ten years younger? Oh, but my husband was mad. 'How so? How is he mad? Chap seems as sane as a radish to me.' And Anthony would pour everyone another drink, fetch out his finest smile, slap his thigh and do all his good-fellowish things so convincingly that the company would murmur, one to another, 'It's her, you know. I always suspected those Garlands had bad blood in them somewhere.' Oh, but he was evil, too, and cruel . . . Mary Dipple would support her. But what would one voice be against such a multitude?

The storm was whipping the branches of the elms into a frenzy. Gusts of snow were driving horizontally past the summerhouse. None of this she really noticed. Everything was somehow muffled and obscured by her preoccupation.

But what should she do? Not tomorrow or in a week, but the instant she rose from the bench. At dinner, with Edward's foot pressed between hers; the next day on the lawn; this morning, the future had seemed to bound towards her with arms of rapture. But supposing, setting aside all other considerations and supposing that he was not as he appeared: that he was grippy and refused her an allowance; or a spendthrift; or liked to carouse all night with his friends; or had no real conversation; or was simply hopeless at living – what then? Was she about to condemn herself to another term of servitude?

She felt bullied by the urgency of it all. Within an hour it would be dark. She had to decide quickly and act before the lanes were closed by snow. She screwed her hands up inside her muff and beat it against her lap. How could she know this minute what would be for the best in five years? How could she see the unseeable, balance all the imponderabilia . . . With an even-tempered gurgle, like a boat launched into a steady ripple, the word lowered itself into her mind and rocked as she laid a hand on it. How could *anybody* know what would be best in five years? Today's happy warrior might be in torment, the greatest ruffian basking in paradise. Anthony might be dead. His fox-hunting neck might be snapping even as she sat there.

Not only did she see this happen, see him pitched to the ground as he jumped a paltry mud-choked ditch at which he had cantered with casual arrogance. Not only did she hear it, a noise like someone breaking a fleshy stick of rhubarb between his fingers. But she saw his cap go bowling off under a bush, she saw his eyes glaze over – and it felt as if a huge boulder had been rolled off her heart.

She leaned back against the gritty ashlar. The ghost of a smile wrinkled her eyes. Why, if Anthony were dead – and now that the thought had come to her, she longed for it to be so with every particle of her mind – she would, without a moment's hesitation, go with Edward wherever he wished. And if that were the case, and if she did not care about appearances – but why ever had she put on her blue coat if she cared about appearances? There was her answer. She had been wearing it all the time without hearing what it said.

She ran to the house, her hand flat on her hat, tufts of wet snow spurting from the tips of her boots. There were lights in the kitchen quarter and the whisper of a glow in the attic. She lit a night candle in the hall and hurried upstairs. The door to Miss Hoole's staircase was half-open. Leaning her shoulder against it, her tongue pressed against the back of her teeth, she noiselessly lowered the catch. The fewer the questions, the fewer the lies. Her wooden, iron-hooped travelling trunk was at the foot of her bed. She took out the blankets that it contained and stacked them neatly against the wall, all except one, which she smoothed out over the bottom of the trunk. She laid her clothes out on her bed. Well, she would look dowdy by London standards and that's all there was to it. Her lilac dress she packed last, folding it carefully between tissues. She gathered up her toiletries, her favourite relics, and all her little needments, and tucked them in round the sides. A malicious gleam of candlelight drew a wink from her wedding band. She wrapped it with her pearl necklace and the rest of her jewellery in a square of brown velvet and wedged it into the toe of a slipper. It would fetch a few pounds if ever she had to sell it. She put her hands on her waist. Small beads of perspiration had formed at her hairline. She would have to help Clayton carry the trunk downstairs, the two of them creeping like thieves. She would say she was taking some clothes to the Dipples, that she didn't want Miss Hoole to be alarmed by the idea of her travelling in the snow.

She glanced round the room. There! Reposing in an alcove above her bed was a mother-of-pearl framed drawing of her parents leaning upon a paddock railing at home. Her father was hatless. They were looking at a sleek, rather moody, cow that was flicking, it seemed, a beehive of foxing off the end of its frayed-paintbrush tail. Had that been Sorrel, her companion on the road to Overmoor? She picked it up and gazed at it. She saw her father's face darken and his jaw muscles bunch. 'No, child, no! Appearances are everything in life. Don't you ever forget that, d'ye hear me?' Her heart did a frantic poussette. She scooped up her dress and put the picture beneath it, between two chemises. She hung up her blue coat and buckled on her woollen travelling cloak. Then she locked her trunk and swung the shutters to. She took a final look around and went to find Clayton.

'It'll be mortal cold,' he said, scraping his chin with one finger. He ran to the saddle-room and returned with a bag of wood shavings. She placed two light fingers on his back as he knelt and fiddled them into her boots. Thank God for a man so able and considerate.

Stop! They'd reached the crest of the avenue. She leaned out from under the hood and looked down at Overmoor. Miss Hoole passed between her candle and the window. I should go back and say something. It is probably the last I shall see of her. She will be disquieted to discover I am missing, and when she learns the truth –. But the time for nannies is past. Oh Peggotty Hoole, may God go with you. She tugged at the sleeve of Clayton's weather cloak and sat back with her arm over the trunk.

They met the turnpike and stopped. Clayton descended to rig up the side sheets. His young face bobbed in and out as he threaded the eyelets and laced the sheets to the frame.

'Terrible night for a man to come home in if he lived on his own,' he said. Daisy watched in a reverie his cold fingers grappling with the knots.

'I'm sorry, what was that you said?'

'I was thinking I wouldn't care to be a single man coming back to his home on a night like this. All barnacled with snow, fires dead, dogs still to be seen to, horses to be fed, no little lady to greet you and make you feel snug. I shouldn't be caring for that, not one bit.' He climbed back and wiped the bench with the back of his hand. 'No, I shall be proper glad to see mother at the door when I gets in tonight.'

He picked up the reins and cocked his wrists. Tib shook the snow off her ears. 'To Michaelmas Farm, then, my lady?'

'One mile this side of the Green Man there is a quarry on the left side of the road. Take me there please.' Her voice was quick and low; her hand rested on his arm. He stared at her wet doeskin glove as if counting its stitches. He half-turned his head. A snowflake landed in his eye and made him blink.

'Oh my goodness, mum.'

Like an eel, the turnpike twisted through the storm. But at last it came to a drift between two hedges at which Tib baulked. Clayton picked up his shovel and jumped down.

'No, we'll try the Britannia road. It's more exposed. It may still be open.'

His cloak cracked in the wind as he uncoupled the trap and hauled it round. His fingers were red against the black wood of the shafts. A crow alighted in a tree above them and, sensing human danger, flew off with a dungeon cry. He reharnessed Tib and they started back up the hill, keeping to the tracks they had already made. The snow raced at them head on.

What if Edward had seen the trap had gone and had ridden on to Winterbourne? It would be the natural thing to do. He'd have to change his clothes and collect his baggage. Then what would he do when he reached the quarry and found no trace of her?

And what if Anthony were at Overmoor when she got there and they met? What should be said if he discovered her with the trunk, on the quayside as it were, on the point of embarkation? She shrank into the corner of the trap. She wished it were tomorrow, that she was coaching into London with Edward, that the deed was done.

Twenty-nine

H E CHOSE to leave Luna hidden among the trees where the back drive joined the Britannia road. He could not say what made him do this. His gloves were sodden, so he took out his spare pair from under the saddle flap. Then he made his way up the lane, past the hound kennel and the walled garden and the dappled, steaming dung heap. He moved stealthily, his boots creaking in the wet snow.

There was a plank laid up the side of the dung heap so that Clayton could barrow the manure to the summit. He looked to see if it had been trodden recently, but the snow was unbroken. Good. Clayton had had no time for stable duties because he was driving Daisy to the quarry. It was an omen pointing in the right direction. It was likely, he thought, that they had gone first to the Dipples so that Daisy could say goodbye to her friend. But even so he should hurry himself.

The yard was empty and its buildings mute. The snow on their roofs was seamed with horizontal wrinkles at each course of slates. He peered into the shed where the trap was kept. It was empty. He noted the faint wheel marks leading out of it. Keeping tight under the eaves, he stole towards the saddle-room. A smudge of light showed in its window. The door was swinging in the wind, its hinges making a sibilant squeak like the call of a sea bird. 'Clayton?' he called out softly. There was no answer. His heart began to pound. The trap had gone and so had Clayton. It was the signal that Daisy had told him to look for. He stuck his head inside. He heard nothing, saw only the shadow of an upraised arm fly down against the candle-yellow wall. He fell unconscious.

He was lying on his side, one ear flat against the damp, chaffy flagstones. By some quirk of the acoustics, he could hear the tiny jaws of mice chittering in the corn bins. First he thought: how long will Daisy wait for me? A moment later: my father would have been agog to understand how this munching echo found a passage from there to here.

His hands and ankles had been tied. His head ached abominably on the left side. His cap would have saved him: he should have stopped to pick it up. The lid of his upper eye was gummed solid, with blood he supposed, so that he could not open it. He looked out of the lower one and saw, behind the slope of his wind-red nose, two small muddy boots rocking impatiently from toe to heel and back again, and a pair of plump legs encased in leather gaiters that were also muddy. He closed his eye and lay still as rough hands rummaged through his clothing. He was rolled on to his back. His hipbone caught on something sharp, a buckle of some sort, and he cried out. His bad eye sprang open.

'I knew it was you, Robert. There's only one man round Buxton who has feet like a woman's.'

'Nothing,' said a voice from behind him which he didn't recognise, 'not a damned thing. How large is the book?'

'About so by so, the size of a thin prayerbook. Have you looked in his breeches?' His shirt was torn out. He gasped as a cold paw groped round his ribs and down his lower stomach.

'Your hands are very intrusive, sir, and you will not find what you are seeking. Tell me, have I had the pleasure of meeting you before?'

'I do not think so,' Archer Appleby said, straddling him.

'It is strange. I could have sworn I have seen your face previously, in a bestiary, I think. Or in the volume of Buffon that deals with the lower order of primates. The resemblance is very strong.'

'This is not a game, Mr Horne. We want my book, the one you walked out of my office with. We are prepared to do whatever is necessary to recover it. Yours is the hand that took it and yours the hand that has placed it somewhere. We are in earnest. My partners and I, we stand or fall together.' Robert made a sign to his cousin William, who began to work the treadle of a circular blacksmith's brazier. The diaphragm rose and fell like an accordion. Its rhythmic gasping pervaded the room.

'How did you know I'd come here?'

'Your man was indiscreet in the inn last night. First there was your commission for a four-wheeler from Derby and then, when he returned and was celebrating the disinterment of Mrs Smith, the information that you and Sir Anthony were to pursue a fox today. Where else would you do that but at Overmoor?'

'You were lucky to find me alone. But what is truly extraordinary is that this morning I rode to the Green Man specifically to return your book to you. Poor Robert, I thought, he'll get a better tune out of the Bank of Buxton than I ever shall. So that was where I went after my breakfast. But you were already on the road.'

'Then the matter is straightforward. You can give it to me now and William can cease his work.'

'But alas I do not have it any longer. You were not there, so I gave it to another.'

'Then it is still straightforward, though it may take us longer. Show Mr Horne what you're doing, William.'

William removed the saddle brand from the coals and held it before Edward's face. At its tip, at right angles to the shank, a small flat A was beginning to glow. A wisp of almost colourless smoke tapered to the roof.

'Dip it in the bucket and let him hear it fizz.' There was a sudden hiss and a billow of steam.

'Another five minutes and it should do. Then we'll hear what we want to hear, won't we, Mr Horne?'

'Five minutes?' snapped Archer. 'Do you think we've got all night for this fiddle-faddle? Apreece could ride up any minute now and then where would we be? Here, William, you hold the iron while I work the bellows.' He peeled off his coat and stepped over Edward's legs. The treadle throbbed beneath his heavy foot, the air gushed through the brazier. A buffet of wind struck the roof and made the slates shiver and the candle flicker. 'What do you think you're doing now?' he shouted to Robert, who was tearing a piece of cloth in two.

'I'm making a blindfold.'

'Have you gone soft in the head? Let him see it coming. He'll

sing the quicker for it, you mark my words. Little wonder you
made such a mess of it at the bank . . . Put it where the coals are
hottest, William. There, dammit, plunk in the centre.'

Hopelessly, Edward looked and listened. Daylight was fading
through the cobwebby windows. Again the wind shook the roof.
Small pieces of mortar fell to the flags beside him and shattered
into fragments.

'How do you know I didn't give the book to Constance?'

Robert squatted down on his hams. 'How do I know you
didn't? Because if you had, you wouldn't have said it like that, not
with Archer heating up a saddle brand. You'd have fairly
squawked it out if you'd given the thing to Constance . . . You
don't believe we'll do it, do you?'

'Not by yourself you wouldn't. You haven't the courage of a
termite.'

'But I'm not by myself, that's the whole point. It's not just me
you have ruined but my partners as well, not to mention
Constance, my children and poor Sophia.'

'I shall cry.'

'Indeed you shall, when we brand your fair skin with the initials
of the man whose wife you are making free with. How will it be
when we plant A for Apreece at the very point on your breast that
a woman likes to kiss when her lover is up to the maker's name
within her? Eh, Mr Horne, how will that be? Are you sure you do
not have something to tell us?'

'Go to hell.'

'Very likely. But it will be in a good cause if we recover my
book.' Then with a soft pursing of his lips, he said quietly into
Edward's ear, 'Tell me where my book is and I will return your
capital plus interest at ten per cent compounded quarterly. And I
will retire my partners so that you and I can be the proprietors.
Their minds, you know, do not have the same communion as
yours and mine. Say you will. I do detest this savagery.'

Behind them William said, 'Let's get it over with. I don't feel I
was made for this sort of business. It's a crime we're committing.'

'Give me that then,' Archer said. 'Go outside for a walk if you
cannot stand the smell of singeing flesh. Though it'll be no
different to taking the bristles off a pig.'

'But I cannot help you, Robert. You must believe me. Your

book is not in my possession. It is somewhere deep, warm and beloved by a man.'

'Apreece has it! You have given it to him. You have come to a bargain with him, to break me and buy my bank cheaply. I always knew there was something between the pair of you –'

'Clayton, Clayton, where the devil are you, man?'

The tired crump of snow-packed hooves trudged up the yard and halted outside the saddle-room. Faintly, from the direction of the house, came Clayton's call in response. His feet tramped through the snow. Harness jingled, leather creaked. 'Careful with that foot, damn you. Don't pull so at my horse's head or he may take off. Now easy does it, one step at a time – careful I said, they may be icy – no, it's not your arm I want but your shoulder – God, you're a fool, Clayton . . .' A confused dragging, shuffling sound approached the door.

Edward smiled up at Robert. 'You may be right, Robert, you may well be right. You must ask him about the bargain that he and I made.'

The latch jiggled in its slit. The door, propelled by Clayton's heel, flew open, struck the wall and flew back. 'Watch what you're doing, man. That could easily have hit my foot.'

Then Clayton backed and crabbed his way in with Anthony draped around him like a scarlet mountain. He glared testily and uncomprehendingly round the small, hot, crowded room. He stared at Edward on the floor, at Archer and William, clouded in steam as they doused the brazier, at Robert Pumfrey staring at him. He swallowed and shook his head. Then a crinkly smile warped across his face. He hopped a pace nearer Robert. ·

'Well, what have we here! Just look at this will you, Clayton, poor Mr Horne in a pickle again . . . Now those two gentlemen all done up in a vapour in the corner, they're roasting chestnuts, I dare say. And this bold gentleman is Mr Pumfrey, whom we may suppose is in command of the excursion. I always thought you'd fare better with a squadron at your heels, Robert. You were never cut out to be a lone warrior . . . Four fine figures whom we discover hugger-mugger in my very own saddle-room! Dear oh dear, *comment c'est drôle* . . . Stick a wedge under that door, Clayton, and let some air into the place. We'll have pineapples growing in it or else. No, wait, bring me that chair first. You don't object, do you gentlemen, if an old man takes the only chair? I apologise that the furnishings are so atrocious. But we are not used to such a welter of bodies. Dear oh dear, how bizarre you all look . . . Now go and fetch me the brandy – yes, of course a glass to go with it. I shall enjoy this, sitting like Methuselah before a first-class piece of theatre. The key? No, I certainly did not give it to Hucknall. What can you be thinking of? Give Hucknall the key to the grog box? You are as demented as the rest of them. Here they are, but mind you bring them right back with the brandy and no monkeying, eh, Clayton?

'Now, you must admit that to someone who has just ridden out of the hills, you form an extraordinary tableau between you. The intimacy of this little scene quite touches me, truly it does. But you must unshackle poor Ned there, for he has an engagement presently –'

'Your pleasantries are completely out of order, Sir Anthony. You must know why we are here.'

'Indeed, indeed,' he said ruminatively, stretching his gouty foot in front of him. 'There were only ever three things to interest mankind, fornication, fox-hunting and money, and I can imagine very easily which you are at here. Your little book, Robert, you still have not found it? So carry on then, my dear fellow. Now your friends have untied Ned, I am sure you will enjoy better sport.'

'But he does not have it. We have searched him and he does not have it.'

'Then it will be in his saddlebag or at Winterbourne.'

'We do not think so. We believe it is you who now hold it.'

'Oh do you?' Anthony said, anger flushing his cheeks. He gripped the arms of his chair and half-rose. 'That is a preposterous suggestion. I would have thought you knew better by now than to cross me.'

Archer stepped forward, waving the saddle brand. 'But Sir Anthony,' he said smoothly, 'you are the one who has most to lose by it not being in your possession. You are Robert's largest debtor. So our suspicions cannot be counted unreasonable.'

'And there is the pact that you have concluded with Edward Horne,' added Robert.

'I, a pact with Horne, a pact with that little coxcomb? I? . . . My

God, I cannot believe my ears.' Roaring and trumpeting, he struggled to his feet. 'Do you know what he has done to me? Do you know that not an hour ago he told me . . . And now you have the insolence to suggest . . . You, you are nothing more than a pack of blackguards. Out with you, you scum. Out! Out! Out!'

With his hand on the back-door latch, Clayton turned and looked across the yard. Knotty shadows gestured threateningly in the window glow. Huge voices stamped and swore. He hurried in to tell Daisy.

She thought again about what she'd do if she met Anthony. It was impossible to reach the Britannia road without driving through Overmoor. It was growing dark. It was as close to a certainty as one could get that their paths would cross. He'd be dismounting, lame and ill-tempered. Where do you think you're going at this time of the day? he'd shout at her. Of course he'd shout. He always shouted whenever she showed any independence. And she'd reply, I'm going, that's what I'm doing and that's all there is to it. Then she'd go down between the trees of the back drive and turn left to Britannia and Winterbourne. Edward would be changing. Perhaps he'd have on the cinnamon coat he'd worn to church. Then someone, one of the Paxtons, would take them to the quarry, where the carriage was waiting.

Or if Edward had been delayed, she'd go in and have a snoop through his things, see what books he read – she wagered *Tom Jones* was among them – what pictures he had on the walls, what sort of colours he liked. She'd catch the drift of what he felt comfortable with. Of course it was possible Mary Paxton would be there, tidying around or stoking the fires. What had he told his people? He must have said *something* to them. He couldn't go away and say nothing. In any case, Mary might be there – and from the moment their eyes met she, Daisy, would be notorious. There would be a questioning look, one would be enough, and everything would be understood between them. Neither obfuscation nor pretence would come to her rescue. Mary would know and she would know that Mary knew. Then it would only be a matter of time before she was arraigned in the pillory for fallen women.

She looked blindly at the buildings of Overmoor, which

squatted toad-like below her as they whisked down the front drive with the snow curving outwards from the wheels.

Clayton took her to the carriage door. She unfastened the flap in the side-sheet and peered out. The steps were virginal, the drawing-room windows unlit. So Anthony had not come in this way. But she wanted to make certain that he wasn't in the stables before she drove through them. It was not like a man with gout to be abroad so late. And she didn't want to think the coast was clear and then be surprised. She didn't like surprises of that sort. She entered and went to the kitchen.

'Neither sight nor sound of him,' Mrs Keech said, slowly putting down the sugar duster beside her new gooseberry cake and gorging herself upon Daisy's bedrabbled cloak, her best gloves, her travelling boots, her taut expression. Your look reminds me of Arthur Smith, Daisy wanted to say.

They heard the back door open, Hucknall tapping the snow off his boots, a grunt as he set down his hods of coal. 'Time to draw the fires up and get a good roar going,' he called through. 'Are you in there, Mother Keech?' He entered and saw Daisy. 'Just riding up the back drive the master was, not ten minutes ago.'

'He'll chase you if the fires aren't ready,' Daisy said.

'How can a man be doing everything at once? Clean the copper for his bath, split the kindling, shake the flies out of the curtains, get in extra coals in case it snows for a week – but he won't get far chasing me tonight, the state he'll be in. Anyway, why pick on me, ma'am, why not Aggie or Elizabeth? I'm not the only servant in the house, even though sometimes it seems I do be,' he finished aggressively, holding Daisy's eyes in his.

Though she did not want it, she gathered a fingertipful of cream and gooseberry jam off the edge of the cake and placed it in her mouth. Mrs Keech and Hucknall watched her lick her finger clean. She took off her hat, smoothed back her hair, and replaced it. 'Was he alone when you saw him?' she said carefully.

'So far as I could make out. Course there could have been someone behind him or there again there could have been someone in front of him. I was shovelling coal and heard a horse go by so popped up and looked over the wall and there he was, gout and all, the poor devil. But that's not to say he was alone.' Hucknall felt something of Mrs Keech's tension and glanced across at her. A look of malevolent pleasure spirtled in his eyes. 'Course if it's Mr Horne you were meaning, ma'am, why, come to think of it – no, I can't rightly say I've seen Mr Horne since he rode across my lawn this morning. Or have I, let me think on that a moment . . .'

'I'm glad you are amusing yourself, Hucknall.'

'Why, thank'ee ma'am. Now where was I? No end to the things that a gentleman has to have done for him . . .' He went through into the cold room, calling with unnecessary loudness for Agatha, who all the time they had plainly been able to hear as she slapped the whey out of the butter cakes between a pair of small wooden paddles.

Daisy and Mrs Keech faced each other across the table. Mary Paxton would have shown a gentler spirit, she thought. But now there could be no secret of what was happening at Overmoor. Perhaps Mrs Keech might think it no more than a woman's seven-day fancy, that she was only toppling, but in her heart she knew herself for fallen. So she would start as she meant to continue. It would be a useful trial, to confront her nerves when the stakes were still low. She looked Mrs Keech in the eye and teased her gloves off, finger by finger. She laid her ringless hands flat on the table. Then she poked her chin forward and said, 'Well, Mrs Keech –?'

'Miss Daisy, please Miss Daisy . . .' Clayton was calling to her from the door. He inclined his head modestly towards the boot room. She picked up her gloves and went to him. He closed the door behind her.

'Mr Pumfrey is here and Mr Horne and two other gentlemen I've never seen before. They've got Mr Horne tied up on the floor. Sir Anthony is in there with them, too. They're all having ever such an argument, about a money book someone's got. I'm afraid they'll do a mischief to Mr Horne unless you come straightaway. Sir Anthony sent me to fetch the brandy and then I heard them all start shouting at each other. You'll hear them yourself if I open the door.'

She snatched at his sleeve. 'You mean, Mr Pumfrey has got Mr Horne in there? – Oh my God, the book, I forgot – quick, Clayton, take them their brandy – did he give you the keys? – and tell them – tell them it is I who have what they want. Now hurry, hurry . . .'

Daisy ran into the kitchen. Mrs Keech was in the cold room whispering to Hucknall and Agatha. Their heads went up like geese as she entered. She ran unheeding along the flagstoned corridor, into the hall and upstairs towards her room. Miss Hoole had just come down from the attic and had paused on the landing, her candle in her hand. They almost collided.

'But why are you hastening so, child? Are we on fire?'

'They'll kill him if I do not give them what they're after. He gave it to me this morning. They're desperate, Mr Pumfrey and his friends.'

'Whom will they kill?'

'Why, Edward . . . Oh, I must hurry.'

Miss Hoole followed Daisy into her room and watched her wrench open the wardrobe door.

'Ah, Edward,' she said with a long sigh. 'The Edward I first met that day among the raspberry canes when he arrived late for luncheon. I have been wondering and now you have told me. That morning after Sir Anthony's dinner, when the two of you were walking on the lawn, I looked down and a hand tugged at my old maid's heart. It cannot be, I said to myself, surely it cannot be. Yet all this time I have hoped it was. He is a good man, he is very like his father . . . Is that what they're making all this noise for, that tiny thing, that tract?'

'I must go or they will do something to him –'

'No, my dear, you must not go until you have soothed yourself. You will look silly if you appear amongst them in a great fluster. Men are brutes and women fools, this at least I have learned by watching them. But now it is they who can be made the fools, for you have something that they want. It does not often happen thus, that a woman has an advantage. You must see if you can use it. Think on it, child. Perhaps for a few moments only, but think on it.'

Daisy looked doubtfully into Miss Hoole's lined face. 'Oh, if only it hadn't been for the snow, I would have been spared all this, and Edward too. I was on my way –'

'Your mind was made up to leave. You had packed, you were ready – I see that now.' She went up to Daisy and took her by the wrist, circling it tightly with her spindly fingers. 'Sir Anthony is with them too? I supposed it would be so. I expect they will all jeer and shout at you, as if you were simple. So you must first fix upon your course and then hold to it. As for the other –'. Her eyes moistened. She clasped Daisy's hand within her two and held its palm flat against her chest. 'You are a woman and a woman needs love. I cannot – you must do whatever you find apt. Remember that it is you alone who can decide on your happiness. It is all I know how to say. After so many years together, it is all I know –'. Her voice faltered. She hugged Daisy's hand and pressed it against her cheek. She ran her hands several times up Daisy's arms, beneath her cloak sleeves, trying to find the courage to put into words what she was thinking. Blinking back her tears, she left the room, pulling the door to without closing it.

Daisy put Robert's book into her pocket and followed her, calmer now. She reached the head of the stairs and sat down. Through the tall landing window she saw that the snow had stopped, except for a few weakening flurries.

Could it really be true that life was a story in which she had been assigned some lines to read but not others? She did not think so. She pondered on what Miss Hoole had said and more than ever she did not think so as she hugged her cloak around her and stared out at the darkening lawn and buildings. Freedom, the rope ladder of escape that she had plaited so artfully for herself at dinner, could not be hers until she was completely the mistress of her own destiny; until, unopposed by doubts, reservations or any of the pack of shibboleths that had hitherto governed her existence, she could say to herself, I am being who I am, this is my nature and I alone am responsible for it. She was conscious that she had already trodden some miles along this hard and pitted road. There was much that she had unravelled during the recent weeks without being absolutely clear as to where it was leading her. But now, as she dwelt on Miss Hoole's words and revolved the possibilities that Robert's book had so unexpectedly presented her with, she saw its end. She saw that after all there was no seamless or incontestable logic by which matters of private and public interest were conjoined. There was no need for her to go on trying to disentangle the great web of what was popularly termed morality. Let it remain as it was, a vast number of subtle yet sinewy filaments by which the generality of opinion sought to enmesh a person within its self-appointed limits of freedom, of thought and thus of action. If people felt more secure when they could see that there were boundaries beyond which no one should trespass in their conduct as individuals, this she could understand, for she, too, had experienced that security. But she had been catapulted by her love for Edward and by the contours of the circumstances around her clean over these man-made palisades into territory where common morality had no guidance to offer her – no, where it was positively her enemy. She saw this quite clearly now. It would neither succour nor defend her. It had made of her an outcast; and, being an outcast, she was free. The bonds of convention had held her within the pale and now chance had severed them. Chance and circumstance, the two of them together. So she would hold the compass herself in future, and the route she would prick off on the map would be of her own making. Her feelings and her nature would be owned by no other person than herself. She would go with Edward because she chose to, exist to the fullness of her powers, make her peace with whatever parts of the unknowable whole lay within her reach, bear his children and die, perhaps in labour. And when she did, when she turned her face to a foreign wall, she would at least be certain that she who was dying, for whom everything was about to cease, had been Daisy Garland and no other. What God, or at any rate someone far above this earthly mêlée, had intended her to be, she would have been.

She rose and went out into a murky pall that was neither day nor night. She walked past Tib and the trap towards the anxious figure of Clayton. The shouting in the stable-room came plainly to her ears. But it did not intimidate her as it would have before. The leather covers of Robert's book were smooth against her palm. In the morning she had tasted the joy of mutiny. Now she held the strap of power.

Clayton pushed the door away from him with the back of his hand and stepped to one side. 'Miss Daisy . . .' he murmured, and snibbed it behind her.

Edward was on the far side, leaning against a saddle rack with his wrist hanging loosely over its ridge. When Clayton had set down Anthony's brandy and, as he stood up, blurted out that Daisy had gone to fetch what they wanted and would be with them presently, he had experienced such an intensity of relief and exhilaration that his legs had started to shake, something that he thought happened only in the pages of fiction. His entire expression softened as she entered and went immediately to his side. He saw she was wearing the same clothes as in the morning, except that she had exchanged her blue coat for a travelling cloak, and understood that she had forgotten about Robert's book when she had changed. Her black, wide-brimmed hat partially veiled her face. But he very much wanted to see it. He flicked away a snowflake and, curling the brim upwards, bent and found her eyes. She smiled up at him: 'Oh, but you have some blood on your temple.' She took out her handkerchief and moistened it with her lips. Archer ran to her side with a pannikin of water.

'Mr Appleby, I believe it must be, such amiability is most winning.'

She dabbled, frowning, at Edward's cheekbone. Behind her Robert coughed. Her husband shifted in his chair.

'I know you are impatient to learn what is important to you, but to me this is more important and so you must wait.'

The stable cat, sleek and possessful, stalked in from the feed room where it had been dozing. Swishing its tail and flicking its paws, as if walking on cinders, it skirted Anthony's legs and padded across the floor, conscious that every eye except Daisy's was on it. It paused to gauge the height of the saddle rack and leaping up, advanced on Daisy, mewing.

'There, and that is more important also,' she said, placing the pannikin on the floor for it.

'Very well, Daisy, very well, but let us come to the point. Do you have it or do you not?' Anthony said.

She straightened and turned in one movement, the hem of her cloak brushing the chaff into the shape of a fan. Edward's stomach rumbled beside her and she was grateful for the humanness of the noise.

'I have it,' she said in her low voice, 'yes, I have it with me.'

'Then you must show it. You cannot toy with us. We are not to be treated as that creature does a mouse.'

She slipped the book from her pocket. One corner had become a little dog-eared. She nursed it back and gave the covers a polish on her cloak.

'I think there can be no mistaking its externals. By their sins shall ye recognise your children. But is it authentic within, you will want to know. Is the record it contains the true one or has the lady been tampering with it to suit her whims? I have thought of this objection and so to validate the proof, I shall read out a summary of each page.

'Page the first deals with the loans made by the Bank of Buxton to my husband for the purchase of Milkwells, the Tor and High Hill. (Your signature was very firm in those days, Anthony.) Page the second with the purchase by loan of Upward, Longbottom and Jericho.' She glanced up. 'Until today I had no idea you owned any of these. Jericho – what a captivating name that is for such an unprepossessing place. Now, had it been Antioch – but that is no concern of yours. Page the third has but one entry, incomplete and in pencil. Winterbourne with a question mark is what I find Mr Pumfrey has written there. Then follows a longer section dealing with miscellaneous loans, commencing with a Mr Cutler, whom I do not know. Do you wish me to enumerate them, gentlemen? Shall I continue? It would not embarrass you?'

Anthony stretched out his hand. 'You are my wife and your property is mine. It is to me that you must give it and that by force of law.'

'But mine is the claim with the greater moral authority,' Robert said quickly. 'The book was taken from me with violence and therefore I too can invoke the assistance of the law. And what is more powerful yet is that without the capital that it represents I am a broken man. I have no estates, no herds of cattle, not even a house to call my own. My wife, my family, your goddaughter, yes, your own goddaughter, my lady, little Ettie whom you have coddled in your arms, without that book we should be punished with a severity that I cannot bring myself to dwell upon.' He took a step towards her, deliberately at an angle so that he obscured her view of Anthony. He abased his head and made a piteous gesture with his palms. His voice trembled. 'Your goddaughter, my noble fellow Andrew, Constance who is your friend, would you have them dredging the gutters for cabbage stalks? I implore you, my lady, to show compassion.'

'But you received good value for your book, Robert. There was never any violence. It was agreed between us that I took your book in lieu of the sum I had deposited with you. Both of us acted in good faith. You are lying to claim otherwise.' Edward jutted his chin; his tone was sharp.

'So, Mr Pumfrey, if we are weighing morality – which in my opinion we would find very fluffy on the scales – then it must be that Mr Horne also has a right to it. (Right and wrongs, I mistrust these words.) It is a conundrum, is it not, gentlemen? If I give it to one, I displease two others. The mathematics alone seem inequitable to me. So what should I do? Should I tear the pages from the binding and distribute them amongst you so that everyone is a little satisfied? But then how am I to select which page will go to which man? Should I start on the right with my husband or on the left with Mr Appleby? Or should I make a judgement as to the neediness of each of you? But what about myself – do I not also have a need? You see what comes of obliging a lady to make a decision.'

She turned to Edward and laughed, a gurgling, resinous laugh that set his heart ringing. 'What must I do? Do you think that perhaps I should take the easy way out and burn it? Then there need be no argument at all for you will have a woman to blame, as is ever the wont of man.' She walked towards the brazier. 'One page at a time. Milkwells – gone. Jericho – gone. Mr Cutler whom I do not know – Mr Cutler gone too. And so on to the end. Up in smoke, each and all of them. Consider how many people would be grateful to me. But it is a method that I fear would not favour you, Mr Pumfrey.'

'It would save you much heart-searching later, my dear,' Anthony grunted from his chair.

'You cannot –' shouted Robert, seizing a handful of her cloak and pulling her back.

She looked at his hand and then into his face, her eyes ablaze with triumph that she wished to suppress but could not.

'I cannot? You say I cannot burn it? Is your meaning that I am too weak in my body or that I am too feeble in spirit? Tell me, Mr Pumfrey, which did you intend?'

'I do not think he meant either of those things, my lady,' Archer said hastily.

'And in any case he is right. I cannot because I wish to keep it for myself. At some future date, Anthony, I may choose to call on you for that portion of the debts which is yours. It will depend on how you conduct yourself. You will do well to remember that. Or I may request that you make over to me these farms. With the exception of Jericho. That you may always keep. Such a buried little place. I warrant that weeks can pass in the winter without it ever seeing the sun. I could not bring myself to deny you so suitable a retreat. And Mr Pumfrey, I have valued much in our friendship. I shall not forget my responsibilities to Ettie, of that you may be assured . . . No, please do not say more. You will only demean yourself. When Constance challenges you, you must emphasise to her that the decision was that of a woman. Then she may excuse some part of its harshness.'

Edward touched her on the elbow. 'It is time,' he said, and went to the door.

She looked at Robert and then at Anthony, who was staring sunkenly at the floor, his hands flat across his stomach. She walked over to him. She had not expected that it would affect her so powerfully, removing herself from this frightful man whom she had never loved, who had given her so little of what a woman needed, who knew as little of happiness as of grief, a man who stood in the path of life like a buttress of salt. She stopped and laid her hand on his shoulder. His hot hand came up and for an instant gripped hers. 'You have a fever,' she said, 'you should be in your bed.' His coat collar was turned up on one side. She folded it down. She fingered a small burn mark on it, thinking, I never noticed this before. Then she left him and went out into the welcome air of the evening, the cat making little pounces at a hay stalk that had attached itself to a loose thread on her cloak.

Clayton was lighting the outside lanthorn, holding the tinder-box between his knees. Edward told him to take the trap and wait for them on the Britannia road. He put his arm through Daisy's and they set out to follow him on foot.

'Luna will be fretting,' he said. After a pause: 'I shall miss her.'

'What else will you miss?'

'Winterbourne – and the small people, the people who are real. Amos, Moley Dibdin, Arthur Smith. That sort of person. And you?'

'My brother and Mary Dipple, that is all. The list is a meagre one for half a lifetime. But they are important to me. Do you think, Edward, that we shall remain away for long?'

'I think that at any rate we should try it. We are the quick, and our lives are before us. We should try it whilst we can.'

'And then we shall return,' she said decidedly. 'I am a woman, and I need to make a home for my family. And a time will come when you, too, hear your father's voice calling for you.'

From among the trees in front of them Luna snickered as Tib trotted past. Suddenly Daisy stopped. 'What do you think you would have found if you'd been able to see inside Nat's head?'

For a moment they looked at each other. The whites of her eyes were stark in the gloaming. Then he gave a great laugh and throwing his arms around her shoulders, crushed her to him. Her hat slid to the ground. With his lips moving against her ear, he murmured, 'I believe I would have seen something like this: a very thick hedgerow, nothing straight, everything tangled and askew, poking up at odd angles. No holly though, nothing spiky like that. Or nettles. Just a jumble of different sorts of bushes, full sunlight on their upper leaves and underneath an army of birds and butterflies, all ahop with excitement and going chatter chatter chatter to each other. Once in a while I see a fox slinking down the middle of the hedge with sharp eyes. It is my mother. Everything falls quiet. A cloud passes over the sun. The butterflies make themselves invisible, you know, become leaves. The birds cock their little heads. Off she stalks in a huff and they all make rude noises at her and then they're at it again, jumping up and down like a set of coronation bells. That's what I think I'd have seen, Daisy my angel.'

She leaned back in his arms, slid her fingers beneath his cherry-pink lapels and gently tugged at them. 'Do you remember that afternoon we were at Winterbourne with Mary and Fuscus Quex-Parker and I asked you what symbol you would choose for the god of optimism? Do you remember that, Edward?'

'Most certainly I do, for I believe it was the opinion of one of the party that optimism was no match for sin. Who can it have been who said that?'

She laughed wryly and beat her fists against his chest. 'I think we should have Nat as our symbol. Let us go into the world a little and return so we can bring up our children beneath the sign of Jupiter. That is what I would like most. Shall we do that, you and I?'

He bent to pick up her hat. Waving it around, he began to tell her what old Mrs Scarlett had said about women and peonies making bad travellers. Side by side they dwindled into the vaulting aisle of trees. From the branches long plumes of snow cascaded to the ground like necklaces of crystal. Above them the moon sped through black streamers of cloud, hurrying towards tomorrow.